BRENDA JACKSON

SEIZED BY SEDUCTION

HQN™

ISBN-13: 978-0-373-79934-3

Seized by Seduction

Copyright © 2017 by Brenda Streater Jackson

Recycling programs for this product may not exist in your area.

This edition published by arrangement with Harlequin Books S.A.

For questions and comments about the quality of this book, please contact us at CustomerService@Harlequin.com.

® and TM are trademarks of Harlequin Enterprises Limited or its corporate affiliates. Trademarks indicated with ® are registered in the United States Patent and Trademark Office, the Canadian Intellectual Property Office and in other countries.

www.HQNBooks.com

Printed in U.S.A.

Praise for Brenda Jackson

"The only flaw of this first-rate, satisfying sexy tale is that it ends."
—*Publishers Weekly*, starred review, on *Forged in Desire*

"Leave it to Jackson to take sizzle and honor, wrap it in romance and come up with a first-rate tale."
—*RT Book Reviews* on *Temptation*

"Brenda Jackson is the queen of newly discovered love… If there's one thing Jackson knows how to do, it's how to pluck those heartstrings and stir up some seriously saucy drama."
—*BookPage* on *Inseparable*

"[Jackson] proves once again that she rocks when it comes to crafting family drama with a healthy dose of humor and steamy, sweaty sex. Here's another winner."
—*RT Book Reviews* on *A Brother's Honor*, 4½ stars, Top Pick

"This deliciously sensual romance ramps up the emotional stakes and the action…. [S]exy and sizzling."
—*Library Journal* on *Intimate Seduction*

"Jackson does not disappoint…first-class page-turner."
—*RT Book Reviews* on *A Silken Thread*, 4½ stars, Top Pick

"Jackson is a master at writing."
—*Publishers Weekly* on *Sensual Confessions*

Also by Brenda Jackson

The Protectors

FORGED IN DESIRE
SEIZED BY SEDUCTION
LOCKED IN TEMPTATION

The Grangers

A BROTHER'S HONOR
A MAN'S PROMISE
A LOVER'S VOW

For additional books by
New York Times bestselling author Brenda Jackson,
visit her website, www.brendajackson.net.

To the man who will always and forever
be the love of my life, Gerald Jackson, Sr.

To all my readers who after reading The Grangers Series
wanted more. This book is especially for you.

And to my readers who will accompany me to Barbados
for Brenda Jackson Readers Reunion 2017.
I appreciate you from the bottom of my heart
for your love, encouragement and support.

For none of us liveth to himself,
and no man dieth to himself.
—*Romans* 14:7

PROLOGUE

QUASAR PATTERSON WAS a man who appreciated anything female, which was why his gaze was focused on
the woman standing within the perimeters of the crime
scene tape. He didn't know her identity, but the one thing
he did know was that she was definitely a looker. She was
so striking that he felt a scorching sensation in his eyes
from staring at her. And he was convinced it had nothing to do with him having run out of a burning mountain
cabin in the Shenandoah Valley just a short while ago.
He would lay the blame solely at her feet. Even from a
distance her facial features were so captivating, so mes-
merizingly beautiful, he felt an intense stirring in his gut.

Her skin appeared the color of creamy cocoa with a
sensual pair of cheekbones, well-shaped lips, a delicate
nose and dark eyes that were either black or brown. From
where he was standing he couldn't be certain. Regardless of their color, her eyes made the entirety of her facial features exquisite.

Long, straight black hair fell to her shoulders, and
even from across the yard it looked thick and silky. The
kind a man would want to run his fingers through…or
better yet, grip while thrusting hard inside her. He usually preferred a woman with bigger breasts but concluded
hers were perfect for her size. The lush curves outlined

in the dark slacks and short leather jacket she wore were appealing as hell.

He'd first seen her after running from the burning house with his friend Stonewall Courson. He and Stonewall hadn't thought twice about running into the blazing cabin to save their friend Striker Jennings, and the woman Striker had been hired to protect, Margo Connelly. Striker and Ms. Connelly were being treated by paramedics, and the body of the man who'd tried to kill them lay covered by a white sheet.

"You okay?"

Quasar reluctantly shifted his gaze off the woman to glance at the man who'd joined him. "Yeah, Stonewall, I'm okay. What about you?"

"We're alive. So are Striker and Ms. Connelly, and that's all that matters. And that bastard over there is dead," he said, indicating the would-be assassin. "Good riddance."

Quasar nodded in agreement and then switched his gaze back to where the woman stood. Three other women had joined her. He recognized Margo Connelly and Detective Joy Ingram, and when the third woman took out a writing pad he concluded she was a federal agent about to take a statement from Ms. Connelly. Federal agents were swarming all over the place. However, Quasar had no idea about the woman who'd caught his eye. Was she a federal agent, as well?

When Stonewall muttered something about it being a pity that such a nice house was burning down, Quasar decided to satisfy his curiosity. "Hey, man, the woman standing over there next to your detective—the one wearing the slacks and leather blazer—who is she?"

Stonewall frowned after glancing over his shoulder.

His friend wasn't all that keen on him referring to Joy Ingram as *his* detective. Stonewall and Joy had met at a party a month ago, and from the first it was obvious Stonewall had the hots for the detective. Probably to the same degree Quasar had the hots for the woman standing beside her.

"She is not *my* detective," Stonewall said, copping an attitude that Quasar chose to ignore.

"You want her to be, though. I know the two of you haven't had an official date yet, but you've met up with her a number of mornings at that café on Monroe Street for coffee and donuts. You also met with her at Shady Reds a couple of times to grab a few beers."

Stonewall's frown deepened. "You know too damn much."

"Not really, which is why I want to know who that woman is. The one in the dark slacks and leather blazer."

"I heard your description the first time," Stonewall snapped.

"Well?"

Stonewall took a huge gulp of water from the bottle he was holding, then swiped across his mouth with the back of his hand. Quasar knew his friend was trying to annoy the hell out of him by deliberately taking his time in answering. Finally he said, "Her name is Dr. Randi Fuller."

Quasar lifted a brow. "The psychic investigator?"

"Yes, the psychic investigator. I admit I was a skeptic at first, but she's made a believer out of me. She led everyone to this place, and just in time. I don't want to think what would have happened if no one had taken Dr. Fuller seriously."

Quasar didn't want to think what would have happened, either.

"Well, let me get back over to Striker," Stonewall said. "He's about done giving his statement to the Feds now."

When Stonewall walked off, Quasar returned his full attention to Dr. Randi Fuller. Randi. He liked that name and thought it was different. Tired of standing, he decided to crouch down a minute, and when he did so, as if the movement carried a sound that floated through the air, Dr. Fuller turned and looked over at him.

The moment their gazes connected, desire with an intensity he'd never felt before twisted Quasar's gut, and primitive male awareness filled his every pore. A throbbing need suddenly consumed his senses, and there was an unmistakable pounding in his crotch. Crackles of sexual energy passed between them, hot, raw and relentlessly carnal. Even across the distance, he swore he could hear the intimate sound of her breathing, the fast pounding of her heart. He was convinced he could even smell her. It was an arousing scent of jasmine and some other entrancing fragrance.

Shit. What the hell was happening? With him? Between them?

She must have been trying to figure out that very same thing, because she suddenly broke eye contact with him. He used that time to suck in a deep breath and to force his aroused state under control. The strange connection they'd just shared was a jolt of sexual energy that rocked him to the bone. Nothing like that had ever happened to him before.

Moments later, when she glanced back his way and their gazes reconnected, his mind conjured up a number of erotic images. Like him burying his face in the hollow of her throat, undressing her, making hard-ass love to her while those long legs wrapped tight around his waist. His penis throbbed at the thought of pounding into her. Hammering hard. Then harder.

When Detective Ingram said something to get her attention, she looked away from him again. But he continued to stare at her, to will her to glance back. Although maybe it was a good thing she didn't. He was so damn aroused he could probably come just from all this sexual chemistry surging between them. Explosive. Fiery as hell. The I-need-to-get-fucked kind.

"We need to talk to Striker," Stonewall said, returning, interrupting Quasar's heated thoughts.

Annoyed, he glanced up at Stonewall. "Why?"

"He's about to make some crazy decisions about Margo Connelly."

Frustrated, Quasar ran his fingers through his hair. "And you know this, how?"

"Because I do. He's crazy about her and is fighting it."

"Not my business, and neither is it yours," Quasar said, standing back up and pulling his shirt down past his pants zipper.

"It will be our business if we're the ones who have to put up with his crappy-ass mood."

Well, hell, Quasar figured Stonewall was right about that. "Okay, so, what's the game plan?"

As Stonewall began talking, Quasar glanced over to where Randi Fuller had been standing. Dammit, she was gone. He anxiously glanced around the crime scene but didn't see her anywhere.

He sucked in a deep breath of disappointment and as he drew the oxygen through his lungs, he wondered if, somehow, someway, he would ever see the beautiful psychic investigator again.

CHAPTER ONE

Three months later

WHY IS THE NIGHT I saw Dr. Randi Fuller still so vividly clear in my mind?

That irritating question nagged the hell out of Quasar while at his home in Charlottesville, Virginia. Getting more annoyed with himself every passing minute, he grabbed a beer out of the refrigerator and a slice of leftover pizza from the microwave. The very idea that any woman could linger on his mind for this long was preposterous. Especially when it was a woman he'd seen only one time.

But damn, she'd been beautiful, and he would admit to being awestruck and mesmerized. So much, in fact, he hadn't been able to stop looking at her that night. She'd caught him staring and had boldly stared back. He'd seen the same interest mirrored in her eyes he was certain shone in his. A part of him wondered if she'd read his thoughts. After all, she was a psychic.

Deep down he knew that her paranormal abilities had nothing to do with why she'd been stuck in his mind for three solid months. For a reason he couldn't explain, he'd felt this strange connection between them. One that had him still thinking of her three months later. As far as he was concerned, nothing about his obsession with Dr.

Fuller made sense. He dated women. He bedded women. What he didn't do was get fixated on one.

His phone rang and he recognized the tone. It was a call from his father. Normally he'd have let it go, but he decided to answer it. Maybe if his mind was full of anger at someone, it would keep his thoughts of Dr. Randi Fuller at bay. He'd never known a time when a phone conversation with Louis Patterson didn't end in shouting.

He looked at the clock. Usually his father didn't call past dinnertime. There was only one way to find out the reason for this abnormality. "Is there a reason for your call, Louis?" He had stopped referring to his father as *Dad* years ago. As far as Quasar was concerned, the man didn't deserve the title when he'd unashamedly picked one son over the other countless times. And unsurprisingly, his father hadn't made a fuss about the change.

"Yes, I wouldn't be contacting you if there wasn't. Doyle has decided to run for public office."

Quasar's stomach clenched at the thought of his older brother. Doyle was and always had been his father's golden child. "Any reason you thought I needed to know?"

"Forever the smart-ass, aren't you, Quasar?"

Quasar managed a tight smile while thinking, *Yes, if it riles you, then it's worth it.* "Why do you think I need to know Doyle has decided to get his hands dirty in politics?" He figured his old man didn't like that question, especially the reference to *dirty hands*.

His father ignored the comment altogether. "The media knows about you. They might want to talk to you. Get an interview."

Quasar chuckled. "Oh, I get it. And you're afraid I'll tell them something. Like the truth."

Once again there was silence on the other end of the call. Quasar liked it whenever he could render the great, all-powerful Louis Patterson speechless. It was always this way between them. He was determined never to be controlled again, and his father was intent on controlling him like old times.

The old man finally recovered and said, "When are you going to forget about that and let it go, Quasar? You know I couldn't let Doyle go to jail."

But you could let me go and waste three years of my life behind bars for a crime I didn't commit. Quasar knew there was no reason to get into an argument with his father about it. The man had wanted to protect Doyle, and Quasar had been the sacrificial lamb.

As far as Quasar was concerned, the only good thing that had come out of those three years in prison was meeting a man who'd proved that not all fathers were assholes. That there were some who loved their sons... no matter how many they had. That man was Sheppard Granger. Like Quasar, Sheppard had been jailed for a crime he hadn't committed.

Shep, as the other inmates called him, was a lot older than most of the prisoners and served time for murdering his wife. It didn't take long for anyone who hung around Shep to know he was a natural-born leader— a positive one. He gained the respect of many and was highly admired.

Before being sent to prison, Shep was the CEO of a major corporation, Granger Aeronautics. While in prison he became a father figure to the younger inmates, their mentor, confidant and role model. Instead of acting resentful for being locked up for a crime he didn't commit, Shep used his time in prison to implement Toastmasters,

Leaders of Tomorrow, GED exams and college programs. Shep was the reason Quasar had walked out of prison a different man. A man who would no longer allow his father to intimidate him. While growing up, nothing he did pleased his father. Louis always made him feel inadequate, as if he would never measure up…like that time he'd become captain of the swim team and the team came in second place in its first competition. Instead of giving him accolades for even making it to the finals, Louis had verbally lashed out at him for not winning.

Prison had also introduced several other men into Quasar's life. Some who were better brothers than Doyle had ever been. The first two who immediately came to mind were Striker and Stonewall.

"Quasar?" His father's voice annoyingly intruded on his thoughts.

"I heard you. Doyle is getting into politics."

"You gonna keep your mouth shut and not bring shame on the family's name?"

"Don't count on it." Not giving his father time to respond, he clicked off the phone.

He laughed, imagining the look on his father's face. Not too many people would have the courage to hang up on Louis Patterson and laugh about it. Oh, well.

Quasar was about to settle down in front of the television with his beer and pizza and see what was happening on the sports channel when his cell phone rang again. It wasn't his father calling back but Roland Summers, his boss at Summers Security Firm.

Not long after being released from prison, he, Stonewall and Striker had signed on to work for Roland's security firm. Since the three of them hadn't known a thing about security work, Roland, an ex-con himself, understood the importance of them having steady and productive employment and had gotten them into one of the top tactical training schools in the country. In addition, Roland had hooked them up for a full year with a former Secret Service agent by the name of Grayson Prescoli. Grayson had a reputation as being one of the best in the business while serving under three presidents.

After Striker was credited with taking down the assassin who'd been terrorizing Charlottesville, Summers Security received national attention and was hailed as one of the top-notch security firms in the country. Since then, the security firm had received numerous requests from around the country for their services. That had prompted Roland to hire additional trained bodyguards to protect celebrities, politicians, and members of wealthy families and handle security details during special events. As of last month, the security firm had gone global, and international requests were rolling in. Stonewall was currently in Paris, acting as bodyguard to some billionaire playboy.

Quasar clicked on the phone. "What's up, Roland?"

"I took a chance in reaching you. It's your weekend off, and I'm surprised you're not out on a date or something."

Quasar chuckled. Roland was not only his boss but also a good friend who knew how much he enjoyed the opposite sex. "I thought I'd hang around home this weekend."

"Oh, I see."

He figured Roland really did see and was fully aware that at times, Quasar slipped into pensive moods. It was during those times he preferred being by himself. "So what do you need, Roland?"

"I just got a call about an event at the Kennedy Center.

They're expecting a ton of celebrities, will be increasing their security detail and need at least three of my men. Since you've done events there before, I'm reaching out to you in case you might be interested."

"When is it?" Quasar asked.

"Next weekend. It's on Friday night, but they're footing the bill for an entire weekend if you want to use the additional two days and do some sightseeing. If you're interested, I'll have the packet ready when you return to the office on Monday."

"I'm interested." He hadn't been to DC in a while. It would give him the chance to check in on Ryker Valentine, a former inmate who, after returning to his home state of California, had entered politics and was now a US senator.

"Good. I'll put you down, Quasar."

"I hope you're not overdoing anything, Roland." The man had been shot earlier that year in an attempted carjacking.

"My last scheduled checkup with the doctor was yesterday," Roland said. "I'm officially released with a clean bill of health."

"Glad to hear it, but still, don't tax yourself."

"I won't. I'll have Carson to deal with if I do."

Quasar knew that to be true. Carson was Shep's wife and Roland's good friend. She doted on Roland like a younger brother. "And how is Carson?"

"Fine. They found out last week that she's having a girl. Everyone is happy. Especially Shep. After three sons, he's getting a daughter. The baby is due sometime in July."

Quasar smiled, thinking of Shep with a daughter. In a way, it was strange to picture Shep and a baby at all,

considering his youngest son, Dalton, would be thirty this
year. Shep was starting fatherhood all over again. "What
about Caden and Dalton? Any word on what they're having?" The wives of two of Shep's sons were pregnant,
as well.

"Caden and Shiloh are also having a girl. Dalton and
Jules aren't saying yet."

Quasar shook his head and chuckled. "Leave it to Dalton to keep everyone in suspense."

"Yes, that's Dalton for you. Talk to you later."

Quasar clicked off the phone. Maybe spending a weekend in the nation's capital, visiting an old friend, was just
what he needed.

"So WHAT ARE your plans for Trey's birthday?" Randi
asked her sister, Haywood, as they tossed their shopping
bags into the backseat of Haywood's SUV. It was a beautiful day in Richmond, although forecasters had predicted
rain later today. Randi loved shopping, and a day spent
at the malls with her sister was the best. Even with the
eight-year difference in their ages, they'd always been
close. Usually their mother would join them, but their
parents had left today to celebrate their thirtieth wedding
anniversary on an international tour of four countries.

"You know your brother," Haywood said, sliding into
the seat behind the steering wheel and buckling her seat
belt. "It's going to be hard to pull anything over on him,
so a surprise birthday party is out of the question. I think
I'll host a birthday dinner instead."

Randi nodded while buckling her own seat belt. Yes,
she did know her brother, and Haywood was right. It
would be hard to pull anything over on Trey. It always
amused her to watch people's reactions whenever they

discovered her sister had married her brother. Then Randi would have to explain, as simply as she could, that she and Haywood shared the same mother, where as she and Trey shared the same father.

Jenna Fuller's first husband and Haywood's father, Steven Malone, had died of a heart attack when Haywood had been four. Randolph Fuller and Jenna, who'd been college sweethearts, reunited and married when Haywood was six. Trey, whose real name was Ross Donovan Fuller III, was Randolph's son from his first marriage and was named after their father's brother, who'd been killed in the Vietnam War.

Thanks to Haywood and Trey, Randi had two nephews—ten-year-old Ross Donovan Fuller IV, who was affectionately called Quad, and seven-year-old Randolph Devin Fuller II, who went by the nickname of Dev. Then there were her identical twin nieces, Brooklyn and Brynn, who turned three a few months ago. Randi adored her nieces and nephews and considered them her joy in life.

"What do you have planned for this weekend?" Haywood broke into her thoughts to ask.

"I'm thinking about painting my bedroom."

Haywood glanced at her when she brought her SUV to a stop at a traffic light. "Why? You know you don't want to do that."

Randi chuckled. "What are you? A mind reader?"

Haywood shook her head, grinning. "No, reading minds is your thing, not mine."

True, Randi thought as she settled back in her seat. After all, she was Dr. Randi Fuller, psychic investigator and behavioral analyst. She'd been fifteen when she'd gotten her first premonition but hadn't told anyone until she was nineteen. That's when she'd confided first in Haywood and then her parents.

No one had been surprised, since it was a known fact that Randolph Fuller's maternal grandmother and great-grandmother had been psychics. Nor had it been surprising when those not close to her family had been skeptical of her abilities. At first Randi had consider her psychic abilities a curse, especially after an incident in college involving her best friend, Georgie Mason, and Larry Porter, the guy she'd convinced herself she would love for life. She'd secretly confided to Georgie she had psychic powers. In her junior year she began dating Larry, and Georgie had betrayed Randi's trust by telling Larry of Randi's psychic abilities before she'd gotten the chance to do so herself.

When Larry confronted her about it, she'd confirmed what Georgie had told him. Larry broke things off with her, saying there was no way he could be involved with a freak. She'd taken their breakup hard, and it was only with her family's love and support that she had gotten through that difficult period in her life.

"I wasn't going to mention it, practically promised Trey that I wouldn't, but…"

Randi glanced over at her sister. "What is it that Trey doesn't want you to mention?" she asked, her curiosity piqued.

"It's about Larry."

Now she wondered if her sister could possibly read minds, since her ex-boyfriend had been in her thoughts just moments ago. "What about Larry?"

"Zach ran into him this week. Seems he's moved to DC and works for an IT company there."

Zach was Senator Zachary Wainwright, Trey's best

friend. Zach was also married to their cousin Adrianna, whom everyone called Anna. "Why would Larry moving to DC bother me?"

Haywood shook her head. "Come on, Ran, it's me you're talking to. I of all people know how much you loved Larry and how badly he hurt you."

Larry *had* hurt her. "I've gotten over him, Haywood. It wasn't easy, but I did." What she said was true. She'd taken a year off college just to get herself together. That time spent on Glendale Shores had been just what she'd needed. Located off the South Carolina coast, Glendale Shores was one of the most beautiful of the Sea Islands and had been in her family for generations.

"Are you sure?"

Randi glanced over at her sister. "I'm positive."

Haywood didn't say anything for a minute. Then she said, "I'm glad, because according to Zach, he's married. Larry mentioned to Zach that he's attending that big bash at the Kennedy Center this weekend with his wife. Since you have plans to go as well, there's a chance you might see them there."

Randi drew in a deep breath and felt…nothing. Not even that painful ache in her heart that it had seemed would take forever to go away. But it was finally gone. Who would have thought she would actually feel zilch upon hearing the man she once loved so deeply had committed his life to someone else?

"Randi?"

She heard the worry in her sister's voice and glanced over at her. "I heard you, Haywood. So Larry's married. I'm happy for him. Truly I am. And it wouldn't bother me in the least if I saw him."

She paused a minute, then added, "I got over Larry.

I now understand that not all men could handle a girlfriend having psychic abilities. I shouldn't have expected
Larry to be different."

"Well, I did," Haywood said with indignation. "He
claimed he loved you."

*Yes, he had claimed that, and when I needed him to
be supportive and understanding, he'd been neither. In
fact, he was a total ass.* "Well, like I said, I'm over Larry,
and no one has to be afraid to mention him around me
or freak out at the thought we might run into each other
someplace whenever I'm in DC."

"I'm glad to hear that, Randi. I know getting over
Larry was not easy for you. But I'm still concerned, because you haven't dated much since your breakup with
him, and it's been close to four years."

Reaching up, Randi adjusted her sunglasses. Had it
been that long? "I date."

"I didn't say you hadn't dated at all. I said you don't
date *much*. There's a difference."

"I date enough. Criminal cases take up a lot of my
time, Haywood. You know that." After college she'd gone
to work for the FBI as a behavioral analyst. She'd found
the position too restricting because she couldn't assist
other law enforcement agencies. That's when she'd made
the decision to freelance. In between job assignments, she
used her time writing books on psychic criminology that
were being used at the FBI Training Center at Quantico.
And on occasion, she would teach classes there, as well.

"Speaking of cases, you haven't said much about the
last one you worked. The one in Charlottesville," Haywood cut into her thoughts to say.

Randi shrugged. "Wasn't more to tell. All the details
were blasted on television and in the newspapers." It had

been crazy when a mobster who'd been found guilty had put a hit out on everyone in the courtroom the day of his sentencing. Close to ten people had been assassinated before it all ended.

"The media gave you a lot of credit."

"They shouldn't have. It was a team effort."

"Yes, and with all the cases you've helped solve, you'd think people's skepticism of an investigative psychic's abilities would have lessened."

Randi was well aware that most people didn't believe or accept the possibility that some individuals were born with psychic gifts. Over the years she'd gotten used to closed-minded people. "It's not always easy to have an open mind to the unknown…especially when it contradicts what you think you know or believe," she said in defense of the doubters. She would admit that in the beginning, she'd had a hard time accepting people's attitudes about that. Now she mainly ignored them.

"Why do I get the feeling that there's something you're not telling me about that case in Charlottesville?"

Randi started to speak, to deny there was anything she wasn't telling her sister, but she knew there was no point. Her sister could read her like a book. "I saw him."

Haywood had pulled her SUV into the parking lot of one of their favorite dress shops. She brought the car to a stop, cut the ignition and turned to Randi. "You saw whom?"

When Randi felt a part of her breath backing up in her lungs, she let out a whoosh; otherwise, what she was about to say would overwhelm her. It practically did whenever she thought about it. "While in Charlottesville, I saw the man Gramma Mattie told me in my dream that I would one day meet."

As Randi expected, Haywood was quiet for a minute, allowing what she'd said to sink in. Then her sister lifted her brow, stared at her with that thoughtful expression she could wear so well and asked, "You saw *him*?"

The corner of Randi's mouth lifted into a smile. "Yes. And it happened pretty much like the dream said it would."

In actuality, it had been a vision instead of a dream, but she'd told everyone it had been a dream so they wouldn't ask too many questions about the experience. It had happened during that year she'd spent on Glendale Shores while getting over her breakup with Larry. Her deceased great-grandmother, who'd also been blessed with psychic powers, had come to her in a vision. Gramma Mattie had told her Larry was never meant to be her mate, and there was a man chosen just for her.

Her great-grandmother further said that Randi would know him when she saw him. Although no physical description of him was given, it was revealed that the first time she saw him, he would be wearing all black, and when their gazes locked, she would feel the connection.

And she had.

"I don't understand, Randi. If you met him, then why isn't he here with you? Why haven't you introduced him to us?"

Randi smiled, hearing the excitement in Haywood's voice. "Mainly because I haven't officially met him myself. I saw him one night at the crime scene, and he saw me. Something passed between us just the way Gramma Mattie said it would. I'm sure he thinks it was nothing more than sexual attraction."

"And you didn't say anything to him?"

"No. It was the same night the assassin was killed, and

everyone's attention was focused on what had happened. Two people had come close to losing their lives that night in a fire. Besides, according to Gramma Mattie, he has to make the first overture. The only reason I know his name is that I overheard someone call out to him."

Randi didn't say anything for a moment. Then she added, "And another thing, the most important thing Gramma Mattie said, was that I have to earn his love, and he has to earn mine."

"How?" Haywood asked.

Randi answered thoughtfully, "I don't know. But what I do know is that if one of us fails, then we both lose out on love. There's not anyone else out there for either of us. If not together, then we will live apart and forever alone."

CHAPTER TWO

RANDI LOVED ATTENDING galas at the Kennedy Center, especially when they were honoring a well-known humanitarian who deserved the award. Since her parents were still out of the country, she was attending with Trey and Haywood and her godbrother and her cousin, Zach and Anna. It was a dressy affair, and she'd enjoyed going shopping to buy what she thought was the perfect outfit.

She glanced around, remembering the first time she'd come here. It was with her parents and paternal grandparents when the Kennedy Center had honored the Performing Arts. She'd been eight at the time and had been starstruck, not only by the performances but also by the notoriety of her father. That night, she realized Randolph Fuller might be *Daddy* to her, but to others he was a world-renowned defense attorney. She had been amazed at the number of people who'd admired her father and whose lives he'd touched.

She couldn't help noticing how close Trey was sticking by her side tonight and was about to ask why when she remembered Haywood's heads-up that Larry and his wife might make an appearance. Since she wasn't supposed to be privy to that information, she had no choice but to let him play the role of big brother and protector.

"You okay?" Trey leaned down and asked her for what seemed like the tenth time that night. It was intermission and they'd stepped out into the lobby. She was glad to see so many people were in attendance. Security was high due to the number of celebrities and dignitaries in attendance, including the President.

"Any reason why I wouldn't be, Trey?" she asked, reaching up and giving him a sisterly pinch on the cheek.

"None that I can think of."

Yeah, right. She glanced over at Haywood, who looked as though she was trying hard to keep a straight face. "I guess it's time to go back to our seats," she said. At that moment, Trey and Zach left Haywood's and Anna's sides to flank hers.

"Good evening, everyone."

Randi recognized the masculine voice immediately. Glancing up, she took in Larry's face as well as the woman by his side. His wife.

THERE IS A big crowd tonight, Quasar thought, glancing around the huge lobby. The celebrities and dignitaries sitting in the balcony areas were now mingling upstairs. He was posted by the bank of elevators to make certain that only those with VIP passes got past him. Several young women had tried him, all but offering him a hot night in their beds if he looked the other way for a minute so they could sneak up to socialize with the rich and famous. Of course he'd turned down their offers. They would have to hobnob on someone else's time. He had a job to do.

He glanced around, not for the first time admiring the beauty of the inside of the Kennedy Center. The decor was colorful with beautiful, gigantic chandeliers hanging from the high ceilings, which gave the lobby an intrinsic charm. His attention went to the huge bust of President John F. Kennedy. He recalled the first time he'd come here and seen it. He'd been around ten at the time, and his mother had brought him for his first tour of DC.

His mother.

Not for the first time, he wondered how different things might have been had cancer not claimed her at forty. He'd been fourteen, and a part of him would forever feel the loss. His life had gone downhill after that. With his mother gone, there was no one to protect him from Louis's verbal abuse or Doyle's bullying. At some point, his godmother, Lucinda, had stepped in, giving him the love and support he'd desperately needed and wasn't getting at home.

Checking his watch, he noted intermission would end in ten minutes. Already the crowds were dispersing as individuals began leaving the lobby to return to their seats. In a few hours he would be able to go back to his hotel and rid himself of the suit and tie. He'd decided to take advantage of Roland's offer and stay in town until Sunday. He'd contacted Ryker, and they would be hanging out on Sunday. Tomorrow he would take in the sights. The last time he'd been in DC, he'd been with Striker and Stonewall. They'd eaten breakfast at a café in Georgetown, and he planned to revisit it tomorrow morning.

Several crowds lining the lobby floor shifted, and suddenly his breath caught. He did a double take to make sure he wasn't seeing things. Standing across the room was the one woman he'd assumed he would never see again, although he'd hoped otherwise. The woman who'd stolen her way into his thoughts for the past three months. Dr. Randi Fuller. Psychic investigator extraordinaire.

He studied her profile, willing her to turn ever so slightly. Then he would know for certain it was her and not a figment of his imagination. She was standing in a group. Friends of hers, he assumed. Or was one of the men standing so close to her side more than a friend? A lover, perhaps? The thought of her involved with someone tightened his gut.

She looked beautiful, and her gown flattered her body in a way that had every cell in his body responding to her curves. A deep sexual hunger surged to life within him, and there wasn't a damn thing he could do about it. How could a woman he didn't know arouse him to a degree no other woman ever had? And why did the very thought that they were standing under the same roof practically thicken the air flowing through his lungs?

What were the odds that he would see her again? Here? Tonight? Was she a resident of DC? Or was she, like him, just in town for the gala? More than once he'd been tempted to research her, to see what he could find. But to do so would put too much importance on the night he'd seen her and the connection he'd felt, so he hadn't. Now a part of him wished he had.

Then he wouldn't have been wondering where she lived. Where had she grown up? Was her family as fucked-up as his? Did she have a lover? He continued to look at her while those questions went through his mind.

He was about to force his gaze away, fix it on something else—like that huge bust of President Kennedy—when something happened to halt those plans. As if she felt the caress of his gaze, she tilted her head in a way he thought was sexy as hell, such a damn turn-on. And then, as if she had a sensor detecting his exact location, she looked over at him.

RANDI DREW IN a sharp breath when something akin to an electric current passed between her and the man standing across the lobby.

Quasar Patterson.

Where had he come from? Why hadn't she detected his presence before now? And why was she tempted to leave everyone standing right here and cross the room to him? She then quickly remembered one of the things Gramma Mattie stressed in the vision. *He* had to make the first overture.

"I guess we'll head back our seats now," Larry was saying. "It was good seeing you again, Randi."

She quickly broke eye contact with Quasar to look at Larry. "Same here." Giving Larry's wife a gracious smile, she said, "And it was good meeting you, Yvette."

"You, too, Randi. I hope everyone enjoys the rest of the show."

When the couple walked off, Randi quickly returned her gaze to Quasar. He was standing in the same spot, staring at her. He looked blatantly male, handsome as sin in a dark suit. He broke eye contact with her when a well-dressed, very attractive woman approached him. It was obvious the woman wanted to use one of the elevators, and he was denying her the right to do so. It then occurred to Randi why he was here. He was part of the security detail. When the woman walked off, Quasar returned his gaze to her. Why hadn't she seen him when they'd come down from the balcony? She then remembered they had used the escalator instead of the elevator.

"You handled that well," Trey said, interrupting her thoughts.

She broke eye contact with Quasar, a little annoyed that she had to. She glanced up at her brother. "What?"

"Seeing Larry Porter again."

Randi shrugged, shifting her gaze from Trey back over

to Quasar. He was busy sending a group of ladies away. "I told you I was over him, but you didn't believe me."

"Only because I know how much he hurt you."

The very fact that Trey had fought to be cordial and not take Larry apart meant he had let her handle her business, like their father had told him to do if they ever ran into Larry again.

"That year I spent on Glendale Shores helped me realize it wasn't meant to be for me and Larry. He's married now and looks content. I'm happy for him."

The lobby lights blinked. "That's our cue to get to our seats," Haywood said quickly, taking Trey's hand and giving Randi an I'm-proud-of-you smile.

Trey led the way. "We'll take the elevator back up," he said. "It will be faster."

Randi felt a quickening in her stomach. That meant she and Quasar would be in proximity to each other. Would he acknowledge her presence? She could feel blood rushing through her veins when the group got close to where he was standing.

They had been to enough of these events to know the procedure. Only VIPs were allowed upstairs in the balcony area, so she, like the others, took out her badge. When he stood directly in front of her, she showed him her pass. He nodded, and before she moved to pass him, he inconspicuously slid a card into her hand. Not wanting to call attention to what he'd done, she tightened her hand on the card as she stepped on the elevator with her family. When she was certain no one was watching, she slid the card into her purse.

"Wow! He was definitely a handsome guy," she heard Anna say.

"Who was?" her husband, Zach, asked.

"That security guy. He's hot."

Trey chuckled. "You might want to be worried, Zach. Your wife and mother of two is checking out other men."

"So was your wife, who's the mother of four," Haywood said, smiling. "A man who looks that good would be hard to miss. So what do you say about that, Ross Donovan Fuller III?"

Trey frowned at his wife. "You and Anna are married. Neither of you have any business checking out other men. On the other hand," he said, glancing over at Randi, "Randi is single and has every right to look, but I doubt she even noticed the dude."

The elevator door opened and Randi quickly stepped out. Otherwise she would have to tell her brother just how wrong he was.

IT WAS THREE HOURS later when Randi was able to pull Quasar's card from her purse. Everyone was crashing at Zach and Anna's home across the Potomac in National Harbor, Maryland. The tri-level house was huge and had plenty of room for the sleepover guests, which included Randi, Trey and Haywood and their four kids. Zach and Anna both worked outside the home. Zach as a senator and Anna as a physician. Carole, a woman in her fifties who'd been their live-in nanny since their first child, had kept the kids while everyone had gone out tonight.

Randi thought it had been a nice evening spent with her family. After leaving the Kennedy Center, they had stopped at a café for coffee. When they returned to Zach and Anna's home, an announcement was made. Anna had found out a few days ago that she was pregnant. This would be their third child, and they were hoping for a girl. Their news prompted a celebration and calls to Zach's parents, who resided in Miami, and Randi's parents all the way in Rome.

Randi stared at the card Quasar had slipped into her hand. It was his business card representing Summers Security Firm.

She flipped the card over and read the message he'd scribbled on the back.

Please call me tonight. No matter how late.
Quasar Patterson

Underneath his name was a phone number. Randi tapped the card to her chin as she felt a slow roll in her stomach. This was the overture she was to wait for. She figured he was probably wondering why there was such a strong attraction between them. It was more powerful than just sheer sexual chemistry. Both times she'd seen him, what had passed between them had stimulated her senses and made her realize something she'd conveniently not dwelled on for quite some time. The fact that she was a woman.

She'd appreciated how Quasar had filled out that suit with such a powerful, sexual physique. Not all men wore a suit well, but Quasar didn't just look good—he looked breathtaking. The suit had appeared tailor-made for his body. For all she knew, it could have been.

She looked back at the card and then at the clock on the guest bedroom nightstand. It was after midnight. Although he'd said she should call him tonight, no matter how late, she couldn't do that. The last thing she needed was to hear his voice. She'd bet it was as sexy as the rest of him and then she was certain not to get any sleep for thinking about the sound of it.

Drawing in a deep breath, she placed the business card on the nightstand. She would call him first thing in the morning. Tonight she needed to get some sleep and accept the realization that, for better or worse, her life was about to change.

CHAPTER THREE

QUASAR TOSSED THE empty coffee cup in the trash can to join three others. If his friends had told him he would stay up half the night, guzzling caffeine while waiting for some woman to call, he would have told them they were out of their ever-loving minds. But here he was, four cups of coffee later and still waiting for the call.

It had been past midnight when he'd left the Kennedy Center. As a rule, none of the security detail could leave until the last car was out of the parking lot.

Once back at the hotel, he had quickly gotten out of his suit and showered, anxiously checking the phone. No call. So he decided to kill time by getting on his computer. He'd convinced himself that had she read the message scribbled on the back of the business card, she would call.

So far she hadn't.

Granted, they hadn't officially met, but he figured she had to remember him from that night in Charlottesville at the crime scene. Maybe not to the same extent he'd remembered her, but still. And then, hours ago at the Kennedy Center, with all that sexual chemistry flowing between them, she had to have found what was happening between them just as bizarre as he did.

On the other hand, maybe she hadn't. After all, she was a psychic. For all he knew, she could get this type of reaction from men all the time. But for him, it was the weirdest thing he'd ever encountered. If he assumed the first time had been nothing more than getting caught up in the moment, what happened at the Kennedy Center pretty much dismissed that idea. It had nothing to do with the moment but with her, and he was determined to find out why.

Quasar checked his watch. It was close to seven in the morning, which meant he'd been up all night. But at least it hadn't been a total waste. He'd finally decided to research Dr. Randi Fuller. When he couldn't pull up anything but professional information, he contacted the headquarters of Summers Security, knowing that someone was on call twenty-four hours a day. It was Roland. More than once he and the guys had told their boss he needed a life, and Roland would give them some smartass response that Summers Security was his life.

If Roland thought it odd he'd called at two in the morning for access to GRETA, he didn't let on. GRETA was a state-of-the-art search engine that specialized in information you couldn't find anywhere else. It was a great tool for those doing investigative work. All you had to do was tell GRETA what information you wanted, and within minutes she would recite all you needed to know.

According to GRETA, Dr. Fuller made her home in Richmond. She was the daughter of famed defense attorney Randolph Fuller; sister to Ross D. Fuller, who was making a name for himself as a top corporate attorney; goddaughter of retired Senator Noah Wainwright and godsister of Senator Zachary Wainwright. He recalled Senator Zachary Wainwright had been among the group she'd been with last night. Connected to that much fame, he understood why she preferred protecting her personal data.

Quasar stretched out on the bed. He was filled with too much caffeine to sleep, so he might as well watch the news. He grabbed the remote. From his hotel room window, he had a view of the Washington Monument standing tall against the bluest sky he'd ever seen.

It was at that moment his phone rang, and immediately he felt a stirring sensation in the pit of his stomach. It was a number he didn't recognize. "Quasar Patterson," he said.

There was a brief pause before a feminine voice replied, "Yes, Mr. Patterson, this is Dr. Randi Fuller."

Quasar sat up in the bed, wondering how any woman could sound ultrasexy and impressively professional at the same time. He immediately remembered her as he'd seen her last night, in that beautiful blue gown. The material draped her curves, and he'd thought she'd looked absolutely stunning in it. For a minute he'd ignored the lobby filled with people, his total concentration on her.

"Thanks for calling, Dr. Fuller."

"Although you said to call anytime, when I settled in for the night by my standards it was way too late."

"I understand and I appreciate you calling now. What I didn't have time to write on the card is that I want to get to know you."

For the first time in his life, Quasar felt like a man on a mission.

RANDI NERVOUSLY NIBBLED on her bottom lip. Twenty minutes ago she had still been debating the merits of making this call. Now that she had, she wondered how much, if anything, she should tell him. And just like he wanted to get to know her, she wanted to get to know him. What woman wouldn't? But for now, she'd let him lead the conversation.

"Dr. Fuller?"

She swallowed. Why did he have to sound so darn sexy? Especially this early in the morning. She hadn't been able to sleep and had gotten up before seven o'clock to wash her face, brush her teeth and make a cup of tea before calling him. "Yes?"

"Do you have a problem with me wanting to get to know you?"

She considered his question thoughtfully. "It depends on why you want to."

"I believe you know the reason."

"Do I?"

"Yes, I think you do."

Randi drew in a deep breath, deciding for the time being to play coy. "And just what reason do you assume I know?"

She heard him chuckle and knew he was well aware she didn't intend to make anything easy for him. "Although we haven't officially met, something is going on between us that defies logic," he said.

Maybe in his world it did, but not in hers. "Does it?"

"Every time we look at each other, it's like we're the only two people in the universe."

She would admit that was true. "It's called chemistry, which is a normal, healthy attraction. It happens."

"Not to me. At least not this way, and not this intense. Has it ever happened to you before?" he asked her.

Randi didn't say anything for a minute. She could say yes, it happened to her all the time, but that would be a barefaced lie. Her attraction to him was just as intense as he'd described his to her. "No," she finally said. "It's never been this way for me before, either."

He didn't say anything for a minute, as if he was trying to digest her response. "Don't you think we owe it to ourselves to find out why it's happening?"

Truth was, she already knew why, but he would need to discover the reason for himself. "How do you suggest we go about solving the problem?"

"I didn't say it was a problem. In fact, I find it quite stimulating."

"Do you?"

"Yes, which is why I want to get to know you. You intrigue me."

Randi took a sip of her tea. It wouldn't be the first time a man said she'd intrigued him. He wanted either to get inside her head or to try his luck getting her into his bed. She couldn't help wondering why, of all the men out there, he had been chosen to be her mate for life.

"I think we owe it to ourselves to explore what's going on between us," he said, pulling her mind back into the conversation. "To meet finally would be a great start. However, if you're seriously involved with someone, then of course I understand."

Seriously involved? She'd forgotten just how that felt since it had been so long. "No, I'm not involved with anyone." *Seriously or otherwise.*

"In that case, will you join me for breakfast? Let's say in an hour? There's a wonderful café in the heart of Georgetown. Rocs. I've eaten breakfast there before, and it's good."

Trey, Haywood, Zach and Anna were taking the kids on a train ride to Delaware today, and she had told them she would join them. Randi figured she could certainly change her plans. She would be honest with herself and admit she wanted to see him again. "Yes, I'll join you for breakfast. However, you need to make that in two hours instead of one." She had promised to go jogging with Trey this morning.

"Fine." He gave her the address. "And another thing."

She pushed to her feet to get dressed for jogging. "What?"

"I'm Quasar, and I hope it's okay to call you Randi."

"It is."

"Great. I'll see you in two hours, Randi."

"Alright, Quasar."

After Randi disconnected the call, she couldn't stop the butterflies from swirling around in her stomach. She would get to see Quasar Patterson again. And soon.

CHAPTER FOUR

QUASAR FELT RANDI FULLER'S presence long before he saw her. Since it was a gorgeous day in May, he'd chosen to sit at an outside table in the beautiful historic section of Georgetown. His gaze searched up and down the cobblestone sidewalk, but he didn't see her.

He would have been the first to admit that nothing about his attraction to Dr. Randi Fuller was normal. He'd been attracted to beautiful women before, but this was different. It was something he couldn't explain...like what was happening now. When had he actually been able to feel a woman without being buried deep inside her body? All he knew was that he was convinced Randi was close by, either parking her car or coming up the sidewalk...although he had yet to see any sign of her.

"More coffee, sir?"

He glanced up at the waitress, who was smiling at him. She'd been to his table three times now, and his coffee cup was still pretty full. She was young, probably no more than twenty-two. And more than likely a student. He'd seen her looking at him a couple of times, and he'd felt nothing. Not even a twinge of excitement or a flutter of desire. "No thanks. I don't want any more coffee."

She gave him a sexy look...or at least she tried to. "Would you like anything else, then?"

He didn't have to ask, *Anything like what?* "No thanks. I'm good."

"Yes, I'll just bet you are." And then she walked off, deliberately sashaying her hips as she moved toward another table.

"I hope I'm not interrupting anything."

Quasar quickly switched his gaze from the waitress to the woman standing beside his table. He couldn't keep his eyes from dragging all over her before staring into the most gorgeous pair of brown eyes he'd ever seen. Up close they were lighter than he'd thought they were. "No, you're not interrupting anything," he said, standing.

He liked everything he saw. Smooth, creamy, cocoa-colored skin; high, perfectly sculpted cheekbones; a cute nose; a pair of lush lips and pretty ears with dangling gold earrings. He thought she was gorgeous. Irresistibly hot.

And there was no way he could overlook the thickness of the black hair spilling to her shoulders and framing her face in such a sassy and sexy way. He could imagine her raking her fingers through it or pushing it back off her face. She was wearing a yellow print sundress with spaghetti straps that highlighted beautiful shoulders. And he couldn't help noticing she had a gorgeous pair of legs. She managed to look both graceful and sensual at the same time.

He extended his hand to her. "Randi."

She took it. "Quasar."

Why did his name sound so damn sexy on her lips? And why were they standing there holding hands while something akin to hard-core sexual chemistry flowed between them?

"I hope I'm not late," she said, finally easing her hand from his.

"Not at all," he said, sitting back down after she'd taken her seat. "What would you like to drink? Coffee? Tea? Juice?"

"Tea will be fine."

"Anything else?" he asked, handing her the menu.

"What do you suggest?" she asked, placing it aside and looking over at him.

Quasar focused his gaze on her too-luscious lips and thought he honestly didn't want to go there. The first thing he would suggest was for them to go back to his hotel room. He could visualize her naked and stretched across his bed while he kissed her all over. He would see if all that creamy cocoa-colored skin was as sweet as it looked. Deciding not to let erotic thoughts get the best of him, he said, "They have delicious pancakes here."

"Then that's what I'll have with my tea."

"Okay." He motioned for the waitress, who, unlike all those other instances, seemed to take her time coming to his table. He gave her their order and was glad when she finally left. He liked being alone with Randi. Although there were people sitting at other tables, it seemed as if she was the only one in his little corner of the world.

He knew how dangerous getting this caught up in a woman was, but he brushed the concern aside. He was a man and she was a woman, and the strong attraction between them was nothing more than a normal aspect of human sexuality, right? Even she'd alluded to that. However, he couldn't shake the idea that the chemistry between them was way too explosive, and there had to be more to it. Randi Fuller was too deeply embedded in his system, and for the life of him, he didn't know how she got there.

Or how long she would stay.

Other than dealing with an annoying ache in certain places, though, he had nothing to worry about thanks to Lilly Alpine, the woman he'd planned to marry. She'd known the reason he'd gone to prison and had promised to wait for him. She hadn't. Instead she'd married the person he'd gone to prison to protect. His brother, Doyle. Because of Lilly's betrayal, Quasar would never share his heart with another woman. So whatever this thing was with Randi, he was fine with it since he wasn't doing anything foolish like putting his heart on the line again.

He felt his stomach clench when she nervously licked her lips. "Thanks for agreeing to join me for breakfast, Randi. Did you enjoy the gala last night?"

"I did. There was a large crowd."

"Yes, there was," he said, leaning back in his chair.

"What about you? I know you were working, but I hope you managed to enjoy some of it."

"Yes, I did."

Their gazes held, and he felt a tightening in his chest. He wished at some point he could be unaffected by her but had a feeling that wasn't possible. Especially when his fingers were itching to run through all that hair on her head. He couldn't help but be drawn to how it cascaded around her face.

"You did an outstanding job assisting law enforcement with the Erickson case," he said. "I don't want to think of what would have happened to Striker and Margo Connelly had we not gotten to the cabin when we did."

"I'm glad I was able to assist. I got a call from Ms. Connelly thanking me personally, and I enjoyed our conversation. I understand she and Striker Jennings are seeing quite a lot of each other these days."

Quasar chuckled. "Yes, they are." There was no need

to mention that he had a feeling a wedding would be in the works before the year was out.

"I could tell that night that you, Striker Jennings and Stonewall Courson are close friends. I watched you and Mr. Courson race into that burning house to help get Mr. Jennings and Ms. Connelly to safety."

Quasar thought about the night and the fear racing down his spine that he and Stonewall would not be able to get Striker and Margo out alive. "The three of us are more than that. I consider them as close to me as brothers." Then, deciding to be up front with her in case she didn't know his history, he said, "We served time together in prison."

He watched her features for some kind of shock. When that didn't happen, he waited for the questions. They didn't come, either. He could only assume that she'd known. Evidently her psychic powers were at work.

"Not sure if you've heard the federal government has completely taken over the Erickson case," he said. "They're determined to find out how he died while locked up at that federal prison. It's still all a mystery."

She nodded. "Yes, I heard that."

"It seems the murderer covered his tracks well. So far there aren't any leads."

"Well, I'm sure justice will prevail and the killer will eventually be caught," she said, tilting her head in that sexy way of hers.

The shrill ring of his mobile phone disturbed the comfortable conversation between them. He tried to hold his anger at bay when he recognized the ringtone. The call was from his father.

"Do you need to get that?" she asked him.

He shook his head. "No. I have the rest of the weekend off," he said, although he knew the call was personal and not business.

"I like this place," she broke into his thoughts to say. "It reminds me of a restaurant back home."

"And where is home for you?" he asked, knowing already but wanting her to tell him anyway.

"Richmond. But I love coming to DC. I attended college here at Howard for my BS, and then Georgetown for my master's and PhD. Georgetown is my favorite part of DC."

He nodded. "You come to the nation's capital often?"

"Often enough. I have family here, and I like visiting them as often as I can. Sometimes my work can take me away a lot."

"You have a big family?"

She smiled, and he could feel his stomach tighten even more when that smile produced beautiful dimples. "Depends on what you mean by *big*. Compared to most, I don't consider it big, but when my parents have family get-togethers, inviting both my mom's side of the family—the Haywoods, and my father's side—the Fullers, there are a lot of us. We're a close-knit group."

"Is it a coincidence your sister's name is Haywood, after your mom's family?"

Her smile widened. "No coincidence. Mom says she'd always been proud of being a Haywood and wanted to pass the name on to her first child, whether it was a son or daughter."

She'd angled her head to look at him, making a mass of hair cascade even more over her shoulder. "What about you, Quasar? Do you have a large family?"

He could feel his jaw tighten at the question. "No,"

he said and decided not to add they were definitely not close-knit.

"Any siblings?"

He immediately thought of his brother. His one and only brother…at least biologically. "Yes, I have a brother. An older brother by four years."

"And where did you grow up?"

Quasar loved her smell. Why did her scent have such sexy undertones? "Los Angeles."

"You're a long way from home."

And he wouldn't want it any other way. Instead of telling her that, he said, "Yes, I am."

Wanting to shift the focus from him back to her, he said, "So tell me some more about you, Randi."

She laughed and the sound fired his blood. "I would bore you."

"I doubt that. Try me."

TRY ME.

Randi didn't want to think of all the ways she could try him, and they were ways she'd never thought of until now. She never considered herself an overly sexual being, even when she and Larry had been together. But the man sitting across from her looked so ridiculously sexy, it was hard not to fantasize a little. Um, maybe a lot.

His chestnut complexion, aquiline nose, sharp cheekbones and strong chin were what female fantasies were made of. Then there were his brown bedroom eyes and chiseled jaw that made him appear too handsome to be real. The straight texture of his dark hair that stopped at his shoulders made her curious about his ethnicity. Mexican? Italian? Or other? His mouth was holding her senses captive, namely the shape of his lips. They were the kind of lips a woman would want to kiss and lick until she was sexually silly. Pretty much how she was feeling now.

And when he'd stood, he appeared to be around six feet two or three inches of solid muscle, a lean, well-built physique with great broad shoulders. She couldn't help but appreciate a body that was so powerfully male. And why did his scent, a masculine blend of soap, aftershave and cologne, travel along her nerve endings? What she found so mind-boggling was the fact that the man sitting across from her, playing havoc on her body from top to bottom, was meant for her.

"I'll tell you what," she decided to say. "If I tell you a little about me, then you have to tell me things about you." This meeting between them was important and would establish the framework for the rest of their lives. Of course there was no way for him to know that.

He shrugged, smiling over at her. "With your psychic abilities, I'd think there's not much about me you wouldn't know already."

Searching his eyes, she considered his words and knew she needed to nip that assumption in the bud. "You're not showing up on my mental radar," she said truthfully. "I don't have the ability to read every single human being."

"Then how did you know I was an ex-con?"

She tilted her head. "I didn't until you mentioned it. I had no idea."

He held her gaze as if trying to divine the veracity of what she'd said. "Then why didn't you react when I told you?"

She lifted an eyebrow. "How was I supposed to react? Did you expect me to run out of here hollering and screaming?"

After huffing out a short laugh, he shook his head.

"Nothing that drastic, but experience has taught me to expect some sort of reaction."

Randi wondered what kind of response he was used to getting. Was it similar to the one she got whenever it was revealed she had psychic powers? She decided to explain a few things to him. "My father is a defense attorney, probably one of the best…at least I think so. And the one thing he's instilled in me is the belief that not all people in jail are there because they are guilty. Not saying whether you were guilty or not. All I know is that you're sitting here, which probably means you served your time."

"I did. And that's good enough for you?"

"Yes, Quasar. That's good enough for me." *When you want to tell me more about that time in your life, you will*, she thought to herself. When he didn't say anything but continued to look at her, she said, "I wanted to follow in my father's footsteps and become a lawyer."

"You did?"

"Yes. From the time I found out what he did for a living. I was so proud of him. That wasn't in someone's plans for me. But in all fairness to my *gift*, which I am now very proud to have, I learned early on that it's meant to help others more than to help myself, which is why I probably can't read you. I'm meant to find out some things on my own."

She'd discovered this when Georgie betrayed her and Larry broke things off with her. She'd felt with her paranormal abilities that she, of all people, should have known Georgie couldn't be trusted and Larry would end up being a jerk.

"You said that now you are proud of your gift. Does that mean that hasn't always been the case?"

"Yes," she said, nodding her head. "What fifteen-year-old wants something like that dumped on her? The realization that she has psychic powers? To be considered a freak of nature?"

She forced to the back of her mind Larry's cruel words to her that day. She figured if Larry saw her that way then others would, as well. "I knew my great-grandmother was psychic as well as her mother, but not in a million years did I think the gift would be passed on to me."

"How did you come to terms with it?"

Randi immediately recalled that year spent on Glendale Shores. That had certainly helped. But more important had been her relatives. She decided to credit the latter. "My family's love and support."

"Then you should consider yourself fortunate to have such a wonderful family."

At that moment, the waitress returned with her tea and Quasar's cup of coffee. That was good timing since it gave Randi a chance to dwell on what he'd just said. His words led her to believe that his family was anything but wonderful, not even close.

A part of her wished she didn't have a mental block where he was concerned. But then, maybe it was for the best. It was up to her to get to know Quasar Patterson and break down any barriers he erected. She had a feeling that doing so wouldn't be an easy task. He had invited her to breakfast under the misconception that whatever was drawing him to her was purely sexual. Eventually he would discover that wasn't totally true.

"You know what I think?" he asked.

She met his gaze. "No, what do you think?"

"I think with your proven track record as a psychic assisting law enforcement, especially with the Erickson case, anyone who doesn't appreciate your gift would be crazy. What you're doing is pretty awesome."

A smile touched the corners of her lips. Randi didn't say anything, but she appreciated his compliment. There was no reason to tell him that although she did have a proven track record, some of her cases weighed her down. She often dealt with the struggles of not having every single case laid out for her, like Erickson's death. She hadn't seen it coming. And then there was Levan Shaw, the one who got away. "Thanks."

"I spoke the truth, Randi," he said softly.

And what was so utterly amazing was that deep down, she knew he had. He was definitely nothing like the last guy she'd gone out with, about six months ago. The one who thought a date with her was a sure win at lotto. Colin Kennesaw had spent the majority of his time during dinner trying to get her to give him the winning numbers for Powerball.

"What about your mother? Does she work outside the home?"

She positioned her mind to return to their conversation. "Yes. She's an architect and has her own firm in downtown Richmond. She loves what she does and designed the house my parents live in." Randi rook a sip of her tea before asking, "What about your mother? Does she work outside the home?"

She noted the drooping of his shoulders when he said, "My mom passed away when I was fourteen."

"Oh, I'm sorry."

"Thanks. It's been a long time, but I still miss her. She and I were close." And then, as if he needed to switch topics, he said, "I shouldn't be drinking this."

She watched him add sugar to his coffee and stir it with a spoon. "Why?"

"I've consumed too many cups already, starting when I returned to my hotel room last night. I wanted to be awake in case you called. My only regret in not getting any sleep last night was that I missed having my dreams," he said in a deep, throaty tone.

Randi lifted a curious brow. "Your dreams?"

"Yeah. My dreams of you. They've been coming pretty steadily since that night I first saw you."

"Oh." She didn't know what else to say and honestly couldn't believe he would admit such a thing. No way would she confess that he'd been invading her dreams pretty steadily, as well.

"To be honest, they should be classified as hot fantasies rather than dreams," he added in a voice that had gotten even huskier.

Hot fantasies? Randi swallowed when she felt a swelling in her nipples and heat settling between her legs. All the dreams she'd had of him could have been considered hot fantasies, as well. Last night's dreams had been hotter than ever after seeing him again at the Kennedy Center. But nothing could compare to seeing him today, this close-up while sharing space with him.

When she'd come up the sidewalk and seen the waitress flirting with him, admittedly she'd gotten jealous. But what woman wouldn't be tempted to flirt when he was such a gorgeous specimen of a man? Even Haywood and Anna had commented about him last night. And now this handsome hunk just admitted to having fantasies about her? Hot fantasies?

"How's your tea, Randi?"

It took her a second to realize she'd been caught staring. "Excuse me?"

"I asked how your tea is," he said, not taking his eyes off her face.

"Delicious." She picked up her cup to take another sip. Although she knew she shouldn't ask, she couldn't help doing so. "You want to tell me about those hot fantasies?"

She noticed his eyes suddenly shone with wicked pleasure. "I'd rather not. There are some things a woman shouldn't know. Especially if it's a woman a man desires."

Whew. She needed more than hot tea right now. A cold glass of iced tea might have been better. But she took another sip anyway, enjoying the taste, and licked her lips afterward. When she saw his gaze lower to her mouth, her skin began tingling.

"Delicious?"

She felt that unmistakable connection whenever their eyes locked, and it resulted in a shiver oozing down her spine. "Yes. Very delicious."

Her belly clenched, and she broke eye contact with him. She was grateful when the waitress appeared with their pancakes.

CHAPTER FIVE

"Thank you for breakfast, Quasar. I enjoyed it."

He pushed his plate aside. "So did I." More than anything, he had enjoyed her company. The sexual attraction hadn't lessened; if anything, it was stronger than ever. She was beautiful, and as a man, his entire body couldn't help reacting. There was something about her eyes that seemed to smile at him whenever he talked. Then there were the times her brows creased when she was concentrating on what he was saying.

He'd dated woman who'd pretended to do both, feign interest just to score brownie points. Women who really hadn't a clue what he was talking about. That was not the case with Randi.

Whenever their gazes locked, something akin to a sharp electrical current would zap him. And the thought that she wasn't involved in a serious relationship, didn't have a significant other in her life, a lover of any kind, gave him pause. Any man would want her in his bed. Not just sometimes but all the time. Every night, if possible.

She had to know that he wanted her, just like he could tell she wanted him. He had the hots for her, and every time he looked into her eyes, he could tell the desire was reciprocated. He would have given anything to seduce her.

It was hard as hell to push those thoughts from his

mind. And when she'd asked about his hot fantasies, he'd gotten an erection just thinking about them. It had been difficult sitting across from her and not suggesting they go somewhere and take care of their desires. That might be all it took to get her out of his system.

They'd eaten their pancakes and had refills on coffee and tea. Now they were just sitting and talking, taking their time. Neither seemed in a hurry to leave, knowing when they did they would be going their separate ways. The breakfast crowd was moving out and the lunch seekers were arriving. Waiters and waitresses were hustling about, clearing off tables, passing menus, serving drinks and food. Randi was glancing around, watching all the activity. And he was watching her.

"Why aren't you involved in a relationship, Randi?" he decided to ask. He had speculated long enough.

"Why aren't you?"

He hadn't expected her counter or the intensity in her gaze when she made it. He had no problem giving his answer first. He could say he just hadn't met the right woman yet. The woman he'd want to settle down with, have his babies, share his life with, yada yada. Or he could tell her the truth. That at one time he thought he'd met such a woman and had been wrong. And it was a mistake he wouldn't make again.

Quasar decided to be honest with her.

"I was involved in a long-term relationship at one time." No need to tell her it was a relationship that had started in high school. The kind you'd think would last forever. "Less than a year after graduating from college, I was jailed for a crime. I spent three years in the slammer, and she decided not to wait. Since then, I've decided long-term doesn't work for me."

No need to elaborate that he much preferred casual relations, and one-night stands were even better. He didn't need to get caught up in anything other than the moment. Which just went to show how mixed up his mind was when it came to her, because she definitely didn't look like a casual dater or a one-night-stand sort of woman. "So what's your reason?" he asked her.

Randi met his gaze and tried to ignore the sizzle she always felt whenever she did. "I guess you can say the reason is mostly my work. I'm not sure when I might get a call asking for my assistance, or where that call might take me and for how long. And then…"

He lifted a brow when she paused. "And then what?"

She lifted her cup of tea, took a sip and eyed him over the rim. "And then there are the guys who see me as a freak for having such a gift. Those who don't see me as a freak consider me a threat."

"Why?"

"They assume I can read their minds—would undermine their every male maneuver or be aware of their every planned move. Although I try assuring them that's not how my gift works, they don't believe me."

His jaw tightened. "Any insecure, weak-minded man would think that way."

She placed her cup down. "Should I assume you don't fall in that category?"

He smiled warmly. "I don't consider you a freak or a threat. I admire you and your gift and have seen firsthand how remarkable it is. You assist law enforcement in saving lives and getting hard criminals off the streets. I don't want to think of the outcome had you not alerted the authorities about that assassin's next move. Your psychic powers should be commended, not scrutinized."

She smiled, please by his words. "Thank you."

"You don't have to thank me," he said, pushing his cup of coffee aside. "But there is something I would like to ask of you."

"What?"

"Would you spend the rest of the day with me?"

Randi's stomach fluttered at the same time she felt her heart rate kick up a beat. "The rest of the day? "

"Yes."

"Why would you want to spend the rest of day with me, Quasar?"

He smiled, and the fluttering in her stomach increased. "Because I'm not ready for our time together to end. I have nothing else to do today and would love spending more time with you."

She considered him for a moment, trying not to get giddy because of what he'd said. "What do you have in mind?"

"We could visit that new museum, for starters. And no matter how often I come to DC, I enjoy visiting the National Zoological Park. I understand two new pandas were added since I was here last."

When she didn't say anything, he leaned forward. "One day, Randi, is all I'm asking for," he said softly.

Would that really be all? she wondered. What if he invited her to his hotel room at the end of the day? She would decline, of course. It would be as simple as that. But then, nothing about the strength of their attraction to each other was simple.

Randi met his gaze, felt the heat of his desire but refused to be overtaken by it. She had to keep a clear head. Drawing in a shaky breath, she said, "Okay, Quasar. I'll spend the day with you."

RANDI SURMISED QUASAR was a touchy-feely person since he liked touching her every chance he got. While at the museum, his hand had stayed at the center of her back as they viewed one painting after another. At the zoo, as if it was the most natural thing, he'd taken her hand in his. The contact caused all kinds of heated sensations to cascade through her body and made her even more aware of him.

More than once she found herself studying Quasar instead of the animals at the zoo. Whenever he looked back at her, she would quickly avert her gaze. She figured he knew she was checking him out, but she hadn't been the only one. Other women, both young and old, were eyeing him, as well. Some inconspicuously and others openly.

And then there was that bold, heavy-breasted woman in the tight jeans and too-revealing top who seemed to appear wherever they went. Randi thought she was stalking them, and that suspicion proved true when the woman finally got the nerve to approach and ask Quasar if he was some actor from one of the soaps. Even when he took off his aviator sunglasses and assured her he wasn't, she tried flirting with him right in front of Randi.

Randi couldn't help but admire how Quasar shut the brazen woman down by letting her know he was annoyed with her lack of respect for his girlfriend and she should take her bullshit elsewhere. Of course she wasn't his girlfriend, and Randi knew the lie had been told mainly to get the woman out their faces. He had spoken to the woman in Spanish and afterward, apparently assuming Randi didn't understand the language, had given her a cleaner version of what he'd said. She decided not to tell him she spoke fluent Spanish and had understood what he'd said. What mattered was that what he'd told the woman had worked, since they never ran into her again after that.

Randi looked at him as they walked from one habitat to another while holding hands. His hair fell to his shoulders, and more than once today she was tempted to reach out and run her fingers through the silky strands, wondering again about his ethnicity, especially since he'd spoken Spanish earlier.

Deciding to satisfy her curiosity, she asked, "Where is your family from originally?"

He glanced over at her and smiled. "Depends on what side. My mother's parents are from Cuba. They were Afro-Cubans who fled the Castro regime years ago. They made it to the United States just in time. My grandmother gave birth to my mother a couple of days after their arrival in Miami."

"So she was born an American."

"Yes. My father is white and is proud to claim a little bit of Irish in his blood."

Intrigued, she asked, "How did your parents meet?"

They stopped at the monkey pen and watched as the animals scampered about when other people tossed them peanuts. "Like many Cubans, my grandparents settled in Florida. Years later after finishing high school, my mother decided to attend college in Los Angeles. While at UCLA, she met a young woman by the name of Lucinda Coker, and they became the best of friends. My mother was introduced to Lucinda's cousin Louis, and the rest is history."

Randi nodded. She always enjoyed hearing a good love story. "Are your grandparents still living in Florida?"

He shook his head. "No, they both passed away years ago."

Then, as if he wanted to change the subject, he asked, "Want to grab something to eat before we take the trolley back to our cars?"

Instead of driving either of their cars, they had taken one of the DC sightseeing tour trolleys. It was great since it allowed them to hop on and off at various sites. "Yes. That would be nice."

It was getting close to five, and she had gotten hungry. Other than grabbing a few snacks from vending machines, they hadn't eaten a meal since breakfast. When she left that morning, she'd told everyone she was meeting a friend for breakfast. After agreeing to extend her time with Quasar, she had texted Haywood that she wouldn't be returning until around six or so that evening. Other than telling her to enjoy herself, no one asked the identity of the friend, and she hadn't provided any information.

"How about you suggesting a place we can grab a bite to eat this time?" Quasar asked.

She smiled up at him. "What about Marlon's Seafood? Their crab cakes are to die for."

He chuckled. "So you've got a taste for seafood, huh?"

It was on the tip of her tongue to confess that what she really had a taste for was him, but she figured that would be too scandalous. Her body had felt like it was in heat most of the day. Just being with Quasar Patterson set off intense desire. This was a unique experience for her. One she intended to take full advantage of…within reason. She was a woman, and as far as she was concerned, there was nothing wrong with appreciating a good-looking man who could fill out a pair of jeans like he did.

"Yes," she said, "I like seafood. Do you?"

"I happen to love seafood. I'd take a bucket of raw oysters over a steak any day," Quasar said, grinning.

His smile spiked another kind of hunger inside her. Sexual hunger. Whenever she looked at Quasar she felt it. And it didn't help matters when she recalled that raw oysters were considered an aphrodisiac.

"You won't be disappointed. Their oysters are amazing," she said.

"Then let's head on over there." He tightened his fingers around hers and began leading her toward the zoo's exit.

"Auntie Rand! Auntie Rand!"

Randi stopped walking and turned upon recognizing the chorus of voices. Two little girls, namely her nieces, rushed over to her. "Brooklyn! Brynn!" Sliding her hand from Quasar's, she bent down to give the girls hugs.

She glanced around and saw the group—Haywood, Trey and their sons, Quad and Dev; along with Zach and Anna and their sons, Zach Jr., who was seven, and Noah, who was five. From their expressions, the adults were as surprised to see her as she was to see them. And of course they were curious about the man she was with.

"Hi, guys," she said, smiling at everyone when they reached her. "I didn't know you all planned to come to the zoo today."

"We hadn't," Trey said, looking from Randi to Quasar, more than a little bit curious. "It was the kids' idea."

"Oh." Randi knew introductions were in order. "Everyone, I'd like you to meet a friend of mine, Quasar Patterson. Quasar, this is my family." She then went around and introduced everyone.

Randi didn't miss how both Trey and Zach kept staring at Quasar as if they knew him from somewhere. She

wondered how long it would take before one of them figured it out. She could tell Haywood and Anna had already
done so by the way they were smiling all over themselves.

Randi should have known it would be Trey who remembered. "Hey, man, didn't we see you last night at
the Kennedy Center?"

"Yes," Quasar said. She could tell from the look passing between Trey and Zach that they were recalling their
wives drooling over Quasar when she'd pretended non-
chalance. And now, after telling them she would be
spending the day with a friend, here she was with Quasar, and chances were they'd seen them holding hands.
She decided it was time to split.

"Quasar and I need to leave or we'll be late for dinner."

"Dinner where?" Trey asked, giving her a look that
clearly indicated he was about to flex his big brother
muscles.

"Not that it's any of your business, Ross Donovan
Fuller III but Quasar and I are dining at Marlon's."

"How long have you lived in DC?" Trey asked Quasar.

"I don't. I live in Charlottesville. I came into town
Friday night for security detail."

Randi knew Trey was about to get in his interrogation
mode, so she said quickly, "I'll see you guys later." She
then leaned down to give the kids kisses on their cheeks.

"At a reasonable time, we hope," Zach threw out.

Leave it to Zach to be just as bad as Trey today. Figured. Grinning, she did likewise to Trey and Zach, kissing them on the cheeks and then saying, "Don't wait up."

She grabbed Quasar's hand, and this time she was the
one leading them toward the exit.

CHAPTER SIX

AFTER RIDING THE TROLLEY for a half hour, Quasar and Randi finally walked through the doors of Marlon's Seafood. The place was packed, and Quasar immediately knew they would be in for a long wait.

"Do you want to go someplace else?" he leaned down to ask Randi. His lips came so close to her ear that he was tempted to lick it. Instead he quickly seized the opportunity to grab her by the waist and pull her closer when the man standing in front of them turned abruptly, almost colliding with them.

"Sorry," the man said.

"No problem," was Quasar's response.

Randi looked up at Quasar. "Thanks."

He smiled down at her. "Don't mention it."

"We don't have to go anyplace else," she said.

"Okay." He didn't mind the wait if she didn't. Besides, he hadn't removed his arms from around her yet. The way she fit against his body was sending all kinds of sensations rippling through him.

The door behind them opened and more people came in. He moved, edging her in front of him to accommodate the new arrivals. He inhaled sharply when her perfectly shaped backside pressed against his groin. Her intoxicating scent filled his nostrils and her beauty almost blinded him. Suddenly a big, tall, brawny older man came barreling through the crowd, a mass of blond hair flying around his shoulders. Quasar was about to pull Randi aside, out of the giant of a man's path, when unexpectedly the huge hulk stopped in front of them. The smile on his face was so huge his blue eyes seemed to illuminate the entire area.

"Little Randolph! One of the waitresses sent word to me that you were here," the brawny man said before grabbing Randi in a massive bear hug, lifting her feet off the floor in the process.

Little Randolph? Quasar watched the affectionate exchange between the two.

When Randi's feet were planted firmly back on the floor, Quasar noted her smile was almost as big as the giant's. "Uncle Marlon! How are you?"

Uncle Marlon? Quasar glanced from the man back to Randi, definitely not seeing any family resemblance.

"Quasar, I want you to meet my Uncle Marlon Farentino. Uncle Marlon, this is my friend Quasar Patterson."

They shook hands, and Quasar felt the man's strength in his handshake. "Nice meeting you."

"Same here." Marlon turned his attention back to Randi. "Come on, girl. I'll take you to your special place."

Marlon led, and they followed through the crowd of people who seemed to open up a pathway like the parting of the Red Sea. Although Quasar was wondering where the man was taking them, he decided not to ask. Not even when they went through the double doors that led to the kitchen. An older lady and younger women noticed the procession and happily waved at Randi, who waved back and threw kisses.

They exited the kitchen and entered a huge dining room set up for a private party. Quasar barely had time to take in the beautiful view of the Potomac through the private dining room's large windows before Marlon led them up a set of stairs to another room with more tables set up. But they didn't stop there. Marlon kept walking until they reached another room where only one table was set up. This room also had a gorgeous view of the Potomac.

"You want your usual?" Marlon asked, pulling the chair out for Randi.

"Yes," she said, sitting down. "And Quasar has a taste for raw oysters."

An even bigger smile crossed the man's ruddy features. "We serve the best in the city. Did you tell him that?"

Randi chuckled. "Yes, I told him."

"Good. Now, what would you two like to drink?"

"Beer is fine for me," Randi said.

"Same here," Quasar said, looking around. This was a nice room that provided privacy.

When Marlon had left them alone, Quasar glanced across the table at Randi and quirked a brow. "Little Randolph? Uncle Marlon?"

The cutest smile curved her lips. "Yes. Before I was born, when Uncle Marlon was in his twenties or so, my father defended him in a homicide case. Dad was able to prove it was self-defense. The Farentinos adopted Dad as one of their own, and when I was born, Uncle Marlon began calling me Little Randolph, after Dad. His daughter, Avona, is my age and is an attorney at my father's law firm. His son, Damon, has his own seafood restaurant, and it's a very popular place in South Miami Beach."

Quasar nodded. "Marlon looks like he ought to be a ship captain."

"He was a fisherman for years and still loves the sea. I've gone out with him and his family on his huge boat."

"You must come here a lot for him to consider this your room."

She smiled. "At one time I did, while attending college at Howard and Georgetown. Whenever I needed to escape, this room became my study room, my eating room and, on occasion, my nap room. Uncle Marlon put a cot in that corner for me to use whenever I needed it. And whenever I could, I helped out on the weekends, waiting tables."

At that moment, a waiter appeared with their beers. Quasar watched as a slow, delightful smile touched the corners of Randi's lips. "After all that walking we did today, I need this."

She lifted the ice-cold mug to her lips and took a sip. Then her tongue licked the sudsy residue from around her mouth. Quasar's breath hitched in his throat as he watched her. The lingering erection he'd gotten when her body had been pressed close to his earlier was now beginning to throb all over again.

Quasar knew he needed to think about anything but her mouth right now, so after taking a sip of his own beer, he said, "Earlier, when you introduced your family at the zoo, did I misunderstand or did you say Haywood was your sister and Trey was your brother?"

"No, you didn't misunderstand. Both my parents were married previously, and Haywood and Trey were products of their first marriages. So I'm sister and brother to both. While Haywood and I were growing up, Trey didn't live with us. He lived in California with his mother and her second husband."

"They have a beautiful bunch of kids. All of them."

Another smile touched Randi's lips. "Yes, they do, and I love all of them to pieces. Aren't the twins adorable? I got to name them," she said proudly. She took another sip of her beer. "Are there any little ones in your family?"

"None that I know of." If she found his response strange, she didn't ask him to elaborate. He appreciated that, because the topic of his family was one he preferred not to discuss.

IT HAPPENED AGAIN.

Randi sensed a high degree of pain and sadness within Quasar whenever he spoke of his family. She couldn't help wondering why. He'd gotten quiet since diving into his bucket of oysters. All the members of her family were seafood lovers, and she'd seen them eat live oysters many times. But there was something about watching Quasar that spread intense sexual heat through her. She'd never thought that shucking oysters could be erotic until now.

She watched as he expertly used the oyster knife to open the oyster, and when he placed it to his lips and sucked the oyster into his mouth, she pressed her thighs together where she felt a deep throb between her legs.

"Something's wrong?"

She blinked when he asked the question, and she knew she'd been caught staring. "No, nothing is wrong," she said, turning her attention to her plate of crab cakes, fries and coleslaw. And because Uncle Marlon knew how much she liked his fried shrimp, he'd given her a huge side order.

"The oysters are good," Quasar said, taking another sip of his beer.

"I told you Uncle Marlon serves only the best."

"Do you like oysters?"

"I like all kinds of seafood. You can't know Marlon Farentino and not do so. I ate my first piece of gator here. It wasn't bad."

"Here. Taste."

Before Randi knew what he was doing, Quasar had scooped some oyster into a spoon to feed to her. Automatically her lips parted, and she sucked the oyster into her mouth, knowing he was watching her. She then took her tongue and licked around her lips. She couldn't help noticing his gaze followed every movement of her tongue.

"Do you want to try some of my crab cakes?" she offered.

"No thanks, but you can feed me a fry." When she reached for her fork, a crooked smile touched his lips. He said, "Use your fingers."

His words sent her already throbbing center skyrocketing. The air between them was sizzling. And why did her mind pick that moment to remember how her bottom had felt plastered against him downstairs earlier? There was no mistaking his huge erection pressing against her.

Knowing he was waiting, she lifted what she thought was the longest fry between her fingers and leaned toward him, directing her hand to his mouth. It opened. She slid the fry inside and nearly moaned when his tongue came into contact with her fingers. It had been deliberate. She was sure of it, and it only made the sexual awareness between them that much more keen.

"Thanks," he said, and that single word spoken in a deep, husky voice washed over her like warm honey.

She stared at him, breathless. Hot. Totally turned on. "You're welcome."

She nervously ran her tongue over her lips, tempted to lick the spot on her finger where his tongue had touched her, as well. Just looking into his eyes all but told her he wanted her just as much as she wanted him. But she knew neither of them was ready for that part of a relationship.

Deciding they needed to talk about anything that wouldn't stir the intense attraction between them, she asked, "So, Quasar, what's your favorite sports team?"

IT WAS CLOSE to eleven when Quasar walked Randi to her car. After sharing a meal at Marlon's, he'd suggested they take in a movie. Convincing herself that the new James Bond movie was something she truly wanted to see, she'd agreed with his idea.

It had been a unique experience for her to sit in the theater, sharing popcorn with Quasar and pretending to watch the big screen, while her entire focus was on him. She had sat there remembering how he'd fed her a few of his oysters at Marlon's and she'd done the same with him and her fries. And the more they'd done so, the more the air surrounding them became electrified to the point that temptation, the likes of which she'd never felt before, had rocked through her veins.

After the movie, they'd stopped at a café for coffee and shared a slice of lemon pound cake. Deep down she had a feeling he wasn't ready for their day together to end any more than she was and was merely drawing out their time.

They hadn't engaged in much conversation since getting off the trolley a few blocks back. Instead they walked to her car in intimate silence. Even now she could feel tremors spreading low in her belly with every step she took beside him.

He was holding her hand as they walked. He'd done the same while sitting beside her in the movies. There had been something about their fingers entwined that made every nerve ending in her body ripe with passion. The man was temptation, walking or sitting.

"Nice night," he finally said.

She glanced around. "Yes, it is, isn't it?"

Other people were walking about, taking advantage of the beauty of the night. Pools of light from the street lamps shone on various car tops, while the intense glow from a full moon illuminated their paths. The scent of some flowering plant floated in the air, and the low hum of insects invaded the night.

"This is my car," she said, coming to a stop in front of the white Lexus two-seater.

He studied the car appreciatively, then smiled at her. "This looks like you."

She chuckled. "Does it?"

"Yes. Sleek, stylish and seductive. I like it."

Randi couldn't help but smile, pleased he thought she was those things. "Thanks, and I'm glad you like my car."

"I like you even more."

A part of her wished she could dismiss his charm. "Do you?"

"Yes. And I enjoyed my time with you today, Randi."

She decided to be honest. "I enjoyed my time with you today, too."

He stared down at her with an intense expression, then reached out and touched her cheek, caressed it. "I want to see you again."

She shoved her hands into the back pockets of her jeans. It was either do that or be tempted to reach up and wrap her arms around his neck. "Why?" She needed him to tell her the reason.

"Because after spending time with you today, I'm not

ready to let you drive away with the thought of not seeing you again. If I didn't know better, I'd think you cast
a spell on me."

Her lips tightened. "I don't have the ability to cast
spells, Quasar. Nor do I predict lotto numbers or fore-
cast the outcome of elections."

Evidently something in her tone alerted him that she
hadn't found his statement amusing. He touched her arm.
"Hey, I was just joking," he said softly. "Sorry. I didn't
mean to offend you."

She drew in a deep breath and shook her head. "No,
I'm the one who should apologize," she said softly. "Your
words reminded me of the ridicule I got when certain
people, those I considered friends, found out about my
psychic abilities. I heard the jokes about casting spells,
sharing winning lotto numbers and forecasting elections.
It made perfect sense to them that if I had these psychic
abilities, I should be able to do all those things and more.
If I couldn't, that meant I was a fake."

He was quiet for a moment and then said, "Again, I
apologize for the thoughtless tease, Randi. I want to see
you again. It has nothing to do with any spell. I find you
desirable. More desirable than any woman I've known. So
if you're okay with it, I'd like to visit you next weekend."

"You live in Charlottesville, and I live in Richmond."

He nodded. "You're talking about an hour's drive. You
would be worth it."

"Would I?" She wished he wouldn't stroke her cheek
like that or look at her with those dark eyes that could
spin her body into a mass of sexual need, something she
wasn't used to experiencing.

"Most definitely."

Was she imagining it or had he shifted his stance,

leaning in a bit closer to her? Needing to keep her sanity, she said, "Correct me if I'm wrong, but didn't you tell me earlier today that you didn't do long-term relationships?"

He held her gaze. "Yes, I did say that."

"In that case, why are you suggesting that we see each other again?"

He slowly dropped his hand and shoved both in the pockets of his jeans, like she'd done with hers. His gaze held hers, as if her absolute attention was totally and completely necessary. As if he'd given what he was about to say some serious thought. "The reason I want to see you again is that the thought of not doing so is something I can't handle right now."

He paused a moment and then continued, "Don't ask me to explain, because I can't make you understand when I don't fully understand myself. All I know is that since that night we saw each other in Charlottesville, you've constantly been on my mind, even when I didn't want you to be. I've thought about you more than any woman I've ever met. I know I've told you all this before, and I was hoping that today would…"

Quasar went quiet. His words had been drawing her in, and she didn't intend for him to leave her hanging now. "Would what?"

He drew in a deep breath. "Purge you from my system. Help me see that what I thought was real was nothing but a fluke. That there was no way I could have met a woman who would make me consider something more than a toss between the sheets at night and a don't-call-me, I'll-call-you in the morning."

Randi tried controlling the beat of her heart. She knew the stipulations regarding her and Quasar about earning the other's love. Was this their first step in achieving those goals? What if the time was right for them to meet but not for them to do anything else, like move forward? What if the latter was supposed to take place at another time, or in another place? For the first time, she regretted not being able to know his inner thoughts.

She swallowed. "I told you why I'm not seriously involved with anyone."

He nodded. "Yes, and I told you I don't have a hangup about your psychic abilities, and what I thought of the men who did. And as far as your work interfering, I understand, because I'm in a similar predicament. My work can take my anywhere at any time."

Quasar took a step closer. "Can you look into my eyes, Randi, and tell me that we don't need to explore what's happening between us further? That you don't agree that today wasn't enough time?"

She knew there was no way she could do that. "But what if things don't work out?" *Especially if our timing is wrong.*

"Then we will know."

Will we? she wondered. Rushing into things now would be a mistake if this wasn't the right time for them. She knew they were sexually attracted to each other, but they also had to earn each other's love. What if they got caught up in the sex and didn't focus on the love?

"When are you returning to Richmond?"

His question made her blink. She was finding it difficult to concentrate around him. "Excuse me?"

"Home? When will you return home?"

"Tomorrow. In the afternoon. After I attend church with my family, I'll be driving back."

"Do you have a problem with me coming to Richmond to see you next weekend?"

Her entire body reacted at the thought that she would see him again, and so soon. "No, I don't have a problem with it."

He smiled. "I'll call you later in the week to get your address."

At that moment, a couple passed them. The man had the woman curled into his side with his arm draped over her shoulders. The love Randi felt flowing between the two almost melted her insides. Funny how she was able to pick up the emotions of strangers, but she got a mental block where Quasar was concerned.

"It's late. I'd better go," she said quietly.

"Alright."

He took a step closer to her, and when he began lowering his head toward hers, instead of taking a step back, she moved nearer. Bracing both hands on the roof of her car, he pinned her, caging her in his delicious strength and heat.

CHAPTER SEVEN

THE MOMENT QUASAR slanted his mouth over Randi's, she couldn't hold back the moan. It was the kiss she'd been waiting for all day. A kiss that robbed her of her senses while it overwhelmed her. She closed her eyes, and whatever strength she had left drained from her body. It was a good thing his arms had moved from the roof of her car to her waist to support her. Otherwise, she would have sunk to her knees the moment his tongue entered her mouth and began mating with hers.

She'd wondered about his taste since that first night, and now, the way his tongue was thrusting in and out of her mouth, she knew how he tasted. He shifted, and his body pressed hard against her. She could feel him— aroused. His erection was poking her in the belly. She became consumed by the heat of him with every languorous stroke of his tongue. Desire began coiling deep inside her.

Randi wrapped her arms around his neck while thickened blood rushed through her veins. She knew for certain that she'd never been kissed like this before. Instinctively she eased up on tiptoes, determined to return the kiss with the same hunger. Her tongue became the aggressor as it battled for control, but he refused to give her any. Instead he was proving that when it came to kissing, he had the skill. The know-how. Definitely more experience, and he intended to make her understand that. She figured her whimpers were a sign she had no problem conceding.

The pressure of his mouth eased up somewhat as slow, deep strokes replaced the intense, hungry ones. But pleasure continued racking her body, and when he finally released her mouth, she slumped against him, feeling totally drained.

And he held her. Even leaned in and licked her bottom lip a few times while telling her how good she tasted. Quasar Patterson had practically devoured her mouth and she'd not only let him, but she'd tried devouring his, as well. Intoxicated by lust, she breathed in his scent, removing her arms from around his neck, knowing he was still holding her up.

She released a deep, satisfied sigh when he took a step back. She figured it was a good thing he'd done so. Otherwise they might have gone after each other's mouths again.

"You can follow me back to my hotel if you like," he invited in his sensual voice.

Randi shook her head. God knew she was tempted, but this was meant to be more than just sex between them. "Thanks for the offer, but I need to go." *Away from you and the way you make me feel.*

"Okay."

She heard the disappointment in his tone. "How far is your car from here? Do you need a ride to it?" she asked him.

"Naw. It's just a few cars up from yours. Since it's so late, if you give me a minute to get to it, I want to follow you to make sure you get home safely."

Follow her? From the look in his eyes, she knew there was no need to tell him not to bother. Besides, the thought that he was concerned for her well-being moved him up a notch. "Alright, if you think you can keep up," she teased.

"Hey, no speeding. The cops in DC don't play."

Randi couldn't help laughing. "Don't I know it."

"Hmm, sounds like a person who's gotten a ticket or two."

"Or three," she said, fishing the car fob from her purse.

Quasar grinned. "With this car, I can see how that's possible."

He stepped back to allow her the space to unlock her car door and slide inside before he shut the door for her. "Thanks," she said, tugging the shoulder harness in place before buckling her seat belt.

"Anytime."

Placing both hands on her steering wheel, she told herself not to look back up at him, just to turn the ignition, say goodbye and drive off. But she couldn't. Nor could she stop herself from rolling her window down. "Thanks for a wonderful day, Quasar. I really enjoyed myself."

He crouched down, bringing his face level with hers, just outside the window. Their mouths were in kissing range. "So did I. Drive carefully."

"Okay."

He leaned his head in the window and copped a quick kiss from her lips...just like she'd been hoping he would do. "And no speeding, Randi."

She was tempted to stick her tongue out at him, but it was still tingling from the force of his kiss. Instead, in an authoritative voice meant to mimic his, she said, "And no speeding, Quasar."

He threw his head back and laughed. She started the engine and saw him move away and sprint ahead. She couldn't help but appreciate how agilely he moved in his jeans. When she saw him get into his car, she pulled away from the curb. As she passed his SUV, she watched in the rearview mirror and saw him pull behind her.

The drive to Zach and Anna's home took about thirty minutes, and each time she glanced in the rearview mirror, Quasar was behind her, right on her tail, figuratively speaking. A comforting feeling filled her, knowing he was there.

When she drove into Zach and Anna's driveway to park right behind Trey's car, she turned off the ignition, unbuckled the seat belt and got out. He'd stopped at the end of the driveway and had rolled down the window. "I'll sit here until you go inside."

"Alright, and good night, Quasar."

"Good night, and I'll see you next weekend."

She nodded and hurried up the walkway to the door.

QUASAR STAYED PUT until Randi had opened the door and gone inside. It was only then that he drove off. He'd gone half a block when he remembered the phone calls he'd gotten today. Twice. He had ignored both, not the least bit curious why his father had been trying to reach him. Didn't matter. He'd had no intention of letting Louis intrude on his time with Randi.

Since the drive back to the hotel would take a good thirty minutes, and considering the time difference between DC and California, he thought he would return the old man's call now. When he came to the first traffic light, he used the car's hands-free system to dial his father.

"About time you returned my call."

Quasar chuckled, deciding not to tell Louis blatantly

that in all honesty, he was lucky to get this phone call. "And the reason you tried reaching me?"

"Doyle intends to announce his candidacy for mayor of Beverly Hills next weekend at the house. I want you here."

You can hold your breath for that to happen, Quasar thought. That's how it had been in the past, though. Louis gave an order and he obeyed. Even if he had to jump through hoops to do so. Even if it meant spending three years in jail. "Sorry to disappoint you, but I'm busy next weekend." Already he was looking forward to visiting Randi in Richmond. "Besides, I'm surprised you'd want me there, being an ex-con and all."

"You served your time. And I want to show family unity."

"Family unity doesn't really exist with the Pattersons. Count me out."

"Look, Quasar, this is a serious matter," Louis snapped.

"Like I care. I haven't been back home in ten years and I have no reason to return now, so like I said, count me out."

"It was your choice not to return to LA. We would have been glad to see you."

Yeah, right. When he'd been released seven years ago, he'd taken Shep's advice and joined Striker and Stonewall in Charlottesville. There was nothing for him to return to in LA. It was a decision he'd never regretted making.

"Tell that to somebody else, Louis. You haven't seen me in ten years. Another ten won't bother you."

"It's not like I haven't tried keeping the lines of communication open. I do call to check on you and make sure you're okay. It's not like I haven't tried getting you to come home. Hell, you wouldn't even tell me where you moved after you got out of jail or even how to reach you, for that matter. I probably still wouldn't know if I hadn't hired that private investigator."

Quasar drew in a deep breath, trying to keep his anger at bay. Yes, his father called from time to time, but usually it was with some BS. The old man always bragged about Doyle's successes and highlighted what he saw as Quasar's failures. The phone conversations were so draining mentally that Quasar regretted answering the calls.

And the old man was right. He hadn't let him know his whereabouts after leaving prison. He hadn't seen the need. Neither his father nor Doyle had visited him or communicated with him while he'd been locked up. Not even during the time he'd nearly lost his life in jail and had to be hospitalized. Other than his godmother, no member of his family had given a damn. That was the main reason he had wanted to put as much distance between them as he could once he became a free man. He'd wanted a new life, one without the stench of them in it. He was determined to make something of himself without their criticisms, and to come to terms with the fact that he had a father and brother who didn't give a fuck about him. He'd been able to do that by getting a surrogate family. Shep was the father figure Louis could never be, and Striker and Stonewall were the brothers Doyle had never tried being. Quasar was satisfied with his life.

"Don't you think it's time for you and Doyle to call a truce?" his father asked.

Truce? Honestly, Quasar didn't think he and his brother were at war. Doyle was probably the same ass he'd been all his life. And as far as Doyle marrying Lilly, well, they were welcome to each other. It hadn't taken him long to realize she'd just wanted to be married to a Patterson.

"If it's about him marrying Lilly," his father continued, "then you need to get over it. They love each other."

He doubted Doyle or Lilly truly knew what love was. They equated love to opportunities. "Glad to hear it. Now, if you don't mind, I need to—"

"I need you to come home, Quasar. You should come home. Think about it."

Quasar shook his head. *He should come home?* There was no reason why he should. Over the years, Louis had said the same thing a number of times, and Quasar knew it was a biting burr in his father's ass that he wasn't there under his thumb for him to manipulate and control. "There's nothing to think about. I've made plans for next weekend and don't intend to change them."

He heard his father snort. "Why are you wasting your time working at that job? You're my son. You should be working alongside Doyle to run Patterson Industries and—"

"And do what? Wait for him to stick his hand in the cookie jar again so I can go to jail to protect him? No thank you. I'll pass. Three years of serving time for a crime I didn't commit was three years too long. But I don't expect you to understand that. Now, goodbye." Not giving his father a chance to say anything when there was nothing that could be said, he clicked off the phone.

Plans were still on for him and Ryker to get together tomorrow. Then he would head back to Charlottesville by evening time. For now, he intended to put his father as well as his phone call, out of his mind. The only person he wanted to think about was Randi. He'd never been involved in a long-distance affair. In a way, long-distance equated to long-term, but would that be such a bad thing? At least he wouldn't have to worry about her showing up unexpectedly at his place, and while he was on assignments, out of sight would mean out of mind. Then, whenever he felt the urge to spend time with her, mainly sleep with her, he could take the drive from Charlottesville to Richmond. He figured it wouldn't be more than an hour on Interstate 64. Unless he decided to take the scenic route for a more relaxed drive. Either way, the destination was the same. Randi's arms and her bed.

He licked his lips, thinking of the kiss they'd shared. He was convinced he could still taste her and hadn't wanted their kiss to end. And the way she'd wrapped her arms around his neck, clung to him, plastered her body against his, had made blood pump through his veins like crazy, especially in his groin. Hell, he was still throbbing down there. Hard as a rock and causing an ache against his zipper.

The instant he'd inserted his tongue inside her mouth, he'd known heaven. Her taste had been delicious, and he had deepened the kiss on instinct to get more of it. His greedy-ass tongue had shifted from one side of her mouth to the other while exploring and tasting as much of her as he could. Desire for her must have practically taken over his senses since they'd done that standing in a public place. But at the time, he hadn't given a damn. The only thing he'd wanted was her. A part of him had known she would turn down his offer to go to his hotel with him, but shit, you couldn't blame a man for trying.

When the car behind him blared its horn, Quasar realized the traffic light had turned green. He smiled as he headed to his hotel while thinking next weekend couldn't get there quick enough.

RANDI WAS STILL floating on a cloud when she entered the guest bedroom. The house was quiet, which meant everyone was asleep. *Evidently not*, she thought moments later upon hearing the knock on her door.

Placing her purse on the dresser, she crossed the room. She hoped she hadn't awakened anyone when she came in. Easing open the door, she really wasn't surprised to see Anna and Haywood standing there. Anna was holding a bottle of wine and a bottle of grape juice, while Haywood was dangling three wineglasses between her fingers.

"Is there a reason for this late-night visit, ladies?" she asked, moving aside to let them enter.

"What do you think?" was Haywood's flippant reply. "You owe us an explanation."

"Do I?" Randi asked, closing the door behind them. "And aren't the two of you worried you'll be missed by your husbands?" The last thing she needed was for Trey or Zach to show up knocking on her bedroom door, looking for their wives.

A smile curved Anna's lips. "We intended to talk to you, so we concocted a plan to wear them out tonight. It worked. They're sleeping off all those org—"

Randi held up her hand to stop her cousin from providing any further details. "Too much information. Besides, I get the picture."

A part of her was happy for her sister and cousin and for the close and openly affectionate relationships they shared with their husbands. But then, she'd have been the first to admit she'd grown up around a mother and father who'd raised the bar when it came to love, happiness and being openly affectionate. There was so much love displayed between her parents that it was something she'd gotten used to over the years, and she couldn't imagine it any other way. Because she'd grown up around so much love, she naturally wanted the same thing for herself. That was one of the reasons she'd found Larry's rejection so painful.

Randi crossed the room to sit on the edge of the bed while watching Anna pour wine in two of the glasses and grape juice in the third. Not for the first time, she couldn't help but admire her cousin's beauty, a result of her mixed heritage of black American and Vietnamese. "I don't recall asking for a nightcap," she said, knowing the only reason Anna and Haywood were there was to pump her for information.

"Chill, sis," Haywood said. "You owe us some answers as well as a debt of thanks for keeping Trey and Zach from drilling your guy. And don't pretend he's not your guy. I saw you before the twins did, and the two of you were holding hands, looking all lovey-dovey."

Randi didn't say anything as she accepted the glass of wine from Anna, who only smiled at her, obviously satisfied with letting Haywood handle the inquisition. "So what do the two of you want to know?"

"Who is he and how did the two of you hook up when you just saw him the other night?" Haywood asked.

Randi took a sip of wine, appreciating the tingling flavor on her tongue. However, she was certain that nothing could replace the taste Quasar had left in her mouth. "Remember when, a few weeks ago, I told you about that guy I met in Charlottesville?"

Haywood raised a brow. "Yes. The one from your dream. Your intended at the crime scene." She paused midsip of wine, and Randi knew Haywood had connected the dots when she placed her wineglass down and stared at Randi. "That was him, wasn't it? He's the guy."

"What guy? What dream? What intended?" Anna asked, looking back and forth between Haywood and Randi.

"You can fill her in," Randi told Haywood. "I'll be back after changing into something more comfortable." She grabbed the mini caftan from the foot of the bed and headed for the connecting bathroom.

Closing the door behind her, she leaned against it. She was still in a state of euphoria from a day spent with Quasar, and she needed some pull-yourself-together time and not interrogation time with her sister and cousin. But still, their untimely interruption couldn't eradicate the memories of Quasar's kiss. She felt as if she was in some sort of daze whenever she thought about it. All she had to do was close her eyes to remember how masterfully he had taken her mouth and the sensations that had swept through her body.

She knew all the time they'd spent together that day should have prepared her for the moment of the kiss. After all, she'd been drawn to his mouth practically all day. Her entire body had literally throbbed every time she looked at it...especially while watching him eat those oysters and drink his beer.

But nothing could have prepared her for that kiss. And it was a kiss that still had her insides tingling something fierce. A kiss that had scorched her all over and branded her mouth permanently. The moment his tongue entered her mouth, her senses had shut down and wicked temptation had taken over. She'd even heard herself purring.

Drawing in a deep breath, she pushed away from the door and eased her jeans down past her hips. It had been her intent to shower and go to bed to dream and fantasize about the coming weekend, when she would see Quasar again. Now thanks to Haywood and Anna, the shower and bed had to wait until she appeased their nosiness.

She slid the caftan over her head, loving the smoothness of the silk fabric against her skin. Drawing in a deep breath, she left the bathroom to rejoin Haywood and Anna. She could tell by the look on Anna's face that she had questions. "Okay, Anna, what do you want to know?" she asked, grabbing her wineglass off the nightstand.

"Does Quasar Patterson know that the two of your futures have been pretty much mapped out?"

The answer to that question was simple. "No. Right now all he knows is that we're very much attracted to each other. The reason we spent the day together is that he's trying to figure out why."

"Wouldn't it be easier if you told him?"

Randi settled back on the bed. "I can't do that. There are circumstances we have to overcome before we can have a future together. Namely, we have to earn each other's love. If I were to tell Quasar that he and I are destined to have a future together, what do you think he'd do?"

Haywood chuckled. "Probably run in the other direction, fight it like hell or try to prove you're wrong."

"Yes, he would. Right now he thinks the attraction is of a sexual nature, and he's operating on that assumption. It will be up to him to discover different."

"What about you?" Anna asked after taking of sip of her grape juice. "How do you feel about all of this? Hav-

ing the man you'll spend the rest of your life with chosen
for you, instead of you choosing him yourself?"

"I chose Larry and look what it got me," Randi said,
sipping her wine. "I admit it's kind of overwhelming, but
I've known that's the way it would be for some years now.
That year spent by myself on Glendale Shores and having
Gramma Mattie come to me the way she did helped me
not only understand my gift but also accept and appreci-
ate it for what it is. It wasn't love at first sight for me or
Quasar. What we are is sexually attracted to each other.
That much is pretty obvious and what's driving things
right now. I have a mental block where he's concerned,
and it's deliberate. Maybe that's a good thing. But then,
I had a mental block when it came to Larry, as well."

After taking another sip of wine, she said, "I have to
believe my future is being directed for a purpose, and
in the end, if things work out and Quasar and I do earn
each other's love, then it will be well worth it."

"He's certainly not a hard man for a woman to love,"
Haywood said, fanning herself. "Looks good to any female's eyes. The man is definitely hot. How did you manage keeping your hands to yourself today?"

Randi chuckled. "Who said I did?"

Haywood's eyes widened. "Does that mean the two
of you—"

"No! How could you think such a thing, Haywood?"

"Easily. Like I said, he's hot. And…you've been gone
all day. When we saw you this afternoon, you said the
two of you were going to Uncle Marlon's for dinner. I
doubt you closed the place down, so I can only assume
you went back to his hotel with him."

"Well, you assume wrong. We took in a movie, and

afterward we stopped by a café for coffee and dessert," Randi said, shaking her head.

"Sounds like the two of you enjoyed yourselves."

Randi smiled. "It was nice. However, I know that I have my work cut out for me. I'm well aware that Quasar's main interest in me right now is all about getting me into his bed. We have to develop a relationship not centered on sex."

"When will you see him again?" Haywood asked.

"Next weekend. He asked if he could visit me in Richmond, and I told him that he could."

Anna placed her empty glass aside. "Well, I think the two of you looked good together. He's handsome and you're a natural beauty. The two of you will make beautiful babies."

Randi nearly choked on her wine.

CHAPTER EIGHT

"I SAW HER this weekend."

Lamar "Striker" Jennings paused from taking a huge bite of his pizza to look at Quasar. They had met for lunch, like they normally did on Tuesdays, at a place that was fast becoming one of Quasar's favorite fast-food dining places. They not only served the best hamburgers but also had some damn good barbecue ribs and pizzas. "You saw who?"

"Dr. Randi Fuller."

Striker lifted a brow. "The psychic?"

"Yes, the psychic."

Striker recalled that night Quasar had first seen Dr. Fuller at the crime scene. He had talked about nothing else for days. Then he stopped talking about her...or maybe Striker had stopped listening, since he was so wrapped up in Margo Connelly at the time. He was still wrapped up in Margo. "I hadn't heard she was back in town."

Quasar took a swig of his beer. "She's not. I ran into her in DC while doing that security gig at the Kennedy Center Friday night."

"And she remembered you?"

Quasar's lips twitched in a smile. "Let's just say that we remembered each other."

Striker snorted. "What the hell is that supposed to mean?"

"Just what I said. The sexual chemistry between us was still too strong."

Striker rolled his eyes. "I bet more on your end than hers."

Quasar lifted a brow. "Why do you think that?"

Striker grinned as he took a swig of his own beer. "Damn, Quasar, she's a psychic. Helping the police rescue me and Margo made a real believer out of me about her paranormal abilities. So there's no reason for me to believe she doesn't know what's on your mind. Every damn horny detail."

Quasar's frowned. "For your information, Mr. Know-It-All, her psychic abilities have nothing to do with me. She says that she has a mental block where I'm concerned."

Striker had been dousing his pizza with more parmesan cheese when he shifted his attention back to Quasar. "She says? Mental block? WTF? Did the two of you engage in conversation?"

Quasar shrugged. "I guess so."

Striker frowned. "Stop being a smart-ass and answer the question. Did you and Dr. Fuller converse?"

Quasar couldn't help shooting Striker an amused look. Ever since he'd hooked up with Margo Connelly, Striker was getting way too serious. "Yes, we talked. In fact, we did more than that. We spent the entire day together on Saturday."

Quasar had Striker's full attention. "How did you manage that?"

Quasar saw no point in telling Striker every single detail of what happened, so he decided to give him a shortened version. "I asked her to breakfast, and we decided to make a day of it."

"Day? Not night?"

Quasar rolled his eyes. "We spent only the day together, Striker."

After taking another bite of his pizza, Striker asked, "Whose idea was it…for the two of you to spend *any* time together?"

"What difference does it make?"

"None, I guess. I merely asked out of curiosity."

"Okay, it was my idea," Quasar admitted.

"Hmm."

Quasar's lips tightened. "What's the *hmm* for?"

"No reason." Then Striker asked, "And you really believe she has a mental block where you're concerned?"

"Yes. She said that she did."

Striker shook his head. "She was probably pulling your leg, man. I doubt psychics can turn on and off their telepathic abilities that way."

Quasar shrugged. "I'm just stating what she told me, and I have no reason not to believe her."

A slow grin curved Striker's lips. "Just as well. Good thing she had no idea what you were thinking while you were with her. Those horny details I mentioned earlier."

He wouldn't admit it, but Striker was probably right. Most of the time he was thinking of her in his bed. "Whatever."

"Aren't you the least bit curious why you aren't on her telepathy sensor? What makes you so special?"

"It's not that I'm special, Striker," Quasar said, trying not to get annoyed. "From the way she explained things to me, her psychic powers are meant to help others more than to help her."

Striker's smile faded. "Are you saying that she fore-
sees danger for others but not for herself?"

Quasar frowned thoughtfully. He hadn't looked at it
that way. Leave it to Striker to analyze every damn thing
and come up with possibilities Quasar didn't want to
think about. The mere thought that Randi could be vul-
nerable to the crazies out there was unsettling. "I guess
so. Hell, I don't know. All I know is what she told me."

"And like I said, she was probably pulling your leg
about what she could and could not do."

Quasar honestly didn't think that she was. "She didn't
know I was an ex-con."

Striker lifted a brow. "Are you sure of that?"

"Pretty much." Quasar bit into his own pizza.

"Did she ask you any questions about the time you
were locked up?"

"No," Quasar said, picking up his mug to wash down
the pizza with beer.

"Then consider yourself lucky. When I told Margo
about me being an ex-con, she didn't give me a minute's
rest. She wanted to know every single detail." Shaking
his head, Striker then downed the rest of his beer.

Quasar eyed his friend over the rim of his beer mug.
"You love Margo, don't you?"

Striker scowled over at him. "Why are you asking me
that? Damn right I love her. I told you and Stonewall I
did. Hell, you two were the first people I told…after telling Margo, of course."

"That was almost three months ago. Nothing has
changed?"

Striker burst out laughing. "Shit, Quasar, falling in
love doesn't work that way. It's a lifetime commitment.
It took me forever to find a woman I'd want to spend the

rest of my life with, and I can't imagine that being any woman other than Margo. She totally has my heart."

Quasar didn't say anything. Striker was the last person he'd thought would admit such a thing. But then, Quasar liked Margo, and he knew that she might have Striker's heart, but Striker had hers, as well. He'd seen how they interacted. It was easy to tell they cared deeply for each other.

"Don't worry. Your time is coming, Quasar."

Quasar lifted a brow. "How you figure that?"

A smile touched Striker's lips. "Not sure. I just do."

Quasar didn't like that prediction. He leaned over the table, got almost nose to nose with Striker and looked him dead in the eyes. "What are you now? Some damn psychic?" he asked angrily. Any other man with a lick of sense would have thought twice before getting in Striker's face. He was just as tall as Quasar—in fact, maybe a few inches taller—and was a total badass who worked out a lot, rode his motorcycle like a bat out of hell and spent a lot of time at the gun range, perfecting his aim.

Instead of knocking the hell out of him, Striker merely sat there grinning like he enjoyed getting a rise out of Quasar.

"If figuring that out makes me a psychic, then so be it."

As if anticipating a brawl was about to take place, a man Quasar assumed was the manager of the establishment rushed over to their table. "Not in here, guys. Take it outside."

Quasar sat back down in his seat. "No need. I'll put off his ass-whipping for another day."

Ignoring Striker's laugh, Quasar resumed eating his pizza.

Randi's fingers paused on the keyboard of her laptop as she gazed at the huge arrangements of fresh flowers that had been delivered to her earlier. They had certainly brightened up her Wednesday morning. They were from Quasar and the card simply read,

> *Thanks for spending the day with me, and I'm looking forward to seeing you this weekend.*

She couldn't help smiling as she recalled the last time a man had sent her flowers other than her father or her godfather, Noah. Larry had never sent her any. Probably couldn't afford to as a college student. To say the delivery had been a pleasant surprise would definitely have been an understatement.

A few hours later, after completing her project, she swiveled her chair around to pull her cell phone out of her purse. There was no reason she couldn't take the time to thank Quasar now. It was polite and had nothing to do with the fact that she'd thought of him a lot since Saturday. More than she really should have with all the work she had to do. Next month she would be teaching a class at Quantico. She needed to get prepared and not daydream about Quasar every chance she got.

"Hello, Randi."

She wished she could ignore the warm sensation that flowed through her. Why did he have to sound so sexy and say her name with so much sensuality? "I got the flowers, Quasar, and they are beautiful." She refused to trot out the old cliché *You shouldn't have*, when she was glad he had. "Thank you so much."

"You're welcome. Like I said on the card, I enjoyed my

time with you Saturday and look forward to this weekend."

And I enjoyed my time with you. "Is there anything in particular you'd like us to do while you're here?" Too late she realized how that might have sounded. Given the opportunity, she'd bet any man could come up with several things, all sexual in nature.

"Um, I'll leave the plans to you," he said in that ultra-sexy voice stirring her in places that hadn't been stimulated in years.

"So tell me, Randi, how have you been?"

She leaned back in chair while gazing at her flowers. "Great. I'm teaching a class at the FBI Training Center next month, and I'm getting prepared for it. New recruits always try to challenge my mind."

"In what way?"

"By attempting to test my abilities. They figure if I'm a psychic, I should know everything, including who's winning the Super Bowl next year."

"A few skeptics, huh?"

"More than a few, but I'm used to it. What I do is use my degree in analytical behavior to smooth out the doubters. I explain that not all psychics are alike and not all of them can do the same thing. Every gift is pretty personalized. And then, unfortunately, there are the great pretenders. They give those of us who are legitimate a bad rap. That's something the doubters see as logical and making sense."

"You're the real thing. I'll admit, I was a skeptic at first, but you made a believer out of me."

"Glad to hear it. Well, I need to get back to work. I just wanted to thank you for the flowers."

"You're welcome, and while I have you on the phone, what's your address?"

She rattled it off to him.

"Thanks, and I'll see you Friday around seven."

"Okay, I'll see you then."

After hanging up the phone, she picked up her cup of tea and took a sip while trying to ignore the giddy feeling in the pit of her stomach. She almost jumped at the sound of her phone ringing. She glanced at it, not recognizing the number. "This is Dr. Randi Fuller. May I help you?"

"Yes, Dr. Fuller, this is Special Agent Jarez Riviera of the Los Angeles FBI."

She leaned back in her chair. "Yes, Agent Riviera?"

"You came highly recommended from Special Agent Tommy Felton in Charlottesville. He said the two of you worked together on a couple of cases."

Randi doubted she could forget Special Agent Felton and his blatant dislike of her, mainly because he had chosen not to believe in her capabilities. The first time had been a case involving a human trafficking ring. If the Bureau had taken her findings seriously, they could have captured the leader of the group, Levan Shaw. They had managed to rescue over fifty kids and young women. However, Shaw remained at large. He was out there involved in no telling what types of criminal activities. He hadn't resurfaced in over two years. Some thought he was dead, but a part of her knew the man was very much alive.

Shaw was the one person she'd never been able to get a clear read on. However, when it came to his criminal activities of kidnapping kids for the slave trade, she'd been able to key in. It had been the children crying out to her for help that had aided her with the case.

Because Agent Felton had blown the chance to apprehend Levan Shaw, the director of the FBI had come down hard on him, and he'd gotten overlooked for the big promotion he'd felt he deserved. He'd blamed her for it.

She would admit that in the course of the last case they'd worked together three months ago, the Erickson case, she felt she'd finally gained his respect. In a move that had surprised her, Agent Felton had approached her during her last day in Charlottesville, thanked her for all her help and apologized for his past hard-hearted behavior toward her.

"By the way, Agent Felton told me to tell you that he sends his best regards."

"Thank you, Agent Riviera. How can I help you?"

"Rival gangs are about to go head-to-head here in Los Angeles unless we can stop them. The mother of the Westside Warlords gang leader was brutally murdered a few days ago. The rival gang, the Eastside Revengers, claim they had nothing to do with it and are being set up. We have reason to believe that's true. We need to find the perp and make an arrest before this city is covered in blood."

Randi closed her eyes, and immediately an image of Esther Emiliano flashed through her mind. She could see the woman clearly, lying on her back, naked, with the blue dress she'd been wearing ripped into shreds. Hair that had been cut from her head lay scattered on her naked stomach, and her once angelic face was sadistically carved up.

A chill went through Randi. Esther Emiliano's murder had been the work of a coldhearted, bloodsucking, merciless bastard. And the perp was not a member of the Eastside Revengers.

"Dr. Fuller?"

Randi set her mind back on the phone conversation. "Yes, Agent Riviera. You're right. The person who killed Esther Emiliano is not a member of the Revengers."

He didn't say anything, and she knew he was trying to digest the fact that she'd given him the name of the victim when he hadn't mentioned it. "I also know she was wearing a blue dress at the time she was brutally raped and that the perp all but cut her hair off at the scalp after shooting her in the head. Four times. Her face was carved up to the point that it was unrecognizable. She died on her back, legs sprawled open in a pool of blood. It was an execution-style killing."

Randi heard the sound of the agent's sharp gasp. Without being given any specifics of the case, she'd described things to him as if she'd been there at the crime scene. "And you know all this from my phone call?" he asked with utter amazement in his voice.

"I'm able to tune in to the crime from a phone call most of the time, but not always. I also know that currently you don't have any tangible leads. And although you know the type of gun used, you haven't been able to find the murder weapon." She let out a long sigh. "You and your men are looking in the wrong places."

"We are?"

"Yes. I see water, beautiful blue waters. Not the ocean. Not that large. It's in a smaller body of water. Like a small lake or pond."

"Around LA, that could be a number of places. We have lakes and ponds all over." He paused a moment, then asked, "Do you know who did it, Dr. Fuller? The person or persons responsible?"

"Not yet. But I feel certain I can assist you."

"Any help you can give us will be appreciated."

"I don't feel I will be able to provide any additional revelations over the phone. I need to come to LA and visit the crime scene."

"How soon can you get here?"

Randi glanced over at the flowers. Regret touched her deeply. "I can fly out there first thing in the morning."

"Thank you, Dr. Fuller."

CHAPTER NINE

QUASAR'S SPIRITS SANK while listening to what Randi was telling him. This weekend was off. She was needed in LA to assist the local authorities and FBI in stopping bloodshed between two rival gangs.

"I'm sorry, Quasar. I was really looking forward to seeing you again this weekend."

He heard the sincerity in her voice. "Same here. Do you know how long you'll be on the West Coast?"

"Not sure. Ideally for no more than a week or so. The key lies in the murder weapon, and we're racing against time. One gang is convinced the other one is guilty and plans to retaliate. Innocent people could get hurt."

You could get hurt. Quasar blinked, wondering why such a thing had popped into his head. He knew Randi handled these types of assignments all the time. That was her life with the gift. So why was he suddenly remembering what Striker had theorized?

She can foresee danger for others, but not for herself.

"Will you have protection?"

"Protection? What kind of protection?" she asked.

"Bodyguard protection. Someone watching your back." Suddenly the sight of her backside filled his mind. He couldn't dismiss the image of her hips swaying with each and every step she took. He'd seen a number of asses in his day but was convinced he'd never seen anything as sensual as hers.

"No, Quasar. I don't need a bodyguard or anyone watching my back." She chuckled. "If I did, you'd be the first to know."

Would I?

"I've done all this before, and my life has never been in danger," she added.

"Just being concerned," he said, not liking all these thoughts going through his mind.

"That's awfully sweet of you. I need to start packing since I'm flying out in the morning. I'll call you when I get back. Then I hope we can reschedule things. Okay?"

"Sounds like a plan, one I'll look forward to. Have a safe trip, Randi."

"Thanks, Quasar. Goodbye."

"Goodbye."

Quasar clicked off his cell phone and didn't place it back on the table. Every ounce of good sense warned him to let it go. Randi was right. She didn't need protection. She did this sort of thing all the time, assisting law enforcement in capturing the bad guys. Hadn't she done the same thing while in Charlottesville? She hadn't needed protection then.

Okay, she might not need protection, but…he wanted to see her and would probably use any flimsy-ass excuse to do so. He'd never been obsessed with a woman to the point of considering following her across the country to sniff her out.

But then, Louis had invited him home this weekend. To some damn party to kick off Doyle's political career. His first thought had been that there was no way in hell he would attend the party. But he would admit that spending time with Randi, seeing her interact with her family and hearing about how close they were had ignited struggles within him. He needed to do what he'd put off doing for years—coming face-to-face with the old man to get some answers once and for all. It was time he dealt with the demons from his past in order to move on fully.

He shook his head. Another flimsy-ass excuse when he knew his main reason for even thinking about hopping a plane tomorrow for the West Coast was Randi.

Quasar paced around his living room a few times, talking himself out of going and then talking himself right back into going. *What the hell*, he thought, finally making a decision he intended to stick with. He punched in Roland's number, and it was answered on the first ring. "This is Roland."

"Roland, this is Quasar. I need to be taken off the work schedule for two weeks starting tomorrow."

"Is everything okay?"

"Yeah, things are fine."

Since there was no way he'd tell Roland he was going to LA for a woman, he told Roland something that wasn't the total truth but wasn't a complete lie, either. "The old man's been calling. He wants me to come home this weekend. At first I turned him down, but I've changed my mind. So I'm going to LA, after all."

"You okay in doing that?"

Roland was one of the few people in his circle of close friends who knew his history. Namely, the truth about his confinement and his dysfunctional family. "Yes, I'm okay in doing that. About time, don't you think?"

"Yes, Quasar. I think it's about time."

"Is there anything you need me to do while you're gone?"

Randi glanced over at Haywood. "No, and you didn't need to put yourself out to drive me to the airport. I could have taken my own car and left it there until I returned."

"No problem. Besides, we haven't had a chance to talk."

Randi chuckled. "You mean since last weekend when you and Anna had me in the interrogation room?"

Haywood laughed. "Hey, we weren't that bad, were we?"

Randi shrugged. "No, I guess not. It's been a long time since the two of you got all into my business that way."

"Mainly because you hadn't had any business for us to get into. And speaking of getting some business, are you on the Pill?"

Randi was certain if she hadn't finished her coffee already, she probably would have choked on it. "The Pill? What brought that question on?"

"A sexy, hot man by the name of Quasar Patterson. Remember him?"

Randi doubted she could forget him. "First, you assumed I went to his hotel room and did the nasty Saturday night. Now you're asking me if I'm on the Pill. What's up with you?"

"I figured you went off birth control after your breakup with Larry, thinking you'd never sleep with another man again and all that craziness."

"You sound like someone who's been there."

Haywood chuckled. "How do you think Quad was born? That's what happens when you hang around a sexy man. Sexual chemistry can be deadly."

Randi looked at her sister. "I'm a big girl. I can handle it."

"That's what I thought, so do your big sis a favor. If you haven't done so, please go back on the Pill."

Randi shook her head. "I'm not sexually active. However, I've been getting injections for a couple of years… just to be on the safe side."

"Great! Then you're good to go."

Good to go? Randi shook her head again. "Thanks for the words of encouragement. Most big sisters wouldn't entice their little sisters to go out and act so…"

"Horny?"

Randi smiled. "The word I was thinking of was *promiscuous.*"

Haywood brought the car to a stop at a traffic light. "Sweetheart, you don't have a promiscuous bone in your body. You were a virgin before Larry, and you haven't shared a bed with anyone since."

"You sure of that?"

Haywood chuckled. "Yes, unless you're living a double life, which I doubt. And although some of those FBI agents and detectives you get to work closely with at times are probably hot, I just can't see you getting buck wild."

Randi couldn't see herself getting buck wild, either. "So why are you willing to throw me out there to Quasar, spread-eagle and all?"

"Because he's your mate. Or he will be when the two of you begin seriously dating."

Randi sighed deeply. "Not sure when that might be since I had to cancel this weekend. I was looking forward to seeing him again. I'll call him when I get back and try to reschedule his visit."

Haywood pulled the car up to the curb at the airport for Randi to get out with her luggage. "Give me a hug, sis, and stay safe."

Randi leaned over and hugged Haywood. "I will, and take care of my brother, nieces and nephews while I'm gone."

"I can't imagine my life being any other way. My man and our babies are my heart."

Randi knew that to be true and looked forward to the day when she would say something like that about *her* man. An image of Quasar flashed in her mind, and she couldn't help but smile.

QUASAR MOVED ASIDE to let the two men enter his apartment. He shook his head as he closed the door behind them. "One day you guys are going to learn to call before just showing up."

"Why?" Stonewall Courson asked, glancing around. "You have a policy of not bringing women back here anyway."

Quasar continued walking to his bedroom and wasn't surprised when they followed. He was packing and didn't intend to let them slow him down. His plane left later that day. "When did you get back, Stonewall?" His friend had been gone for three weeks, providing bodyguard services to some billionaire playboy who was jet-setting all over the world.

"This morning, and it's good to be back."

Quasar chuckled. "Why? You missed your detective?" He was teasing Stonewall about Detective Joy Ingram again since it was no secret Stonewall had the hots for her. Like it was no secret that due to both Stonewall's and the detective's crazy work schedules, they still hadn't gone out on an official date.

"No, I missed you guys."

"Liar," Striker said.

Quasar looked at Striker, thinking that was his first word since walking into the apartment. "What's wrong with you, Striker? Margo decided not to marry you, after all?"

"No. Roland told us you're headed to Los Angeles."

"What about it?"

"If you're finally going back home to give your brother the ass-whipping he deserves, then we need to go with you…"

"I can handle Doyle," Quasar said, lapsing into Spanish, something he had a tendency to do whenever his strong emotions kicked in about anything.

"I assume you said you can handle Doyle. What about your old man?" Stonewall asked. "Can you handle him, as well? And for heaven's sake speak English so we can understand you."

"Yes, I can handle him, as well," Quasar said, easing back into English. "Any more questions?"

"Yes, there's another one," Striker said, pulling a folded piece of newspaper out of the back pocket of his jeans. "According to this article, Dr. Fuller is on her way to Los Angeles and will be working with the FBI on a gang-related case. Now, isn't that a coincidence that the two of you will be in LA at the same time?"

Keeping a straight face, Quasar said, "Yes, it is, isn't it?"

"Don't test my intelligence by saying you didn't know," Striker said, narrowing his gaze.

"Wouldn't think of it."

"So you're going to LA mainly for her and not your fucked-up family?"

Quasar tried keeping the grin off his face. "For both."

Stonewall ignored the back-and-forth banter between the two and glanced into Quasar's luggage. "I hate to interrupt such interesting conversation, but is there a reason you're taking your Glock with you to LA? Expecting trouble, Quasar?"

Quasar leaned back against the bedroom dresser and crossed his arms over his chest. He was tempted to tell them about the weird dream he'd had last night. In his dream, Randi had been running—from whom, he didn't know. But every time she looked over her shoulder, there was a look of intense fear in her eyes. He didn't know why he'd dreamed such a thing and figured it might have to do with that damn pizza he'd eaten before bedtime. All those onions, peppers and garlic might have gone his brain. But still, he'd awakened that morning with a funny feeling in his gut about it that wouldn't go away.

"I take my Glock whenever I travel," he said. "And as far as expecting trouble, the answer is no. However…"

Both men stared at him. "However, what?" Striker asked.

Quasar met both men's gazes in turn. "However, trouble has a way of sneaking up on you when you least expect it."

CHAPTER TEN

"DR. FULLER?"

Randi, who was in baggage claim waiting for her luggage to appear on the conveyor belt, had to strain her neck to look up into the man's face. He had to be every bit of six-four, probably thirty-five or -six years in age, and was ruggedly handsome with a charming smile. "Yes, I'm Dr. Fuller."

He extended his hand. "I'm Special Agent Jarez Riviera. Welcome to Los Angeles. We appreciate you coming."

"Thanks."

"I'll grab your bags off the carousel. How many do you have?"

"Just one. It's that twenty-one-inch piece coming toward us now."

She moved aside as he effortlessly snagged her luggage, which she knew was close to the fifty-pound max limit. "Thanks."

"No problem. I have a car waiting for us at the curb."

Instead of relinquishing his hold on her luggage, he pulled it for her. She appreciated it since that meant she needed to maneuver only her carry-on while she did everything she could to keep up with his long strides.

"Sorry," he said, glancing back at her when he noticed

she had fallen behind. "I have a tendency to walk fast." He then slowed his pace for her benefit.

"That's okay."

"First time in LA?" he asked her.

She shook her head. "No. I've been here a few times."

Randi was curious about the status of the gangs, but with so many people around, she knew that now was not a good time to discuss it. "So, Agent Riviera, were you born and raised in LA?"

"As a matter of fact, I was. However, I've been back only three years now. That's how the FBI operates. They seldom allow you to remain in the same place more than two to three years. They like moving you around."

"I know. I used to work for the Bureau full-time as a behavioral analyst." She'd gotten to know a lot of agents while at Quantico.

"So I heard. I understand you stayed for only two years."

"Yes. They had restrictions about me assisting other branches of the law with my psychic abilities. I agreed to continue to be an instructor for them as a freelancer. That way I'm not limited on whom I can help."

"Here we are," he said, stopping at a black sedan parked at the curb. He opened the trunk and placed her luggage inside. "We've made reservations for you at a hotel close to headquarters. You had a long flight, so we want you to relax and get some rest. We'll be by in the morning to take you to the crime scene."

When he opened the door for her, she slid inside the car. "There's really no need to rest up since I slept a lot on the plane. If it's all the same to you, Agent Riviera, I'd rather check into my room to freshen up a bit and then meet with your team. If possible, I'd like to look at the crime scene today. The sooner we can bring to justice the person or persons responsible for the death of Esther Emiliano, the sooner we can head off a gang war."

A relieved smile touched Agent Riviera's lips. "I was hoping you'd say that. And just so you know, as much as we wanted to keep your involvement in the case under wraps, it's now public information. It was mentioned on the news this morning that you were coming, and there was also an article in this morning's paper about it."

Randi nodded. "That's the least of my worries. My main concern is to help stop any unnecessary bloodshed."

"I HEARD ON the news that the Feds have called in a psychic investigator." Shane Griffin had to talk louder than normal since the arcade was noisy.

The man he was talking to didn't even look up. Instead he proceeded to drop more change into the pinball machine for another game. "Did you hear what I said, Rick?" Shane asked, just in case he hadn't been heard over the blaring sounds from the speakers.

Rick Constantine excitedly jumped up and down when he got a free game. It was only then that he turned to Shane. "You think I give a shit about some psychic? That just shows the Feds have nothing. They must be pretty damn desperate to go out and solicit the help of some loony with a crystal ball."

"Hey, man, I heard she's good and the real thing. That reporter on TV claims she helped save some political figure from the clutches of ISIS."

"You sure about that?"

"I heard it myself. The reporter said that more recently she helped the Charlottesville Police and FBI nab a serial assassin. What if she fingers us, man? Hell, we'll all be dead if Maceo discovers we're the ones who killed his mother. I shouldn't have let you talk me into getting involved with your crap."

Rick frowned. "You got involved because the money was good. I bet you've spent your share already."

"Hey, don't worry about what I did with my share. Just make sure that psychic doesn't nail us." Shane then turned and walked out of the arcade.

Rick's frown deepened. Some guy who called himself the Big Man had approached him last month with a plan to start a war between the Warlords and the Revengers. Rick didn't know Mr. Big's real name or where he'd come from, but Rick could tell he was used to being in charge. And the guy was loaded. Hell, Rick had gotten fifty grand just to kill Esther Emiliano and make it look like a gang hit—something Mr. Big was sure would push the Warlords to the brink—and would be paid another fifty when the war led to the deaths of both gang's leaders. The war would also take out most of the members of the two gangs and then a new gang, headed by the Big Man, would take over the streets of LA. Rick had given Shane half of the money for his help and the promise of more once the Warlords retaliated for Esther Emiliano's murder. Rick knew Shane was regretting his part in knocking off the old woman, but the deed was done, and they needed to keep their mouths shut. He didn't want to think about how Mateo would react if he discovered his mother's murderers were members of his own gang. Traitors.

The one thing Rick hadn't counted on was the FBI bringing in a damn psychic. He needed to let the Big Man know right away.

RANDI AND AGENT RIVIERA had just entered the hotel's lobby when his cell phone went off. "Riviera."

Although Randi could not hear what the caller was saying, she could tell from Agent Riviera's expression that it wasn't good news. She hoped the Warlords hadn't retaliated already.

He clicked off the phone and said, "Looks like we'll have to put off going to the crime scene until the morning after all, Dr. Fuller. I just received word that the mayor is calling an emergency meeting in an hour about the gang activities in the city. That meeting will be followed by a press conference, after which the FBI and LAPD will hold a joint meeting. If it's okay with you, we can go first thing in the morning. Say around ten?"

She nodded. "That time works for me."

"Great, and thanks for your understanding. When you get hungry, there's a pretty nice restaurant in this hotel. If you prefer something else, just call me," he said, passing his business card to her. "If I don't answer by the second ring, the call will be transferred to my personal assistant. She's been given strict orders to give you anything you need. If you leave the hotel for any reason, a private car will be at your disposal to take you anywhere you want to go."

"Thank you, Agent Riviera. I appreciate that."

"You're welcome. I'll check on you later, after my meetings. I hope you find the accommodations here to your satisfaction."

Randi glanced around. It was a beautiful hotel. There was a huge spectacular atrium populated with numerous flowers and plants, and the ultramodern decor spoke of class. If this was a sample of what awaited her in her hotel room, she couldn't wait to get up there. Smiling, she turned back to Agent Riviera. "I'm sure that I will."

"So Mr. Big, you got this, right? You're going to take care of that psychic so she doesn't mess up our plans?"

Our plans? Leo Stillwell fought hard to keep the smile plastered on his face. The punk standing in front of his desk had no idea he was nothing more than a pawn being used to carry out *his* plan. There was no *our* in it, but he wouldn't tell the fool that yet. In the end, Rick Constantine would be disposed of like the others.

He stood. "I said I did, didn't I? But of course I'm going to need my right-hand man. Let me figure a few things out. I'll call and let you know when I want to make a hit."

"A hit? So you intend to kill her?"

He heard both surprise and excitement in Constantine's voice. For someone so young, he had a killer instinct that Leo admired, but Rick Constantine couldn't be trusted. If he could so easily betray his gang for money, then there was no way Leo could fully trust that Rick wouldn't do the same to him if given the chance. "Yes, I plan to kill her."

There was no need to explain to this nitwit that now he would get his revenge. He had read the papers this morning and had seen the news about Dr. Fuller being brought in to assist the FBI in circumventing a possible gang war. Things couldn't have worked out more to his advantage if he had planned them himself. He could start the gang war and finally settle the score with Dr. Fuller.

"Leave so I can set our plans in motion."

Constantine gave him a huge, silly-looking grin. "That's what I like about you, Big Man. You don't waste time taking care of business." The cocky young man then turned and walked out the door.

Leo leaned back in his chair, thinking Constantine would see firsthand just how fast he worked when it was Constantine's time to get a bullet blown in his damn head.

CHAPTER ELEVEN

RANDI TOOK IN her surroundings. Just as she'd figured, the suite was simply beautiful. The furnishings, especially the king-size bed, looked comfortable and inviting. Instead of carpeting on the floor, the set of rooms had rich-looking hardwood floors, a fireplace and tray ceilings with exquisitely crafted crown moldings. A set of French doors led onto a balcony that provided a scenic view of downtown Los Angeles.

She'd been to Los Angeles several times. As far as she was concerned, there was nothing more majestic than downtown LA at night. All the skyscrapers and brilliant steel beams cast a beautiful reflective glow of the moonlit sky.

A part of her wished she had someone to share the experience with, and for the first time in a long while, she felt the pangs of loneliness. She had her work to keep her busy, and that had always sufficed.

But that was before she'd met Quasar.

Unpacking her luggage, she paused as she felt a deep flutter in her heart. How could a man she'd spent only one day with have such an impact on her state of being? Could it be that she'd looked forward to this weekend with him more than she'd realized? She shook off the thought. She had work to do and couldn't let thoughts of Quasar fill her mind. She would get a good night's sleep and be well rested when she went to the crime scene in the morning.

She had finished unpacking and was about to open the reference guide of all the dining places in the hotel when her cell phone rang. She reached out, picked it up and tried to slow the pounding of her heart when she saw it was Quasar.

It was as if he'd known she'd been thinking of him and had called. "Hello, Quasar."

"Hello. How are you?"

She couldn't help wondering how any man could have such a sexy voice. "I'm fine. I made it to LA, and the hotel the Bureau has put me up in is simply gorgeous."

"Is it?"

"Yes."

"And what hotel is it?"

"The Westwind."

"I've heard that's a nice one."

"It is. I love my suite, and the balcony view of downtown LA is stunning. I'll bet it looks gorgeous at night from here. I can't wait to see it."

"Wish I could see it with you."

His words warmed her body, heightened the beat of her heart and filled her with a passionate sexual aura. "I wish you could, too." Too late, she realized she'd spoken her covert thoughts out loud. She should have regretted saying them, but a part of her couldn't when she'd stated the truth.

"I can make that happen, Randi."

She chuckled softly. "How can you when you're in Virginia and I'm in California?"

"Um, good question. You must be pretty high up to have such a view."

"Not too high. I'm on the thirtieth floor."

"That's pretty high up."

A corner of Randi's lips curved into a smile. "Don't tell me you're afraid of heights."

She could hear him chuckle, and the sound made her stomach do a quick somersault. "Naw, I'm okay with heights, but I refuse to sleep in a hotel room with the number nine anywhere on the door. The last two times I did, by the time I checked out, I was sick."

"Poor baby. Then I guess I should appreciate I don't have a nine in mine. In fact, my room number is kind of neat since the last two numbers represent both my parents' birthdays, April 4. I'm in room 3044."

"Your parents share birthdays?"

"Yes, same day but different years. That makes it pretty easy when we do birthday parties for them."

"I'll bet. Well, I just wanted to check and see how you were doing. May I call you later? Will you be in?"

"Yes. The plans to go to the crime scene were postponed until tomorrow, so I'll be here for the rest of the day. I'm ordering room service so I can stay in and relax."

"Alright. Enjoy your time."

"I will, and thanks for calling."

Randi clicked off the phone and drew in another deep breath. Quasar had called to see how she was doing. She shouldn't have been so moved by the gesture but she was.

QUASAR CLICKED OFF the phone and maneuvered the rental car out of the airport's parking lot and into LA traffic. He couldn't wait to see Randi, especially the shock on her face when she opened her hotel room door. He knew she had her work to do and didn't intend to interfere with that. All he knew was that he wanted to see her. Breathe in her scent. Hold her in his arms. Taste her lips.

He also knew that at some point while in LA, he would contact his family. And he used the term *family* loosely because as far as he was concerned, his true family was back in Charlottesville. He tried to recall the first time he'd noticed his father preferring Doyle over him and quickly concluded there had never been a time when he hadn't. For years Quasar had questioned whether he was Louis Patterson's biological son, but knew there was no way he wasn't. Although he and Doyle had inherited Elaina Martinez Patterson's chestnut-brown Afro-Cuban coloring, their facial features were those of his father. There was no way he wasn't Louis Patterson's biological son, and the reason behind Louis's blatant disregard of him remained a painful mystery. A mystery he was ready to have solved.

Pushing those thoughts away, he shifted his mind back to Randi. Before leaving Charlottesville, he had felt the need to research the two LA gangs involved in her case just to see what she was getting into. GRETA had provided data, stats and images of the Warlords and Revengers. He'd read the majority of the report on the flight here. It had practically chilled his blood learning about some of the things both groups were accused of doing. And that dream last night hadn't helped matters. He still had that funny feeling in his gut. It was unsettling and he wasn't sure what it meant. At least he and Randi would be at the same hotel. Now that he knew her room number, he hoped to get a room on the same floor.

Sensations unknown to him before meeting Randi curled his stomach. Quasar knew beyond a shadow of a doubt that there was something drawing him to her in an unprecedented way. He'd thought of her nonstop since last weekend. She'd been in his hot fantasies during practically every waking thought. Their time together on Saturday had been meant to purge her from his mind, but instead it had only solidified her presence there. Why?

And why had he caught himself smiling like a stupid fool whenever he remembered something she'd said or done on Saturday? How they'd walked side by side holding hands at the museum and the zoo. How they'd fed each other at her uncle's restaurant. And then there had been the kiss that bathed him in both heat and desire. How perfectly their tongues tangled, and how well she fit in his arms with their bodies pressed together. Solid against soft.

Half an hour later, thoughts of Randi still filled Quasar's mind as he walked into the Westwind Hotel. He glanced around, impressed by the decor as he walked over to the check-in desk, where a middle-aged woman was smiling at him. "Welcome to the Westwind."

He returned her smile as he looked at her gold-plated name tag. "Hello, Angela. I need to check in for a few days."

The woman beamed when he called her by her first name. "Certainly. How many days will you be with us?"

"I hope to have business wrapped up in a week."

"Okay. Would you prefer king or double?"

Although Quasar figured it was wishful thinking on his part, he couldn't help but envision Randi in that bed. "King will work. And if possible, I want to be on the thirtieth floor. Room 3044 if you have it. I stayed in it the last time I was here," he lied. "The view outside my balcony window was awesome."

He watched as the woman's fingers typed something

on the keyboard of her computer. Moments later she lifted disappointed eyes to his. "I'm sorry, sir, but that room is presently occupied."

He plastered a crestfallen look on his face, as well. "Oh. Do you have a room close to that one with a balcony?"

"Let me check." Within moments she looked at him with a huge smile. "I have something, Mr. Patterson. The room next door to 3044 is available. Will that room work for you?"

A grin touched Quasar's lips, too. "That hotel room will be perfect."

RANDI WALKED OUT of the bathroom feeling relaxed after taking a leisurely soak in the tub. Deciding it was too early to put on her pajamas, she had changed into a pair of floral print palazzo pants and a yellow cold-shoulder tunic. For simplicity's sake, she had twisted her hair into a knot atop her head.

She checked her phone and saw she hadn't missed a call from Agent Riviera. She could only assume his meetings were taking longer than expected. She had, however, missed a call from her parents. She returned it, glad to hear their voices. They were now in China and would leave in a week to return home. Her mother put her on speakerphone, and from the sound of her parents' voices, Randi could tell they were enjoying their anniversary trip.

After talking with her parents, Randi called Haywood to let her know she had arrived safely. She talked longer than anticipated when Haywood told her about the plans she'd made for Trey's birthday dinner and began soliciting ideas.

When she finished talking to Haywood, Randi was about to pick up the phone and order room service when her cell phone rang. Thinking it was Haywood calling her back, without checking her phone ID, she clicked on and said, "What now, Haywood?"

"This isn't Haywood."

No, it wasn't. The deep, sexy voice was undeniable, and she recognized it immediately. "Quasar?"

"Yes?"

Two phone calls from him in the same day? She wondered what was going on...not that she was complaining. "Hi. Is anything wrong?"

"It depends."

She tried to downplay the effect the sexiness in his voice was having on her. "Depends on what?"

"Whether you were serious about wanting me to view downtown LA from your balcony with you tonight."

Her mouth quirked into a smile. "If I say yes, what do you plan to do? Materialize inside my hotel room?"

Before he could answer, there was by a knock at her hotel room door. "Excuse me, Quasar. There's someone at the door."

"Sure. No problem."

Holding her phone in her hand she crossed the room to the door and looked out the peephole. She blinked, wondering if she was seeing things. Standing in front of her door, smiling at the peephole while holding a phone to his ear was...

Quasar?

CHAPTER TWELVE

RANDI SLOWLY BACKED AWAY from the door, semishocked, slightly dazed. Drawing in a deep, I-must-be-seeing-things breath, she lifted her phone to ask, "Do you have a twin, Quasar?"

She heard his sensual chuckle. "No. It's me at the door."

Randi returned to the door quickly to open it. For the longest time she just stood there. All she could do was stare at the handsome man dressed casually in a pair of jeans and a sports jersey. She thought the same thing now that she had the night she'd first seen him. Quasar Patterson was so ridiculously handsome she could barely keep breathing while looking at him. He made true the statement that a man could take a woman's breath away.

"Are you going to invite me in, Randi?" He slid his phone into the back pocket of his jeans, and her gaze was drawn to his taut muscular thighs when he did so.

She blinked after realizing how long she'd been staring. But there was so much to stare at. Quasar was causing her womb to contract, while lust to a degree she experienced only around him rushed through her veins. "Yes, come in," she said, stepping aside.

She closed the door behind him and leaned against it when he walked into the middle of her suite. He turned to face her, and she could feel the heat of his brown bed-room eyes roam over her outfit. "You look nice, Randi."

"Thanks. You look nice, too." She shook her head to clear her brain. "How did you…? When did you…?" Randi wondered if he was following her clipped questions.

The smooth smile that appeared on his face indicated he was. "How did I? By a straight flight from Charlottes-ville," he said. "When did I? I arrived in LA a little over two hours ago."

It took her a moment to digest what he'd said. "So when we talked earlier, you were already in LA?"

He shifted, and when he did, her gaze was drawn to the breadth of his shoulders beneath his jersey. "Yes. I wanted to surprise you. I'd arrived half an hour earlier and had just picked up my rental car. You told me everything I needed to know during our conversation. By the time it ended, I knew what hotel you were staying in and your room number."

She quickly did a mental recap of their conversation and realized she had supplied him with all that info. "But why are you in LA?"

He shifted to stand with his legs braced apart in a stance that made him appear even more imposing. "I think I mentioned I had family here."

He had mentioned that, although she'd gotten the distinct impression he and his family weren't close. "Yes, but when I talked to you yesterday, you didn't mention anything about coming to LA to visit your family."

"I decided after we talked that maybe it would be a good time for me to come to LA, as well. I'm glad I did."

She raised a brow. "Why?"

"Because I get to stand out on the balcony with you tonight."

With supreme effort, Randi forced herself to continue breathing when he moved forward, covering the distance separating them. Coming to a stop directly in front of her, he reached out and used the pad of his thumb to gently stroke the side of her face.

"So you decided to visit your family during the same time I'm here?" she asked. All kinds of emotions were swirling inside of her from his touch.

"Not exactly."

Randi was trying to follow him. Hadn't he said he was in town because of his family? "Seriously, Quasar, why did you come to LA? Are you here to visit your family or not?" She could feel the air sizzling between them. And was that a little purr that sounded in her throat just now?

The eyes staring back at her were dark, intense and mesmerizing. The force of his gaze seemed to touch her all over. "Not. I'm in LA because I wanted to see you again," he stated in a deep, throaty voice. And then he came a step closer, leaned down and slanted his mouth over hers.

Sensations began flowing through Randi the moment Quasar slid his tongue inside her mouth. Sparks of arousal began escalating all through her body. He wrapped his arms around her waist and began mating greedily with her mouth. The kiss was fiercely hot, hotter than any she'd indulged in before. He was using his tongue in a way that was sending an intense throb of desire through her bloodstream.

When he tightened his arms around her and drew her closer, on instinct she wrapped her own arms around his neck as even more desire clawed at her insides. It was then that she felt the heavy bulge of his erection through his jeans. Evidence of his desire for her was awakening a multitude of feelings within her. Feelings she'd thought she'd put to rest after he left last weekend. But they were back and in full force. Driving her to return his kiss, stroke for stroke.

There was no telling how long they would have stood there, devouring each other's mouths, if her phone hadn't rung. Quasar broke off the kiss and when it rang again, he whispered against her moist lips, "Are you going to get that?"

Honestly, the only thing she wanted to get was more of the luscious taste of his mouth. Without answering him, she walked over to the table and grabbed her cell phone on the third ring.

"Yes?"

"Dr. Fuller? Are you alright?"

She had been more than alright moments ago…before being interrupted. "Yes, Agent Riviera, I'm alright. Why do you ask?"

"You took a while to answer your phone."

"I was in the middle of something, but I'm fine."

She glanced over to where Quasar was standing. He hadn't moved from that spot in the middle of her hotel suite, and he was staring at her. Was he waiting for her to come back to him? To continue their kiss? She should have been using this time to reclaim her senses, but for some reason she wasn't able to do that. All she could think about was returning to him and kissing him some more. Was that crazy or what?

"Sorry I got detained by those meetings, but I wanted to check and make sure you're okay," Agent Riviera said, pulling her concentration back to his phone call. "Do you need anything? Have you had dinner?"

"I was about to order room service, and no, I don't need anything."

"Okay. If you do, let me know. Otherwise, I'll see you in the morning at ten."

"Alright. Goodbye, Agent Riviera."

Randi clicked off the phone and turned to Quasar. He had shoved his hands into the pockets of his jeans and was still standing there, staring at her. He was gorgeous. Her gaze moved up past a pair of jeans-clad masculine thighs, a lean waist, a firm stomach and wide, muscled shoulders to focus on his facial features. She studied his lips, the same ones that had melted her insides moments ago.

She hadn't known that a man's tongue could go as deep into a woman's mouth as his had. And when he'd held her tight, she'd felt how hard and powerful his body was. Yet he'd held her with a gentleness that had surprised her.

"Is everything alright, Randi?"

She tried to ignore all the heated sensations rolling around in her stomach. "Yes. That was the FBI agent I'll be working with while I'm here, Special Agent Riviera. He wanted to make sure I was okay and have everything I need."

He crossed the room to her. "*Do* you have everything you need?"

"ASK ME AGAIN in a few minutes." In a move that surprised him, she rose up on tiptoes, lifted her arms around his neck and planted her mouth on his.

Quasar took it from there. Pulling her into his arms,

he deepened the kiss, trying to ignore the tumultuous emotions that were battling to overtake him. He loved the way her mouth felt beneath his. He loved her taste. He broke off the kiss to nibble greedily around her mouth before sucking her bottom lip back into his mouth. The moment he did, he could feel something—he wasn't sure what—bind him to her in a way he'd never been with another woman.

He wanted to pull back, break off the kiss to get his senses under control. Instead he continued kissing her like there was no tomorrow, the taste of her mouth driving him.

This time it was the ringing of *his* phone that intruded into the moment. He wanted to ignore it but couldn't when he recognized the ringtone. It was a call from Sheppard Granger. He broke off the kiss and pulled back. "Sorry, I need to take this," he rasped, pulling his cell phone from the back pocket of his jeans.

"I understand," she said, backing away.

He wanted to reach out and grab her hand, coaxing her not to go anywhere, but she was too quick and moved across the room to sit down on the sofa.

He kept his gaze trained on her as he clicked on his phone and placed it to his ear. "Yes?"

"Quasar, I hope this isn't a bad time to call."

Had it been anyone else, he would have said it was. "No, it's not. What's up?"

"I just got a call from your father."

Anger sliced through Quasar. "Dammit, he had no right to call you. How did he get your number?"

"Calm down, Quasar. It's okay that he called me. And as far as getting my number, I'm still at the office, and he phoned me here."

Quasar pulled in an irritated breath. "What did he want?"

"He said he asked you to come home this weekend for some kind of family function and you refused. Since I know you flew to LA this morning, I can only assume he doesn't know you changed your mind about coming."

"No, he doesn't know."

"And I didn't tell him any different. I just wanted you to know."

"Thanks. I appreciate that. We'll talk when I get back to town."

"Okay. Talk to you later, and you take care of yourself."

Quasar drew in a composing breath, trying to get his anger under control. A family event—what a bunch of bullshit. The only reason Louis wanted him to come home was control. The old man had given an order that he wanted obeyed.

"Quasar? Everything okay?"

He glanced over at Randi, and a semblance of calm ran through him. He could see concern line her features. When had anyone other than the select few he'd allowed to get close been concerned about him? "Yes, everything is okay."

Not wanting to go into any details about the call he'd received, he slid his cell phone back into the pocket of his jeans. The moment she'd opened the door, sexual chemistry had seemed to overpower them. It had made him kiss her to see if the taste he'd remembered from last weekend was as powerful as he thought. It was.

"Did I hear you tell that FBI agent you hadn't eaten yet?" he asked. The room had become too quiet, and he could feel the sexual chemistry beginning to build between them again.

"Yes. I was going to order room service."

"May I join you?"

She didn't say anything. Given the degree of sexual chemistry between them, he wondered if she saw them dining together in her hotel room as not such a good idea. He held his breath for her answer.

"Yes, Quasar. You can join me."

Standing from the sofa she crossed the room toward him, and he actually felt his throat convulse with every sexy step she took. Coming to a stop in front of him, she gave him a pointed look and said, "And over dinner, you can tell me the *real* reason you came to Los Angeles."

CHAPTER THIRTEEN

"THIS IS DEFINITELY BETTER than any of those microwave dinners I usually eat," Quasar said, sliding another piece of steak into his mouth. Room service had delivered their dinner, rolling a linen-covered table set for two into the room. He'd ordered prime rib with vegetables, and she'd ordered seafood pasta.

"You do a lot of those? Microwave dinners?"

"Yes," he said, watching how she twirled the pasta onto her fork. "Not because I have to, since I consider myself a pretty good cook, but for me it's usually more convenient."

"Same here. They are quick, easy and definitely convenient. But unlike you, I don't consider myself a good cook."

He grinned over at her. "So there's not an apron hanging somewhere around your place?"

She grinned back. "Definitely not. And I refuse to lie and say I wish there was. I'm definitely not a kitchen girl. While I lived with my parents, all that was required of me was a spotless bedroom. I'm glad Mom didn't pester me about learning kitchen duties. She was a great cook, enjoyed doing it and made sure we ate delicious meals every day."

There was a lull in the conversation, and he glanced across the table to find her studying him. He figured she was curious about that phone call he'd gotten earlier. Undoubtedly she was curious about a number of things.

"So why are you really in Los Angeles, Quasar?" she finally asked, after taking a sip of her coffee.

He understood she wanted answers, but the big question was how much to tell her. What he wouldn't go into, at least not tonight, was that crazy-ass dream and all those negative vibes he had about her being in LA unprotected. It would be hard to explain to her when he didn't fully understand it himself.

He took a sip of his own coffee and said, "Like I told you earlier, the reason I came to LA was that I knew you would be here, and I wanted to see you again. And since I have family here whom I haven't seen in a while, I decided to pay a visit. But make no mistake, Randi. I came to see you. Had you not been here, I would not have come."

He didn't miss the flash of incredulity in her eyes. "You actually want me to believe you got on a plane and flew to LA because of me?"

"Yes, I want you to believe it because it's the truth, no matter how crazy it sounds. I was looking forward to seeing you again this weekend. When you called to cancel, I came up with a plan."

"To follow me here?"

"Yes."

Like he'd told her, he knew it sounded crazy, but it was the truth. He had wanted to see her again and hadn't realized just how much until she'd opened the door.

"What about your family?"

"What about them?"

"I would think they would rank higher on your list than me."

"Unfortunately, they don't." *And for good reasons.* He could tell her that his family was none of her business, which is what he'd told other women who'd inquired. But for some reason he didn't want to handle her like all those other women. He wouldn't tell her all the sordid details about his family, but he wanted to tell her something.

"I'm sure you've figured out by now that I'm not close to my family," he began.

She nodded, eyeing him speculatively. "Yes, I gathered as much. When was the last time you saw them?"

He shrugged. "I haven't seen them in ten years."

Her eyes widened in disbelief. "Ten years?"

"Yes. I was locked up for three, and I've been free for seven. For reasons I don't care to go into, when I left Glenworth Penitentiary, I didn't return here, and I deliberately did not let them know where I'd gone. A couple of years ago, my father hired a private investigator to find me. We talk every so often, but that's it."

She tilted her head, staring at him, and he figured her mind was at work, mentally calculating what he'd said and coming up with the fact that his family hadn't visited him while he'd been confined. "Well, I'm glad you've returned home and truly hope whatever kept you and your family apart will be resolved," she said.

He couldn't help but smile. She could hope, but he was a lot more skeptical. "Are you always so optimistic?"

Cute little dimples appeared in her cheeks. "I try to be. In a way, I can't help it, and it has nothing to do with being a psychic and everything to do with wanting the best for everyone."

He didn't say anything for a moment as he took another sip of his coffee. In the short time he'd known her, he'd gathered that much about her. She was also friendly.

Sometimes he thought she was too friendly. Like on Saturday. He doubted she'd ever met a stranger. She would engage in conversation with just about anybody. People visiting the museum. Families at the zoo. Waiters and waitresses at her uncle's restaurant. It had been enough for him just to stand on the sidelines and observe her unguarded nature. More often than not, she had pulled him in and included him in the conversations. He'd reluctantly participated. It was definitely not in his nature to be so social. He knew that she couldn't read everyone she met, and she had explained that more times than not, she didn't read anyone…just a select few…and only when it was for their sakes and not hers. Yet she was more open and honest than most. There was probably not a deceptive bone in her body. He inwardly shuddered when he thought of all the deceitful people he'd met in his life. It was refreshing to find someone so authentic.

"And what about that phone call you got earlier?" she asked. "The one that got you upset?"

He held her gaze. "What about it?"

"Was it someone from your family? Should you be dining with them instead of me?"

He again saw that concerned look in her eyes. She didn't want to get into his business. She simply cared.

"That call was from a good friend. He was giving me information I didn't want to hear." And that was all he intended to share.

"Oh."

"So tell me more about your psychic abilities, Randi."

She chuckled and then shook her finger at him. "I know what you're doing, Quasar."

He plastered an innocent look on his face. "And what am I doing?"

"You're trying to shift the conversation from you to me."

"Am I?"

"Yes. I don't have to be a psychic to see that."

She didn't miss much. "I gather you have more questions?"

"Yes," she said, twirling more pasta onto her fork. He wasn't sure why it was such a turn-on to watch her do something like that. "I want to know more about your family," she said, pulling his mind back to their conversation. "You mentioned last week that you had a brother. One four years older. What's he like? Do the two of you favor? What about your father?"

"Wait…*whoa*." She wanted too much information. Definitely more than he intended to tell her. Rubbing the back of his neck, he fought off a rising feeling of annoyance. She wanted a *tell-all* conversation, and that was the last thing he intended to engage in with her, or anyone. The people who needed to know his business knew it. He didn't allow others into his private domain.

But he couldn't help dropping his hand when he saw the look of genuine interest in her eyes. Quasar knew at that moment he had to get his priorities straight regarding her. And to be honest, hadn't he told her that she was essentially more of a priority in his life than his father and brother, that she was his main reason for flying across the country? As far as he was concerned, she was more of a priority than any woman had ever been. Otherwise, he wouldn't have been there. In LA. Sitting across the table, sharing dinner in her hotel room.

Besides, she'd shared a lot about her family with him. But then, hers wasn't fucked-up like his. Whenever she spoke of anyone in her family, he saw the love, warmth and adoration shining in her eyes. Her relationship with her family was one to envy.

He decided to try changing the subject one more time. Flashing a cool smile, he said, "Anything about my family would bore you to tears."

She flashed a cool smile right back at him. "Let me be the judge of that, Quasar."

He held her gaze for a long moment. *Alright, then. Here goes.* "I told you my mother died when I was fourteen. Had she lived, my parents would have been married forty years this year."

"Did your father remarry?"

He shook his head. "No. He hasn't remarried. Her death took a toll on all of us. She was a special woman who was so full of love." Sometimes he would wonder what his mother ever saw in Louis. The two were as different as day and night.

"You still miss her."

He wasn't sure if she'd made an observation or asked a question. He answered anyway. "Yes, very much so."

She reached across the table and took his hand. When she would have pulled it away, he decided to hold it hostage and keep it for a while longer. He loved the connection. The feel of their hands entwined. That was one of the reasons he'd held on to it so much on Saturday.

"The two of you were close."

She said it like she knew. "Yes, we were extremely close. As a kid, she was my world."

Randi nodded as if she understood, and a part of him wanted to believe that she actually did. "So that left you, your brother and your father."

He chuckled. Maybe in her world, that's how it would have been. "No, actually it left me. Then there were my father and brother. Don't get me wrong. I'm sure they felt the pain of Mom's loss, as well. But her death made my father and brother's relationship that much closer."

"You didn't feel close to your father and brother?"

Good question, he thought, releasing her hand and leaning back in his chair. "There was a time we were close. At least I thought we were. But even then I knew Doyle was my father's favorite. That didn't bother me because I had such a strong relationship with my mom. It was only after she died that it became quite obvious just how close was Doyle and Louis's relationship, and I was merely being tolerated."

"Sounds like sibling rivalry. That's nothing new, Quasar. It happens in the best of families."

There was no need to tell her what happened in his family was a lot more than that. "Does it?"

"Yes. It even happened in mine," she said, placing her coffee cup down. He could tell by the look in her eyes that she was remembering the times when it had.

"While growing up," she said, "I never could understand why Dad and Haywood were so close. We were both daddy's girls, but the two of them shared a special bond, and at times I felt that I didn't fit in. I knew my father was not Haywood's biological father. She was only eight or so when our parents married. He wanted to adopt her, give her his last name since her father had passed away when she was only four."

"Why didn't he?"

"Because doing so would have hurt her paternal grandparents. Her father had been their only child, and Haywood was their only grandchild. As a girl, she was close to her father and wanted to keep his name. And in spite of that…maybe, in a way, because of it…Dad worked extra hard to make sure that Haywood felt included in the family. That in his heart he would always be more than a stepfather. He knew that he could never replace her father, but he wanted to be the next best thing. And I believe that he was. I didn't understand his motives at the time. However, when I got older, I did. Instead of getting jealous, I—"

"I never said I got jealous of my father and Doyle's relationship," he said, his jaw tightening defensively.

"No, you didn't."

"But you think I did," he said in an accusing tone.

"It doesn't matter what I think, does it?"

His brow bunched into a frown as he stared into his coffee, as if there was something to discover in the liquid. No, it didn't matter what she thought. At least it shouldn't have mattered. She'd said her psychic powers were blocked when it came to him, but she did have a doctorate degree as a behavioral analyst. Was that what she was doing? Trying to figure him out that way?

"What does your father do for a living?" she asked.

He returned his gaze to her face and locked eyes with hers. "He owns a film company, specializing in supplying American movies to an international market and vice versa."

"Sounds interesting."

"It is."

"I assume your brother works there."

He took a sip of his coffee. "You assume right. And before you ask, the answer is yes, I did work there for a while, as well. Right out of college." *Long enough to be thrown under the bus as Doyle's scapegoat.*

At that moment, he decided that he'd told her everything he intended to. "Enough questions about my family,

Randi. Over dessert, how about you tell me about the case that brought you to LA? Those slices of key lime pie look delicious."

Her lips curved into a smile. "I'm a woman who refuses to stand between a man and his appetite, even when I know he's trying to change the subject."

"I'm not changing the subject, Randi. I'm closing it." He thought he would make that point clear in case she assumed she could reopen it later.

Seemingly impervious to what he said, she gave him a sweet smile and said, "We'll see."

OVER DESSERT, RANDI told Quasar what she knew about the street gang situation. Since it was an ongoing investigation and there were certain aspects of the case she couldn't divulge, she made sure she stuck to the facts that had been provided in the media. She then told him why it was imperative for her to visit the crime scene tomorrow. "The sooner I can help find that murder weapon, the better."

He nodded as he slid a piece of pie into his mouth. "So, like the Feds, you think someone is deliberately starting a gang war?"

Disgust etched her features. "Yes. Usually that happens when an outsider comes in, determined to hustle in on territory rights."

When Quasar shifted in his chair, Randi tried not to notice how his muscular shoulders and powerful-looking arms rippled with the movement. And why were her fingers itching to reach out and touch his hair, thread her fingers through the silky strands?

She jumped when he waved his hand to get her attention. Apparently he'd said something while she'd been staring. "Yes?"

A grin touched his lips as if he'd known where her thoughts had been. "I asked if you've done research on the gangs so you'll know what you're dealing with."

She tried not to focus on him sliding another piece of pie into his mouth. Her muscles clenched when he licked the fork. "Yes," she said in a voice that might have sounded breathless. "I stayed up most of last night researching, which is why I slept the entire time on the plane."

He released a long, dramatic sigh. "Then I don't have to tell you how ruthless the two leaders of those two gangs are."

"No, you don't." She glanced over at him curiously. "But how would you know?"

He shrugged those massive shoulders. She recalled that when they'd kissed, she'd placed her hands on those shoulders, and they'd felt taut beneath her fingers. "I did my research, as well."

She lifted a brow. "Why?"

"I wanted to see what you would be dealing with."

"You're still worried about me being here, aren't you?" she asked, finding the fact that he cared rather touching. When he'd mentioned his concern during their phone conversation yesterday, she'd figured it had everything to do with what he did for a living. His job as a body-guard was to protect people from the crazies out there.

"Not anymore," he said, giving her one of those smiles that would make a woman want to curl up in his lap and do all kinds of naughty things to his mouth. To him, pe-riod.

"Why *not anymore*?" she asked, eyeing him intently.

For some reason he looked like the cat that not only drank all the cream in the bowl but also took his time and licked the bowl clean.

"Because I'm here, and I don't intend to let anything happen to you. And don't let that sweet mind of yours try to convince you the only reason I came is to play bodyguard. I told you why I'm here. It's all about my need to see you. But if I need to step into the role of protector, Randi, I will."

Randi heard his words and knew that nothing she said would put his mind at ease. Her family had acted the same way when she'd taken her first assignment involving that serial killer. They'd been so certain the killer would add her to his list of strangled young women. She should not have been surprised when Trey popped up at FBI headquarters in Memphis a couple of times, making sure she was okay.

It looked like she needed to tell Quasar the same thing she'd told her brother. "I'm here to do a job."

He shrugged those massive shoulders again, but this time his chin tightened right along with the movement. "I don't recall saying that you couldn't or I would interfere."

No, he hadn't, but she could read between the lines. She had dealt with Trey and Zach long enough to recognize an alpha male when she saw one. "It's what you're not saying that concerns me, Quasar."

He was silent for a minute and then reached across the table to brush the back of his knuckles across her cheek. "Don't let it. I promise not to interfere with the work you came here to do, Randi. Okay?"

He sounded so convincing that she found herself nodding. "Okay." What else could she say when he was looking at her like that, with those brown bedroom eyes, and touching her skin, making her feel sensations all through her body?

"I've got an idea," he said huskily as he continued to stroke her cheek.

She swallowed, not wanting to admit she had a few of her own, and all of them had something to do with them getting into something wicked. "What's your idea?"

"After we enjoy the view of downtown LA from your balcony, how about I take you for a drive, show you the city up close and personal?"

Randi stared at him and realized that all the time he'd been talking, his gaze had been on her mouth. Her entire body warmed under his regard. "I'd love that."

"Then consider it done."

CHAPTER FOURTEEN

QUASAR WATCHED RANDI as she stood at the balcony's minibar, pouring two glasses of wine. He really liked that outfit on her. Her long blouse had cutouts on the shoulders revealing bare skin, and the soft-looking fabric of her slacks flowed sensually over her curves. He even liked the way she'd styled her hair, pulled up on a twisted knot on her head as if to emphasize her beautiful neck. Time and time again his gaze was drawn to her mouth as he remembered how he'd kissed it and how much he'd enjoyed doing so.

Deciding he'd stared at her long enough, he leaned against the rail to look out over the city. He could understand why she wanted to see LA at night from here. It was beautiful. The way the skyscrapers lit the sky was simply awesome.

At that moment he didn't want to remember why he had left here years ago and vowed never to return. But today he *had* returned, for the woman coming toward him.

"Here you are."

"Thanks," he said, accepting the glass of wine she offered and fighting to ignore the zap in his body when their hands touched.

He met her eyes and knew she felt it, as well. And that's how it had been most of the evening in her presence. Nothing new. But what *was* new was his inability to retain a tight grip on his sanity around her, especially when he was known as a man who could take rationality to a whole new level.

"It's beautiful, isn't it?" Randi asked, turning to look out over the brightly lit city.

Quasar fought back saying *You're beautiful.* Instead he answered, "Yes, and I can't wait to show it to you by car."

She glanced back at him. "I can't wait, either."

He studied her when she switched her gaze from him to look back over LA. She took a sip of her wine, and he thought there was something significantly sexy about her when she did so. His gut tightened as he watched how her mouth fit on the rim of the wineglass, and his mind was suddenly swamped with images of all the other things she could do with that mouth. When he felt heat begin to spread through his body, he knew it was time to suggest that they leave and go for that ride. Or else it would be hard to control his desire for her.

"I remember the first time I came here and saw this," she said softly. "I was amazed at all the tall buildings and bright lights."

In a way, he was glad her words had interrupted his thoughts. He took a sip of his wine and asked, "How long ago was this?" He wondered if another man had shared the view with her as he was doing. Why did the thought of that possibility bother him?

"It was years ago. I was probably nine or ten. I came here with my parents and Haywood."

He chuckled. "Let me guess. Your parents took you and your sister to Disneyland. Right?"

She looked over at him and smiled. "Yes, but that's

not the reason we came. We flew to LA to see Trey. He lived here with his mother and stepfather."

Quasar nodded. He recalled her mentioning last week that her brother had grown up in California. "Do his mother and stepfather still live here?"

She shook her head. "No. Trey's mother passed away a few years ago, and Harry died last year. Trey was close to his stepfather."

Quasar thought her brother was a lucky man to have had a close relationship with both his biological father and stepfather. When she took another sip of her wine and the gesture caused arousing sensations in his groin again, he knew it was time to leave her hotel room. "Ready to take that car ride?"

A smile touched her lips at the same time those dimples he'd gotten overly fond of appeared in her cheeks. "I'm ready when you are, Mr. Patterson."

A SHORT WHILE LATER, Randi was convinced more than ever that Los Angeles was one of the most beautiful cities she'd ever visited. The streets after dark were just as stunning as the view from the hotel balcony. For the past hour, Quasar had covered a lot of miles, and she'd taken in numerous sites. Traffic wasn't too bad this late. LA was known for its traffic congestion until around nine at night.

Now they were on Sunset Boulevard and headed toward Beverly Hills. It was a beautiful night for a car ride, and they decided to cruise with the windows down instead of using the vehicle's air conditioner. He had pointed out a lot of places he used to frequent while living here.

She knew them leaving her hotel room had been for

the best. There was no telling what kind of trouble they would have gotten into had they stayed there any longer. More than once she'd seen the heated look in his eyes and felt in response a rush of stimulating sensations invade her body. He wanted her, and she wanted him just as much.

"Before we leave LA, I'm hoping we can dine at Hollywood and Vine."

She glanced over at him. She'd heard about the legendary restaurant but had never eaten there. "That would be nice. I would like to add Roscoe's to the list, as well. I love their chicken and waffles."

"So do I. I use to eat there a lot back in the day."

"How was it growing up in Los Angeles?"

He smiled. "I loved it. A lot to do, beautiful beaches, Hollywood. At the time I couldn't imagine myself living anywhere else."

"But now you consider Charlottesville your home."

When he brought the car to a stop at a traffic light, he glanced over at her. Was that sadness she noted in the dark eyes staring back at her? "Yes, Charlottesville is my home now."

When the traffic light changed, he turned his attention back to the road. The next few miles took them into Beverly Hills. She would periodically glance over at him, and more than once he'd turn his head and catch her staring. He wouldn't say anything but would flash a sexy smile that set off a spark of reactions within her.

They had left the city and were traveling up some mountain road. Beautifully lit homes that cost millions flashed by. She should have asked where they were going, but instead she turned to him and asked the one question she really wanted answered. "Why did you go to jail, Quasar?"

He didn't say anything for a long moment. "The state of California claimed I was involved in land fraud."

"Claimed? Were you or weren't you?"

He shrugged. "Doesn't matter. I served the time."

The time instead of *my* time? His choice of words made her think he'd been accused of a crime he hadn't committed. She was about to ask if that was the case when he spoke first. "What do you think of the view now, Randi?"

She glanced out the window. They had driven to the top of a mountain that overlooked the entire city. It was the most beautiful view she'd encountered. She saw not only the brightly lit skyscrapers but also several other glittering buildings and homes. The view was simply breathtaking.

"Where are we?" she asked, leaning forward to take it all in.

"Mulholland Drive Overlook. It's one of the most popular places in LA to park."

She could see why. "Um, sounds like you've been here before."

He chuckled. "I could deny that I have."

"Don't bother. You took those winding roads too much like a pro for it to be your first time up here."

"Thanks, and I have been up here a few times."

"Lucky girls," she said, grinning.

Although the interior of the car was somewhat dark, the moon shone enough to see the tightening of his jaw. "One girl. I dated the same girl all through high school."

"Oh. Then, lucky girl. What was her name?"

He was quiet a moment, as though he might not answer, before saying, "Lilly. Her name was Lilly."

Why was she feeling slightly jealous of a woman from his past? She evidently had meant a lot to him for him to have dated her all through high school. She then remembered something he'd told her last week. "Is Lilly the one who wouldn't wait for you while you were in jail?"

Again there was a pause. "You have a good memory, and yes, she's the one. She promised to wait for me and broke her promise. I guess you can say she had a change of heart."

As far as Randi was concerned, it was Lilly's loss. In all actuality, it wasn't Lilly's loss, because she had never been meant for Quasar anyway. His destiny was tied to hers. But that wouldn't stop him from falling in love with a woman he'd assumed was his future. Did he still love her?

"I'm sorry, Quasar. About what happened with you and Lilly."

He looked over at her. "No reason for you to be sorry. You didn't know me or Lilly. It was her decision. She said she couldn't wait any longer and wanted to marry someone else. I gave her my blessing."

Randi didn't say anything. Was that the reason he hadn't returned to LA all this time? "Does Lilly still live in LA?"

"Yes, she still lives here."

There. She pretty much had her answer. "Is she still married?"

"Yes, she's still married."

How did he know? Were they in each other's lives? She couldn't help but think of her own parents' story. How Jenna had broken things off with Randolph right after college, thinking she was doing the right thing. But her father had loved her mother too much to sever the cord entirely, keeping tabs on her all those years, even when Jenna married another man. And as fate would have it, they'd reunited after twenty years and married. Was Quasar Patterson another Randolph Fuller? A man who could love only one woman? The woman who'd been his first love? The woman who was married to another man? Where would that leave Randi?

Fate had been on her parents' side, but she knew it wasn't for Quasar and Lilly. He wasn't meant to marry Lilly. He'd been chosen for Randi. But did it matter if his heart belonged to someone else? How was she to earn his love if another woman already had it under lock and key?

"Randi?"

Quasar saying her name broke into her muddled thoughts. Too many of them, all at once. Coming at her with injurious force and making her wonder if she'd been set up for failure. She refused to believe that. She couldn't believe that.

"Yes?" She glanced over at him. She knew the same look was in his eyes that had been there in her hotel room. All she had to do was glance at his mouth to recall the wildness of his taste and how the erotic use of his tongue had nearly brought her to her knees. Made her moan. Filled her with a longing she hadn't felt, ever. She couldn't forget how he'd sucked on her bottom lip while his hand held her chin hostage.

"We can sit here and talk, or we can do other things," he said.

She didn't have to wonder what those other things were. Although she and Larry had never made out in a parked car, she'd had college friends who had. They hadn't minded sharing the details with anyone who cared to listen. "I hope you're not suggesting we make out in the backseat of this car like horny teens. Besides," she said in a lighthearted tone, "I don't make out on the first date."

A smile eased his lips, magnifying the sexual chemistry encasing them. "First of all, Randi Fuller, this isn't our first date. And as far as making out like horny teens is concerned, although the thought of such a thing sounds pretty damn appealing, I wouldn't suggest we go *that* far."

Then what was he suggesting? "I thought you brought me here to enjoy the view."

He chuckled as he released his seat belt and twisted his body to stare directly at her. "I did, and I am. I love the view I'm looking at right now."

She actually liked them being together like this, sitting in a parked car underneath the beautiful moon and stars. There was no way anything would happen as long as she kept a level head and didn't let desire override her common sense. "I meant the view *outside* the window."

"I like looking at you better. Nice blouse, by the way," he said, reaching out and stroking his finger across her bare skin exposed by her cold-shoulder blouse. Shivers raced through her from his touch. Igniting some of the same parts of her that he'd awakened last week. "Thank you. I'm glad you like it."

"Do you know what else I like?" he asked as he continued to stroke her bare skin softly.

Don't ask, Randi, she silently ordered herself. Instead of obeying, she asked, "What?"

"Kissing you. I think about tasting you every time I see your mouth," he said, reaching out and unsnapping her seat belt.

Randi swallowed, feeling the intensity of his gaze on her mouth. "I honestly don't know what to say."

He leaned closer, never breaking eye contact, and filling her nostrils with his manly scent. "Say you want me to kiss you. That you want to feel my tongue inside your mouth, tangling with yours. Sucking on it," he whispered huskily, just mere inches from her lips. "Say it."

That was too much to repeat, so she said, "Just do it."

And he did.

He sucked her bottom lip into his mouth, greedily, as if his desire for her had pushed him to the edge and he couldn't stop falling. Then he covered her mouth with his, devouring the entire thing. Consuming her. Claiming her. Driving her mad with desire. Fogging her brain. And making her body hum. Quasar had the ability to take a single kiss and make it explode like a keg of dynamite even before the fire was lit.

She felt every swirling stroke of his tongue that left no area of her mouth untouched. Blood pulsated through her veins. Hunger pangs were awakened deep within her womb. Her tongue retaliated, and she leaned into him to get farther into his mouth. She grabbed hold of those massive shoulders, loving the way they felt beneath her hands. They were muscular shoulders. Perfect shoulders.

His mouth wouldn't let up. Neither would hers. A battle of the tongues ensued. Both would come out winners…or losers…since this kiss was as far as they could take it. And in knowing that, they were driven to take it to the limit. She was rooted in the scent of man. The scent of him. The sensations of his damp tongue sliding back and forth over hers incited a tempestuous hunger within her. It was then that she became conscious of his hand slipping between her legs. His palm pressed against the fabric of her pants. Right there in the center. In that heated spot. As if he was claiming ownership. Branding her.

And that's when she came.

CHAPTER FIFTEEN

QUASAR WAS AWARE the moment it happened. Felt the tremors that passed through Randi's body, felt the quivering thighs that tightened around his hand. Her tongue had suddenly gone wild. Then wilder. His mouth might be sore tomorrow. But then, so would hers.

He untangled their mouths and nearly grunted in pain at the way his hard erection was jammed against his zipper. He drew in a deep breath as he gazed at her. Her eyes were closed as if she needed to catch her breath. And he heard the jagged murmur of satisfaction in her moan.

He tried to recall if he'd ever brought a woman to climax with his tongue—inside her mouth and not between her legs—and had to conclude he never had. Until now. Randi had to be the most passionate woman he'd ever known. Definitely ever had the pleasure of kissing. And it had been pleasure. All the way to the bone. Nearly more than he could handle. Just hearing her come had fueled that burning ache within him.

And then there was the kiss that had started it all. Her mouth had a unique flavor. One he enjoyed too damn much. He couldn't help wondering how the rest of her tasted, and he became even more aroused at the thought of finding out.

He had intended for this kiss to be slow and steady, but the moment his tongue entered her mouth, all he could think about was how ravenous he was. The more their tongues mated and mingled, the more insatiable he felt. The more every cell in his body erupted in need.

He thought about her breasts. While he kissed Randi, he could feel her hardened nipples poking him in the chest through the material of his jersey. Each poke had affected every nerve ending in his body. Gripped him. Aroused him. Excited him. Driven him to kiss her even harder.

She slowly opened her eyes and looked at him. "I need to get my heart rate back in sync," she said raggedly, drawing air into her lungs.

"Go ahead. Don't let me stop you," he said, sliding his mouth to her shoulders to lick the bare skin exposed by her blouse. He could hear her intense breathing, and when she moaned his name, he lifted his head to look first at her face before moving his eyes downward to her chest. He watched the movement of her breasts while she inhaled and exhaled. The lower part of his body began throbbing under the close observation. Hmm, if he could make her come from kissing her mouth, what would happen if he sucked on her breasts? Licked them all over?

"I can't believe I did that from just a kiss," she said, forcing his attention from her breasts back up to her face. "Who does that?"

His smile stretched wide. "You do. You did. Want to try it again?"

He heard her soft chuckle. "You're insatiable."

"Look who's talking."

Car lights flashed through the back window as another car pulled up to enjoy the view…or for the occupants to enjoy each other. "I really brought you here for the view but couldn't help myself," he said, buckling her seat belt and then easing back to his seat to buckle his. "You're a difficult woman to resist, Randi Fuller."

"Funny you should say that."

"Why?"

"Because you just said the same thing my dad always said about my mother. He said he fell in love with her the moment he saw her because she was a difficult woman to resist."

Quasar didn't say anything as he started the car's ignition. Deep down he hoped Randi realized what was between them was nothing more than a physical attraction, one that went deeper than most. He'd accepted that and intended to stoke the sexual chemistry between them as much as he could. He didn't want her ever to question his motives, so it would be best to reiterate a few things, just to make sure they were on the same page.

"Falling in love is something I don't intend ever to do again, Randi. I'm interested only in the physical aspect of a relationship."

She nodded. "I get that. Which is why you being here now, chasing me across several states, doesn't make sense."

He *had* chased her. Across several states. "I told you why."

"Yes, because you wanted to see me."

Okay, that did sound kind of crazy and misleading. "The reason I wanted to see you is I'm deeply attracted to you…just like I know you're deeply attracted to me." When she didn't deny it, he said, "All that sexual chemistry will eventually lead to one thing. I just don't want you to expect something long-term out of it." There, he'd spelled things out to her so there shouldn't be any misunderstandings.

"I totally understand your position, Quasar," she said, smiling brightly over at him. "And just for the record, I'm not interested in falling in love any more than you are."

Randi's words stayed on his mind during the drive back to the hotel. Did she have to seem so damn happy when she'd said them? He should be glad she had such an accepting attitude about what to expect and what not to expect. Then why was he feeling so damn annoyed?

"You don't have to walk me to my hotel room, Quasar," Randi said, interrupting his thoughts when they entered the lobby.

He hadn't mentioned that he was staying at the same hotel and that his room was right next to hers. Now was a good time to tell her, but he knew that doing so would invite more questions. Questions he wasn't ready to answer. When he saw her tomorrow, he would tell her.

"I wouldn't be a gentleman if I didn't see you to your room," he said as they walked toward the bank of elevators.

When they stepped onto the elevator, he instinctively placed his hand in the middle of her back. Quasar eased them toward the rear, to their own private corner of the elevator, when other couples got on. "I enjoyed spending time with you tonight, Randi," he said, deliberately keeping his voice low.

She smiled up at him. "And I with you."

When the elevator reached their floor, they stepped off and walked side by side toward her room. He had taken hold of her hand in the elevator and hadn't let go. "Chances are I'll be extremely busy for the next few days," she told him while taking the passkey from her purse.

He nodded. "And like I told you earlier, I don't want

to interfere with your work. But I hope you don't intend to work twenty-four-hour days."

She shook her head. "No, usually I don't."

"Good. Ideally you'll have time to join me for dinner tomorrow. You have to eat sometime."

When they reached her room, they stood outside the door. "How about breakfast in the morning?" he asked.

"Not sure I'll have time. Agent Riviera will be picking me up at ten. I'll probably grab one of those breakfast bars from the vending machines. What are your plans for tomorrow?"

"Not sure. I might call my family to let them know I'm here." Why was it that the longer he looked at her, the more he regretted having to let her go into that room alone? Sleep in that big bed all by herself?

"I think that's a good idea," she said.

She would. He took a step closer to her. "Good night, Randi. Sweet fantasies," he said cupping her nape. He then lowered his mouth to hers, kissing her deeply yet tenderly, while wondering why he couldn't get enough of her taste.

Moments later she pulled back from the kiss, drawing in a deep breath. "I'd better go inside. You, Quasar Patterson, can get a girl in trouble."

He leaned in and rested his forehead against hers. He could swear he heard the sound of her erratic heartbeat. "What kind of trouble is that?"

"Trouble that I'm not ready for. And I got a sample of it tonight."

"You shouldn't be so damn passionate," he growled near her ear.

"And you shouldn't be so hot-blooded." Then she

quickly turned and swiped her passkey to open the door. "Good night."

He continued to stand there until he heard the solid click of the lock. It was only then that he moved to go to his own room next door.

IN THE DEEP RECESSES of her sleep, Randi was reliving the first orgasm she'd had with a man in four years. And it had happened from a kiss. But what a kiss. When she'd told Quasar he was hot-blooded, she'd meant it. He had used his tongue in her mouth and made her come. Granted, he had touched her there, between her legs. But she'd been fully clothed.

Her hot fantasies spiraled from there. Yes, that's what they were, and she had no problem accepting Quasar's description of the over-the-top dreams she was having. The ones in which her imagination ran wild. They were naked. In a bed. He'd just finished kissing her into another orgasm and was moving his body lower to kiss her between her legs. She moaned in her sleep at the thought of what would come next...

Randi bolted upright in bed, suddenly awake. She squinted around the dark room, listening. She didn't hear anything but was convinced she'd heard a sound in the living room area of her suite. Then she heard it again and knew for certain that someone was in her hotel room, moving in fluid, near-silent steps.

Hair rising on the back of her neck, she quietly eased out of bed on the side opposite the door and crouched low on the floor...and waited. She didn't know who was out there, or how they had gotten inside her room, and she might not have a weapon, but she could defend herself.

After criminals attempted to kidnap Randi when she

was eight to blackmail her father into dropping a high-profile case he'd taken, her parents enrolled Haywood and her in karate classes. Haywood had lasted only three years, but Randi had continued taking the classes all through her college years. Even now when she had the time, she joined her instructor, Hanshi Decatur, in sparring matches.

A rush of adrenaline sprinted through her veins and her shoulders tightened as she prepared for defense mode. Randi didn't know why people were in her room, but she was determined to make sure they regretted invading her space. She held her breath when she heard the sound of her bedroom door opening. In the sliver of moonlight shining through the curtains, she could make out a figure silently moving toward the bed, evidently assuming she was in it. Did the person have a weapon? If so, what kind? That question was answered when she heard a gunshot through a silencer. The assassin had intended to kill her while she slept. Would the intruder assume the target had been hit and leave?

She saw that wasn't going to happen when the person slowly inched toward the bed as if to verify the kill. Now was her chance, when the element of surprise was still on her side. Knowing timing was everything, she watched, waiting as the slow steps sounded on the carpet, moving closer to the bed. And when the time was right, she ejected her body from its crouch and attacked, making sure her first strike counted.

CHAPTER SIXTEEN

WHAT THE HELL was that?

Quasar came awake with a start. Was that a crashing sound he heard next door in Randi's room? No sooner had that question flashed through his mind than there was another crash. He jumped out of bed, quickly sliding into his jeans. Grabbing his Glock off the nightstand, he raced out of his hotel room, not bothering to put on his shoes.

Quasar immediately noticed Randi's room door slightly ajar and entered as another crash sounded from her bedroom. With his gun drawn, he entered the room and flipped on the light switch in time to see Randi deliver a hard kick to the side of a man's head. When brightness flooded the room, the man's attention wavered, which ended up being a costly mistake. Randi took advantage and whirled her body seemingly in midair. She took aim, and her foot landed right in her attacker's groin, with a swift second kick to his shoulder. A loud snap could be heard when the shoulder dislocated. It was then that she took aim again with her foot, in a hard blow to his face. The man let out a deep howl of pain before crumbling unconscious to the floor.

She jerked her gaze to him, and he saw surprise in her eyes. "Quasar?"

Putting the safety on his weapon and tucking the gun in the back waistband of his jeans, he walked over to her.

"I came to help, but it appears you took care of business on your own."

She shook her head as if she needed to clear it. "What are you doing here?"

"I'll explain things in a second," he said, pulling her into his arms, needing to touch her, feel her to make sure she was alright. "You okay?"

She pulled back and looked up at him. "Yes. He tried to kill me, Quasar."

They heard a groan and saw the man had come to and was struggling hard to get to his feet. When he saw Randi, he snarled and called her a bitch. In the blink of an eye, Quasar had crossed the room and used his fist to knock the man out again.

Glancing around the room, Quasar saw it was in shambles. His gaze snagged on the bullet hole in the bedcovers and the gun with the silencer on the floor next to the nightstand. A Beretta. Striker's gun of choice. Had Randi been in that bed and taken a hit, she would not have survived. Quasar had to fight back his rage so he wouldn't douse the attacker with water to bring him around again, just to dislocate the other shoulder.

He went back to Randi. "Do you know who he is?"

"No. I need to call Agent Riviera," she said, picking up her cell phone off the floor. "And you need to tell me how you got here, Quasar. How did you know I was in danger?"

"I heard the noise coming from this room."

Randi gave him a bemused look. "How? You walked me to my hotel room hours ago. Why are you still at the hotel?"

"I never left," he said, snatching the electric cord from a broken lamp on the floor to bind the man's hands behind his back, not caring about the dislocated shoulder. He was tempted to break the bastard's damn arm, as well.

Randi tapped her phone screen. "What do you mean, you never left?"

Before he could answer, Agent Riviera must have come on the line. Randi lifted a just-a-minute finger to Quasar. "Agent Riviera, this is Dr. Fuller. You need to come to my hotel as soon as possible. Someone just tried to kill me."

No sooner had she clicked off the phone than a man rushed into her hotel room. In an instant, Quasar was on his feet with his Glock drawn.

The man threw up his hands. "What's going on here?" the man asked, seeing the gun aimed at him. "I'm Victor Pierson, head of hotel security. We received several calls that a lot of commotion was coming from this room."

Quasar lowered the gun and tucked it back inside the waistband of his jeans. "Someone broke into this room and tried to kill Dr. Fuller. The authorities are on their way."

AGENT RIVIERA STOOD in front of the man handcuffed to the chair. "You might as well make it easy on yourself and tell us who hired you to kill Dr. Fuller."

The man, who looked like he'd gotten beaten by several men when most of his injuries had come from a single woman, snarled from a bruised lip, "I need medical attention. My shoulder is dislocated. I came into this room by mistake, and that woman jumped me."

From his position leaning against the wall, still barefoot and shirtless, Quasar couldn't help rolling his eyes. Seriously? Was that the story he was going with? The man was beyond stupid if he thought someone would fall for that lie. Especially when it was obvious there'd been forced entry into the hotel room and there was a gun with his fingerprints all over it. Thinking it would be a quick and easy kill, the asshole hadn't bothered to wear gloves. Quasar bet the bastard hadn't counted on the likes of a woman like Randi kicking his ass. And she had definitely kicked it. He'd seen that kick she'd planted in the man's groin. Probably damaged him there for life. Paramedics had been called for his dislocated shoulder but hadn't arrived yet.

Deciding he'd heard enough and wanted to check on Randi, Quasar left the bedroom for the living room area, where Randi was giving a statement to a police detective. The technicians were there, dusting for fingerprints and collecting other evidence. Quasar stepped aside when paramedics burst through the door, wheeling in a stretcher.

Quasar sat down on the sofa. The police officers had given Randi time to change out of her pajamas and into a multicolored caftan. To anyone else she must have looked cool, unflappable and pretty damn composed, considering what she'd been through. But he had a feeling she was anything but those things. He could imagine what she felt, knowing a man had been sent to kill her and would have done so if she hadn't taken steps to protect herself.

He glanced over at the two detectives and saw them watching him. He figured they would want to know the same thing Agent Riviera had asked him. Why did he have a gun?

"Now, Mr. Patterson, we need to ask you a few questions."

Without saying anything, not even giving a nod that he'd heard what they'd said, he moved to switch places with Randi. The questions started off routine. No problem. He'd given statements before. And through all the questioning, he could feel Randi's eyes on him.

"So what brought you to LA? And do you normally travel with a gun?" the detective asked him.

"It's a beautiful city, and I wanted to feel safe." He knew he was being a smart-ass, but at the moment he didn't care. He hadn't liked the detective's attitude when he'd been questioning Randi and had pegged the guy to be a first-class jerk. More than once his line of questioning ridiculed her reason for being in Los Angeles. It was obvious the man didn't believe in or respect Randi's psychic abilities. "And since I know you're going to ask," Quasar decided to add, "I am licensed to carry a firearm in all fifty states due to the nature of my work. I've provided Agent Riviera with all the necessary paperwork."

"And you know Dr. Fuller?"

He looked at Randi, who held his gaze. "Yes, I know her."

"How?"

He returned his focus to the detective and was about to tell him that it really wasn't any of his damn business. However, he figured the man was just doing his job. "We met a few months ago, during another case she was assisting the FBI and law enforcement on." He and Randi hadn't really officially met then, but he wouldn't tell that to this jerk.

"And what about the attacker?"

"What about him?"

"Do you know him, as well?"

Quasar immediately got angry at that question. "No, I don't know the bastard. Am I giving a statement or are you interrogating me, detective?"

"I was beginning to wonder the same thing," Agent Riviera said, entering the room. The attacker, now handcuffed and flat on his back, was being wheeled out of the hotel room. He hadn't looked their way.

"We'll take things over from here, Detective. This is all part of a federal investigation."

The man who'd identified himself as Detective Duke Sutherland cast Riviera a slight smile, and Quasar could feel tension between the two men. "Need I remind you that we're in this together, Agent Riviera? My department is using common sense while you're depending on this quack and her crystal ball."

Quasar was out of his seat in a flash. "You're out of damn line." Cop or no cop, this man was about to get his ass kicked for what he'd just said about Randi. Talk about being disrespectful. Before Quasar could say anything else, Riviera crossed the room to stand in front of the man. Anyone could tell from the set of his jaw that he was angry. "And I agree with Mr. Patterson, Detective Sutherland. You are way out of line and owe Dr. Fuller an apology."

Detective Sutherland glanced over at Randi and, to Quasar's way of thinking, muttered some shitty-sounding, insincere apology.

"Now, get the hell out of here," Riviera told him. "I'll be talking to your superior tomorrow."

The detective turned to Riviera. "Whatever. You're going to regret this when the shit hits the fan and those two gangs go at each other and leave this city covered in the blood of innocent lives." And on that parting shot, Sutherland headed for the door with his partner following him out.

Agent Riviera turned to Randi. "I'm sorry about that, Dr. Fuller."

Randi waved away his words. "No need to be. I'm used to skeptics."

Quasar didn't say anything as he sat back down, pissed off as hell. The man wasn't just a skeptic; he was a damn jerk whose ass needed kicking. How could Randi put up with such crap on a constant basis, people not believing in her abilities to the point that they belittled her? She had the perfect temperament, resilience and strength, and more than ever at that moment, he couldn't help but admire those qualities in her.

"Did my attacker tell you anything?" Randi asked Agent Riviera.

Agent Riviera shook his head. "No, nothing. I've asked my men to haul in the leaders of both gangs for questioning. One of them had better tell me—"

"It's been revealed to me that the gangs had nothing to do with what happened here tonight," Randi said.

"Maybe not, but until we have proof that a third party is involved, they remain our top suspects," Agent Riviera said in frustration.

Randi stood, walked over to the window and looked out. She still had a lot of questions, including those about Quasar. How had he arrived in her room at just that moment? When Agent Riviera had observed Quasar packing a gun, he'd demanded to know who he was, and she'd told him the truth. Quasar was a guy she was seeing who happened to be in LA at the same time she was.

As to why he had a gun, she could only assume that in his line of work, carrying a gun most of the time was something he did. If Agent Riviera really wanted to know, then he needed to question Quasar about it himself. Her mind was still in tatters about what had happened tonight. She could hold things together for only so long. She wanted to go somewhere and have a good cry. After tonight she deserved it.

"Do you have any idea who was behind the assassination attempt tonight, Randi?"

Quasar asked the question, and she turned around and noticed he was watching her intently. She saw his brown bedroom eyes were still filled with fury. Shaking her head, she said, "No, but like I said before, I know it wasn't gang-related. That much was revealed to me through my psychic abilities. I think it's the same individual or group that wants everyone to believe what happened to Esther Emiliano was gang-related, as well."

"That means someone is going to a lot of trouble to make it seem that way."

What Quasar said was true. Someone was going to a lot of trouble. They had killed once and had tried again tonight. They were not going to like that their person had failed. Would they try again? Would whoever was responsible be afraid she could nail him or her with the use of her psychic powers?

"I'm assigning around-the-clock protection for you, Dr. Fuller," Agent Riviera said. "That also means a safe house."

Randi frowned. "Granted, I know I can't stay here tonight, but do you think a safe house is necessary?"

A scowl touched Agent Riviera's features. "Did you not see that bullet hole in your bedspread, Dr. Fuller?"

Randi closed her eyes for a moment and drew in a deep breath as she relived parts of tonight. When she opened them, she saw Quasar and Agent Riviera staring at her closely. "Yes, I saw the bullet hole. If you recall, I was there when it was made. Someone wants me dead. I got that. But I came here to do a job, regardless. If anything, I'm even more determined to go to the crime scene in the morning."

She paused a moment and knew she would probably get some resistance from Agent Riviera with her next request. "And there's something else I want you to arrange for me tomorrow."

Agent Riviera lifted a brow. "What?"

"I want to meet with both gang leaders on their turf."

First, Agent Riviera looked at her as if she'd lost her mind. Then he began shaking his head. "That's too risky, Dr. Fuller. We aren't talking about choirboys gone bad. We're talking about thugs of the worst kind."

"I understand that, but I need to talk to them. It's essential that I do, and you're just going to have to trust me on this."

Agent Riviera rubbed the back of his neck. She would not compromise on this. He must have seen that in her face. "Fine. I'm bringing them in for questioning tonight anyway, regarding what happened here. Although I know you believe they aren't involved, I have to follow procedure, and right now they're my main suspects."

He paused a minute before continuing. "I will come up with a reason to hold them to give you time to meet with—"

"I prefer it be on their turf."

Agent Riviera shook his head. "That's not possible. It's too dangerous."

Randi gave him a stubborn look. "Doesn't matter."

When Riviera was about to say something, she held up her hand to cut him off. "It has to be done, Agent Ri-

viera. Not only to stop all the bloodshed but also finally
to bring peace between these two gangs."

Riviera looked stunned that she could even think such
a thing. "Peace? There will never be peace between the
Warlords and the Revengers."

"How do you know?" she countered. "Has anyone ever
tried? Or has the only thing the authorities tried doing is
containing them? Keeping them in line."

"We are talking about criminals."

Quasar sat listening to the intense conversation between Randi and Special Agent Riviera. As far as he
was concerned, what happened tonight had been a game
changer. Although she'd handled her attacker damn ad-
mirably on her own tonight, she should not have had to
do so. He refused to let her stay in this city unprotected.
What if there had been more than one attacker with guns?
Even with her skill in karate, she would be dead. The
thought of that had pain erupting inside him like needles
piercing his skin.

He did agree with Agent Riviera about the danger of
meeting with the gangs on their turf. But he didn't agree
with the federal agent regarding gangs not being able to
make peace.

"It's happened before," Quasar interrupted the conversation. When both Riviera and Randi turned to him,
he continued. "Gangs can make peace. It was done right
here in LA close to twenty-five years ago. The Crips and
the Bloods became a united front in what was the first
peace treaty between gangs in any city's history."

Riviera rubbed his hands down his face. "Look, Mr.
Patterson, you're talking about over twenty years ago.
I'm talking about the present. Maybe back then some
percentage of gang members were rational, but not now.

They thrive on violence and hate and barely have respect for each other, much less for anyone else."

Quasar watched as Randi's lips, the same ones he loved to kiss, formed a mutinous pout. "I'm sure this city has some sort of gang intervention organization, Agent Riviera."

"Yes, but—"

"Solicit their help. They will be needed after I talk to the leaders of the gangs."

Quasar couldn't wait to hear what the FBI agent's response would be. He was finding all this very interesting. Especially how passionate Randi was about her work. And where had that stubborn streak come from?

"I will have to take your request to meet with the gang leaders to my superior, Dr. Fuller."

"Fine, and make sure you underscore that when I meet with the gang leaders, I prefer it to be on their turf."

Quasar watched as the agent gave Randi a smile he bet the man wasn't really feeling. "Is there a reason you prefer it to be on *their* turf?"

"Yes. I need to feel the vibes of everyone in the gang. Someone, and I believe more than one, has defected and is working with a third party who's trying to overthrow both gangs. Like I said, you're going to have to trust me on this."

Agent Riviera didn't say anything, but he did trust her. Hadn't Special Agent Felton admitted the biggest mistake he'd made in his forty-year career with the Bureau was not believing the full extent of Dr. Fuller's psychic abilities? Riviera didn't intend to make the same mistake.

"Okay. I'll leave you to pack," Riviera said. "My men will be stationed at the door until you finish. I'm taking you to the safe house and—"

"That won't be necessary," Quasar said, standing. "From here on out, I'll be the one responsible for Dr. Fuller's well-being. Officially, starting now, I'm her bodyguard, and I'll be the one protecting her."

CHAPTER SEVENTEEN

QUASAR KEPT HIS EYES on the road, although he was tempted to glance over at Randi. For the second time that night, they were riding through the streets of Los Angeles. She was quiet, and her eyes were closed. He hoped she was getting some sleep and figured she had to be exhausted, both mentally and physically.

Randi hadn't as much as put up an argument when Quasar stated to Agent Riviera that he would be her protector, placing her solely under his care. He'd known she'd had misgivings about going to a safe house. When Quasar said he might have an alternative, the FBI agent hadn't liked the idea, but it had been Randi's call to make.

When Quasar had gone to his room to pack, he had taken the time to call Roland to brief him on what had happened tonight. Roland, who'd met Randi when she'd worked the Erickson case in Charlottesville a few months ago, was outraged.

Roland felt Quasar was doing the right thing by stepping up as Randi's bodyguard and said Quasar should let him know if he needed backup. Roland had a security team ready to catch a flight to LA to lend a hand if needed.

"Where are we going?"

So she hadn't drifted off to sleep, after all. "To my home in Malibu."

He heard her pulling up in her seat. "Your home in Malibu? But I thought you said you hadn't been back to LA since your release from jail."

"I haven't. The house was a gift from my godmother, Lucinda, on my twenty-first birthday. I had every intention of moving into it, but before I could do so, I was arrested and sent to prison. Lucinda hired a property manager to handle things for me, making sure it was rented out all these years. I talked to him before leaving the hotel to let him know I was in town. He said the couple leasing it moved out last month and he was in the process of listing it again as a rental. So it's available for us to use."

Randi nodded. "Lucinda? That was your mother's best friend in college, right? The one who introduced your mother to your father, who was her cousin."

Quasar wasn't surprised that she'd remembered what he had told her last weekend about his godmother, when she'd also remembered what he'd told her about Lilly. "Yes."

"Since you own a home in Malibu, why were you staying at the hotel? In a room next to mine?"

Quasar had figured sooner or later she would get around to asking him that. She'd listened to his statement to the FBI about hearing noises coming from her room. And he'd told her that, as well. She had to be wondering why he hadn't mentioned staying at the hotel, in the room next to hers. He'd had several opportunities to do so.

"I wasn't crazy about you coming here assisting with gangs, but you felt safe and I let it go. Like I told you, I made plans to follow you here because I wanted to see you and spend whatever free time with you you might have while you're here."

"And you intended to try making peace with your family," she inserted, as if he'd forgotten about it.

"Whatever. Anyway, the night before flying out, I had this crazy dream."

Randy lifted a brow. "What was crazy about it?"

"You were in danger. Running away from someone. The next morning I tried dismissing it from my mind but couldn't. I had a gut feeling about it. And it didn't help matters that I kept remembering what you said about your gift being meant to help others more than to help yourself, which is why you can't read me. That made me concerned that although you can detect danger for others, you might not be able to do so for yourself. I'm glad I followed my intuition and stayed at the hotel."

"I am, too."

Quasar was surprised by her easy acceptance of what he'd told her about his dream and his need to protect her. He figured she was too mentally drained to care.

"What about your family, Quasar? Being my bodyguard will detract from the time you could be spending with them."

He figured he should level with her now. "The reason I decided to come visit my family finally, after all these years, was not for a touchy-feely reunion. I need answers from my father about a lot of things. For instance, the way he shut me out after Mom died. What he says will determine my next move."

He could feel her gaze on him. "Your next move?"

"Yes. There are things about my relationship with my family that I'd rather not discuss. But those particular things are the reasons a part of me feels that I can't ever be close to them again, Randi. That it's time I move on and sever the ties. The purpose of this trip is to meet with them to determine which way it's going to go. That's the only way I'll ever have true inner peace."

Randi wondered what could bring Quasar to want to do such a thing with his family. He actually was considering severing ties with them? In her world, family was everything. Even during those years when Trey's mother, Angela, had kept him from their father and had filled Trey's mind with hateful and evil lies about Randolph Fuller, neither Randolph nor Trey had cut the cord.

"Does your family know that you're here to do that?" she asked. "Sever the ties?"

Quasar brought the car to a traffic light. "They didn't know I was coming to LA, but I'm sure they do now since I called my property manager. He handles a lot of business for my father. They're friends, and I suspect he won't waste any time letting Louis know I'm in town."

"Louis?"

"Yes. My father."

She bunched her brows. "You call your father by his first name?"

"Sometimes." Quasar knew by now Randi thought the whole situation with his family was strange. And it was. Even when he'd talked to his property manager, Paul Woodard, the man had tried quizzing him about some things, such as when he planned to visit his family.

He'd always liked Paul. The man was fair and had treated him decently. Quasar had seen no reason to stop him from handling the affairs dealing with the beach house, although Paul was a close associate of Louis's. Even when Quasar had been incarcerated, he'd followed his godmother's advice to let Paul invest the proceeds from the rentals. Paul was also the person he used to invest the trust funds left to him by both sets of grand-parents.

Upon his release from prison, Quasar discovered all the investments had paid off, and he didn't have to work another day in his life if he chose not to. The old Quasar Patterson would have taken advantage of that. But the new Quasar, the one who'd spent three years in prison, the one who'd met and been mentored by Shep-pard Granger, knew money wasn't everything. Peace of mind was.

"Quasar. I need you to hold me, please."

He snatched his eyes from the road to Randi. She was trembling. Not caring that the two FBI agents following them, who'd been instructed by Riviera to tail them until they reached their destination, had to be wondering what he was doing, Quasar eased his car to the shoulder of the road and killed the engine.

He unsnapped his seat belt and pushed back his seat before reaching out to unsnap Randi's seat belt. He pulled her across the console and into his arms. She wrapped her arms around him and buried her face in his chest. She continued to tremble as he alternated between Spanish and English, whispering words to console her, to let her know everything would be alright and he would not let anything happen to her. Surviving an attempted murder had to leave a person traumatized. She was human, and any sane person who'd gone through what she had tonight could hold it together for only so long. And then there had to be that inner fear in knowing the person respon-sible for sending that assassin might try again. But like he'd told her, he would not let anything happen to her.

She lifted her head, and when he saw the lone tear from her eye, he gently wiped it away. She leaned up and covered his mouth with hers. Quasar knew she needed to dominate this kiss, and he intended to let her. Even if it killed him.

He was beginning to think it just might when their tongues mingled and mated in a tango so sensual he could feel a drugging rush of desire flow through his entire body. It was as if the forceful demand of the kiss was trying to claim his very soul while igniting a bone-melting fire that quickly spread through his loins.

He had to remember this kiss was therapy for her. At present, he was her anchor in turbulent waters. Her calm in the storm. And whether she knew it or not, that unexplainable connection he'd felt the night their gazes had met over the crime scene tape was binding them tighter.

She released his mouth, and when she parted her lips to speak, he shushed her by placing a finger to her moist lips. "Don't feel the need to apologize about anything or feel you're not strong. Okay?"

She held his gaze a few moments before nodding. "Okay."

A sharp knock on the car's window had her scampering out of his arms and back to her seat. Quasar rolled down his window. The FBI agent standing there looked at Randi and then back at him. "Is anything wrong, Mr. Patterson?"

Quasar shook his head while putting back on his seat belt. "No, nothing's wrong. We just needed to clear up a few things."

"Oh, I see." Quasar had a feeling the agent saw too much. "We'll continue to follow you when you get back on the road," the agent said.

"Alright."

When the man walked away, Quasar rolled up the window. He glanced over at Randi and waited while she finished buckling her seat belt before he restarted the engine.

"We'll finish clearing things up when we get to the beach house. We don't have far to go."

LEO STILLWELL SLAMMED down the phone. How could Ken Adams screw up killing Randi Fuller? The only good thing was that no matter what, Ken wouldn't talk. His paid assassin had seen firsthand what happened to snitches.

He began pacing, trying to decide his next move. More than likely Dr. Fuller would be going to the crime scene tomorrow. That's how she usually operated, and unfortunately, that's when that damn mind of hers managed to snag clues. If she linked Rick Constantine and his friend to anything, they would spill their guts, and he couldn't let that happen. It was time they were eliminated.

He smiled when a plan popped into his mind. He would make it seem as if their deaths were retaliation by the Revengers. That would throw even more grease on the fire.

Leo picked up the phone to place a call.

"What do you need, Leo?"

"I got a job for you."

LOUIS PATTERSON HUNG UP the phone and smiled. At first he'd been annoyed to have his sleep disturbed, but the news that Paul had delivered had more than excused the intrusion. Quasar had returned to LA just like Louis had ordered him to do.

He chuckled. For years he'd believed prison had changed his youngest son, had given him a mind of his own. Evidently not, at least not to the degree that it mattered. Oh, he knew Quasar had grown up, was a changed man, but some things couldn't change, and one was the control he'd managed to maintain over both his sons.

Louis eased out of bed and slipped on his robe to go downstairs to the library. He needed to start putting plans in place for his prodigal son's homecoming.

He would welcome him back with open arms...just long enough to make sure he played his part.

CHAPTER EIGHTEEN

"I HOPE YOU like the place," Quasar said, leading Randi into his beach house. He noticed she had managed to get at least thirty minutes of sleep in during the drive, and he regretted having to wake her when they'd reached their destination.

She glanced around as she moved past him to walk inside. "I'm sure I will. I can hear the sound of the ocean. How close are we?"

"Just through those sliding doors," he said pointing across the room. "It's a private beach, and most of the homes, including this one, have a boat dock. You can't see much of anything tonight, but you'll get a good view when you wake up in the morning."

"From what I see in here, this is a really nice place. It's hard to believe you've rented it out all these years and haven't used it. You weren't ever tempted to come back?"

"No, I was never tempted." No need to tell her that he'd been here in this house, spending the weekend with friends, when the police had shown up to arrest him.

"Come on, I'll take you to your room. You have to be exhausted."

"I am."

He led her upstairs, and when they entered the room, he stood back while she placed her overnight bag on the bed. "I'll bring the rest of your luggage in. You have your own private bath if you want to take a shower or anything."

"Thanks."

He watched as she took in the room, and when he saw a semblance of fear in her eyes, he felt anger coiled in the pit of his stomach. "You're safe here, Randi." She jerked her head up and met his gaze.

"I won't let anything happen to you," he added.

She drew in a deep breath and then nodded. "I've never had reason to be afraid before."

He leaned back against a wall. "You have no qualms about meeting with the leaders of the gangs who are undoubtedly dangerous. You're not scared about that?"

Jamming her hands in the pockets of her jeans, she said, "No. I guess it's because I feel I can control that situation to a degree, but I had no control or forethought that someone wanted me dead."

"Well, I think you did an admirable job kicking his ass. Who taught you martial arts?"

"I took classes from the time I was eight after someone tried kidnapping me. The kidnappers thought they could force Dad to withdraw from some high-profile case. It was Uncle Marlon's idea that I learn to defend myself." A small smile touched her lips. "At the time, I thought it was better than those piano lessons I dreaded."

For some reason he couldn't envision her docilely sitting at a piano while her fingers glided over the keys. "What degree black belt are you?"

"Fifth."

He knew reaching that level had to have taken a lot of hard work, commitment and dedication. "I'll bring the rest of our stuff inside."

"Okay, and thanks for earlier, in the car when I came

apart. I appreciate everything you said. Some of it was in Spanish."

He nodded and decided to explain, especially since according to Striker and Stonewall it could drive some-one who wasn't familiar with the language nuts. "I have a tendency to switch to Spanish at times whenever my emotions are running high." In a way he was glad she hadn't understood what he'd said since the Spanish words he'd spoken to her hadn't been just comforting. A few had been pretty damn sensual.

"Oh."

He hesitated, not wanting to leave her but knowing he had to. But just like at the hotel, he intended to sleep in the bedroom next to hers. Her safety meant every-thing to him.

RANDI'S EYES FLEW OPEN and she bolted upright in bed, her breathing erratic. Frantically looking around, she saw that she was not in her hotel room and she was alone. There was no attacker with a gun.

But there had been.

Closing her eyes, she remembered it clearly, especially the man firing that shot into the bed, thinking she was in it. He'd had no reservations about ending her life. He'd been sent to kill her and had tried doing just that. She'd been involved with dangerous cases before while assist-ing law enforcement, but she had never been a deliber-ate target. And the thought that someone would attempt to end her life sent cold shivers through her body. The same as last night, when she'd asked Quasar to hold her.

She had needed to feel safe. To be held by him. He would never know the relief she'd felt when he'd burst into her room with his gun. She'd known that even if she hadn't been able to down the attacker, he would have.

More shivers shook her body, uncontrollably so. Burying her face in her hand she tried getting a grip on reality. She was alive and at Quasar's beach house in Malibu. The thought that the man who was destined to be a part of her future was the one protecting her now was almost too overwhelming to digest. And he said he'd had a dream the night before leaving Virginia that she would be in danger. Did he have the ability to detect such a thing when she herself couldn't? Was that a sign? A part of their connection? That during their lifetimes, he would always be her protector?

Dropping her hand, she lifted her face to stare out the window. Dawn was approaching, which meant she hadn't gotten a lot of sleep since her head had hit the pillow at close to four in the morning. After bringing in the rest of her luggage, Quasar had told her to get some rest. If she needed him for anything, he would be in the bedroom next door. The thought that he was in a bed so close made something akin to liquid heat flow up her spine.

Just in case what happened last night made the national news, she needed to call her family to let them know she was okay. Reaching out, she grabbed for her cell phone on the nightstand. It slipped from her hand to go tumbling to the floor. "Gripes."

She was about to ease from the bed to retrieve it when there was a knock on her door. "Yes?"

"I heard a sound. Are you okay?"

How in the heck had he heard that? The phone hitting the floor had barely made any noise. Getting out of bed, she grabbed the robe from the foot of the bed and quickly put it on. "Yes, I'm fine," she said, picking up her cell phone before going to open the door. "I dropped my…phone."

The last word stuck in her throat when she saw Quasar standing shirtless with a pair of pajama bottoms riding low on his hips. She couldn't stop her gaze from leaving his face to travel down to his chest and the curly hair covering it. It wasn't too much or too little but just the right amount. Her eyes moved lower to the path of hair that eventually became hidden beneath the elastic waistband of his pants. When he'd burst into her hotel room in his bare feet and jeans with his chest bare, she'd been too traumatized to react to seeing him that way. Now she could appreciate what a nice chest he had.

With a mass of dark hair flowing to his shoulders and stubble darkening his unshaven chin, Quasar looked the epitome of sexy. And the realization that it was the same chest she'd been wrapped up against while he'd held her protectively last night, first while waiting for the authorities to arrive and then later in the car, sent her adrenaline spiking.

"Is it damaged?"

She forced her gaze from his chest back to his face. Why was he so sexy with that little bit of stubble on his jaw? He'd appeared so incredibly handsome before, but now his looks were downright sinful. Her eyes kept returning to his chest of their own accord.

"Randi?"

She snapped her gaze back to his eyes. Those make-a-woman-drool brown bedroom eyes. "Yes?"

"Is your phone damaged?"

He had asked her that before, hadn't he? She needed to take her concentration off his body and put it on their conversation. Floundering mindlessly, she tried to get a grip. Glancing down at her phone, she said, "It's fine. It's in one of those hard cases."

"I see."

"Sorry if the noise bothered you. I'm sure you were trying to get some rest."

He shook his head. "No, I was awake, waiting for sunrise."

She lifted a brow. "Sunrise."

"Yes. See?" he said, pointing at her window.

She turned, and what she saw nearly took her breath away. Now the ocean was visible with the sun rising over it. "Oh, Quasar," she said, rushing across the room to the window. "The view from here is gorgeous. Come see it with me."

She felt heat radiating off him when he stood beside her. "It is beautiful, isn't it?" he asked softly. "I've gotten used to seeing the Atlantic Ocean, but for me, there's nothing more gorgeous than the Pacific."

Randi looked out the window while puzzling over why he had given up his Malibu home for almost seven years if he loved the Pacific. He could have come back after he was released from jail but had chosen not to. "I can't believe how close this house is to the beach. Your godmother must have loved you a lot to give you this place as a gift."

"She never hesitated to tell me that she loved me. She was a very affectionate woman," he said, smiling. "My fondest memories are of spending my summers with her. She was a lot of fun and quite a character."

"In what way?"

"Too many to name. She was an advocate for human rights, animal rights and the environment. I remember her taking on the mayor of LA when he approved plans to demolish her old high school."

"Did she win?"

"Yes, she gathered enough support to pressure City Hall to come up with a new plan. They turned the school into a museum and even named one of the wings after her. I hope before you leave LA I can give you a tour."

"I'd like that."

He looked at his watch. "It's not quite seven, and we need to eat breakfast after our walk on the beach. I talked to Agent Riviera and assured him I would have you back in LA by ten."

"Breakfast? There's food here?"

"Yes. I told my property manager last night to make sure that the place was ready for us and that we had enough food in stock."

Randi wondered if that meant the property manager's employee had gone grocery shopping after midnight. "If you recall, last week I mentioned not being a kitchen kind of girl."

He chuckled. "I remember. I guess it's a good thing that I'm a kitchen kind of guy."

She smiled. "In that case, I would love to go walking on the beach."

At that moment her phone rang, and she knew from the ringtone it was her sister. She glanced at Quasar. "It's Haywood. I was about to call her when I dropped my phone. I'll bet she heard about what happened on the news."

She then clicked on the phone. "Haywood?"

"Randi! You okay? Trey just read what happened in this morning's paper. Why didn't you call?"

Randi drew in a deep breath. Haywood was all but

screaming. She was certain Quasar could hear her sister's dramatics. "Calm down, Haywood. I'm fine. I was about to call. The reason I didn't last night is that my brain was fried and the only thing I wanted to do was sleep."

"I'm glad you're okay. I can't believe someone tried to kill you."

"It's hard for me to believe, as well, but I was able to defend myself with my karate."

"I'm glad those karate classes came in handy."

"Me, too." No reason to admit to Haywood that in all honesty, she'd never been so afraid in her life, taking on a killer.

"Randi, Trey's right here. He wants me to tell you that if you need a safe place to stay, he has friends in LA who can—"

"That's not necessary. I'm already in safe hands," she said, peering up at Quasar.

"I thought so. I told Trey, Zack and Anna that you're probably under tight FBI security and all."

She could let her sister continue to think that way, or she could let her know the truth.

"Not really. I have a bodyguard."

"A bodyguard?"

She heard her brother echo the word and figured he was hovering over Haywood. "Yes," she confirmed. "A bodyguard."

"Is he reliable? We're talking about your life here."

Randi couldn't help but smile as her gaze still held Quasar's. "Yes, he's reliable. In fact, you've met him."

"I have?"

"Yes."

"When? Who is he?"

"Quasar Patterson."

There was a pause, and then Randi chuckled at the flood of questions that poured from her sister's mouth. Just as she'd known would happen. "I have to go, Haywood. I'll call the folks myself, but just in case I can't reach them, if you talk to them, please let them know I'm fine."

"But—but—"

"We'll talk again later, Haywood. I will call you. Don't call me. I'm working, remember? Goodbye."

Randi clicked off the phone and placed it on the TV table as she drew in a deep breath. "Haywood was concerned."

"I gathered. Thanks for believing I'm reliable."

She shrugged. "How could I not? Thanks to that dream you had, which turned out not to be crazy, after all. You figured I was in danger when I didn't have a clue. I appreciated you being my backup last night."

He chuckled. "Like I told you, it looked to me like you were handling things pretty damn well on your own."

"Yes, but what if he'd managed to take me down? You would have arrived at just the right time to stop him."

"Hell, I hope so," he said, gently stroking the bruise on her arm.

His touch sent heat cascading through her. When he reached up and gently cupped her mouth, hot, smoldering air shimmered around them. He didn't say anything, nor did he do anything. He just stood there, staring at her and causing the already fiery temperature surrounding them to rise even more. He had to be, without a doubt, the most virile man on the face of this planet. Any planet. She couldn't help it, but her senses were being overtaken by his scent and his physique. The man was so friggin' hot, blazing with erotic energy and causing stimulating awareness to thrum through every part of her body.

He took a step closer. Or did she? Honestly, it didn't matter who made the move when the lower parts of their bodies touched. The rush of desire that clawed at her just couldn't be ignored or denied.

When she couldn't stand the intensity of the sexual chemistry encasing them any longer, she whispered his name. "Quasar."

As if on cue, he leaned in and took her mouth with a need that she felt all the way to her toes. Was she imagining things or had the floor just shifted under her feet? She soon became disoriented with the languid, swirling strokes of his tongue with hers.

Her phone rang, and she pulled back from the kiss. To keep her balance, she placed her hands on his bare chest and felt the warmth of his hairy skin beneath her fingers.

"Are you going to get that?" Quasar asked in that too-sexy voice.

She looked up at him and thought about ignoring the call but knew better. She recognized the ringtone. This time the caller was Trey. If she didn't answer, he would be on the next plane to LA. Evidently he wanted to speak with her himself to make sure she was okay. "Yes, I'd better. It's Trey."

Quasar swiped a kiss across her lips. Straightening and then taking a step back, he said, "Let's meet downstairs in half an hour for our walk on the beach."

"Okay."

He left the bedroom as she grabbed for her phone.

CHAPTER NINETEEN

QUASAR HAD BARELY made it back to his bedroom when his own cell phone rang. Recognizing the ringtone, he answered, "Yeah, Striker?"

"I heard what happened. Are you and your woman okay?"

Quasar frowned. "My woman?"

He heard Striker's chuckle. "Still in denial, are you? Okay, then, let me rephrase that. Are you and the psychic okay?"

Quasar wasn't sure he liked that any better. The way Striker said it was as if Randi was some delusional person. "We're okay. I'm officially her bodyguard."

"Roland told us. How did the Feds take that?"

"Honestly, I didn't give a damn. As far as I'm concerned, they should have anticipated some craziness happening when they summoned her out here."

"Anticipated it like you obviously did?"

Quasar gave some thought to Striker's question. He couldn't deny the dream and those negative vibes he'd gotten before coming here. But he couldn't help wondering how Striker had figured it out. It never ceased to amaze him how Stonewall and Striker could deduce things when it came to him. "I guess so. All I know is that I'm not letting her out of my sight."

"Do they know who put the hit on her?"

"If they do, they aren't saying. And of course Randi's determined to stay and help solve the case. If it was left up to me, she would have been on the first plane back to Virginia."

"Getting kind of possessive, are we?"

An intense scowl touched Quasar's features. He wasn't in the mood for Striker's wisecracks. "I got this. Don't worry about it."

"And where are you now?"

"At that beach house I own. It's in a gated community with a private beach. But the Feds are parked on the outskirts, keeping tabs on who comes and goes."

"Be careful and trust no one. Not even the Feds."

Quasar knew why Striker was telling him that and was smart enough to heed his friend's warning. "Gotcha. Where is Stonewall?"

"At the barber. He's finally going on a date with his detective tonight and making a damn big production out of it. I guess he wants to look all dolled up and shit. Oh, by the way, Margo and I set a date for our wedding."

Quasar wasn't really surprised. They'd held out longer than he figured. "So when is it?" he asked, sliding off his pajamas and slipping on a pair of shorts.

"Next month. You don't sound surprised."

"If you recall, I'm the one who delivered the meals every day when you were protecting her. I know firsthand how hot things were between you and Margo. And since you claim you love her…"

"I don't claim anything. I love her. Till death do us part and all that shit."

Quasar smiled. He liked getting a rise out of Striker as much as he knew Striker enjoyed getting one out of him. "I thought the two of you had decided to date awhile."

Striker snorted before saying, "We did the dating thing and decided it was a waste of our time. We want to be husband and wife, and there's no reason to wait any longer. It will be a private affair on her uncle's estate, and I want you there. You can even bring the psychic with you."

Quasar fought hard not to grit his teeth. "Her name is Dr. Randi Fuller, Striker."

"Whatever. I'll talk with you later. If you need help, just call. Stonewall and I will be on the first plane out."

"Thanks."

"Hey! Wait! I forgot to ask. Have you made contact with your family yet?"

"No."

"But you will, right?"

"That's the plan."

"Good. Take it from me, closure is everything. I'll talk to you later."

Quasar clicked off the phone and continued to get dressed. *Your woman.*

Striker's words came back to him, but he shook off the stifling thought. He didn't have a woman. Lilly had taught him a lesson he would never forget.

"I'M FINE, TREY. Honest, I am."

"I read the full details in the paper, Randi. Someone broke into your hotel room intending to kill you. The bastard even shot into the bed, which luckily you weren't in."

Why did he have to remind her of all that? "I know. But I'm okay."

"And what's this about you having a bodyguard? Although I think it's a damn good idea, Haywood said it's the same guy you introduced us to at the zoo last weekend."

"It is."

"What is he doing in LA? Did he follow you there? Is he stalking you? Did you invite him along? How well do you know this dude?"

Randi tossed her hair back from her face. "Stop interrogating me, Trey. I'm not your client and you're not my attorney. Quasar works for a security firm. You saw him that night at the Kennedy Center."

"Yeah, I remember. I also remember that for some reason you pretended not to know him. Yet you were with him the next day, all lovey-dovey, holding hands at the zoo."

Of course her brother would remember that. "All you need to know, Ross Donovan Fuller III, is that Quasar knows how to protect people and volunteered to be my bodyguard while I'm here. That's all there is to it."

"Not by a long shot. You left out a few details, sis. Like why the hell he was in LA in the first place."

"Last time I checked, this was a free country. He can go anywhere he pleases. Now, if you don't mind, I have to meet with the FBI Special Agent this morning. I came to LA for a reason."

"And you're determined to stay and help? I read about those gangs. They are ruthless, murderers and—"

"—innocent of any crime until proven guilty. I'm sure the attorney in you knows that, but it just slipped your mind. Love you, Trey. Chat with you later." She made several kissy sounds for his benefit before clicking off the phone. Older alpha male brothers. You just had to love them.

Randi then thought of another alpha male and glanced at the clock on the wall. She'd lost ten minutes talking to Trey, and she still needed to reach her parents.

At that moment she recalled last night and how she'd come apart during the drive to the beach house and the words he'd spoken while holding her, comforting her. More than once he'd used terms of endearment in one of the sexiest voices she'd ever heard. She knew he still assumed she didn't understand Spanish, and maybe it was time for her to tell him about her fluency in the language. But he'd said the only time he spoke Spanish was when his emotions were high. She knew everyone needed an outlet for emotions and didn't want him to stop using his if he knew she understood what he said. So for now, she wouldn't tell him.

Satisfied with that decision, she placed a call to her parents.

QUASAR GLANCED UP when he heard a sound at the top of the stairs. Randi descended, and his heart almost stopped beating. Like him, she had pulled her hair back in a ponytail, which made her features even more captivating. Then there were the shorts and top that emphasized delectable curves, nice full and firm breasts and a gorgeous pair of legs.

His gaze moved upward from her legs to her face and zeroed in on the lusciousness of the lips that he'd had the pleasure of tasting several times and still couldn't get enough of.

"Sorry if I kept you waiting," she said when she stepped off the last stair.

He couldn't help the smile that touched his lips. She smelled as good as she looked. "I just came down myself."

He'd gotten calls from Stonewall and Shep. Like Striker, they'd wanted to know he was okay. He'd also gotten a call from Louis, which Quasar had refused to take. Paul had probably told his father he was in town, and the old man figured Quasar had made the trip because he'd been ordered to do so. Louis didn't know just how wrong he was about that. Quasar would call him back when he got good and ready and not before.

"Nice outfit," he said, while hot and sharp desire clawed at his insides.

"Thanks. I packed a few beachy pieces. I wasn't sure whether I'd get the chance to wear them or not."

"I'm hoping that before you return home, maybe I can entice you to stay for a few days to relax here."

A smile spread across Randi's lips. "I would love to." She then glanced around. "Last night I was too tired to appreciate the beauty of this place. It's really nice."

"Thanks. When we get back from our walk, I'll show you around."

"Okay."

"Ready to go?"

"Yes."

He led them through a set of French doors, and they stepped out on a screened-in patio with a beautiful brick floor. But what captured Randi's attention more than anything was the sight of the ocean that had to be no more than fifty feet away. It was a beautiful day in May, and she thought the weather here was wonderful.

"You might want to take your sandals off," Quasar said, and Randi saw him slip out of his own shoes. He pulled a pair of aviator sunglasses out of his shirt pocket and put them on.

"I have no problem doing that," she said, fully aware every pore in her body was attuned to him as a hot, stunningly masculine man. "I love the feel of beach sand beneath my feet."

Moments later, after she'd shielded her eyes with her own pair of sunglasses, they began walking toward the beach. They didn't hold hands, but just being close to him as they walked, with their shoulders occasionally touching, was temptation enough.

When she'd seen him at the bottom stair looking up at her, she'd almost lost her footing. She'd felt a crackle of sexual energy pass between them with every step she took. But that had given her a chance to drink him in, standing there in a pair of low-rise running shorts and a plain white T-shirt. But there was nothing plain about the massive shoulders and broad chest outlined in sharp relief. And the way he filled out those shorts was sinful.

"Did you get a chance to talk to your parents?" he interrupted her thoughts to ask.

"Yes, but just to assure them I was okay and to let them know I have a bodyguard now. I'll call them back later." She glanced out at the ocean. "It's so peaceful here. Reminds me of Glendale Shores."

"Glendale Shores?"

She nodded. "Yes. It's one of the most beautiful of the Sea Islands off the South Carolina coast and has been in my family for generations."

"Your family owns an island?"

"Yes. Over the years developers have tried their best to buy it, to make it into another Hilton Head, but we refuse to sell. All of us were deeded a piece of the island from our great-grandparents. I built a small cottage on my property. I'd love to return the favor and invite you there one day."

She couldn't see his eyes for the sunglasses, but she

didn't miss his smile, the same one that was stirring desire in her. "That sounds like a plan."

Whether he knew it or not, he was helping to relieve some of her anxiety and tension from last night. A part of her was so glad she was here. She had a feeling this place was special to him, and she appreciated that he was sharing it with her. "What were your favorite places when you lived in LA?" she asked him.

He didn't say anything, as if he was remembering. "I always liked visiting my godmother here. I was glad she gave me this house when she was alive. She loved it so much."

"Why did she leave it?"

"It had always been her dream to live in Paris again, and she decided to move back there."

"She lived there before?"

"Yes, she studied art there for a while. Most of the pieces hanging on the walls at the beach house are hers."

Randi recalled the ones she had admired hanging on the wall in her bedroom. "She did excellent work. It's obvious that she was very talented."

"Yes, she was."

"Is she still alive?"

He hesitated a minute before answering, and a part of her already knew what his response would be. "No. She passed away while I was locked up, but she visited me often. Two to three times a year, coming all the way from Paris each time."

He paused again and then added, "The year she died, she came four times. She knew her life was almost at an end and wanted to see me before dying of colon cancer. She died a month after her last visit with me."

A lump formed in Randi's throat. "I'm sorry, Quasar. Did you know she was dying?"

"Not until that last visit. That's when she told me."

Quasar didn't say anything for a minute as he recalled that visit when his aunt had told him her days were numbered. She'd also said that in addition to a trust fund she'd set up for him, he would inherit all her possessions, including her bungalow in Paris. She never had any kids, nor had she ever married, although he'd known her to have a number of lovers over the years. His godmother had always been there for him after his mother's death, and for that he would be eternally grateful.

The one thing he remembered more than anything about that last visit was asking for her total honesty about whether or not there was a chance he really wasn't Louis's biological son. She had assured him he was, but that she couldn't…or wouldn't…tell him why his father preferred Doyle over him. She had suggested he ask his father the reason. He hadn't done that. Instead he'd made the decision to cut the ties and move to Charlottesville without letting his family know where he was. Even after the private investigator found him and he and his father began communicating, Quasar hadn't asked. Maybe he should have, but a part of him didn't want to know what his father's answer might be. Now he wanted answers, no matter what they were.

Randi didn't ask him any more questions, and he welcomed the silence. He wondered if she'd caught on to the fact that he would occasionally brush his thigh against hers. Earlier he'd stopped short of taking her hand. The last woman he'd gone for a walk with on the beach while holding hands had been Lilly. Thank God it hadn't been this particular beach.

He glanced at his watch. "Time to go back. I want to give you a tour of the place before we eat breakfast."

"Okay."

"Do you still intend to push the issue with Agent Riviera regarding meeting with those gang leaders?"

"Yes. For some reason, the ambiences I'm getting on this case are stronger than they've ever been for me."

"Why?" he asked her, taking in the moment of sizzling awareness each time their shoulders touched.

"It's complicated, and I'm sure you don't really want to hear about it."

Quasar wondered if others had brushed her off when she'd tried discussing her work with them. He would admit she was the only person he knew who was involved in the paranormal, but he couldn't help but be fascinated by it. Nor could he help being fascinated by her. "It's your work, and I do want to hear about it. So tell me why the ambiences are so strong."

They kept walking a few steps before she said, "Both gang leaders had mothers who were extremely close to their sons. It's the mothers who're sending me messages."

He raised a brow. "The mothers?"

"Yes. The most recent victim, Esther Emiliano, as well as the other gang leader's mother, Donna Naples. Donna died years ago in a car accident. Her son didn't join a gang until after her death."

He didn't say anything for a minute. Then he asked, "How do you handle all that? Your mind being infiltrated by messages from dead people?"

She looked up at him. She wasn't annoyed by his question. A smile teased across her lips. "It's not like my life is anything close to that kid's from the movie, *The Sixth Sense*. I live a normal life until I'm called on. If it's law enforcement calling, I refuse to let them tell me anything about the case."

"Why?"

"Because I don't want anyone's opinion or thoughts influencing me. I'm able to tell them how things went down, describe the crime scene to a tee over the phone, mention details about the crime scene they haven't released to the public yet. Sometimes I can give them vital info they might have overlooked. I did that with Esther Emiliano."

"In that case, why did you come? Why do you need to go to the crime scene at all?"

"Because of the murder weapon. It can't be found."

"And you think it's still at the crime scene?" he asked, trying to follow her.

"No. But I believe it's somewhere nearby in a body of water. According to Agent Riviera, there are a number of lakes and ponds in the area. Revisiting the crime scene will help me pinpoint which one."

As they headed toward the beach house, he had a better understanding of the case from her perspective. "Come on, I'll race you back to the house."

She laughed. "You're on."

CHAPTER TWENTY

THE FIRST THING they did upon reaching the beach house was use the outside shower to wash the sand off their feet. Then they grabbed towels from a nearby rack to dry off. Quasar won the race, but Randi was convinced it was because hunger pangs had slowed her down.

Placing his hand in the center of her back he guided her inside and proceeded to show her around. She *oohed* and *aahed* at every room they came to. She hadn't realized how large his beach house was. There were three bedrooms and each had its own private bath. There were two other bathrooms, a spacious kitchen and a dining room. Instead of a living room, there was a massive great room completely surrounded by windows, providing a panoramic view of the Pacific Ocean.

Quasar told her that the year before his godmother died, to make the beach house more attractive to long-term renters, she'd hired a decorator to give both the interior and exterior a face-lift that included painting and new furnishings throughout the house. This was the first time he was seeing the makeover and agreed with Randi that the decorator had done an awesome job.

"So that's the last room," he said at the end of their tour.

"Everything is simply beautiful, Quasar."

"Thanks."

"What can I do to help with breakfast?"

"Nothing. I've got everything covered. How do blueberry pancakes sound?" he asked as they began walking down the stairs toward the kitchen.

"Delicious. Yum-yum."

He threw his head back and laughed. She couldn't help admiring how doing so made his ruggedly handsome features even more pronounced.

"Is that what you're feeding me?" she asked. "Blueberry pancakes?"

"Yes. And how do you like your eggs?"

"Scrambled." She was already licking her lips. When they walked into the kitchen, she said, "I was just thinking that I haven't heard from Agent Riviera. Did he mention anything when you talked to him earlier this morning?"

"No. But then, I doubt that he would have told me anything. It was obvious last night he didn't like me stepping in as your bodyguard. He much preferred that his men keep an eye on you."

Randi had picked up on that, as well. Deciding to change the subject, she asked, "Is there anything I can help set up?"

"You can set the table and pour the juice if you like."

"Okay."

She moved over to the cabinets, opening the doors and retrieving dishes and glasses. She turned around and found him staring at her. He quickly switched his gaze away to open the refrigerator. Too late. Randi had actually felt the heat of his gaze on her backside. "Do you want me to make coffee, as well?" she asked him.

He turned back to her. "Can you make coffee? I mean, good coffee?"

She held out her hands in front of her. "See these hands, Quasar Patterson? They are capable of doing a lot of things."

"Are they?"

She heard the deep huskiness in his voice, and the tenor sent quivers all through her belly. She could just imagine what thoughts were running through his mind. Namely, what other things her hands could do. "Yes."

"I intend to find out if that's true one day, Randi."

"I'm counting on it, Quasar." She quickly turned back to the cabinets or else he would see the heated desire in her eyes.

"Do we need to talk about it, Randi?"

Randi knew what *it* he was referring to. The sexual chemistry between them that just wouldn't go away. It was expanding by leaps and bounds. He'd given her a sample of the passion she could share with him. Unfortunately, sexual chemistry or passion was the last thing either of them needed right now. She had a job to do. And there was also the issue that someone wanted her dead. But when everything was over with the gangs and the danger in her life had passed, she had no problem with them confronting all that passion and sexual chemistry head-on. They needed to make sure none of it went to waste.

She turned around to face him, leaning back against the counter. "No, we don't need to talk about it. Let's just make our plans now, via mutual agreement. When this situation with the gangs is over and before we return to our homes, let's seize the moment. What do you say to that?"

A seductive smile touched his lips. "I say, hell yeah. Let's do it."

His words smoothed over her like a heated promise, filled with all the hot and urgent pleasure she could anticipate. She walked over to the table and began setting it, knowing his eyes were on her.

She looked up and met his gaze. "I think I need to warn you about something, Quasar," she said softly.

"What?"

"I haven't slept with a man in over four years. I might be a little rusty."

Randi didn't miss the look of surprise on his face before he slowly crossed the room to her. "No worries. If you're rusty, I'll slick you down with pleasure oil."

She smiled. "Pleasure oil? I like the sound of that." Knowing what could happen if he stood in front of her much longer, she asked, "You about ready to start on those pancakes?" Randi skirted around him to go start coffee.

Over breakfast he told her about places in LA he'd enjoyed while living here. He told her about the Walk of Fame and some of the celebrities who'd gotten stars.

Breakfast was wonderful, and she thought he was a great cook and told him he could prepare breakfast for her anytime. They had stood to remove their plates from the table when her phone rang. She looked at the caller ID. "Yes, Agent Riviera? I hope you have good news for me."

Listening to his response, she quickly said, "We're on our way."

"Randi? What is it?"

Her expression must have given her away. "Two members of the Warlords were brutally murdered. Execution-style. The Warlords think it's the work of the Revengers, and all hell is about to break loose."

On the drive to LA from Malibu, Randi alternated her gaze between the scenery outside the window and the man sitting behind the steering wheel. What was there about Quasar—in addition to his sinfully handsome looks and hot body—that made her ache? She figured any other woman would think those two things were enough. Problem was, she wasn't just any other woman.

She was a woman who had decided a few years ago, no matter what that vision from her great-grandmother had foreshadowed, that loving Larry had taken a lot out of her, had made her see things with a different pair of eyes. She still believed in happily-ever-after; there was no way she couldn't with so many happily married couples in her family. But still, she'd thought that sort of relationship was out of her reach. And she'd accepted that.

Until now.

That night she'd seen Quasar at the crime scene in Charlottesville, it had been pure feminine interest that had made her check him out. And then it had been all the sexual chemistry and physical attraction that had kept her looking.

A decision was made that before she returned to Richmond, they would make love. Just knowing it would eventually happen sent a restless throb of desire through her veins whenever he looked at her. Was she wrong for looking forward to it with such longing and wild anticipation?

He had changed into a pair of khakis and a shirt. The gun strapped in a holster on his shoulder didn't detract from his sex appeal. In fact, it made him look like a kickass kind of guy. His hair was still in the ponytail, and she thought for now it suited him, but she couldn't wait for the day she could run her fingers through those strands.

"I hope you enjoyed breakfast."

She pushed her hair from her face. "I did. Who taught you how to cook?"

"I learned while serving time. More often than not, I got assigned kitchen duties."

That piqued her interest. "They weren't leery with you being around knives or anything you could use as a weapon?"

He chuckled. "No. I was in the slammer for what is considered a white collar crime. Typically I would not have been imprisoned with violent offenders, but Glenworth had an overcrowding problem. As a result, some of the lower-level offenders like myself had to be housed in the higher-security section of the prison. I mostly stayed to myself, until that time I got into trouble."

"What kind of trouble?"

"A couple of guys planned a jail break and figured I could help them by stealing some of the items from the kitchen they would need. I refused, and one day they jumped me…with the intent of killing me. They wanted to show other inmates what would happen if anyone ever thought of refusing them anything. My death would be a message."

Randi's felt her skin crawl as the blood rushed to her temples. "Oh, my God," she said, twisting around in her seat to stare at him. "They tried to kill you?"

"Yes, and would have if Striker and Stonewall hadn't saved me. The bastards tried drowning me in the pool."

She lifted a brow. "Your prison had a pool?"

He nodded. "Yes, an Olympic-size pool. We even had a swim team. Those two guys caught me unawares while swimming in the pool and kept me submerged underwater. I would have been dead if Striker and Stonewall hadn't seen what they were doing and come to my rescue."

He didn't say anything for a minute and then added, "Striker had to perform CPR. But the worst thing is that I developed a water phobia. I freak out if I get in water above my waist. It was a long time before I was able to take tub baths again instead of showers. That's a lot for someone who was the captain of his swim team in both high school and college to admit."

Her mind reeled with what he'd just confided in her. He had mentioned last week that the three of them—he, Striker and Stonewall—had served time together in prison and what a close relationship they had. Now she knew why. "Those men…the ones who tried to kill you… what happened to them?"

"They got more time added to their sentences, but it really didn't matter, in a way. They were both serving sixty-year terms already and were in their forties. They wouldn't have gotten out anyway unless they lived past a hundred."

"What about you? You said that incident got you in trouble. How?"

She could see the way his hand tightened on the steering wheel. "I had to be hospitalized a couple of weeks because I had a collapsed lung. The incident raised a few brows with the prison commission, which made the warden look bad. He blamed me and I became his target. He was determined to make my life a living hell and was doing a pretty damn good job of it until Shep stepped in."

"Shep?"

"Yes, Sheppard Granger. If it hadn't been for him, I would have gotten into worse trouble that could have made me serve more time. The warden hadn't known

Shep was friends with the new governor. The next thing we all knew, the old warden was out of a job. Thanks to Shep's intervention."

She recalled reading an article in the newspaper about Sheppard Granger. He had been falsely accused of killing his wife and had served fifteen years of a thirty-year sentence. He was eventually found innocent when the real killers had been captured.

"Shep also fought to make sure I got therapy with a counselor for my water phobia. But even with all those counseling sessions, I couldn't put behind me the image of coming so close to dying in water, gasping for breath, having water fill my lungs and not being able to do anything about it. At least I don't have the dreams anymore. The counseling sessions with the therapist did help with that."

Randi reached over and touched his shoulder. She could only imagine what he'd gone through. And in a way, what he was still going through. "I'm glad they did help. And I'm glad Sheppard Granger was there as an advocate."

"What the hell!"

Quasar suddenly swerved the car when another vehicle speeded toward them head-on. Randi was certain if it hadn't been for his skill behind the wheel, they would have gone off the edge of the road, into a ravine.

"Hold on, Randi!" Quasar shouted.

He brought the car to a complete stop and quickly pulled the gun from his holster. When the driver of the other car turned his vehicle around and began hurling toward them again, she fought back a scream at the same time Quasar rolled the window down and begin firing. Apparently he knew just where to hit to blow out the tires.

The car began spinning out of control. Several more shots fired from Quasar's gun hit the fuel tank. The attacker's vehicle crashed into a tree before bursting into flames.

He then quickly backed them away from all the fire and smoke. After bringing the car to a stop, he unsnapped his seat belt and turned toward her. His gaze scanned all over her. "You okay?"

She nodded, unable to speak at that second. A moment later, when she could, she asked in a strained voice, "Where are the agents who were following us?"

"I can only assume they were deliberately cut off from us. This was a setup."

Randi's hand flew to her throat. "A setup?"

"Yes. Someone knew we would be traveling this route and was waiting. That car came from out of nowhere."

She drew in a deep breath, refusing to wonder who and how. She definitely knew why. Someone was determined to start a gang war and wasn't about to let her interfere.

Her gaze roamed over Quasar. He seemed all in one piece, but she had to know for certain. "What about you? You okay?"

He nodded. "Yes, I'm fine."

He'd said it so coolly and calmly, it made her wonder if having something like this happen was a regular part of his job as a bodyguard. Probably.

"I'm calling Riviera." He placed the phone on speaker for her to listen.

"This is Riviera."

"This is Quasar Patterson. Not sure where your men are, but we almost got ambushed."

"What! Where are you?"

"About thirty minutes from LA. We got lucky—if this

had been an hour earlier, more cars would have been on the road."

"Stay put. I'm coming with backup."

"No need. Just be at headquarters when we get there in ten minutes. I know a shortcut. However, you might want to summon the fire department. The car that tried to ram us is in flames."

"Any survivors?"

"I didn't check. At this stage of the game, I really don't give a fuck."

CHAPTER TWENTY-ONE

"ARE YOU SURE you're okay, Dr. Fuller?"

Randi stared into the concerned faces of the FBI agents surrounding her. Beyond them she saw Quasar, leaning against a wall with hands folded across his chest, staring at her. Yes, she was okay because Quasar had her within his scope. That filled her with a deep sense of security and protection.

She noticed no one had asked Quasar how he was doing. Evidently they figured since he'd volunteered to be her bodyguard, whatever came his way was something he had to deal with. And luckily for her, he had, demonstrating true grit. He had stopped the attack with expertise and skill while keeping a level head. He'd done what was needed to keep her safe. Unfortunately, the driver of the vehicle hadn't survived, and the authorities were trying to determine the man's identity.

Knowing it wouldn't be long before the media got wind of this, she had phoned her family. Everyone had been upset but was grateful to Quasar.

"Yes," she finally said to Agent Riviera. "For someone who's had an attempt made on her life twice since arriving in LA, I guess you could say I am okay. Thanks to Quasar, I'm alive."

All the agents except Agent Riviera swiveled their gazes from her to Quasar, sizing him up. They stared at him, and Randi watched as he returned their stares with no expression on his face. Not a smile. Not a frown. Although she couldn't read his thoughts, she could imagine what he was thinking. She could imagine what those agents were thinking, as well. He had accomplished something their comrades hadn't, which was single-handedly stopping the attacker. When the agents' gazes returned to her, she saw the admiration in their eyes. The two agents who'd been assigned to follow them had been ambushed, as well. Both had been checked at the hospital and released with minor injuries. Their attacker had gotten away.

"Due to the three recent homicides as well as what happened last night and today, Dr. Fuller, we can't take a chance on a third attempt on your life," Agent Riviera said. "I hate to suggest this, but maybe you should step back from the case."

Randi shook her head. Too much was at stake. This would not be another case that haunted her because those responsible were not brought to justice. "I can't. Someone is deliberately trying to start a gang war. I'm determined more than ever to expose that person before more lives are lost. And after last night and this morning, for me it's personal."

Agent Riviera sighed. "The LAPD raided the War-lords' stronghold and confiscated enough weapons to start World War III. Just think what can happen if the Revengers have armed themselves to that degree, as well."

Randi didn't want to think about it. "Where is the leader of the Warlords now?"

"He's in police custody. Do you still want to talk to him?"

She had wanted to talk with the gang leaders on their

turf, but with the recent turn of events it was apparent there wasn't time. Regardless, she needed to talk to them. "Yes. After I visit the crime scene."

"Okay, I'll make the necessary arrangements."

She nodded. "And I still want to talk to the leader of the Revengers, as well."

"That might be difficult."

Randi raised a brow. "Why?"

"He's missing. Without any solid evidence to hold him, he was released after questioning. He slipped the tail assigned to him. As of this morning, he can't be found, and his gang isn't talking. Something is up and we don't like it."

AN HOUR LATER they arrived at the crime scene, a warehouse buried deep in LA's Westside borough. The mother of the Westside Warlords gang leader had been brutally murdered in the gang's own backyard. Their own turf. The slap had undisputedly been loud and clear and meant to incite the gang.

After bringing the car to a stop, the first thing Quasar noted was the bright yellow crime scene tape that seemed to cover the entire block. He peered through the windshield and saw multiple dilapidated buildings standing tall and empty. The streetlights, some bent over, a number ripped from the sockets, were an eyesore, and garbage was scattered about. An area that once held so much potential was now an unthinkable waste. The gangs had made this side of town unappealing to anyone who could give the community a revitalization boost, something it desperately needed.

He turned to Randi upon hearing her deep sigh. They hadn't said much during the drive here, especially after she'd shared with him the details of how Esther Emiliano had been killed. It had been one of the most horrendous accounts he'd ever listened to. Just the thought that anyone could kill another human being so brutally actually turned his stomach.

Although their car had been flanked by those driven by FBI agents, Quasar had remained alert and watchful, always expecting the unexpected. He had no intentions of lowering his guard.

"You okay?" he asked Randi, watching her take in the depressing view outside the window.

She turned troubled eyes on him. "Yes, I'm fine, but I feel such tragedy here. A senseless loss."

He didn't say anything but silently agreed with her. Before leaving headquarters, Riviera had told them the authorities had found Ms. Emiliano's body after receiving an anonymous call. So far the tipster hadn't been identified.

As the agents stepped out of their vehicles, Quasar said, "I'll open your door, Randi." It was his way of kindly telling her to *stay put*. After rounding the back of the car, he opened her door and offered his hand. Liquid heat volleyed to his groin the moment their fingers touched. Her gaze shot to his. Somehow he managed to keep a straight face when she said, "Thank you."

"Anytime."

He took a step back when Agent Riviera and another agent who'd been introduced earlier as Agent Claude Bledsoe approached. "Get prepared for what you're about to see," Agent Riviera cautioned. "The building has been kept locked, and no one has been permitted beyond the tape. Not even the cleanup company."

Randi nodded. "Who owns the building?"

"Some outfit in New York. They paid the back taxes to get it, but it's been sitting empty since the purchase a couple of years ago."

Everyone moved toward the building, and the group was met by several police officers. Quasar remembered one of them from last night, Detective Sutherland, the prick. The man approached with a smarmy smile plastered on his face. "Dr. Fuller. Mr. Patterson. Good seeing you two again," Sutherland said. "I understand you ran into a little bit of trouble this morning."

Quasar shrugged casually. "Nothing I couldn't handle."

His words were intentionally cocky to rub Sutherland the wrong way. It was obvious it worked when Sutherland's phony smile was replaced with a deep frown. "You like playing cops, Patterson?"

"No. I like being a bodyguard. No playing in it."

Sutherland shifted his gaze from Quasar to Randi. "So, Dr. Fuller, has the universe sent you any signs yet?"

Before Quasar could speak in Randi's defense and tell the arrogant bastard just what he could do with any signs, Randi beat him to the punch. "Yes, in fact, one came to me a few moments ago. It told me that you could be a pretty nice guy if you stopped being a total ass."

Several agents cleared their throats. A number of police officers muffled laughter with fake coughs. Agent Riviera didn't try to hide his chuckle, and Quasar waited for the bastard's comeback, wondering if he was stupid enough to make one.

As if deciding a verbal spar with Randi wouldn't be in his best interest, Detective Sutherland didn't reply. Instead he turned his attention to Agent Riviera. "There are no new developments. The murder weapon still hasn't been found."

"And that's why I'm here," Randi said. "Shall we go inside, gentlemen?"

RANDI WONDERED IF she was the only one who smelled it. The stench of death. Blood had seeped into the cracks in the concrete floor. Hair shaved from the victim's head along with pieces of torn clothing littered the ground. She stood. Assessing. Measuring. Weighing. And yes, even asking for a sign from the universe. Detective Sutherland's words were meant as a dig, but at the moment, such a sign would be welcome.

Moving toward the area where white chalk marked the location the victim had been found, she knelt and touched the floor, feeling the cold cement against her fingers. Closing her eyes, she pictured what happened that ill-fated day. The visions came to her. At first they were fragmented. Disjointed. Just scraps, really. Then the images became clearer and stronger. At times shivers ran through her body, and at other times she felt so hot she was tempted to remove her top.

Moments later—ten minutes or thirty, she wasn't sure—Randi opened her eyes and glanced around. The interior of the warehouse was deathly quiet, and everyone present—FBI Agents and police officers alike—was staring at her. Waiting expectantly. Some impatiently.

And then there was Quasar.

He was staring at her, as well. She couldn't decipher his look, and for the moment she couldn't concern herself with what he was possibly thinking. This was the first time he'd seen her in her paranormal element, and she was grateful for the two mothers who'd psychically reached out to her, wanting to spare others pain.

Randi stood and spoke, making sure her voice was loud and clear. "It's imperative that what I share with all of you today is kept from the media for now. I'm sure you're aware by now that there's a mole in one of your organizations."

Although no one had mentioned such a thing to her, she knew they had to have reached that conclusion. Otherwise, those attackers would not have had known what route she would be taking this morning or what hotel she had checked into yesterday.

"I don't know which agency yet, or the culprit. But there's a way I can be certain it's no one in this room."

"You have our word that nothing will be released to the media until you give the word," Agent Riviera said, speaking for the group.

Randi shook her head. "No. I need to hear from each man and woman present. If there's a leak, I will know who broke the promise."

All the agents and officers gave their word individually, and as they did she mentally read them, took their measure and sometimes even got a flash into their lives. She had to force back her smile at the number of single men in the room with noncommittal tendencies when it came to women...including Agent Riviera and Detective Sutherland. Quasar was the last person to speak, giving his word. She nodded, knowing he was the one person she couldn't read at all.

Satisfied, she said, "Two men are responsible for what happened in here to Ms. Emiliano."

Agent Riviera asked, "Do you know their identities?"

Randi nodded. She slowly moved toward an officer

who had a copy of that morning's newspaper in his hand. She glanced at his name badge. "Officer Hall? May I see your paper for a moment?"

The man gave her the newspaper. She opened it. Photos of two young men along with the headline, Two Gang Members Brutally Executed, covered the front page. "These two here."

Agent Riviera stared at the newspaper and then back at her. "Rick Constantine and Shane Griffin? The Warlord gang members who were slaughtered last night, execution-style? Are you sure, Dr. Fuller?"

"Yes. I'm positive."

"That would make things convenient, now, wouldn't it, Dr. Fuller?" Detective Sutherland asked with a sneer. "Seeing as both men are dead and can't be questioned. When you need a scapegoat, blame it on the dead man."

No one said anything. Randi had already proven that when it came to Sutherland, she could hold her own. A smile touched her lips. "I'm sure that an intelligent and experienced detective such as yourself won't just take my word for it. But just in case I assumed wrong about your intelligence and experience, I suggest you have your medical examiner run fingerprints and semen samples from both men. Please don't be surprised when both match."

Again, several police officers and agents cleared their throats or fake-coughed.

"If Constantine and Griffin were involved, that meant they'd turned on their own gang. Become traitors. Why?" Agent Bledsoe asked.

Surprisingly, it was Detective Sutherland who answered. "Greed. Must have been promised a whole lot of money."

"They were," Randi agreed. "Check bank accounts...

not in their names but in the names of family members they trusted."

"But who is the money man? The person orchestrating it all?"

Randi drew in a deep breath. For some reason she couldn't get a reading on that person, and she wasn't sure why. All she got when she tried forging through was a strong force denying her entry. It appeared everything had to come together piece by piece. "I'm not sure yet. I can't get a reading on him or her." Turning her attention to Agent Riviera, she said, "I'm ready to go."

He lifted a brow. "Go where?"

"To retrieve the murder weapon. And I suggest you call in the divers."

LEO FUMED AS HE paced around his office. Other than getting rid of Constantine and Griffin, everything had failed. He picked up a ceramic pencil holder on his desk, threw it against the wall and watched it shatter into a thousand pieces while the pencils and pens fell to the floor.

He turned when his phone rang. It was his contact at FBI headquarters. He quickly answered. "Why didn't you call me back sooner?"

"I didn't have time," the deep, throaty voice responded. "A lot of shit's been happening with the discovery of those two bodies. Jesus, did you have to be so damn vicious and inhumane? They were unrecognizable."

"That's the way I intended for it to be. Your weak stomach is not my problem. Grow some balls. Now, tell me what you know. Where is the psychic?"

"I don't know. All I know is that she left an hour ago with an FBI and police escort, I figure to go to the crime scene. And a few minutes ago our divers got word to be on standby."

Leo didn't like the sound of that. Dr. Fuller was no quack like some believed, and for that reason, he had to get rid of her before she started digging too deep. Even if she did recover the murder weapon, she couldn't link him to anything. Constantine and Griffin were dead. But still. He couldn't take any chances. He couldn't forgive her for ruining his business two years ago, sending him into hiding. "I want her dead."

"Your people had their chance and fucked up twice," his contact said. "Now she has a personal bodyguard as well as FBI protection. If I were you, I'd leave town before she nails your ass. Cousin or no cousin, I refuse to go down with you, Leo. And I need to watch myself. They already suspect someone within the agency is a mole. I don't want them to point a finger at me."

"Fuck you."

Instead of a response, there was a resounding click in Leo's ear and then silence. Damn. It amazed Leo how different he and his cousin—friends and cohorts since childhood—had turned out. One on the right side of the law and the other on the wrong side. Well, at least his cousin used to be on the right side. The love of women and money made some men do anything, and his cousin had been no different. All Leo had to do was discover his weakness. After that, it had been easy enough to put him on his payroll and bedroll. Namely, provide him with endless women who enjoyed fucking as much as he did as well as over a million dollars for starters. His insatiable, greedy-ass cousin had been happy. After Leo's human trafficking ring was busted, his cousin had agreed to help him hide out for a while…practically right under the

FBI's nose. He'd even given him a new identity. He was no longer Levan Shaw but Leo Stillwell. Same initials. Different names. If it hadn't been for Dr. Fuller, there was no telling what sort of financial empire he would have accumulated by now.

Angrier than ever just thinking about it, Leo placed another call. As soon as the person was on the line, he said, "We need to talk. Come to my place now."

Less than half an hour later, a woman entered his office. He tried not to dwell on the beauty of her face, the lushness of her figure or the sexiness in her walk. She was wearing a pretty sundress and as usual, she looked good. Shit, he was getting a boner just looking at her.

Taking the seat in front of his desk, she crossed her legs, deliberately flashing a thigh. He watched as she studied her manicured nails. "Why was I summoned?"

Leo knew what he was seeing was all part of the package with her. The package he'd created. They had met about five years ago. After an intense fling she'd become his protégé. She was the one person he could depend on. The only one he could trust. He couldn't even depend on his cousin anymore. "I need you to do something for me. Something very important. You owe me."

She stopped concentrating on her fingers and narrowed her eyes at him. She didn't like being reminded of that. More than obligations were between them, and they both knew it. However, once in a while he liked getting her mad. Before she left, he would put her in a lot better mood. "What do you want?" she asked him.

"Your word."

She lifted a brow. "My word about what?"

"That if something happens and I'm not able to do so,

you will kill a psychic investigator by the name of Dr. Randi Fuller."

She straightened in her chair, her eyes now alert. "What do you mean, if something happens? What do you think is going to happen?"

He shrugged. "You never know, sweetheart." She loved him. He'd always known it and figured that in his own morbid way, he loved her, as well. "Who knows? I might have to go into hiding again. You know me. If the shit hits the fan, I won't be taken alive."

He paused a moment to let what he'd said sink in. "I want your word that if anything should happen to me... you will make it your business to avenge my death."

"By killing this psychic?"

Leo nodded. "Yes. This is something I need you to take care of personally. I won't trust it to anyone else."

She didn't say anything. He knew she'd read the papers and was probably aware two attempts had been made on Dr. Fuller's life already. He would expect her to succeed where others had failed. "And what do I get out of this?" she asked him. "I am a businesswoman, after all."

Now she was trying to rattle him. There had never been just business between them and she damn well knew it. And he knew all about her businesses. He'd set her up in most of them, right under her husband's unsuspecting nose. The man didn't have a clue that she ran a very profitable prostitution ring and was involved in human trafficking and illegal gambling.

Instead of answering, he opened a desk drawer, pulled out an envelope and slid it to her. He watched her open it. Surprise lit her eyes. "You're giving me your list?"

That list contained all the corrupt politicians and law enforcement officials in his pocket. "Just half of it. If anything happens to me, I'll leave my password, giving you access to all the videos and documentation you might need."

She didn't say anything. With that list, he'd handed her a gold mine. Power. Those corrupt officials would be at her beck and call like they had been at his. "One way or another, Dr. Fuller will not leave LA alive," he said.

She slid the envelope in her purse and smiled over at him. "No, she won't. You have my word, Leo."

He returned her smile, believing her. "I knew I could count on you."

He stood and slowly came around his desk. "Now for more important matters," he said, reaching out and pushing the spaghetti straps from her shoulders with one hand while running the other up her thigh.

"I know what you want," she purred. "What if I say I don't have time?"

"I want to fuck you. Here. Now. So I suggest you make time."

A smile spread across Leo's lips, knowing that she would.

CHAPTER TWENTY-TWO

"HERE. DRINK THIS," Quasar said, handing Randi a cup.

She raised a brow. "Coffee?"

"Yes."

"Thanks."

He had been watching her and wasn't sure if her shivers were from the cool breeze coming off the creek or something else. After leaving the crime scene, they'd driven around as she tried to piece together all the information her mind was relaying to her. Her entourage of law enforcement had followed. She'd told them the gun had been thrown in water. Since there were a lot of bodies of water in and around LA, the question became which one.

Her psychic powers had eventually led her here. Copperhead Creek. The creek was also located in the Westside neighborhood but miles away from the crime scene. Divers had been called in and so far nothing had been found.

"This coffee is good," she said. "Where did you get it?"

He worked his shoulders to get the kinks out before saying, "One of the agents brought it. He said usually it takes the divers a while, and he figured everyone would want a cup or two."

"Thanks. I usually don't drink a lot of coffee. Tea is my thing."

"I noticed." The two of them were standing by themselves, off to the side. This was the first he'd had her alone since this morning. And even now they weren't completely alone. FBI agents and local cops littered the shore, most standing close to the water's edge. Agent Riviera was by his vehicle, talking on the phone, and Sutherland was doing likewise. With both men on their phones, Quasar hoped like hell there weren't any new developments.

He switched his concentration back to Randi. She smelled good, and she looked good wearing a pair of dark slacks and a pretty multicolored top. His ever-watchful eye had seen more than one guy checking her out today. He'd noticed that even Agent Riviera's gaze had lingered on her a little longer than it should have a couple of times.

Quasar drew in a deep breath of fresh air along with Randi's scent through his nostrils. Standing this close, the atmosphere surrounding them felt charged, and a shiver raced up his spine. His heart beat faster as a need he always felt but managed to control around her escalated.

"They will find it," she said.

He nodded as he took a sip of his own coffee. "I believe you. I believe *in* you. Never doubt it."

A huge smile touched her lips. "Thanks. I appreciate it." She pushed a curl of hair away from her face. "Will we return to the beach house tonight?" she asked him.

He held her gaze. "Do you want to return there?"

She nodded. "Yes, but will it be too dangerous to do so? Do you think those people who want me dead know where I am? Where I'll be?"

He studied her features and saw an uneasiness lurk-

ing in the dark depths of her eyes. "Doesn't matter what
they know. I'm protecting you and that's all that matters. You're safe."

She stared straight into his eyes, and he felt the strong
connection that always seemed to be there between them.
"Thank you, Quasar. I fear before it's all over, I might
become dependent on you too much."

"I have no problem with that. If I had, I would not be
here. Remember that."

"I will."

At that moment there was a shout when one of the
divers returned to the surface. "We found something!"

Randi and Quasar moved toward the divers. Cheers
went up. The murder weapon had been recovered. Everyone, especially the skeptics like Sutherland, gazed at
her with newfound respect in their eyes.

"We're taking the gun to the lab to verify it's the one
used to kill Esther Emiliano," Agent Riviera said. "I got a
call a few moments ago, and the leader of the Revengers
has been found and brought in for questioning. I know
you preferred talking to them on their turf, but—"

"That's fine," Randi interrupted. "Either way, I need
to talk to them individually. The sooner the better. We
can keep the media in the dark for only so long."

"Okay, let's head on back to headquarters so I can arrange it," Agent Riviera said.

As they headed toward their vehicle, she and Quasar
walked side by side. "Hungry?" he asked her.

Randi glanced up at him. It was a little past lunch-
time, and neither of them had eaten since breakfast. "A
big, juicy hamburger with lots and lots of fries, oozing
with ketchup, and a huge glass of iced tea sounds good
right now."

"No problem. I think they're ordering something in for us." He opened the car door for her, made sure she was safely inside before closing it. "Be back in a second. I'll let them know."

She watched him walk off, thinking not for the first time that he had an ultrasexy walk. His long strides were as masculine and confident as he seemed to be.

"Looks like I owe you an apology, Dr. Fuller."

Randi jumped. She hadn't seen Detective Sutherland approach on the driver's side of the car. He crouched down with his face in the window. "About what?" she asked him.

"For being an ass."

He seemed sincere. "You wouldn't be the first person to think I'm a quack, Detective."

"Well, I regret I was one. To make it up to you, before you leave LA, how about if we go out to dinner and—"

"You're blocking my door, Sutherland," Quasar said in an irritated tone. When Sutherland didn't move out of the way quickly enough, Quasar all but brushed him aside.

An angry frown touched Sutherland's features at Quasar's rudeness. "We'll talk again later, Dr. Fuller."

Before Randi could respond one way or the other, Detective Sutherland walked off. She watched him, thinking there was nothing sexy about his walk compared to Quasar's.

"So the asshole wants to take you out?"

Randi glanced over at Quasar. "He apologized."

"Whatever."

Was that a tinge of jealousy she heard in his tone? "Is there a problem, Quasar?"

He turned those dark eyes on her, igniting a tantalizing sensation in the pit of her belly. And her breasts seemed to have gotten achy. And had his focus shifted to her lips?

"No, there's not a problem. Although for a minute I thought there would be one with Riviera."

She lifted a brow. "Agent Riviera? Why?"

"He didn't like the fact we're returning to my beach house tonight. After what happened this morning, he wants you at a safe house more than ever. Don't be surprised if he approaches you later to convince you to agree to go to one."

"Okay." She didn't tell Quasar that Agent Riviera might try but he wouldn't succeed. She had fallen in love with his beach house, and more than anything she wanted to go back tonight to be with him.

RANDI DECIDED TO meet with Maceo Emiliano first. She read his rap sheet, and he was definitely not a choirboy. He was nineteen and a high school dropout, although it seemed he'd been a pretty smart student when he had attended.

His troubles began after his father died and his mother took on second and third jobs to make ends meet. That gave Maceo a lot of free time to get into all kinds of trouble when he started hanging around the wrong people. His list of priors ran deep, from auto theft to home invasion to weapons trafficking to burglary, among others. In her opinion he was definitely a menace to society. Esther Emiliano wanted to do in death what she'd failed to do in life. Get through to her son and encourage him to do the right thing before it was too late.

Closing the file, Randy felt shivers cascade all through

her body. She muttered softly, "Ms. Emiliano, he's your son. I just hope you can get through to him."

"Did you say something?"

Randi jerked around. She'd forgotten Quasar was in the room. The two of them had been given one of the small offices at FBI headquarters to eat lunch in. The others had been busy following up on the evidence she'd helped uncover that day.

After lunch she'd been given files on both gang leaders, and for the past hour she'd been reading Maceo's. She had spread out the files on the desk. To give her space, Quasar had slid his chair into a corner in the room and used the time to check emails on his phone.

"Sorry, I was just talking to myself," she told him.

"You can talk to me instead if you like."

She shifted her chair around, thinking yes, she could. Quasar was easy to talk to. One reason was that he never doubted anything she said. Never gave her any of those you're-a-loony looks. This morning, during their walk on the beach, she'd told him about the gang leaders' mothers reaching out to her to try and save their sons. He had listened, and not for one minute had she felt he'd doubted anything she said. He respected her work, and that meant a lot.

"I just finished reading Maceo Emiliano's rap sheet. Priors a mile long," she said.

"And you honestly think you can get through to him?"

She shook her head. "By myself? No. But his mother believes I can get through to him with her help and convince him of what really happened." Randi drew in a deep breath of frustration. "That's going to be a challenge when he's convinced she was murdered by members of the Revengers."

There was a knock on the door seconds before Agent Riviera stuck his head in. "Emiliano has been taken to interrogation room G11. Are you ready?"

Randi nodded. "Yes," she said, standing.

Detective Riviera came into the room, closing the door behind him. "Are you sure you want to meet with him? I'm warning you that he's in a foul mood. The worst. He's pissed that he's in here and not out there killing those responsible for murdering his mother."

She could believe that.

"And you were right," Agent Riviera continued. "We heard back from the medical examiner. Both the DNA and fingerprints were matches, which means Constantine and Griffin killed Esther Emiliano. The gun is being checked out to verify it's the murder weapon. But that still doesn't tell us who is the person behind this. The person responsible for butchering Constantine and Griffin. The person who's made two attempts on your life."

"No, it doesn't. I believe more information will come to me, but first things first. I need to deal with the mothers."

Agent Riviera lifted a confused brow. "The mothers?"

"Yes. It's hard to explain right now. You just have to trust me when I say I know what I'm doing."

The agent chuckled. "Oh, I believe you, Dr. Fuller. Thanks to you, this case is finally moving forward."

Riviera paused and glanced over at Quasar, who so far hadn't said a word since he'd entered the room, but was looking at him with deep, penetrating eyes. The man might be Dr. Fuller's bodyguard, but Riviera knew the two were personally involved. Dr. Fuller had practically admitted as much last night. Patterson wasn't just protective. At times Riviera felt the man was downright territorial. He could understand why, since Dr. Fuller was a beautiful woman.

Last night, after Patterson and Dr. Fuller had left the hotel for Malibu, Riviera obtained the key from the front desk and had gone into Patterson's room to lift his fingerprints. He now knew a lot about Quasar Patterson. Even the fact that he was an ex-con. Riviera also knew he was the son of Louis Patterson, one of the wealthiest men in LA. The family owned a mansion in Beverly Hills. He'd been intrigued. Typically the sons of rich men didn't moonlight as bodyguards.

"Is there anything else, Agent Riviera?" Dr. Fuller interrupted his thoughts to ask.

He moved his gaze from Patterson back to her. "Yes. Considering all that's happened, I don't think you should return to Malibu. I can arrange for you to be placed somewhere safe while you're in LA. We'll provide around-the-clock protection."

Randi shook her head. "Thanks, but as you can see, I have a bodyguard who's proven to be very capable at keeping me alive. I want to go back to the beach house. I *need* to go there. My mind needs downtime in a relaxing atmosphere."

Agent Riviera nodded slowly. "I'll be posting more of my men along the routes to ensure nothing happens again."

"And what about the traitor within your organization?" Quasar finally broke his silence to ask.

Riviera returned his gaze to Quasar. "We're determined to identify the mole and deal with that individual.

We have a plan in place and are hopeful he or she will take the bait."

He then glanced back at Randi. "Now, if you will follow me, Dr. Fuller, I'll take you to the interrogation room."

CHAPTER TWENTY-THREE

RANDI PEERED THROUGH the one-way glass to study the young man sitting at the table in interrogation room G11. She wanted to believe that buried somewhere beneath his roguish features was a baby face. No way angelic but nothing close to felonious, either. Judging from his appearance, he was definitely not anyone she would want to encounter at night on a deserted street. The word *badass* was written all over him, from the tattoo of his gang's emblem on one side of his neck and up his arm to the overgrown spiked hair with sections looking whacked off in some places.

He wore a jacket that proudly boasted his gang colors, and his jeans had more holes than Swiss cheese. Impressing anyone wasn't part of what he was about. Intimidation was the name of his game.

It was obvious Maceo Emiliano was angry. He emanated nervous energy, getting up out the chair every so often to pace, looking around as if he needed something to kick—the chair was his victim a few times—before sitting down again to tap his restless fingers on the edge of the table. He would be doubly pissed if he knew he was being watched, studied and analyzed.

"You sure you want to be alone with him in there?"

Randi didn't have to wonder who'd come up behind her. Both his voice and sensual heat gave Quasar away.

And of course there was his scent, masculine and clean with sexy undertones. He was standing close but not too close, although all she had to do was take a couple of steps back and her body would smack up against his. Her backside would be pressed against his hard middle. Just the thought had her senses reeling.

She tilted her head to stare over her shoulder into the depths of his dark eyes. Forcing back the pang of desire that suddenly swept through her, she said, "The question you might want to ask is whether or not he wants to be alone with me."

She heard Quasar's soft chuckle. "You take one man down and you think you're invincible, huh?"

Randi was glad she heard amusement in his tone. "No, but I don't scare easily."

"No, you don't. And I'm trying to figure out if that's a good thing or not."

She slowly switched her gaze from Quasar to the one-way glass. Emiliano was pacing again, and she could tell from his body movements he was getting angrier by the second. "Well, it's time for the two of us to be introduced."

Quasar stepped back to give her space, but when she turned around, he gently grabbed hold of her arm. "Let me go in there with you, as your protector. I won't say a word, and I won't make a move unless I have to."

She patted the hand holding her arm, needing the contact probably more than he did. "Thanks. Agent Riviera made the same offer, but if either of you is there—a man with obvious authority and packing a firearm to back it up—he'll feel threatened and will go on the defense. If I'm alone, he'll think he has the upper hand and might even try using it. He will discover quickly enough how wrong he is."

Randi could tell from Quasar's expression he didn't particularly care for what she'd said or how she intended to deal with Emiliano. "If he gets out of line, his ass belongs to me," he all but snarled.

She didn't like the sound of that. "Don't interfere, Quasar. If I need your or anyone's help, I will give a signal."

He lifted a brow. "What signal?"

She smiled. "You will know it."

She heard Agent Riviera approach. "Sorry for leaving like that, but I got an important call," he said.

"No problem," Randi said. "I was just reiterating to Quasar the same thing I need to stress to you and your team, Agent Riviera. Once I walk into that room, I don't want any interference."

Like Quasar, the agent allowed a rebellious look to cross his gaze. "I can't make you that promise, Dr. Fuller, but I will give you my word to do my best."

It was only moments later, when she was being escorted to the interrogation room, that she realized Quasar hadn't made a promise or given his word one way or the other.

QUASAR STOOD THERE with his arms across his chest and watched her go. A part of him wanted to hit something. Shit, he wouldn't have minded knocking the hell out of Riviera. Quasar hadn't missed how the man had checked out Randi's ass when she began the walk down the hall toward the interrogation room. Male appreciation—he understood it, although he didn't like it when it came from anyone but him.

"We can observe things better from here," Agent Riviera said, intruding into his thoughts.

Instead of saying anything, he followed the man to a connecting room that had a one-way glass. Unlike the one he and Randi had been peering into before, this provided a floor-to-ceiling view. They could observe without missing a thing. And the speakers were great. They could clearly hear an impatient Emiliano cursing under his breath. Quasar meant what he'd told Randi. If Emiliano gave any hint of getting out of line, he would regret the day he was born. He glanced around, and as if Riviera read his thoughts, the man pointed to another door. "That leads into the room if there's a need. But we'll do what Dr. Fuller requested and let her handle things."

Speak for your own damn self.

"How about a cup of coffee?" Riviera asked him.

Quasar shook his head. "No, thanks."

Agent Riviera sat at the table across from him after pouring his own cup. "So you're Louis Patterson's son."

Quasar didn't say anything. Nor did he wonder how Riviera knew. The man was FBI, after all. "What of it?" he asked, meeting Riviera's stare.

"Nothing."

Quasar had to agree with the man. Being Louis Patterson's son meant *nothing*. They both shifted their attention when the door opened and Detective Sutherland strolled in with his own cup of coffee. Without saying anything, he sat down at the table.

Quasar refused to acknowledge the man's presence. Something had Sutherland in a bad mood...not that Quasar could recall ever seeing him in a good one. Except earlier today, when he was hitting on Randi. Quasar leaned back in his chair, thinking that not on the man's life would that ever happen. Definitely not on this planet while Quasar still had breath in his body. He pushed the annoying notion out of his mind that his feelings were totally territorial, possessive, as Striker claimed.

RANDI OPENED THE DOOR and stepped in. "Mr. Emiliano, sorry to keep you waiting and—"

Maceo was out of his chair in a flash, rounding on her. "Bitch, it took you long enough. I want to get out of here, so do what you have to do to make that happen."

If he expected her to cower in fear, he was mistaken. Instead she took a step forward and matched his tone. "First of all, my name is not *bitch*. It's Randi Fuller," she said, deciding for the time being to omit her PhD status. "I'm an investigator, not someone from the public defender's office."

"Then what the fuck are you doing here? I already said I'm not talking."

Randi tilted her head and stared at him. He was only a few inches taller than she was. "Great. I don't want you to talk anyway. I mainly want you to listen." She went around him to sit down at the table.

Maceo stared as if he didn't know what to make of her. And then, regaining his bluster, he said, "Listen, bitch, I told you—"

"And I told you what my name is. I will respect who you are, Mr. Emiliano, and expect you to do the same."

"I don't give a fuck about any respect."

"Maybe you should. And maybe you should listen to what I have to say. I have a message for you."

His brows lifted. He was curious.

Time ticked by and he remained standing there, just

staring at her. Finally he said, "What message and who's it from?"

Now, this was where it could get dicey. He would either believe or not believe. "I told you who I am. What I didn't tell you is what I do."

"Who gives a damn?"

"I suggest you do. Let me reintroduce myself. My name is Dr. Randi Fuller, and I'm a psychic investigator."

That got her the glare of all glares. "Psychic investigator? Then I think your pretty little ass walked into the wrong room," he blasted.

"Not by a long shot," she blasted back.

"I don't believe in all that shit."

She shrugged. "Most people don't. But I'm not the one who's going to convince you I'm legit. Someone else will, and that person will tell you that the Revengers had nothing to do with your mother's death and that the persons who betrayed you and murdered your mother were two of your own trusted gang members."

He was across the room in a flash, anger radiating from him. "None of my members would dare, bitch."

She anticipated his next move, and before he could reach out and jerk her out of the chair, she used her legs to knock his out from beneath him, sending him tumbling to the floor. When he thought to get up, she kicked his legs from under him again and sent him plummeting back down. She stood over him with her arms crossed over her chest. "I forgot to mention that I'm a fifth-degree black belt. You know what that means, since you took karate as a child."

He was about to get up again, but her words made him stay still, a strange look on his face. "Who told you that? That I used to take karate lessons?"

Satisfied that she had his attention, Randi pulled a chair from the table and sat back down. "The same person who told me about your karate teacher, Mr. Hammer, and how much you liked him. I also know about that time when, after your father died, you ran away from home and spent the night at the karate studio before you were found by one of your mother's neighbors."

Maceo slowly eased up, staring oddly. Then in a demanding tone, he said, "Tell me who told you that, bitch."

Instead of telling him anything, she warned, "Don't call me a bitch again or you will be sorry."

After letting her threat sink in, she continued. "Then there was the time you found Ms. Kushner's cat in that sewer and you went in there to get it out and nearly got stuck in there yourself. And the time you got lost on your first trip to the mall by yourself. Or the fact that you and Jason Overstreet, the leader of the Revengers, have history that goes way back, when the two of you were in Mr. Hammer's karate class and were best friends."

He loomed over Randi. "I want to know who told you that."

At least he hadn't called her a bitch again. "First, you will sit in that chair. And the next time you come at me, I will maim you for life. You aren't stupid. You know what a fifth-degree black belt is capable of."

Maceo stood there, sizing her up. Then, as if he'd made a decision, he snagged the chair from the table and sat down. He glared at her. "I'm listening."

She shifted in her chair to look at him. "The person who told me those things is the only person who knew about all of them." She paused to let that sink in. "Your mother."

CHAPTER TWENTY-FOUR

QUASAR WATCHED AS SHOCK followed by denial appeared on Maceo Emiliano's features. Just like Sutherland and Riviera, he'd been observing the proceedings with a keen eye and sharp ear. During that time when it had appeared Emiliano intended to strike out at Randi, Quasar had been the first one out his chair with his gun drawn and heading for the connecting door. With his gun drawn, as well, Sutherland had been right on his heels.

Riviera had shouted at them to stop before either he or Sutherland had reached the door. Riviera had then made them see that Randi had everything under control when she had knocked Emiliano on his ass.

"I can't believe she has him sitting there and listening," Riviera said when they were seated back at the table.

"You would be, too, if Dr. Fuller was telling you the shit she's telling him. Straight from his dead mother. Kind of eerie," Sutherland said. "Damn. I didn't know he and Overstreet had history. Did you, Riviera?"

"No," Agent Riviera replied. "From what I'm hearing, it appears they were recruited by rival gangs."

The room got quiet again as they continued to listen to Randi relaying messages apparently from Emiliano's mother. A dead woman. Quasar agreed with Sutherland that it *was* kind of eerie. But eerie or not, what Randi was saying to Emiliano evidently was getting through to him. For once he was keeping his mouth shut and listening. That in itself was hard to believe.

When Randi revealed the names of his mother's killers and further went on to explain why they in turn had been brutally killed, it was as if pieces of a puzzle were being put together. Emiliano tried holding it together as he stood with his back to Randi, but Quasar, Sutherland and Riviera were able to see his face. Broken. Tormented. Defeated.

Quasar's gaze shifted to Randi. She wasn't saying anything as she gave Emiliano time to compose himself. Quasar continued to stare at her, admiring her ability to do this work. Use her gift in this way. Randi alone wouldn't have been able to reach him. But Randi's words weren't really hers, and Emiliano knew that. Randi was just the messenger. Through Randi his mother had told him that the Revengers were not responsible for her death. This was the first time Quasar had witnessed such a thing, and he figured the same was true for Sutherland and Riviera. Randi's gift was special, and they all knew it.

"I don't know if I could handle something like this if I were in his shoes," Quasar heard Sutherland say. "If that was me, I would want to hurt somebody, namely the bastard who's still out there. Ms. Emiliano's death was brutal and senseless. Damn. Just for power."

"Then we owe it to Ms. Emiliano to arrest the person responsible for her death and bring him to justice," Agent Riviera said. "Randi's done her part in reaching out to her son. Now it's time for us to do ours."

RANDI DIDN'T SAY ANYTHING as she watched Maceo Emiliano. His back was to her, but she knew he was hurting. Hurting for the mother he'd so brutally lost and for two people he'd thought were friends who not only had betrayed his trust but also had been responsible for ending his mother's life.

"Are there others?" he asked.

"Others?" she repeated.

He turned around. "Yes. Are other Warlords besides Rick and Shane responsible?"

She studied his face, his entire disposition, and knew he was fighting hard to hold himself in check. Pain shone in his eyes along with a semblance of regret. "Those two were the only ones your mother revealed to me. But the leader is out there. The man who paid them to start the gang war."

Suddenly his lips tightened with an angry curl. "I want to know who he is."

"We all want to know who he is. He intentionally played the Warlords against the Revengers. Both the FBI and local authorities are trying to gather information to bring that person to justice."

He didn't say anything for a minute. Then, shoving his hands into his pockets, he said, "Do you have any idea what they did to her? I will issue my own justice."

Randi drew in a deep breath. "I know what they did to her. She showed me. Every single detail. And you heard her message, Maceo. She doesn't want you to avenge her death. She wants you to let the authorities handle it."

Maceo stared at her for a long minute, and then he slid down in the chair and covered his face with his hands. "I don't know if I can. She was my mom. What they did to her was inhumane. She didn't deserve that. Mom didn't deserve it."

Randi gave him a moment to collect himself before saying, "You know what you need to do, Maceo. It's what your mother asked you to do now that you know the truth. Only you and Overstreet can stop the war."

Maceo suddenly snapped his head up and quickly stood. "It might be too late."

"What do you mean?" she asked, beginning to feel uneasy.

"We were so sure the Revengers were responsible for Mom's, Rick's and Shane's deaths that we…"

Randi stood, as well. When Maceo didn't continue, she asked tensely, "You what?"

"We put a plan into place. The war starts today, with or without me. And it's too late to stop it."

Randi looked beyond him to where she knew men were sitting on the other side of the one-way glass. Certain they'd heard everything, she motioned for them. Then, looking back at Maceo, she said, "I just summoned men you need to trust. They're the only chance we have to stop that war from happening."

"I CAN'T BELIEVE Quasar hasn't returned your call, Dad. It's just like him to mess something up. I talked to Dwayne Connors yesterday. Everything is all set to go. If we can get Quasar to come back to the company, and anything goes wrong, we'll have him to take the fall like the last time."

Louis glanced up as Doyle walked into the study. He leaned back in his chair. "Hey, don't get upset about anything. Quasar's just being an ass, as usual, Doyle. I told him why he was needed. There's no other reason for him to have come to LA, so the way I figure things, he wants to call the shots. I guess he won't ever learn. And in the end, he will come back. When he does, everything will fall in place just like we planned."

"And you think you can convince him to work for the company?"

"Yes. I'll make him feel needed, especially with you becoming mayor. I'll convince him that his help is required since your time will be tied up in politics. Once he's in place, we will have Connors get things started. Ideally we won't ever be discovered, but if we are, Quasar can take the blame again."

"Good. Sounds like you've got it all figured out, Dad."

"I do. And regardless of whether he attends the party or not, the announcement will be made tonight regarding your political aspirations. If anyone asks about Quasar, we'll say his arrival has been delayed or something." Louis paused before asking, "Did you tell Lilly that Quasar is back in town?"

Doyle frowned. "Yes, I told her."

"And?"

Doyle's frown deepened. "And nothing. Lilly's my wife, not Quasar's. He was a fool to expect her to wait for him. If anything he should be grateful I married her so she wouldn't be alone. Besides, I give Lilly anything she wants. As far as I'm concerned, she was involved with the wrong brother anyway."

Louis had to agree. Initially he'd had his misgivings about Lilly since her family hadn't accumulated the same amount of wealth as the Pattersons, although they hadn't been poor blokes. The woman he'd selected for Doyle to marry, Kendra Biltmore, had turned out to be a real piece of work. She had been the only other person besides himself, Doyle, Quasar, Lilly and his cousin Lucinda who knew the truth that Doyle had been the one guilty of land fraud and not Quasar. Unlike Lilly, who promised to keep her mouth shut about the whole thing, it had taken almost a million dollars to get Kendra to keep quiet. He was glad she'd eventually married some rich bastard so she hadn't needed to hit him up for more money.

Thank God that Lucinda hadn't found out the truth until right before she died. By then, Quasar was less than a few months from being released from jail, and Lucinda was at death's door. There was no doubt in his mind that had Lucinda known sooner or had she lived, she would have done everything in her power to clear Quasar's name and get the verdict overturned. She'd always had a soft spot in her heart for Quasar, and he knew it was due to a promise she'd made to Elaina.

"And you're sure Lilly is okay with Quasar returning?"

"I'm sure. Of course Lilly has blamed herself over the years since she believes she's the reason he stayed away."

Louis chuckled. "She's probably right. Quasar loved Lilly. You and I both know that."

Doyle shrugged. "Well," he said, standing, "you win some and you lose some. I won't be giving Lilly up to anyone. She's perfect for me."

"In other words, she knows to look the other way when it's obvious you're having an affair."

A smile touched Doyle's lips. "Precisely."

"Well, be careful. You're about to become a politician. Mayor today and president tomorrow. Start small but think big, which means we can't afford any scandals, Doyle. No piece of ass is *that* good."

Doyle shoved his hands in his pockets. "I beg to differ with that, Dad," he said with a smirk. "I happen to think it's a pretty good damn piece. But seriously, don't worry about scandals since there won't be any. I know how to handle my business."

"Maybe it's time for you and Lilly to start a family. Voters like that sort of thing. Pregnant first ladies."

"That might not be such a bad idea."

"I strongly suggest it," Louis said, knowing Doyle would follow his directive.

Doyle glanced at his watch and smiled. "I need to get ready for tonight's party."

"You're inviting *her*, aren't you?"

Doyle smiled rakishly. "Yes, she's invited…right along with her husband."

Louis shook his head. "It doesn't bother you to have your whore and your wife under the same roof?"

Doyle shook his head grinning. "Nope, it doesn't bother me at all." He left the room chuckling.

Louis shook his head. He hoped his son knew what the hell he was doing. Once he announced his candidacy for mayor, the media would be watching him like a damn hawk.

An angry Louis picked up his phone and called Quasar again. When he didn't get a response, he called Paul Woodard. "Paul, are you sure Quasar is back in LA? I've been trying to reach him."

"Yes, I'm sure. I talked to him myself last night when he called. I got the feeling he would here for a while since he asked me to make sure the refrigerator and pantry were stocked."

"I was just wondering since we hadn't heard from him yet."

"I might be able to explain that."

Louis lifted a brow. "Oh? What's the reason?"

"You remember Marion Hoffer? She was Lucinda's neighbor who lived next door to her in Malibu. I saw Marion earlier today. She says she saw a man fitting

Quasar's description and some woman walking on the beach early this morning. Marion claims that although it's been years, she still recognized him. If you recall, Quasar hung out a lot on that beach when Lucinda lived there. Her neighbors got used to seeing him, so chances are Marion probably did recognize him. Sounds like Quasar might have a houseguest who's keeping him busy, if you know what I mean," Paul said, chuckling. "Delphine and I will see you later tonight at the party."

Of course you will, since you like parading around with that younger woman you're married to. "Fine. I'll see you then."

Louis hung up the phone and rubbed his chin. So Quasar had brought a woman with him to LA. He found that bit of information amusing since it seemed Doyle wasn't the only one held captive by a piece of ass.

CHAPTER TWENTY-FIVE

"Do you think Riviera and Sutherland will let us know if they're able to stop the gang war?" Randi asked.

"Yeah, they'll call," Quasar said, opening the door to his beach house.

After closing the door behind them, Randi was about to move ahead when he stopped her. "Wait here while I check out things."

She nodded, watching as he drew his gun from his shoulder holster and moved stealthily forward. From where she stood, she watched him stalk like a panther, going from room to room. She couldn't help but appreciate the well-defined masculinity of his pectorals and biceps in the shirt he wore. He was solid muscle and, as far as she was concerned, an amazing specimen of a man.

"Coast clear," Quasar said, returning and placing his gun back in the holster, drawing her attention to his shoulders, even more impressive evidence of his strength. Annoyance filled her. Her mind should have been off him and on the danger at hand.

"Any reason you're frowning, Randi?"

Quasar was studying her features with penetrating dark eyes. During the drive home he had released the band holding his hair, and now it flowed in a mass of glossy strands around his face, making him look wildly sensual and heart-stoppingly gorgeous.

"Randi?"

And why did she feel a pull in her midsection whenever he said her name? "A part of me feels frustrated, Quasar," she finally answered him. "More than anything I wish I could get a reading on the person who ordered the hits on me, Ms. Emiliano and those two gang members."

He came to stand directly in front of her and reached up to massage her temples gently. She wondered how his large, callused hands could feel so gentle as his fingertips caressed her skin. "Don't worry about it. You might get one later. Personally, I think you accomplished a whole hell of a lot today. You located the murder weapon and convinced Emiliano the Revengers weren't responsible for his mother's death."

"I wish I could have done more. I haven't met with Overstreet yet to give him his mother's message."

"But you will. Sutherland and Riviera had to cut out quickly to defuse those gangs from going head-to-head. I'm glad Emiliano admitted to you what was about to go down."

"I'm glad he did, too," she said, noticing how Quasar's fingers had shifted from her brows and had moved downward to trace across her cheeks. "I hope Sutherland and Riviera will get there in time. I wish I could have gone with them."

"It was too dangerous. Besides, you needed to come back here and get some rest."

I'd rather get some of you, she thought, feeling the heat of Quasar's gaze shifting to her mouth. It surprised her how a woman whose sexual activities were limited to her college days could become such a sexually needy person around Quasar. But then, she really shouldn't have been surprised. She doubted very many women could resist such a prime example of raw, male power.

"You've got another busy day tomorrow," he interrupted her thoughts to say. "Ideally you'll get to talk to Overstreet. I heard you ask Riviera about going to the crime scene where those two gang members were murdered."

"Yes, maybe I'll be able to pick up on something there."

"Maybe."

Was she imagining it or had his head shifted closer to hers? She knew she hadn't imagined it when his mouth was right there, so close she could almost feel his breath on her lips.

Her chest was heaving laboriously, like she'd been sprinting on the beach for over an hour, and her nipples felt hard, like pebbles pressing against her shirt. And she didn't want to think about that throbbing ache at the juncture of her legs.

"Quasar?"

"Hmm?"

"Are you going to kiss me or are you just going to stand there and do nothing?" she asked boldly and watched the corners of his lips ease into a wicked, feral smile.

"It's not that I'm not doing anything, Randi. What I'm doing is thinking really hard about what will happen if I kiss you the way I want."

She swallowed deeply as the ache between her thighs intensified and her nipples seemed to get even harder. "And what do you think might happen?"

He chuckled softly, and the sound lightly stroked across her skin. "What I know will happen is that I won't be able to stop with just a kiss."

Bring it on, she thought, tempted to lick across the lips that were so close to hers. "And you think that's a bad thing?"

"Not for me, but considering how much I want you, it might be for you."

She lifted a brow. "How so?"

He shifted, and she could actually feel him. His hard erection was pressing against her, right at the juncture of her throbbing thighs. "Remember our discussion this morning in my kitchen? You suggested we wait until all this was over before we...indulge."

Yes, she had suggested that, and at the time she'd figured she could wait. Preplan their bedroom activities for a future date. Only thing was, she no longer wanted to wait. She wanted to indulge now.

She shifted her body to press even closer to his. "What if I said that I don't want to wait any longer and that you couldn't possibly want me more than I want you?"

She could tell her words had the intended effect when his eyes darkened even more.

"In other words, Quasar," she continued, "my body is ready for that pleasure oil."

And then, leaning up on tiptoe, she pressed her mouth against his.

QUASAR'S ARMS TIGHTENED around Randi the moment her mouth touched his. It was like a match igniting a keg of dynamite. Never had he felt this obsessed with a woman, filled with this degree of sexual need. The luscious taste of her tongue was drawing everything out of him, making his desire for her intensify, enthralling him to the point that even his shoulders burned in agony for wanting her.

And speaking of shoulders...

He suddenly broke off the kiss, and she looked at him with questioning eyes and dewy lips. "I need to take this off," he said, sliding the holster and gun from his shoulders and placing both on a table within reach.

"Now, where were we?" he asked, pulling her back into his arms and lowering his mouth to hers in an open-mouthed, deep-as-you-could-go wet kiss. He preferred going slow for starters, but his hunger for her overrode any thought of dawdling. Especially not when rushes of desire were clutching and clawing at his insides. His hands spread wide across her backside as their tongues mingled and mated in a way that had blood whooshing through his veins.

Quasar felt his erection throb hard against his zipper. He felt it expand to the point that it was almost painful. The only comfort was in the way it felt pressing against her.

When was the last time he'd been this aroused? Sizzling heat was flowing through them, and she had to feel it to the degree he did. Then there was the feel of her nipples pressing hard against his chest.

And as if his sanity being tested wasn't bad enough, she shifted her stance to part her legs, cradling his erection between them. At that moment, need for her thickened his blood and sent shivers of desire plowing through him.

He momentarily broke off the kiss and rested his forehead against hers. He'd become a man drowning in the taste, scent and feel of her. A man caught between the edges of too much and not enough. "If you keep this up," he whispered close to her wet lips, "you're liable to get more from me than pleasure oil."

"What else will I get? Spell it out for me."

He did.

While holding her gaze, he told her in explicit terms while intermittently placing kisses around her mouth. He told her exactly what he intended to do, how he intended to do it and for how long. The heated licks and greedy strokes of his tongue around her mouth only added to the narrative.

He felt her quivering in his arms from his descriptive words. She even moaned a few times, when he told her how he planned to go down on her, use his tongue to taste her between her legs and make her come. And when he told her how he would enter her body and just how deep he intended to go. And when he told her that he wanted to get her from behind and tilt up her ass at just the right angle to pump inside her while thrusting hard and hearing the sound of flesh slapping against flesh. Repeating the process over and over. The sinfully erotic movement of her hips against his middle indicated she was able to picture it and was turned on by what he was telling her.

He soon discovered his own body wasn't exactly immune to what he was saying, either. He could feel his erection get harder, and the need to make love to her was hammering sensations all through him. This was the first time he'd ever done such a thing—tell a woman his sexual plans. He was typically an I-will-show-you sort of guy. However, with Randi he wanted to tell all, show all and do all.

"You're planning on every bit of that, huh?" she asked in a breathless whisper.

Quasar couldn't help but smile. She evidently hadn't expected his candidness. Instead of answering, he continued to use his tongue to lick across her lips, cheeks and jaw before leaning in close to nibble her earlobe a few times. He whispered, "I'm planning on every bit of that and then some. This will be a night you'll remember for a long time, Randi Fuller."

With that said, he swept her up into his arms and headed for the bedroom.

RANDI SHUDDERED WHEN Quasar placed her on the huge bed—one that neither of them had slept in the night before. If he did even half the things he'd told her moments ago, she figured her entire body would collapse in pleasure to an extent she wasn't certain she could bear.

"Whatever you're thinking, hold those thoughts for a second. I'll be right back." He moved quickly to the door. Before reaching it he stopped and added, "Don't remove your clothes, because I want to do it. Stripping you naked is something I've dreamed about for months."

And then he was gone. A rush of desire raced through Randi at what he'd said. He'd dreamed of stripping off her clothes *for months*. Her pulse kicked up a notch…not that it needed any more jolting. Sitting up, she removed her shoes and pulled the band from her hair before lying back down. He'd blatantly painted all those erotic scenarios, and lying here waiting for him to return was filling her with sexual excitement. Anticipation was curling in her stomach.

After such a hellish day, she would have given anything for a night to remember in Quasar's arms. The intensity of her need for him should have blown her away, definitely rocked common sense back into her brain. But the only thing rocking was the buildup between her legs. When it came to her desire for him, there was no restraint or control, just a convulsion of sexual energy that couldn't be contained. It had been that way from the first, and three months later, nothing had changed. If what he'd said was true, it had been the same for him.

Their mating would've happened eventually. He didn't know all the things that she knew about them. What the future could hold. In a way, she could say it was for her to know and for him to find out. It would be up to her to earn his love, but she knew at that moment he had already earned hers. She had fallen in love with him.

Suddenly all those what-ifs tried clamoring to the forefront. She deftly pushed them to the back of her mind as she said softly to herself, "I want my night to remember."

"And I intend to give it to you."

She gasped and quickly pulled herself up in bed. Quasar was standing in the doorway with his hair around his shoulders, looking wild, untamed and so powerfully male that she had to fight back a groan. "How long have you been standing there?"

"Not long," he said, moving toward the bed with his gun and holster in one hand and packs of condoms in the other. She pointed at the latter. "Thinking to use all of those?"

He gave her a grin as he placed the gun and holster on the nightstand and dropped the condoms beside them. "A man can hope."

He sat on the side of the bed and surprised her when he said, "I think I covered a lot earlier…about what I want to do to you and all the pleasure I intend for you to get out of it. But if there's something I said that you're uncomfortable with, then…"

"No," she quickly said. "I'm not uncomfortable with any of it." She knew some men would not have cared one way or the other, and that endeared him to her even more.

If he hadn't earned her love before, this doubly swung the pendulum his way.

She scooted closer to him and looked into the dark eyes staring at her. Eyes belonging to the man she'd fallen in love with. "I want you to make love to me," she said softly. "I want you to do all those things you said, Quasar."

A smile touched his lips as he stood and pulled her up with him. "And tonight you'll get all you want."

CHAPTER TWENTY-SIX

QUASAR INWARDLY TOLD himself to slow down. It was still evening and they had the entire night. But the minute he'd removed Randi's blouse and slacks and she stood before him in nothing more than her bra and panties, a matching set of icy blue lace, he wanted to rip them off her body. He hadn't made love to a woman in months, but this was the woman who'd dominated his thoughts, the only woman he desired.

Honestly, he didn't understand it, but he would accept it. There had to be a reason he was drawn to her, wanted her, was attracted to her and desired her more than any other woman who walked the earth. Not since Lilly had he allowed a woman to get into his mind like Randi was doing. And in a short time, she was more deeply embedded than Lilly had ever been.

His gaze roamed her body, and he wasn't sure what he wanted to remove first. If he took off her bra and saw her breasts, he would want to take several licks, feast on her nipples, suck on them like a newborn baby. The very thought of doing such things increased his breathing and heart rate.

On the other hand, he knew the moment he lowered her panties down her legs he would be a goner. He would want to bury his head between her legs and do all those things he'd told her he would do with his fingers and tongue.

Drawing in a deep breath, he took her scent into his nostrils. The scent of a woman who was ready to be made love to. Her sensual aroma had sexual sensations overtaking his senses. Looking at her and the dark, lust-filled eyes staring back at him—silently urging him to make a move—prompted him not to keep her waiting.

He reached up and skimmed his finger around the front of her bra, loving the feel of the lacy material beneath his fingertip. When he reached the center of her breast and saw the hardness of her nipple pressing against the lace, he used the pad of his thumb to move in circular motions, feeling the nipple harden to a pebble underneath the material.

"Quasar?"

He lifted his gaze to her face. "Hmm?"

"Are you trying to torture me?"

"Torture you? No. My goal is to pleasure you." With that, Quasar shifted to the other breast and did the same thing with the pad of his thumb. He stared into her eyes and watched the lust darken them even more. And when his tongue felt heavy in his mouth with an urgency to sample her breasts, he reached behind her to work the clasp open easily.

"You seem to be pretty good at that," she said when he slid the bra from her shoulders and tossed it across the room on a chair.

"I do my best," he said, feasting his gaze on what he'd exposed. Her breasts were beautiful. They were full and firm, and her nipples were swollen like hardened nubs. Reaching out, he cupped the twin globes in his hands, his fingers brushing across the nipples.

"You have beautiful breasts, Randi."

"Glad you like them," she said through a choppy breath.

"I do. Let me show you how much." He lowered his head and, after making circular motions with the tip of his tongue around her nipples a few times, he eased a turgid bud between his lips.

THE MOMENT QUASAR'S mouth touched Randi's breast, a blast of heated desire ripped through every part of her. She closed her eyes, cradling his head in her hands while his hot, wet tongue feasted mercilessly on a nipple, gently sucking on the budding tip.

She moaned his name, which she could barely get past her throat. Pleasure spread through every part of her body, especially that part of her breast he was sucking hard. Larry had been a below-the-waist kind of guy and rarely gave attention to her breasts, and never like this. Quasar was showing her just what she'd been missing. And he was unknowingly demonstrating that point in a deliciously heated way. When he moved to the other breast, she heard herself moan again as hot and sharp sensations began slicing through her.

Moments later he released her breast and took a step back to stare at her in such a sexual way, her body actually felt heated under his scorching regard. "Now for your panties," he said in a deep, husky voice.

Randi could barely stand when he crouched down in front of her. Sliding his fingers beneath the waistband of her panties, he slowly tugged them down her legs. She could actually hear his breath catch when he uncovered her feminine mound. He stalled for a minute, staring at her there. When he looked up at her and deliberately licked his lips, she could feel a hot blush color her cheeks. He hadn't said a word and really hadn't needed to. He'd already told her what he planned to do to her there…with his fingers and mouth.

His gaze released hers and he resumed slowly easing her panties down her legs. When she stepped out of them, he tossed them to the chair to join her bra.

He remained crouched. Desire and need thickened the air, and while she waited for him to make his next move, several spikes of heat caught her in the area between her legs. When she thought that she couldn't stand the wait any longer, he reached out. Using his fingertips, he started from her toes and slowly trekked upward, skimming a path toward her center. The feel of his fingers and the provocative movements on her skin sent a thrilling awareness through her. And when both of his hands clutched the cheeks of her backside, she drew in a deep breath.

"You are walking temptation," he said in a throaty voice. "Never have I seen anything so beautiful and desirable," he said. "And I can't wait to taste you here." He released a cheek to fondle the curls between her legs in languid, swirling strokes. *"Quiero tanto follarte que me duele,"* he whispered in Spanish.

Tremors began jolting her, which increased the ache within her womb. Her skin seemed to sizzle where he was touching, bringing every single nerve ending to life beneath his fingers. And just when she thought he couldn't possibly do anything else to get her more delirious, he slid a finger inside her.

She sucked in a deep breath when his finger began stroking her intently while his eyes held her gaze. "I love how wet you are, Randi. The wetter the tastier," he said, and she couldn't say a thing to that.

With his finger stroking her senseless, he leaned forward and brushed his lips there, practically grinding the bridge of his nose in her curls. Randi grabbed hold of his shoulders to remain standing and then, as if her touch pushed him over the edge, Quasar replaced his finger with his tongue.

Oh, God. A sensual tremor shook her to the very core that was the recipient of his tongue's lusty greed. At the moment she couldn't stop moaning as her fingers dug into his shoulders. It seemed that the more she moaned, the deeper he buried his tongue inside her.

Randi wondered if Quasar had any idea how he was making her feel. And then there were the sounds he was making while lapping her up, sounds that were inciting her adrenaline and igniting even more passion.

Suddenly, something akin to an explosion detonated inside her. She screamed his name as she shook violently with her release, tumbling over the edge of more pleasure than anyone had a right to have. But thanks to Quasar, for the second time in her life, she was the recipient of a bone-chilling orgasm. He didn't remove his tongue from inside her until the last spasm passed through her body.

Randi felt herself being swept off her feet and placed on the bed. She heard the sound of a condom packet being ripped and opened her eyes to watch him tear off his clothes. And when he sheathed himself, she whimpered his name.

"I'm right here," he said, coming back to the bed and joining her there. He lifted his body over hers, and she looked up into the penetrating eyes of the man looming over her. Lowering his head, he took her mouth with a hunger that she found hypnotizing. He was deliberately rebuilding her need and her desire to a pitch even higher than before.

She felt him, his engorged penis probing around her womanhood. He released her mouth to look at her while he slid inside her, burying himself deep. Deeper than she'd thought possible.

Wrapping her arms around him, she clung to him as he began moving his body. He pumped in and out, thrusting hard while her inner muscles squeezed and clenched him, while her hips rocked repeatedly against him. The feel of him swelling even more inside her gave her the full effect of being taken by him.

"Had enough?" he asked as he continued to pump into her in a steady rhythm that had sensations curling through her.

"No," she said breathlessly. "Please don't stop."

And he didn't.

He kept pounding hard inside her, thrusting deeper. Only when her body exploded into yet another orgasm did he throw his head back and give in to his own release. Lights seemed to flash in front of her, all around her, and moments later her body became boneless and limp.

Then she was gathered into strong arms and held in a way she wished could last forever.

LEO PACED THE ROOM, waiting for the phone call he figured would come. Not that he was looking forward to getting it. All his plans had been ruined by one person. Dr. Randi Fuller. She was the reason he was in exile now, and when he thought he'd gotten the chance to end her life, he had failed. Twice.

He sat down in the chair and touched the side of his

neck. Bite marks deliberately left there by his recent bed partner. The one person he could count on finally to get rid of Fuller if for some reason he failed again.

He touched the sore side of his neck. She'd been horny as hell with all intentions to outfuck him. He chuckled when he'd shown her that wasn't possible, although he'd enjoyed her trying. Sadly, her insatiable state was a testimony to what the bastard she was married to wasn't doing. He didn't have a problem with that since the thought of the man touching her was a bitter pill to swallow. He'd tried getting her to leave him, but she'd refused, and a part of him understood. She had the perfect wealthy lifestyle and the perfect cover. Very few people knew what she was involved with behind the prick's back. Or whom she was fucking on the side.

The ringing of the phone jolted his mind back to the business at hand. He clicked on the phone he'd been holding. "What?"

"This is the last time I'm going to tell you anything, Leo."

Whatever. "What do you have for me?"

"It's about that damn psychic. I just heard they're taking her to a safe house tomorrow."

Leo raised a brow. "Aren't you worried they'll figure out who leaked the information?"

"Not this time. There was a meeting of the top two special agents, and I eavesdropped. They have no idea I overheard their plan."

Leo smiled. "Good. Now tell me where this safe house is located."

"You're going to send your goons again just so they can fuck up?"

"No. I'm taking care of her myself as well as anyone

who tries getting in my way." He intended to be successful, but if not, he would go down knowing that either way, Dr. Randi Fuller's time was running out. He would be avenged.

CHAPTER TWENTY-SEVEN

RANDI SLOWLY OPENED her eyes to the delicious view of the man standing next to the bed. Shirtless with a pair of jeans riding low on his hips, he was a lot for a woman to take in. And he smelled just-showered good. Gone was the dark stubble around his jaw. She sort of liked the bearded shadow he'd worn yesterday. Had loved the feel of it on her skin last night and early this morning when he had kissed all over her stomach and butt cheeks. And now he was standing there with a tray of food in his hands?

Pulling herself up in bed, she glanced at the clock. It was close to ten. Could that be right? She recalled waking around seven and dragging herself out of bed—sore muscles and all—and up the stairs to shower, leaving Quasar in bed. By the time she'd returned downstairs, he was standing in the bedroom doorway naked and waiting for her with an erection she couldn't believe. They had ended up making love again...several times. That was the reason she was back in bed. After yet another vigorous lovemaking session, she'd dozed off. The last thing she recalled was having a blowout of an orgasm. She'd lost count of how many she'd had over the past fourteen hours.

"Breakfast in bed, Quasar?"

He placed the tray across her lap. "It's the least I can do after you gave me such a wonderful night."

She'd given him a wonderful night? If only he knew what he'd given her. It had been one lovemaking session after another. Her sore muscles could attest to that. As far as she was concerned, what they'd shared was beyond wonderful. "You gave me my night to remember."

"And you gave me mine. You seduced the hell out of me. I was held captive."

She smiled. Yes, she had resorted to seducing him. Whenever he figured she'd had enough, she intentionally did something to turn him on all over again. Some of the things she'd done colored her cheeks just thinking about them. She'd never been that bold or brazen.

"If you want to claim you were seized by seduction, then go ahead," she said. "But you wanted to make love to me as much as I wanted to make love to you, if for no other reason than to find out what all that sexual chemistry between us is about."

He sat down on the edge of the bed and pushed a few strands of hair from her face. "If for no other reason…" he said, as if rolling her words around in his mind. "Sounds like you think that was the main reason. Well, just to set the record straight, I wanted to make love to you because you're sexy as hell. But speaking of all that sexual chemistry, do you think we figured out why we're so attracted to each other?"

Randi could only speak for herself and knew in her heart that she definitely had. She'd found out he was a man she could easily love. Knowing she couldn't look at him any longer for fear he might see a lovesick expression in her eyes, she muttered, "Not sure," before glancing down at the tray in her lap.

"Eggs, bacon, toast and coffee. Boy, you've been

busy," she said, hoping he hadn't noticed that she'd deliberately changed the subject.

"It was either prepare breakfast or wake you up to make love again. *Quiero saborearte entre tus piernas otra vez.*"

She couldn't stop looking at him and feeling love she hadn't felt in a long time. Or ever. More than once over the past couple of years she'd wondered if she had truly loved Larry or it had merely been the idea of being in love with him. Granted, his rejection had been devastating to the point that she'd taken off a year from college. But now she realized that year spent on Glendale Shores hadn't been as much about him as it had been about herself. Hadn't Gramma Mattie revealed in the vision that Larry had never been the man for her?

"Have you heard any news reports?" she asked, biting into a piece of bacon.

"No," Quasar said as he stood. "We can watch together." He grabbed the remote off the nightstand to turn on the wide-screen television in the room.

"Nice bedroom." *Definitely a nice bed with an excellent mattress.* It was a comfortably furnished room, and she liked the color scheme of black and gold. It was her guess the bed was a California king. All the furniture in this room appeared large and elegant. She figured Early American.

"Thanks. This used to be my godmother's room. When she left me the house, it included all the furnishings. People want to rent nicely furnished beach houses like this for their vacations. And for longer-term renters, the price includes a weekly cleaning service."

"That's a nice perk."

"It was my godmother's idea, and I agreed. She wanted

this place to remain in great shape until I could get out of jail and move in."

But you never did, Randi thought, taking a sip of coffee. "Why didn't you sleep in here last night?"

He shrugged those shoulders she liked holding on to when he went down on her or when he was on top of her. They were massive and had felt good beneath her fingers. "Even though I own the place, to me this has always been Lucinda's room. I recall as a kid running in here at night after a bad dream and jumping into bed with her, hiding beneath the covers. She would always say something to comfort me and take my fears away."

In her mind she could see him as a toddler, running in here to feel safe with the godmother he adored. "Did you have bad dreams often?"

"No. Only when my brother was a prick and would do things to scare me. He did that a lot. I've never slept in this room without Lucinda."

"So we ended up in here last night because this bedroom was closest?" she asked.

"No, that's not why I brought you in here."

His words surprised her. "Oh? Then why did you?"

For a minute she thought he wasn't going to answer. "I've made out with other women in both rooms upstairs…in my young, oversexed and naughty-as-sin days. I didn't want you to be just another—"

"—notch on the bedpost," she finished for him.

"Yes. I'm older, wiser…"

"But just as oversexed," she decided to throw in.

He chuckled. "Considering all we did last night, I can see why you would think that. But over the years, I've acquired more discriminating taste in women."

"Gee, I should hope so."

They chuckled together, and to Randi, that sounded good. Yesterday had been traumatic for her, but last night in his arms, in this bed, had been wonderful. He had given her a part of heaven in the most sinful way. "Thanks for not thinking I was just another lay."

"Never," he said, reaching out and wrapping his finger around a strand of her hair. He'd done that a lot. Pulled on her hair while thrusting in and out of her. Pumped hard into her every time she drew a breath. No need to wonder why her scalp was a little tender this morning.

Her attention was suddenly snagged by the news break that came on the television. Agent Riviera had called before midnight to say that they'd successfully stopped the gang war. Like the Warlords, the Revengers had had an arsenal of guns. Several gang members had been arrested, and warrants were out for the ones who'd evaded capture. With the use of dental records, Riviera had also identified the driver of the car who attacked them on the road yesterday morning. The driver was a man by the name of Alonzo McKee. He was a killer for hire who'd eluded the FBI for a few years. The question that remained was who had hired him.

Although she hadn't sorted out all the pieces in her mind, Randi was certain it was the same man who had orchestrated the hit on her two days ago as well as the man responsible for all the other vile incidents. She refused to return home to Virginia without bringing him to justice. Otherwise she would always be looking over her shoulder.

She was about to compliment Quasar on how good her breakfast was when she saw him tense. His eyes were glued to the television. It was a local news report about a man by the name of Doyle Patterson who had announced his candidacy for mayor of Beverly Hills.

The photo that flashed on the screen made it obvious the man was related to Quasar. He was an older version, possibly four or five years older. Quasar's brother? The one he thought his father had always favored over him? Randi didn't say anything as she listened to the report with the same rapt attention as Quasar.

"Doyle Patterson made the announcement last night at a lavish party in his home in Beverly Hills. Only selected members of the media were invited onto the Patterson Estate. One can only speculate that last night's affair was the beginning of numerous fund-raisers."

The picture of Doyle Patterson was replaced with one of Doyle Patterson with a beautiful, chic and elegantly dressed woman on one side of him and an older man on the other. Randi knew immediately that the older man was Quasar's father. Although neither of his sons had taken his coloring, the facial features the three shared were uncanny.

She switched her gaze from the television to Quasar. He wasn't so much as blinking an eye, and he'd balled his hands into fists.

"Quasar? Are you alright?" she asked him.

"I'm fine," he said, not taking his gaze off the television to look at her.

She returned her attention back to the television as the reporter said, "Here you see a photo taken last night when the campaign was announced. Flanking Mr. Patterson are his father, Louis, and his wife, Lilly…"

Lilly? Randi swallowed. What were the odds of Doyle Patterson marrying a woman who had the same first name as the woman Quasar had planned to marry? The same woman who hadn't waited for him? Shivers raced up Randi's spine because she knew they weren't different women but the same woman. Lilly had broken things off with Quasar to marry his brother.

Randi glanced at Quasar and knew his focus on the television screen had nothing to do with his father or brother but with the beautiful woman standing by his brother's side. The woman Quasar had loved. The woman he probably still loved, and she had married his brother.

Randi recalled the night they'd parked on the Mulholland Drive Overlook, when he'd told her about his ex-girlfriend. At that moment she couldn't help but remember the conversation...

"Is Lilly the one who wouldn't wait for you while you were in jail?"

"You have a good memory, and yes, she's the one. She promised to wait for me and broke her promise. I guess you can say she had a change of heart."

"I'm sorry, Quasar. About what happened with you and Lilly."

"No reason for you to be sorry. You didn't know me or Lilly. It was her decision. She said she couldn't wait any longer and wanted to marry someone else. I gave her my blessing."

"Does Lilly still live in LA?"

"Yes, she still lives here."

"Is she still married?"

"Yes, she's still married."

At the time, Randi had wondered how Quasar had known so much about Lilly. Now she knew. Lilly was married to his brother. No wonder he'd stayed away from his family so long.

"Well, we got the news about the gangs," Quasar said,

breaking into her thoughts and turning off the television. He looked at his watch. "I'm going upstairs to dress. If you want to meet back down here in around twenty minutes, then we—"

"Why?" she interrupted. It was obvious he was upset. Her heart was breaking at the thought that he might still love Lilly, but she'd known from the first time he'd brought up Lilly's name that there was a possibility.

He looked at her, confused. "Why? Do I need to remind you that Riviera said you could talk to Overstreet at one o'clock today?"

She shook her head. "That's not what I'm talking about. That's not what I'm asking you."

He looked even more confused. "Then what are you asking?"

"Why are you pretending you didn't see your father and brother on television?"

A wave of uneasiness washed through her when he narrowed his eyes. "How did you know we're related?"

Duh, that was obvious, and she wondered why he wasted his time asking. But since he had, she would respond. "Same last name and the three of you favor. You and your brother have your father's features, although you have darker coloring."

A fierce frown covered Quasar's face, and there was a moment of tension-filled silence between them before he said in a dispassionate tone, "So I saw my father and Doyle. No big deal."

"Wasn't it? And is your brother's wife, Lilly, the same Lilly who was once your girl? The one you wanted to marry?"

Randi knew he might tell her none of that was any of her business and she had no right to ask. But at the moment, she was given the right by every sore muscle she felt in her body, all those passion marks up and down her inner thighs and the taste of him on her tongue that no amount of brushing could eradicate. They had made love more times throughout the night than she could count. Had tried more positions than she'd thought possible and had even said a few dirty words she would need to seek salvation for the next time she attended church. So if he was about to start pining away over the love he'd lost, or more specifically, the love his brother might have deliberately taken from him, then she felt she had a right to know. Her heart needed to know.

He placed the remote on the nightstand and shoved his hands into the pockets of his jeans. "Yes, she's the same Lilly."

Without saying anything else he left the room. And she watched him go.

QUASAR WALKED INTO his bedroom and drew a deep cleansing breath. He could admit while watching the news report his attention had been focused on Lilly. The reason he'd watched her so closely was to assure himself that his feelings for her were as they should be. Over. He could honestly say that he no longer had any feelings whatsoever for the woman he'd once loved. None.

He'd always suspected that was the case; however, seeing her on that television screen had confirmed it, verified it beyond a shadow of a doubt. He had watched her with Doyle and his father, smiling perfectly for the camera as she stood by her husband's side. She was in her element as Doyle's wife, and he was happy for her. From the looks of it, she loved Doyle…or she loved his money. As far as Quasar was concerned, she and Doyle deserved each other.

She'd known what a total ass Doyle could be, just like she'd known how Doyle and his father had willingly let Quasar go to prison and serve time for a crime Doyle committed. Yet she had married Doyle anyway. And yes, like she had moved on with her life, Quasar had moved on with his. Not returning home to LA had been the best decision he could have made.

Even now he could recall how naive he'd been years ago. Fresh out of college, he'd been given an important position within his father's company. He'd actually assumed his relationship with his father and brother would improve. That he could prove his worth to them and to the company. He should have suspected something. And when his father walked into his office that day, told him what Doyle had done and said that to protect the family name and the integrity of the company, they needed him to confess to land fraud, he'd done so.

His thoughts shifted to Randi. He would talk to her on their drive into LA. The last thing he wanted was for her to think he still had feelings for Lilly. Especially after what the two of them had just shared. They'd made love all through the night. Occasionally they would doze off, taking power naps, only to wake up and make love again. He'd gone through the six condoms he'd originally brought into the room and at some point rushed upstairs to grab more. He was more than glad that before leaving Charlottesville he'd purchased a twelve-pack box. He hadn't been sure they would become intimate but had wanted to be prepared just in case.

Okay, he would admit he was a greedy ass. She'd even teasingly called him that at one point during the night. But typically, he'd never been so needy for sex that he wanted to make love nonstop. But he had been with Randi. And he'd wanted to learn everything there was about her body, which was why he had touched and licked her all over. Now he knew about that pretty seashell tattoo on her hip and the cute little mole on the underside of her upper arm. He knew her every erogenous zone, and once he had discovered where they were, he had made sure he exploited them to full advantage to give her pleasure.

It was hard to describe how he felt each and every time they made love. There was something about their bonding, their joining, their mating that still had him in total awe just thinking about it. He had never experienced anything like it before. He'd always thought of himself as a breast man. A nice pair of boobs could turn him on in a heartbeat, but when it came to Randi, he'd found he was an any-part-of-her-body guy. Every place on her body had set him on fire. Made him burn hotter. And each time she had an orgasm and shattered in his arms, he'd wanted to make love to her all over again. It was a wonder either of them had energy left to do anything today. But he knew she had a full agenda, which meant he needed to get dressed.

He had grabbed a shirt to tug over his head when his phone rang. He knew without checking caller ID that it was Louis calling him again. He'd noticed his father had called several times yesterday, but he hadn't bothered to return any of those calls. He would answer this one.

"Yes?"

"Where the hell are you? You have a lot of damn nerve coming to LA and not bothering to see us."

Quasar leaned back against the TV table. "Careful, Louis, or else I'll begin to think you care."

"Of course I care. You're my son."

Quasar rolled his eyes. "Whatever."

"You should have been here for the campaign kick-off last night."

"No, I shouldn't have. I saw the three of you on television. You and Lilly did a great job giving Doyle your support. I didn't need to be there."

"Doyle will make a great mayor."

Quasar rubbed his hand down his face, trying not to get frustrated. "And knowing you, you've already set your sights on the White House." He checked his watch. "Look, Louis, I need to go."

"Go where? Why did you come to LA if it wasn't to spend time with your family?"

Spend time with his family? The same family who hadn't visited or sent a card or letter during the three years he'd been locked up? "I'm in LA on business."

"On business?"

"Yeah. But I will drop by before returning to Charlottesville."

"What about the woman?"

Quasar raised a brow. "What woman?"

"The one staying at the beach house with you. One of Lucinda's neighbors claims she saw the two of you walking on the beach yesterday morning."

Did his father have the neighbors spying on him? "Why would anyone have reason to tell you that?"

"The neighbor didn't tell me. She told Paul, and he mentioned it to me."

"Still have your paid informers, I see."

"Don't be an ass, Quasar. Do you have a woman with you or not?"

Every nerve in Quasar's body was primed with anger. "I do, not that it's any of your business."

"Everything about you is my business. Bring her when you come. Unless you don't want her to meet Lilly."

Everything about him was Louis's business? Quasar wondered what kind of game his father was playing. "Why would I have a problem with her meeting Lilly? Lilly and I broke up years ago."

"No, Lilly dumped you for Doyle. That's a big difference. And they are happy."

"Goodbye, Louis."

"So when will I see you?"

"Not sure it'll be soon, but you will." *Because you and I definitely need to talk.* "Goodbye."

He clicked off the phone, shaking his head. His old man was a piece of work. Thank God for men like Sheppard Granger who'd been there and was still there for him as a role model for what a real father stood for and represented. He knew Sheppard would never intentionally play one of his sons against the other.

Pushing the thought of his father, Doyle and Lilly from his mind, he was about to slip out of his jeans to put on a pair of khakis when he was interrupted again by his phone. This time it was Stonewall.

"What's up, Stonewall?"

"Why don't you answer your damn phone? You okay?"

Quasar couldn't help but smile. "I'm fine, and please stop screaming in my ear."

"Oh. Sorry."

"The reason I missed those calls yesterday was that I had my phone turned off. A lot has been happening."

"So I heard. There haven't been any more attempts on Dr. Fuller's life, have there?"

"No, but the person who organized those hits is still out there. I plan to continue to protect her until he's caught."

"I don't blame you."

Wanting to change the subject, Quasar asked, "So, Stonewall, how was your date with the detective? The one you got all dolled up for?"

"It didn't happen."

Quasar heard the deep disappointment in Stonewall's voice. "Why?"

"She got called away on a homicide at the last minute. And now, unfortunately, I'm leaving today for New York to handle security detail for that Dakota Navarro again. I'll be gone for a couple of weeks."

He knew Navarro to be a wealthy businessman Stonewall had been protecting off and on for the past few months. "What is this now? The fourth canceled date for you and Detective Ingram?"

"Something like that. We both have crazy schedules. I've been out of town on assignment most of the time, and according to Joy, the city's budget took a hit with all the expenses for extra cops and such during the Erickson case. To compensate, they are making the detectives take on double the homicide cases they usually have."

"From the sounds of it, you and your detective might never move beyond meeting for coffee and donuts in the mornings."

"When I get back, I'm going to make it my business that we go out…even if I have to kidnap her."

"And you'll be going to jail by yourself. Striker and I won't be there to protect your ass."

He heard Stonewall laugh. "I recall things differently. I was the one who protected you two."

"Whatever."

"Stay safe."

"You, too."

After Quasar ended the call, he rushed to finish dressing.

CHAPTER TWENTY-EIGHT

"You did an amazing job with Overstreet, Randi."

Randi glanced over at Quasar. "Thanks. My degree as a behavioral analyst came in handy when he simply refused to believe in psychic powers."

They had left FBI headquarters and were now headed to the crime scene where those two gang members had been brutally murdered. FBI agents were in the vehicles in front of them and behind them.

Due to lack of sleep the night before, she had caught a few winks during the car ride from Malibu into downtown LA. No matter how short, she'd needed the nap to deal with Jason Overstreet. Like Emiliano, he had priors a mile long, but unlike Emiliano he hadn't easily accepted that she had a message from his mother. He had initially accused her of being a phony. It had taken a while, but when she began sharing things with him that only his mother could possibly know, he had settled down and began listening.

When she told him the FBI had conclusive evidence that someone was deliberately manipulating both gangs to start a war, he'd admitted he had reached that conclusion himself and that several of his gang members had begun their own investigation. The only thing he'd discovered was that the deaths had been set up by some person who'd called himself Mr. Big. It was rumored the man was into all sorts of criminal activities and wanted the gangs' territory for himself.

"I just hope I can pick up on something when we get to this crime scene," Randi told Quasar. "The last thing we need is for the gangs to take things into their own hands and render their own brand of justice." The view of LA through the car's open window on this beautiful day, with sunny skies and a light breeze, felt at odds with the harsh reality of violence and death she was facing. Still, the flowering plants and trees lining the roadways and perfuming the air calmed her.

"I hope the Feds can get something on this Mr. Big," Quasar said. "They are treating him as a person of interest."

Randi felt there was no need to mention to Quasar that the minute Overstreet had said the name Mr. Big, a cold chill had come over her. Why that had happened she wasn't quite sure. She had racked her brain to recall if it could possibly be a name she'd heard before.

"Randi?"

She looked over at Quasar. "Yes?"

"About last night…"

She swallowed, hoping he wasn't about to tell her that he regretted anything they'd done. Quite honestly, she didn't know how to proceed with him. She'd witnessed his reaction upon seeing his old girlfriend. His brother's wife. Did he plan to get her back? No, she refused to believe that. Quasar was not the home wrecker type. "What about last night?"

"I want to tell you again how wonderful it was."

She wondered if a *but* would follow. When he didn't say anything, she asked, "But?"

He took a quick glance over at her. "But what?"

"That's what I'm wondering."

He gave her a quizzical look. "You think there's a *but*."

"Isn't there?"

"Not that I know of. You think there should be?"

Randi honestly didn't know what to think. "The woman you love is now married to your brother."

"Yes. But what does that have to do with us and last night? And you phrased that wrong. Lilly is a woman I *once* loved. There's a difference."

"Is there?"

"Yes. And like you said, she is married to my brother." The same brother he'd gone to jail for. Even now he wondered if his brother still had his hands in illegal activities. If he did, it would be just a matter of time before he got caught. A part of Quasar couldn't help but hope that one day he would.

"And how do you feel about that? Him marrying your girlfriend?" she asked, wanting to know.

"Accepting." He paused a minute and then added, "I stopped loving Lilly years ago, but she taught me a valuable lesson."

And Randi knew what that lesson was. He'd said as much on their first date. He didn't ever want to give his heart to another woman again. She felt an explosive shake in her chest with the realization that the man sitting beside her could never love her. He would never trust her with his heart.

RANDI TOOK IN the crime scene while rubbing her arms. The moment she'd gone beyond the yellow tape, she had felt the hair stand up on the back of her neck. She encountered vibes so strong she stood rooted to the same spot.

"What's wrong, Randi?"

She drew in a deep breath. Although Quasar had asked the question, she noticed Agent Riviera and Detective Sutherland and other agents and officers staring questioningly at her, as well.

"I feel so much negative energy in here," she said, glancing around the empty building. "As soon as I stepped beyond the tape, I felt a connection. Somehow I've locked in on both victims, Griffin and Constantine."

She didn't say anything for a minute. "I had a flash vision of the execution. It was awful. They begged for their lives."

"Do you know who did it?" Sutherland asked anxiously.

She closed her eyes for a minute and gasped when she reopened them.

"What's wrong, Randi?" Quasar asked her for the second time.

She met his gaze. "Mr. Big. Overstreet was right. The man behind everything, the man who paid Constantine and Griffin to betray their gang, was someone Constantine knew only as Mr. Big."

"And how do you know that?" Sutherland asked.

Randi glanced over at him and wondered if Sutherland felt stupid for asking her that when the others around looked at him strangely. To them it was obvious how she knew it. Her psychic powers were at work. However, she decided to answer him anyway.

"Constantine. He's reaching out to me. Griffin never met this Mr. Big, but Constantine had. Several times. And Constantine just warned me. Mr. Big wants me dead. An old score to settle."

"An old score to settle?" Riviera repeated.

Randi didn't say anything as she closed her eyes again. "I see him. I see Mr. Big through Constantine's eyes."

"And do you recognize him?" Riviera asked in a voice just as anxious as Sutherland's had been moments ago.

"Yes," Randi said in barely a whisper. "The face Constantine is staring into belongs to a criminal by the name of Levan Shaw."

"Levan Shaw?" Riviera asked in astonishment.

Randi nodded and reopened her eyes. "Some still wonder if he died in that FBI raid a few years ago, but his body was never found."

Quasar said, "Now we know why."

BY THE TIME they returned to the beach house that evening, Randi was mentally drained. After leaving the crime scene, she met with several agents, all determined to bring Levan Shaw to justice. She explained that she'd never come face-to-face with Shaw. The last time she'd gotten a psychic reading on him had been through one of his human trafficking victims.

The woman's detailed reading had provided enough information for Randi to lay out the facts to the FBI agents she'd been assigned to work with. Things would have been more successful if Agent Felton had believed in her. He hadn't. And although she'd all but led them to the compound where those women were being held against their will, Shaw had escaped. The man she'd seen through Constantine's eyes looked a little older and was wearing his hair shorter. But she remembered him from those horrible visions.

"You want something to eat?" Quasar asked. "I can whip up some—"

"No, I'm fine. I'm still full from lunch." Riviera had

ordered in again. This time it had been a huge seafood platter. "My sister called a few times, so I need to return her call before she panics. And I want to take a nice long soak in the tub."

"Okay. I need to make a few calls of my own."

"Okay. I'll see you later."

Quasar watched her walk up the stairs. Was Randi putting distance between them, or was she so mentally drained she simply needed time to recharge? He'd seen her today with Overstreet and then at the crime scene. The woman was remarkable. Her psychic powers were truly a gift. Any man who didn't think so or felt threatened by them wouldn't deserve her.

He frowned, wondering how he could so easily think such a thing. Randi and another man. He would admit that today he had been more territorial than ever. He blamed it on the fact that last night they'd shared a bed. It had annoyed the hell out of him when he'd noted how often Sutherland had stared at her with lusty eyes when he thought no one was watching. More than once he'd been tempted to knock the hell out of the detective. And what really pissed him off was when Sutherland had invited himself to join them for lunch in that conference room.

When the detective had suggested Quasar leave them alone for a while to discuss the case, Quasar had refused to do so. He'd told Sutherland whatever he needed to talk to Randi about needed to be said in front of him, because he wasn't going any damn place. Since Randi hadn't argued the point in favor of the detective's request, evidently she hadn't wanted to be alone with Sutherland any more than Quasar had wanted her to be alone with him.

Although Randi said she wasn't hungry, Quasar

headed for the kitchen, deciding to prepare a meal anyway. Her powers might be a gift, but he could see they
took a toll on her.

"So THERE YOU have it, Haywood. Quasar will never fall
in love with me. I'll be living a miserable life alone for
the rest of my days."

Randi had spent the last twenty minutes giving her
sister an abbreviated version of today's activities before
confessing to last night's. She needed a shoulder to cry
on, and she knew Haywood's shoulder was always available. She couldn't help but recall the words she'd spoken to Quasar the first night in LA when he'd taken her
sightseeing at Mulholland Drive Overlook. She'd told
him that she hadn't been interested in falling in love any
more than he had. She saw now how wrong she'd been.

"I never knew you were a quitter, Randi."

Randi frowned, somewhat irritated by her sister's as-
sessment. "What are you talking about?"

"I'm talking about the fact that years ago, you were
given a vision of the man who would be your mate for
life. You knew you would have to earn his love and he
would have to earn yours. A few months ago you finally
met the guy, and the two of you were instantly attracted
to each other. You got a chance to spend a little productive time together and bam! He's earned your love without much effort and without knowing he had to."

"So I'm easy to please. Sue me."

"Don't want to sue you, but I do want to knock some
sense into you. Listen, kiddo. Men are funny creatures.
Sometimes they don't even know what's good for them.
Some of the time—hell, most of the time—women have
to be the ones who go after what they want. Men can be

so damn clueless. I refuse to allow you to grow old alone, so take my advice. You're there with him, so seize the opportunity. Use all that woman power. Let him earn your love but give him a reason to want to earn it. Seduce the hell out of him."

Randi shook her head. "Honestly, Haywood? Seduction?"

"Yes, seduction. Think about it. Lilly is no threat. But she did leave scars. It's up to you to erase those scars."

Randi drew in a deep breath. "That won't be easy."

"Never known you to be afraid of a little hard work. Just think of all the benefits and your reward in the end. There has to be a reason that of all the men in this world, Quasar was chosen for you. Evidently the powers that be think the two of you are right for each other. Need each other. So don't turn your back on him."

Randi nibbled on her bottom lip. "Seduction? I'm not good at that sort of thing."

"All women are good at that sort of thing, thanks to Eve. How do you think she got Adam to take a bite of that apple? Try it. You did say he was horny as hell."

"I didn't say that."

"You didn't have to. I can read between the lines. Sounds like you've kicked his libido into overdrive. Take advantage of it."

Randi finished removing her clothes for her bath. "I'll think about it."

"Don't think. Act."

After her soak in the tub, her conversation with Haywood remained on Randi's mind. She'd even closed her eyes and envisioned a number of hot scenarios while submerged in her bubble bath. The last thing she wanted was just sex between her and Quasar, although she had to admit the sex had been off the charts. But she knew she had to start somewhere, and if that meant she could get the ball rolling by seducing him, then she would try.

LIKE SOMEONE WHO was part of the night, Leo moved around in the darkness, through the trees and thickets, being careful not to make a sound. The house hadn't been difficult to find. The FBI had established a roadblock to stop anyone driving down the long dirt road, like his contact had said, but too bad they hadn't counted on anyone traveling on foot.

Leo had parked his car at a rest stop at the base of the mountain. When he was certain no one was watching, he had gotten his gun case containing his high-powered rifle and swung it across his back. Appreciating the skill he'd obtained in the military as a Green Beret, he had set out on foot and disappeared into the darkness.

He knew it was hard for some to believe that at one time he'd served his country and had intended to make a career out of it. That was until the brass found out he was making a little profit on the side with a prostitution ring he'd set up in Beirut. Who gave a fuck that most of the women had been used against their will? They weren't American women, so why give a damn? He found out the hard way that quite a few people did, and he ended up court-martialed.

It was while in federal prison serving time that he met a man by the name of Orson Pinkney. Orson had been into gambling and racketeering. After serving five years of a ten-year sentence, Levan hooked up with Orson the minute he was out, right under his parole officer's nose.

He and Orson worked well together and began making money right and left, until the Feds started busting up their operation. They retaliated and killed a couple of agents and robbed a few banks to replenish their capital. They expanded into casinos in Vegas, they paid off government officials in DC, they helped fund an illegal war in the Philippines. Their biggest moneymaker was the human trafficking operation until Dr. Fuller came in and messed things up. Orson had gotten killed in a raid. Luckily, Levan had been tipped off and had left right before things went down.

He finally saw the lights of the house ahead. More FBI cars were parked outside. He figured everyone was inside and getting ready to eat dinner. He chuckled. They had no idea this would be their last supper.

Taking the rifle case from his shoulder, he pulled a beauty of a high-powered rifle from the case. It was loaded, and he had more ammunition if needed. He intended to take them by surprise. There wouldn't be any survivors.

He'd expected agents on the perimeter, but there were none. Evidently they felt confident in the roadblock. Fools, all of them.

Crouching low, he eased toward the side of the house. His contact hadn't said anything about special security devices monitoring the yard, but you could never be sure. Hell, for all he knew, there might be patrol dogs somewhere. He had made it across the yard, relishing that he would do what those imbeciles he had hired had failed to do. End Dr. Randi Fuller's life.

He had made it to a good spot and had lifted the MCX rifle when a bright beam illuminated the entire yard, lighting his position up. "What the fuck!"

A booming voice came through a megaphone. "This is the FBI, and you're under arrest. Drop your gun, Shaw!" Instead of doing as ordered, he began shooting.

CHAPTER TWENTY-NINE

"Mmm, something smells good."

Quasar looked up from the pot he was stirring on the stove and drew in a sharp breath. Over the breakfast counter of the open concept house, he could see Randi as she came down the stairs. She was wearing one of those tops with spaghetti straps and a long flowing shirt that seemed to wrap around her legs with every step she took. She looked absolutely gorgeous, and the closer she got, he more he decided the aroma of the food had nothing on her. She wore that perfume he liked, and the scent had a hypnotic effect. There was no mistaking all that combustible chemistry gliding right along with her.

She looked refreshed, well rested. She'd been upstairs for over an hour, and he wondered if she'd snuck in one of those power naps she told him she occasionally took. He was getting tired of asking himself just what there was about Randi that could make his libido go wild. So he would stop asking and accept it as one of those things that just couldn't be explained. If he still couldn't figure it out after their sex marathon last night, then he wouldn't lose any more sleep about it.

He turned back to the stove or else she would clearly see evidence of his desire for her. "I know you said you weren't hungry, but I figured you might be after your bath," he said over his shoulder.

"Is it safe for you to stand that close to the stove wearing your gun?"

He wanted to glance around to see if that had been a serious question, but even the sound of her voice could make him hard. "It's safe," he replied over his shoulder. The sound of silky material sliding across leather let him know she'd sat down at the breakfast counter on one of the bar stools.

"What are you cooking?" she asked.

"Everything's all done," he said, slowly turning around. He couldn't stand with his back to her forever. Besides, it was no secret they generated a lot of sexual energy. They'd tried working it out of their systems last night and failed miserably, but he'd enjoyed every minute.

"I thought I'd introduce you to my godmother's favorite soup. Usually she prepared it during the winter months, but since she claimed it was an energy picker-upper, I thought you might need it. You had a full day." *That kicked off from a full night*, he decided not to add.

"Thank you, Quasar. You take such good care of me."

If she'd only known just how much more he wanted to take care of her, and in what way, she would have been shocked. But then, after last night, maybe she wouldn't.

"Here," he said, walking over to place a bowl and spoon in front of her. "Try it. Tell me what you think. And be careful. It's hot."

"I like it hot."

The heat of her gaze touched him in places already sizzling. He didn't need to deal with any more surges of desire in his body right now or else he just might overload. "Do you?"

"Didn't I prove that last night?" she said with sultry humor in her voice and a sexy smile on her lips.

Why did she have to go and mention last night? Although he'd been remembering it a lot today, now that he knew she was thinking about it, too, a sexual explosion was bound to happen. He doubted he would ever forget the feel of thrusting in and out of her, their bodies gyrating, the sound of her screaming his name while shattering in his arms…

"Well, didn't I?"

She really wanted an answer? In that case, he would give her one. "Yes, you proved a lot of things last night, Randi."

She held his gaze. "All good, I hope."

"Very good. Too damn good." Then he added in Spanish, *"Quiero meterme todo dentro tuyo otra vez y no me importa si nunca vuelvo a salir."*

Quasar thought she looked pleased with his response, and she picked up her spoon. It was a good thing she didn't understand Spanish because he'd just told her that he wanted to get inside her body again and wouldn't care if he never came out.

He watched as she placed the spoon to her lips and blew on the soup a few times before sliding it into her mouth. He felt a stirring in his groin as he recalled that same way she had slid him into her mouth last night. He hadn't expected it but had gotten a whole hell of a lot of enjoyment from her doing so. She had licked him all over…the same way she was licking that spoon now.

He swallowed as she ran her tongue across her bottom lip and then the top. In a husky voice he asked, "So what do you think?"

"I think it's delicious, Quasar, and I want some more."

Why was she still licking her lips? And the spoon?

Had the soup been *that* good? "I'll give you some more. As much as you want."

"You promise? As much as I want?"

They were still talking about the soup, weren't they? To be quite honest, he wasn't sure. His erection evidently thought their conversation had shifted to something else, which would account for the way it was throbbing. "Yes, I promise to give you as much as you want," he said.

She eased her bowl and spoon aside and placed her elbows on the countertop while resting her chin on her clasped hands. The eyes that looked at him were so heated he almost felt scorched. "So tell me, Quasar, what do I need to do to get you naked?"

If her question was meant to set off a keg of dynamite in his gut, then she succeeded. Rounding the breakfast bar, he turned the stool with her on it to face him and said, *"Quiero follarte por todo la casa, en cada habitación y en cada posición conocida por el hombre y en posiciones que solo muy pocos hombres han probado alguna vez en una mujer."*

A smile touched the corners of her lips. "Maybe I should have told you this sooner but just so you know, I speak fluent Spanish. That means I was able to understand all the words you've ever said."

He was surprised and a little chagrined. "I was wrong for not asking if you spoke Spanish and was wrong for assuming you didn't. Like I said, I have a tendency to lapse into Spanish when I'm running on high emotions. And you, Randi Fuller, have the ability to bring out very high emotions in me. Some of which I'd never had to deal with before. In a way, I thought you were better off not knowing what I was saying." He drew in a deep breath. "So now you know what I just said?"

Blushing all over the place with eyes darkening with desire, she whispered, "Yes. You said that you wanted to eff me all over this house, in every single room and every position known to man and a few man might not have tried on a woman."

He moved a step closer to her, placed his hands on her thighs. He leaned forward, his mouth just inches from hers. "Yes, that's what I said. In that case, Randi Fuller, do you still want me naked?"

EVEN MORE SO. "YES."

"Then undress me."

Randi had no problem doing that, although she'd never undressed a man before. She slid from the stool, causing Quasar to back up just a tad. She didn't mind his closeness and liked having her body pressed to his, cradling his huge erection between her legs.

She'd seen the flare of heat in his eyes the moment he'd turned from the stove. She'd also seen the erection pressing against his zipper. The man was incredibly well endowed, and last night she'd been the happy recipient of that endowment.

Her gaze shifted from his eyes to his shoulder. Namely the gun in the holster. She'd been around guns. Owned a small-caliber handgun that she kept in her bedroom. She knew how to shoot, although she was far from being an expert. However, when it came to handling one, she preferred her much smaller one than the huge Glock he was packing.

"I'll let you remove that," she said, pointing to his gun and holster.

"No problem." He took a few steps back, and she

watched as he removed both from his shoulder and place them on the breakfast bar.

She'd seen him use his gun yesterday morning. It was obvious he knew how to use a firearm. From the first she'd felt safe with him. He hadn't ridiculed her for knowing how to defend herself like Larry had once done. Larry had somehow thought being a fifth-degree black belt lessened her femininity. Not Quasar. He'd complimented her on her skill and said he thought she'd looked sexy as hell while kicking her attacker in the balls.

With his gun safely out the way, he retraced his steps to return between her parted thighs and wrap his arms around her waist. "Before you get started, I really need this," he said, lowering his head and sliding his tongue in her mouth.

He deepened the kiss, took her mouth with a greediness that almost brought her to her knees, would have had her sinking to the floor had he not been holding her around the waist. She heard all those lusty groans and goaded sighs coming from her. Quasar definitely had a way with his mouth, his hands, his body, and she loved whenever he used all three on her.

He broke off the kiss and leaned in to lick the side of her face, right below her ear, and whisper in that husky voice that could make her wet, "I love kissing you. Your taste and your scent drive me wild, Randi."

If only he knew what his taste and scent did to her, as well. Whatever cologne he used was seductive as sin, and his taste was in a league all by itself. "You've had your kiss, Mr. Patterson. Now it's my time to be in control," she said, reaching up to unbutton his shirt. She took her time, loving how each open button revealed more of his hairy chest. A chest she'd rubbed her breasts against last night and in the wee hours of the morning. The contact had elicited sensations she'd barely been able to contain.

When the last button had been undone, she pushed the shirt from his shoulders. Unable to help herself, she buried her face in his hairy chest, deeply inhaling the scent of him. The scent of man. But that wasn't enough. She needed his taste, as well. Lifting her head, she used her tongue to lick around his jaw and the underside of his neck before tracing a path around his lips.

"You're killing me, you know." He practically growled out the words.

"I plan to keep you very much alive. There's so much I intend to do to you."

"You're testing my control, sweetheart."

Sweetheart? She tried not the let that term of endearment affect her but couldn't stop it from doing so. She continued to lick around his mouth while lowering her hand to his zipper. Before easing it down, she cupped him through his jeans. "Mmm, big and hard," she whispered while fondling him.

He groaned, and she loved the sound. "I hope you're enjoying this." She really meant that. She wasn't used to seducing a man, but more than anything, she wanted to seduce him.

"You're torturing me," he accused her in a strained voice when she finally eased down his zipper and slid her hand beneath the waistband of his briefs.

"Torture now, pleasure later. Isn't that what you told me last night?"

"I told you a lot of things last night," he moaned.

"Yes, you did. Some in Spanish and some in English. I must say the ones in Spanish burned my ears. I'm sure if you knew I understood what you were saying, you would have toned them down. Right?"

Not giving him a chance to answer, she pulled her hand away. Glad she didn't have to remove his shoes since he was in his bare feet, she crouched down and began tugging his jeans down his hips. He kicked them aside.

Looking at him standing there in a pair of black briefs, she felt moisture gather between her thighs. He was such a sinfully built Adonis of a man. Staring at him, seeing his massive, swollen erection barely contained in his briefs, made her light-headed. Hard to believe she'd taken it into her mouth last night. Inside her body. Had even slid it back and forth on her chest between her breasts, loving the feel of it touching her there.

"You do know that after last night it has your name all over it, right?"

She smiled at that assertion, wondering if he realized he'd basically admitted she'd claimed that part of him. And she would again. "Glad to know I branded it. I hope you remember that, because I will."

She figured he hadn't understood the full extent of what she'd meant when he replied, "Trust me, I'll remember."

A part of her wondered for how long. Until they left LA to go their separate ways? Pushing that thought to the back of her mind, she took a step closer, crouched down in front of him. She began easing the briefs down his robust thighs and muscular legs.

And just as she'd done with his chest, she buried her face in the hairy thatch surrounding his manhood, breathing his scent. She wasn't sure what it was about Quasar's manly aroma, but it only drove her to want him, all of him, every last inch. To taste. To touch. To devour.

She wanted to touch him like she had last night. All over that huge penis, jutting proudly so close to her head. Tilting her face ever so slightly, she began stroking him with her tongue, gliding all over the engorged head and along the protruding veins.

"Don't think I can last much longer," he said, and the words seemed forced from deep within his throat.

"I promise to hurry," she said, knowing she didn't intend to do any such thing. "But dammit, Quasar Patterson, you taste so good."

And on that note, she slid him fully into her mouth.

HE WASN'T GOING to last.

Quasar knew it and had tried to warn Randi, but she was intent on having her way with him. And now her way was literally driving him crazy. With a mind of their own, his hips began moving in a sinfully erotic motion as she continued to do all those naughty things to him with her mouth, while using her fingers to stroke his balls. And each time he tried pulling out of her mouth, she did something with her tongue to make him push back in. And those sounds she was making...it was as if having her mouth on him was supplying her with an overabundance of sexual energy.

She was drawing everything out of him, and suddenly a rush of intense desire pushed him over the edge as primal need clawed his insides. He tried pulling out of her before he exploded. However, it was apparent she had other ideas and intended for that not to happen. He looked down and saw the way her head was bobbing up and down while he was fully planted inside her mouth.

He made another attempt to tug away, but it was too late. Rapture tore into him, ripped through every part of his body like an explosion that splintered him in a thousand pieces. He closed his eyes and threw his head back, shouting her name as sexual pleasure consumed him. Like a flame it nearly burned him alive, making him groan over and over in raw primitive satisfaction.

At some point she finally released him, and when he opened his eyes, she was there, back on her feet, standing in front of him and licking her lips. Too much. And he found himself being pushed over the edge again. Sweeping her off her feet, he set her on the table, then quickly removed her clothes. Reaching down, he grabbed his jeans from the floor to retrieve a condom packet. Tearing it open, he quickly sheathed himself.

"Aren't we going from room to room?" Randi asked.

He shook his head as he moved toward her. "We'll get there eventually. But I want you here. Now."

Grabbing hold of her legs, he gently drew her toward the edge of the table, widening the space between her thighs in the process. Then he reached out and slid his fingers between her feminine folds. He began stroking her, fondling her clit in a way that made her moan before tossing her head back to moan some more.

"You have the ability to drive me crazy, Randi," he said, leaning in and using his tongue to lick around her mouth, using the same measured tempo he was applying with his fingers.

She felt his fingers replaced by the thickness of him as he slowly thrust inside her to begin hammering inside her mercilessly. She felt him lower her back on the table as he continued to pound inside her nonstop. Hammering deep with every hard, solid inch of him.

Quasar held tight to her pelvis as unrestrained passion took over his body and mind. He could not recall ever being this ravenous with any other woman. Only with her. Whenever his shaft was inside her, he could feel her inner muscles clench him, milk him, pull everything he had out of him. As if she was priming him for the blastoff.

He felt himself enlarge even more inside her, wanting her to feel the thickness of his hard length. He intended to brand her the way she'd branded him earlier. He would accomplish the deed with his tongue, his shaft, every tool a man possessed to leave his mark on a woman.

Quasar wanted her to enjoy having him between her legs, just as much as he enjoyed being here. Her fingers were digging deep into his shoulders. He should have felt pain, but he felt a stimulation of every male cell in his body.

He heard that little moan Randi gave when she was about to come, and it triggered something within him that made his balls detonate. There was no way to stop it from happening. He released a deep growl, and the sound seemed to deplete the air of oxygen at the same time pleasure ripped through his body.

"Randi!"

"Quasar!"

Simultaneously, an explosion hit them both, shattering their world. The lower portion of Quasar's body jolted, then bucked as he continued to hammer hard inside her.

And then he was kissing her with an intensity that he couldn't control when his body was bombarded by sensation after sensation. He pulled away enough to meet her eyes, and from the dark gaze staring back at him, he knew she'd felt those sensations, as well. The sexual chemistry that just wouldn't dim, no matter how often they made love would always be there.

Gathering her into his arms, he moved toward the bedroom.

SPECIAL AGENT WALLACE CONWAY checked his watch, unsure why he felt uneasy. He expected Levan to have knocked off the psychic by now. News of the hit should have spread around headquarters an hour or so ago. Had something gone wrong? He didn't see how it could have when he'd given his cousin Dr. Fuller's location.

He glanced up when he heard the knock on his office door. Maybe this was it. Notification that something bad had gone down. That Dr. Fuller was dead.

Wallace braced, knowing he needed to display a degree of empathy that he really didn't feel. "Come in."

The door opened and Special Agent Riviera walked in, flanked by two agents he didn't know. Their expressions were unreadable, which made uneasiness within him surge.

"Jarez, you still here?" he asked Riviera, forcing a smile to his lips while rising to his feet.

"Yes, I'm still here. And I'd like you to meet these two special agents from national headquarters. Special Agent Holiday and Special Agent Wells."

Wallace lifted a brow as he came around his desk. "All the way from DC? What brings you to LA?" he asked, shaking both men's hands. Was he imagining it or did they not give him much of a firm handshake?

"We're following up on a lead," the one named Holiday said.

"A lead?" Wallace asked, trying hard to read the man.

"Yes," the one who'd been introduced as Wells responded. "We heard Levan Shaw was in the area."

Every nerve in Wallace's body filled with alarm. "Levan Shaw," he repeated. "The name sounds familiar, but I can't recall who he is."

"Then let me help," Riviera said. "For the past seven

years, he's topped our most wanted list. We almost had him in a human trafficking bust, but he got away. We suspected he had inside help but could never prove it. But we got him this time."

Wallace swallowed as he felt tension tighten his stomach. "He's been captured?"

"No," Holiday said, looking straight at him without blinking an eye. "He refused to be taken alive."

A blinding flash of light streaked before Wallace's eyes. "He's dead?"

"Yes."

He wasn't sure which of the three men answered. He was still trying to wrap his mind around the fact that his cousin was dead. "I guess that's good news. Was anyone hurt?"

Agent Wells lifted a brow. "Anyone like whom?"

Wallace shrugged. "Dr. Fuller and the agents protecting her."

Too late he realized his mistake when the three agents exchanged glances. Riviera asked, "What makes you think Shaw's death has anything to do with Dr. Fuller?"

Wallace wondered how he was going to talk his way out of this one. No doubt Riviera had figured out Levan had been tipped off by someone. Otherwise, how would he have known where Dr. Fuller was being held? He eased a slow smile to his lips. "Lucky guess."

None of the men returned his smile. "We don't think so. In fact, we know so, Wally," said Riviera.

Wallace chuckled, trying to dismiss the feeling of being cornered. "What are you talking about, Jarez? Of course it was a lucky guess. What else could it have been?"

"Betrayal," Agent Wells said in a voice shimmering with anger.

Wallace frowned. "Betrayal? What the hell are you talking about? Look, I don't know you and you don't know me. I'm a damn good agent who wouldn't betray anyone, especially the people I work with. Tell them, Jarez. We've been together for years. First in Knoxville and then here."

Jarez Riviera stepped forward. "Sorry, Wally. I can't vouch for you. Dr. Fuller wasn't at the safe house. We set a trap, and you took the bait." Riviera swallowed, visibly enraged. "We've suspected you for a while but couldn't prove anything until now. You betrayed every agent not only in this agency but also in every agency across the country. You not only harbored a fugitive who didn't give a damn for human life but also told him about the safe house, knowing that when he went there to kill Dr. Fuller, it would put your fellow agents' lives at risk."

Wallace pretended to be taken aback by the accusations. "Hold up. Wait a damn minute," he said in an angry tone. "I don't know what you're talking about. You're trying to pin something on the wrong man."

Agent Wells stepped forward. "You'll have your day in court to tell that to a judge and jury. Special Agent Wallace Conway, you're under arrest."

CHAPTER THIRTY

QUASAR SLOWLY OPENED his eyes to the bright sunlight shining in through the window and the feel of the woman close beside him. Their limbs entwined, she was wrapped around him, and the feel of her velvety sex was pressed against his thigh. He immediately felt his own sex harden.

After two straight nights of mindless and endless love-making, his desire for her hadn't weakened one iota. If his goal had been to get her out of his system, all he was doing was embedding her deeper into it. He enjoyed making love to her and would do so morning, noon and night and anytime in between if given the chance.

He closed his eyes again and drew in a deep breath, absorbing her scent into his nostrils. She smelled so damn good. Citrus, jasmine, roses, violets—hell, he wasn't sure what. All he knew was that her aroma was a boner builder.

Memories of last night washed over him, filled him with a state of contentment he hadn't felt in a long time, if ever. What had started in his kitchen had continued here, in his godmother's bedroom. By rights, it was *his* bedroom now, and he was here in bed with the sexiest woman alive.

Quasar opened his eyes and stared at her sleeping peacefully. He fought the urge to wake her and start again what had ended with an orgasm so powerful his thighs shook remembering it. All through the night, her need had matched his own, giving, taking and then giving again. He could vividly recall when he'd knelt behind her, skin to skin, flesh to flesh, and poised in position to mate. She had tossed her hair back, glanced over her shoulder with desire shrouding her gaze and whispered, *"Tómame duro o házmelo sentir duro."*

He'd lost it and had thrust into her hard, just like she'd asked him to in Spanish. Like a jackhammer he kept driving into her hot, wet heat, pounding relentlessly. It seemed that every ounce of desire he had for her had pulsed through his engorged penis. That particular mating session had gone above and beyond his expectations.

"You're smiling."

His gaze moved over her face. "So are you," he countered.

"Yes," she agreed. "Your lovemaking was off the charts, but then that phone call from Agent Riviera definitely put the icing on the cake."

It certainly had. According to Riviera, the agent they'd suspected of being the mole had taken the bait. He'd passed false information about Randi's whereabouts to Levan Shaw. As they'd hoped, Shaw decided to take care of Randi himself and had shown up unaware of the setup. Determined not to give up without a fight, Shaw had opened fire, and in the exchange he'd been killed. Two FBI agents had gotten injured in the battle. Both had been treated at the hospital and released. During his interrogation last night, the mole had confessed to everything.

"So it's over," Randi said.

His smile widened. "Yes, it's over. You no longer have to look over your shoulder. You're safe now." He pushed the thought out of his mind that being safe meant she no longer needed him to protect her.

"Thanks to you, a gang war was averted and a dangerous criminal was taken out," he added. "According to Riviera, they gave Shaw the opportunity to be taken in alive, but evidently that's not what he wanted."

Randi drew in a deep breath. "You can't give me all the credit. Agent Riviera and his men as well as Detective Sutherland, worked with me. I could not have done it without them. They believed in me, and that made my job easier."

Quasar frowned. "Sutherland didn't at first. He was an ass."

She chuckled. "Yes, but he came around and even apologized."

"Yeah, and in the same damn breath he hit on you."

She eased closer to him and draped her arm across his shoulder. He still felt her velvety sex against his thigh, and now he could tell she was wet. Just as wet as he was hard. "Doesn't matter. You're the only man I want to hit on me. And hammer into me."

Her nails began grazing a slow, seductive path up and down his shoulder, while thoughts of hammering into her now took over his mind. They lay there staring at each other, and whenever she inhaled and exhaled, the sound of her raspy breaths made his erection thicken even more.

She claimed she couldn't read his mind, so he figured her thighs parted of their own accord. Just like his penis automatically slid into the wet folds of her womanhood. It was then he realized he hadn't put on a condom. He was about to pull out of her when her next words stopped him.

"I'm taking injections, and I'm healthy and safe."

He groaned at the feel of her inner muscles clamping him as he began sliding deeper inside her instead of pulling out of her. "And I'm healthy and safe, as well," he said, beginning to move in and out of her in slow, languorous thrusts.

"Then I guess that settles it," she said as she began rocking her hips in perfect rhythm to his strokes.

Before lowering his head to hers for the kiss he so desperately wanted, he whispered, "It most certainly does." He loved the feel of being skin to skin with her in the most intimate way. "We agreed after everything was over that we would stay a few days and enjoy the beach," he reminded her in a deep, throaty voice.

"And enjoy each other," she added in between moans when his thrusts became steadier and harder.

"Yes, and enjoy each other."

He leaned in and captured her mouth with his.

THE WOMAN STARED at the television. The FBI had called a news conference to report that a man who'd been on the Ten Most Wanted Fugitives list was dead. That man was Levan Shaw.

She fought back both tears and anger, barely listening to the details the FBI director was providing about Shaw's sinister plot to cause a gang war in order to gain control of their territory. The director also mentioned Shaw's two attempts on the psychic's life. The same psychic they'd brought to LA to help solve the case.

A photo of the psychic flashed across the television screen. The director praised the psychic's assistance as well as the hard work of his men and the LAPD.

Already the woman was remembering a promise she'd

made. A promise she intended to keep. She would succeed where Levan had failed. The psychic's days were numbered, and she wouldn't leave Los Angeles alive.

CHAPTER THIRTY-ONE

RANDI GLANCED ACROSS the room at Quasar. They'd rented several movies with plans to curl up on the sofa, eat pop-corn and watch a few later tonight. He was stacking the movies in the order the flicks would be seen. After much sensual coaxing, he had agreed a chick flick would be first, followed by an action thriller and then a comedy. They would keep rotating in that order until all the mov-ies had been watched.

The three days they'd spent here at his home in Mal-ibu had been outrageously idyllic. More than once she'd pinched herself just to make sure she wasn't dreaming. They would wake up each morning wrapped in each other's arms and enjoy an early-morning walk on the beach before returning for breakfast. Then it was back to bed, and they'd wake up in time for lunch. Yesterday he had taken her to LA to purchase a swimsuit. While downtown they decided to do some sightseeing near the Fashion District.

When they returned to Malibu, she had tossed a salad—something he'd shown her how to do—while he grilled steaks. As he tended to the meat, he'd told her about the family he still had in Cuba, some he had yet to meet. She noticed he'd said nothing about his family right here in LA. She'd shared more tidbits with him about her own family. He seemed interested in knowing about her paternal great-grandmother and great-great-grandmother from whom she'd inherited psychic powers. First, she told him about her great-great-grandmother, Minnie Farley, who was said to be clairvoyant and psychic. Her great-grandmother, Mattie Farley Dennison, was born the seventh daughter of a seventh daughter. Although she never claimed to be a psychic per se, she would admit to having the ability to read strong emotions in people.

"Are you ready for your swim?"

Quasar's question returned her thoughts to the present, and she saw he'd finished arranging the movies for tonight. They usually headed for the beach early in the day while the water was still moderately warm. Although he didn't get into the water, he would change into his swim trunks, sit by the water's edge and watch her swim. She was hoping that one day his love for swimming would return. "Yes. I need to change into my swimsuit. I also need to call my parents back. They called when we were at the concert."

The concert she was referring to was a noonday musical featuring several popular R & B, jazz and pop music groups performing at the Staples Center. They had gotten tickets compliments of the mayor of LA as a way to thank Randi for her assistance with LA law enforcement.

Thirty minutes later, she and Quasar were walking on the beach while holding hands. "How're your parents?" he asked her.

"Fine. They're back in the States now. Everyone is gearing up for Trey's birthday celebration next weekend." She was quiet a moment and then asked, "Would you like to attend with me?"

She had no idea what his response would be. Although she thought she'd done a pretty good job with all her seduction attempts, she had no idea if they were breaking down any of his walls. So far he hadn't given any indication that he wanted more than they were sharing now. Namely a bed. As far as she knew, when they parted company this weekend, she would go her way and he would go his.

"I'd love to go to your brother's birthday party with you."

She smiled. His words gave her hope. "Thanks."

"And now I'd like to invite you to go somewhere with me."

She lifted a brow. "Where?"

"A wedding. Striker and Margo have set a date. It's the fourth Saturday next month."

Randi's smile widened. She knew how close he and Striker were. To ask her to attend with him meant something, didn't it? "A June wedding. How wonderful."

Quasar nodded. "Yeah. He's found true love, and I'm happy for him and wish him the best. It could not have happened to a more deserving guy." He paused before adding, "But then, he's never had a woman break his heart. If he had, I doubt he would be so quick to chance it again."

His words tore into her heart. Their time together in Malibu, all her seductive efforts, hadn't done anything to change his mind about love. Had all her efforts only shown him the physical side of a relationship and not the emotional? Regardless of his feelings for her, she was convinced she loved him more today than she had yesterday. Her love for Quasar increased daily. Every hour, minute and second.

When they reached the water, he plopped down to sit

in the sand. "I love watching you swim," he said, gazing up at her.

She chuckled. "Is it that or the skimpy bikini I have on, especially when wet?"

"I admit that it's both."

She laughed. "At least you're honest. Okay, here goes," she said, removing her wrap and loving how he tilted up his aviator sunglasses to gaze appreciatively at her. What made her swimsuit even more special to her was that when they'd gone shopping, this was the one he selected, saying he thought it would look good on her.

"Just remember, Randi. I am watching you."

She smiled. "And I hope you enjoy doing so."

"Trust me, I love every inch of everything I see."

Randi tossed her head back to laugh, and then she raced off toward the cool ocean waters. It did something to her knowing he was sitting there, watching her every move.

She started off doing backstrokes, breaststrokes, the butterfly, sidestrokes and freestyle. From the look of admiration in his eyes, she could tell that he was impressed with her swimming skills. A short while later, she swam over to him.

"You're good," he said, smiling.

"Thanks." Deciding to be mischievous, she splashed some ocean water on him.

"Hey, you're getting me wet."

"That's the idea," she said, dousing him again. "If you can't get the man in the water, then you bring the water to the man."

He grabbed at her, but she was too fast and took off running along the water's edge. "I'm going to catch you."

She glanced over her shoulder while laughing. "No, you're not."

At least she had gotten him to move deeper into in the water, she thought, running from him. Even while walking on the beach, he had refused to wade. Thinking of that made her slow her pace, and the next thing she knew, he'd grabbed her.

"So you want to get me wet, do you?" he asked, bringing her dripping body close to his.

She wrapped her arms around his neck. "And why not? You get me wet all the time," she said, smiling at him, knowing he understood her play on words.

"Let me see if I can make you wet now," he murmured huskily, leaning in and capturing her lips. At that moment, she forgot everything except his taste and his touch. All she could do was concentrate on how his tongue was taking over her mouth. This was the kind of kiss that could spiral her straight into ecstasy. It had happened a number of times they'd been together. He'd made her come just from his kiss.

She wasn't sure how long they stood in the waist-deep water, kissing like it would be their last time to do so. When he finally released her mouth, she felt rapid sensations of need infiltrate her entire body.

Evidently he was experiencing the same sensations, because he leaned close to her lips to whisper, *"Me vuelves loco."*

He might think she was driving him crazy, but he was definitely doing the same to her. She loved him and knew she would always love him.

"Come on. Let's head back," he said, draping his arm over her shoulders as they began walking.

He stopped halfway to the house, turned and pulled

her into his arms to kiss her again. She had a feeling he enjoyed devouring her mouth, kissing her with an urgency and greed that had quakes of desire rushing all through her.

"Maybe we shouldn't watch any movies tonight," he suggested after breaking off the kiss and taking her hand to continue their walk toward his home.

"Quasar! Quasar! Is that you?"

They both turned at the sound of the feminine voice to find a blond-haired woman walking quickly toward them. The first thing Randi thought was that she was model material. Simply gorgeous. Even in the afternoon heat, there didn't appear to be a strand of her hair out of place. Definitely not wet and limp like hers was now.

The woman was wearing a pair of white shorts showing long, tan legs and a short blue midriff top that nearly matched the color of her eyes. She was also wearing a huge smile on her attractive face.

When she got within a few feet of Quasar, she released a loud shriek. "It is you!"

And then, nearly knocking Randi out of the way, the woman threw herself into Quasar's arms.

QUASAR PRIED HIMSELF out of the woman's embrace and took a step back as a smile touched his lips. "You're getting all wet, Kendra."

"I don't care. It's so good seeing you again. It's been years."

"Ten exactly," he said. "And you look the same. Beautiful as ever."

"Liar, although I will accept your compliments. I heard you were back."

He lifted a brow. "Did you?"

"Yes. You remember Ms. Marion who lives a couple of doors down? She mentioned that she thought she saw you on the beach."

"I see." Quasar glanced at Randi, who was standing to the side. It hadn't gone past him that Kendra was deliberately ignoring her. Typical Kendra. Some things never changed and her wanting to be the center of attention was one of them. She was beautiful but spoiled rotten to the core.

"Randi," he said, reaching his hand out to her. "Come here a minute, *mi tesoro*."

Randi tried keeping the look of surprise from her face when Quasar referred to her as his treasure. She took the hand he offered. "Randi, I want you to meet an old friend. Kendra Biltmore. Kendra, this is Randi Fuller."

As expected, she and Kendra exchanged polite pleasantries. Although Randi couldn't get a read on the woman, she didn't miss Kendra's close scrutiny of her. A part of her felt immediate resentment from the woman. Why? Randi knew about Quasar's past relationship with Lilly. Was this someone he'd conveniently not mentioned? Another old girlfriend, perhaps?

But then Randi had to admit she was doing her own scrutinizing. She'd already accepted the woman's beauty. However, up close she noted signs of Botox. Also, she hadn't missed the wedding ring on Kendra's finger.

"Randi, you look familiar. Are you from around here?" Kendra asked as she studied her features.

Randi pasted a smile on her face. "No, I'm from Virginia."

"Oh." The woman continued to stare at her, and then her eyes lit up. She said, "Wait a minute. You're *that* Randi Fuller. The psychic. A photo of you has been plastered all over the television this week. You helped the FBI and LAPD catch some hideous criminal."

Quasar pulled Randi closer to his side while draping his arm around her shoulder. He leaned in and pressed a kiss to her forehead. "Yes, she did."

"Wow. It must be kind of weird going through life doing stuff like that. Sounds pretty bizarre and creepy."

So Kendra thought she could jab at her that way, did she? "Weird? Bizarre? Creepy? No, it's not really," Randi said, forcing a smile. "In fact, I feel lucky to have been chosen to have such an extraordinary gift. Some people live their lives each day with nothing to show for it. No real purpose. I'm glad I don't have that problem."

Quasar placed another kiss to her forehead. "Well said, which is why I think you're the most terrific woman I've ever met."

"But she goes around predicting people's futures, forecasting stuff and reading people," Kendra accused.

Randi laughed. "I'm not that good or else I would have won the lotto many times over. However, I do confess that on occasion, I can read some people, but not everyone. I can't read you. Usually that's the case when there's too much negative energy. I'm sure with you, it must be something else."

Randi didn't miss the daggered look in the woman's eyes. "Yes, it must be something else, since I'm the most positive person you'll ever meet."

And then, as if dismissing Randi, she turned to Quasar. "How long will you be in town? Have you visited your family yet? Have you seen Lilly?"

Randi wondered why Kendra would ask him about Lilly. "I'll be in town until the weekend," Quasar responded. "And no, I haven't seen the family yet, but I will before leaving."

"Well, I would love to have you over for dinner. What are you doing tomorrow night? Byron is out of town on business, and he will hate that he missed seeing you."

Quasar chuckled. "Unless your husband has changed his attitude over the years, I seriously doubt that."

Kendra reached out and touched Quasar's arm. "But you will have dinner with me tomorrow night, won't you? For old times' sake. We can catch up on stuff," she said, batting her long eyelashes at him. "I'm one of your neighbors now. Mom and Dad gave me the cottage when they purchased a bigger place in Pacific Palisades."

Quasar held his smile. "Thanks for the invite, but Randi and I must decline. Our visit here is packed with too many activities already."

Randi drew in a deep breath. The woman's invitation hadn't included her and Quasar had known that. Yet without missing a beat, he'd let Kendra know if he was invited, that meant the invitation extended to Randi. The realization sent a warm feeling rushing through her.

"Well, maybe next time. I hope this is just the beginning and you plan to come back home more often."

Quasar's smile was noncommittal when he said, "Maybe and maybe not. Now, if you'll excuse us, Randi and I have plans for the evening. It was good seeing you again, Kendra. Give my best to your parents…and to Byron."

"Oh. Yes, of course."

Taking Randi's hand, he led her back toward his beach house.

CHAPTER THIRTY-TWO

"So was Kendra one of your girlfriends back in the day?"

Quasar slid another movie into the DVD player. He returned to his seat beside her on the sofa, lifting Randi to place her in his lap as before. He enjoyed having her snuggled close to him like this, where he could kiss her any time he wanted.

He rested his chin on top of her head, loving the smell of her and the silky feel of her hair. When they returned from the beach they'd showered together, which had taken longer than usual since they'd also used that time to make love. Then she had assisted him in the kitchen. After dinner they got ready for movie night. He was a little surprised she hadn't asked him anything about Kendra before now.

"What gave you the idea she's an old girlfriend?"

She tilted her head back to look up at him. "She was kind of huggy, touchy and grabby. And you did introduce her as an old friend."

"She is. At least she was once, but not that way. In fact, for years she was Doyle's girlfriend. I was surprised to hear they'd broken up and he'd married Lilly." At least he *had* been surprised until Lucinda's last visit to him in prison. When he'd asked her about it, she'd been truthful. It seemed Doyle had bragged to Kendra that he'd beat going to jail when the old man had persuaded Quasar to be the sacrificial lamb. Kendra threatened to tell the authorities the truth unless they paid her to keep quiet. His father had, to the tune of a million dollars.

"Oh. I take it that you and her husband, Byron, didn't get along."

Quasar shook his head. "In school Byron and Doyle despised each other. Since I was Doyle's brother, Byron pretty much gave me grief any time he got the chance."

He was glad when the movie began playing and stole Randi's attention. However, his thoughts remained not only on Kendra but also on the phone call he'd gotten earlier today. Louis again, assuming he was still calling the shots. He had stated there would be a dinner party in Quasar's honor tomorrow night and all but demanded he bring *the woman* with him.

Quasar knew with only three days left in Los Angeles, he couldn't put off visiting his family any longer. He preferred Randi not meet his over-the-top family. He had to prepare mentally for the reunion himself. But then another part of him felt she needed to meet them to understand the dysfunction. It would be up to her if she wanted to go or not.

By the time they'd watched two movies, it was close to two in the morning. He couldn't blame the late night entirely on the flicks since he'd paused the DVDs a few times while they'd made love right there on the couch. Whenever she was in his arms or he in hers, an aura of completeness always filled him.

"You're thinking too hard," Randi said, interrupting his thoughts and sitting straight up in his lap to massage his temples.

"I have a lot to think about."

She lifted a brow. "Do you?"

"Yes. Louis called today. He's planning a dinner party tomorrow night to welcome me home."

"That's nice."

He ran his fingers through the tendrils of hair that fanned her face. Were her lips still wet from their earlier kiss? Certainly looked that way. Seeing evidence of his desire increased his longing for her even more. "He asked me to bring you," he said, trying not to think too hard about kissing her again. Especially when they needed to talk.

A look of surprise shone in her eyes. "Me?"

"Yes."

"He knows about me?"

He continued to run his fingers through her hair. "He knows I'm here with a woman, thanks to one of the neighbors."

She was peering at him intently. "And what do you want, Quasar?" she asked softly.

He fought back the urge to say, *To kiss you again. All over. Taste you. Especially between your legs. Then make love to you all night long.* Instead he removed his fingers from her hair and said in a frustrated tone, "Honestly, I'd rather you didn't get caught up in my father's manipulations and his craziness, but you were invited. Whether you go is your decision. But if you do accept his invitation, don't be surprised when the place is filled with all that negative energy you told Kendra about today."

He watched her nibble on her bottom lip, followed by a sweep of her tongue. It was a purely innocent yet erotic gesture that had even more desire twisting his insides.

She wrapped her arms around his neck. "I'll go. I want to be there for you. Besides, I want to meet the man who fathered you."

"Why?"

"I just do, so yes, I will attend the dinner party with you."

He searched her face. "You sure?"

"Yes, I'm sure."

"Okay," he said, pushing her hair back from her face. "Tomorrow we'll go to the dinner party together."

HOURS LATER, RANDI felt content lying naked in Quasar's arms. She had enjoyed their time together last night. The movies they'd watched and all those naughty activities in between. A part of her could feel their relationship shifting. He had accepted her invitation to attend Trey's birthday celebration, and he had asked her to attend his good friend's wedding. She saw that as a promising start to something beyond what they were sharing here in LA.

Tomorrow she would meet his family, and she couldn't stop the tingles of excitement flowing through her. What she'd told him earlier hadn't been the total truth. Yes, she looked forward to meeting his father. But more than any-thing, she couldn't wait to meet Lilly. The woman who'd promised to wait for him but had married his brother in-stead. Randi didn't want to form negative opinions of the woman who'd broken Quasar's heart but was finding it difficult not to do so.

Since she hadn't brought anything dressy enough to wear to a dinner party, especially one held in Beverly Hills, she intended to go shopping tomorrow. She wanted Quasar to be proud to be seen with her.

And speaking of Quasar…she felt his body shift and the arms around her tighten. She loved sleeping nude with him with her back brushing against his hairy chest. And she definitely liked the way his leg was thrown over hers and his hand rested mere inches from her sex. More than once she'd come awake during the night with his hands stroking her down there.

He'd awakened. She knew it from the sound of his breathing. And then there was that telltale sign of his huge erection poking into her backside. After all they'd done last night, she would have thought sex was the last thing on his mind at six in the morning.

Their normal routine in the mornings had been to watch the sun rise while sitting on the beach, drinking coffee. But not this morning after going to bed so late. And then, once they'd gotten into bed, they hadn't gone to sleep.

"You're awake?"

His husky voice close to her ear sent desire racing through her loins. She couldn't help but smile at how quickly her body responded to him. "Who wants to know?"

"My friend down there. Feel him?"

Yes, she felt him. He seemed to have gotten bigger and harder. Quasar was such a virile man, and his libido was unlike any she'd ever heard about. "Yes, I feel him."

"He wants you again."

"He's greedy," she said, feeling his erection enlarge even more.

She heard a soft chuckle. "Yes, he's greedy. But only when it comes to you, *nena*."

Now that he knew she understood Spanish, he spoke it more often. Mostly while making love. There was something about talking naughty in Spanish. Especially when the words came from Quasar's lips. The thought that he found her so desirable, that she was a woman who could stoke his fire, only made her savor her time with him even more.

"Te echo de menos," he whispered hotly, shifting his body and hers to straddle her.

She smiled up at him. "How can you miss me when I haven't been anywhere but right here, lying beside you?"

He returned her smile, and her heart pounded in her chest. Randi loved his unshaven look and the way his hair looked tousled around his face. She reached up and pushed a few strands out the way so she could see his eyes. His sexy brown bedroom eyes.

"Can't explain it, but I do."

She didn't say anything but inwardly wondered if he would miss her as much after they parted ways. Would she remain in his mind? His thoughts? When he lowered his mouth to hers, she hoped that one day she would somehow wiggle her way into his heart.

CHAPTER THIRTY-THREE

"I'M READY, QUASAR."

Quasar's gaze slid over Randi as he rose from the sofa. For the longest time all he could do was stand there and stare. What had she done to herself? She was a beautiful woman, but now she looked even more so. Her hair was no longer straight but was styled in bouncy curls that framed her face.

And her outfit…

He'd gone shopping with her today and was with her when she picked this particular dress off the rack to try on. But she hadn't wanted him to see her in it until now. All he'd known was that it was red. The color suited. The dress fit her figure perfectly, molding to all her luscious curves in a sexy yet not too provocative way. The hem hit her just above the knees and showed off the beauty of her legs in a pair of high heels. A wrap was draped across her shoulders, covering up skin he loved to lick.

"What do you think?" she asked, slowly twirling around so he could see her from front to back.

He shoved his hands into the pockets of his dress slacks. "I think maybe we should cancel and stay here and do other things."

She laughed. "Honestly, what do you think?"

A smile curved his lips. "Honestly, I think we should cancel and stay here and do other things."

She waved off his words dismissively. "We can't disappoint your father."

Quasar snorted. "Trust me, I can and wouldn't lose any sleep over doing so. You look beautiful. I'm tempted to strip this dress off you right now. But I'll be patient. Consider yourself forewarned."

"You have patience?" she asked jokingly. Now it was her gaze roaming over him. "You look awfully handsome."

He glanced down at himself and chuckled. "Just a little something that I threw together." He'd purchased a dinner jacket to go with the dress slacks he'd packed.

"And you threw it together so well," she said, looping her arms through his. "But then, Mr. Patterson, I've discovered you have a knack for doing things well." She leaned up and placed a kiss on his cheek. "I'm looking forward to the evening."

As they headed for the door to leave, Quasar was surprised to realize he, too, was looking forward to the evening. Why not? He had a beautiful woman by his side. One he trusted and knew would have his back regardless of what went down tonight. Over the past few days he'd compared Randi to Lilly and knew there was no comparison. The thought that she was beginning to mean a lot to him didn't bother him as it once did. His thoughts then shifted to Louis. He intended to get some answers tonight and would not be putting up with his father's bullshit anymore.

RANDI SHOULD NOT HAVE been surprised at the sprawling mansion they pulled up to an hour later. After all, this was Beverly Hills, and every estate they'd passed had circular driveways and similar massive structures. During the drive, Quasar had told her that both he and his brother had been born in this house and had grown up with a household staff, various on-premise cooks, gardeners and the like.

"It seems a lot of people were invited this evening," she said when he came around to her side of the car to open the door for her. There were a number of other cars and valet parking.

"I'm not surprised," Quasar responded dispassionately when the valet attendant arrived. "I haven't been home in ten years and he intends to put me on display."

She didn't say anything as he took her hand and gathered her close and they began walking toward the massive front door.

A dismal-faced butler opened the door and smiled when he saw Quasar. The man had to be in his seventies, or even close to eighty. "Mr. Quasar, it's so good to see you."

Randi saw the huge smile that touched Quasar's lips before Quasar reached out to hug the man. "Barnes, I can't believe you're still here. I figured you would have retired by now. And how's Queenie?"

The smile on the older man's face sobered, and Randi saw the flash of pain in his eyes before he said in an anguished tone, "I lost Queenie to cancer three years ago."

The smile left Quasar's lips, as well. "I'm sorry to hear that. Queenie was a special woman."

A slight smile returned to the older man's lips. "Thank you."

Turning to Randi, Quasar said, "This is Barnes, and his wife, Queenie, used to be head of housekeeping here. Barnes, this is Randi Fuller."

Randi smiled as she offered the man her hand. It was easy to see Quasar thought a lot of the people employed by his father. She could imagine how difficult it had been to cut ties with them, as well. Whether he'd done it to protect himself from his father and brother or to protect the staff really didn't matter. Either way, he'd had to separate himself from people he cared about. "It's nice meeting you, Barnes, and I'm sorry for the loss of your wife." Although his handshake was strong, Randi thought his hand felt frail in hers.

"Thanks, Ms. Randi. Queenie and I had fifty-eight good years together."

"You still think it's okay to fraternize with the hired help, I see."

Randi turned when she heard the booming masculine voice. Standing less than ten feet away was the same man she'd seen on television, Quasar's brother, Doyle. Even if she hadn't known the relationship between the two beforehand, it would have been easy to tell they were brothers. The two had the same stature and build, although Quasar seemed to have outgrown his older brother by a few inches. And they had similar facial features and skin coloring. However, in her opinion, Quasar was more striking.

Her gaze moved from the man to the woman standing by his side, whose arm he seemed to be clutching possessively. The woman stared at Quasar with what appeared to be both regret and remorse in her eyes. This was Lilly. And in Randi's opinion, she was even more stunning in person than she had been on television. She was absolutely, positively beautiful.

"And evidently you haven't been fraternizing enough," Quasar said. "Still consider yourself above others, I see, Doyle."

Quasar's biting words cut into Randi's curiosity about Lilly. She had to agree that Quasar's theory had been

right. She was unable to read Lilly or Doyle due to the
negativity surrounding them. In fact, she'd picked up on
it the moment Barnes had opened the door. She had a
feeling this had not been a happy place for Quasar while
growing up, and his brother had had a lot to do with it.

She watched as the couple moved toward them, their
every step in sync as if the measured movements had
been choreographed.

When the couple came to a stop in front of them,
Randi noticed the woman's gaze hadn't moved off Quasar. She decided not to check whether Quasar was studying Lilly just as intently. Up close Randi saw that, like
Kendra, Lilly had blond hair and blue eyes. But Lilly's
beauty appeared more natural, and unlike Kendra's, it
hadn't been enhanced with Botox.

"Welcome home, Quay," the woman said softly, ef-
fectively slicing into the tension surrounding Quasar and
his brother.

"Thank you, Lilly. You're looking well."

"And so are you."

Randi continued to watch the scene played out before her. The two brothers had yet to shake hands, fist-
bump or bear-hug. They stood facing each other as if
adversaries.

After a long moment, Quasar finally stretched out
his hand as if it took him a lot of effort. "Doyle, you're
looking well, also."

It seemed as if Doyle had no intention of accepting
the hand Quasar offered, but then he did. "No reason
why I shouldn't." And then, without as much as returning Quasar's compliment, he looked at his watch. "Glad
you're on time. Had you been late, the old man wouldn't
have been happy."

"And you think I give a damn?" was Quasar's smooth-as-silk comeback.

"No, you never did."

Evidently deciding to intervene before the tension between the brothers could boil over, Lilly extended her hand to Randi. "I believe introductions are in order, Quasar," Lilly said.

"Randi, I'd like you to meet my brother and his wife, Doyle and Lilly Patterson." He then said, "Doyle, Lilly, this is a good friend of mine, Randi Fuller."

Doyle's head snapped up. "Randi Fuller?" Then, for the first time, he gave her more than a mere cursory glance. "You're the psychic. Your photo has been all over the news the last couple of days. As the future mayor of Beverly Hills, I want to add my thanks for what you did to keep Los Angeles safe. Nothing like getting the undesirables off the street and in jail where they belong," he said, offering her his hand.

"Glad I could help."

Instead of releasing her hand, Doyle held on to it, smiled and said, "So did Quasar bring you here to do a reading on us?"

"No," she said, pasting a smile on her lips. "It's Saturday. My day off. I don't work on weekends."

Doyle stared at her blankly, and she knew he was trying to figure out if she was joking or not. He quickly recovered and said, "I like you, Randi Fuller."

She didn't say anything to that because already she knew she definitely didn't like him.

A SHORT WHILE LATER, Randi discovered she disliked Quasar's father even more. Although Louis Patterson was a handsome man for his age and exuded an air of charismatic kindness, she could easily pick up on another aspect of his character. She could tell he was an unscrupulous SOB. Now she knew what Quasar meant when he'd said the man was controlling. It was obvious he was in command and running the show when it came to Doyle and Lilly. Randi could only surmise it had been that way once with his handling of Quasar. Tonight the man's frustrations were quite obvious with Quasar's outright refusal to be manipulated or intimidated.

Quasar hadn't left her side. She couldn't help but notice the guests steered clear of her and Quasar after polite introductions. Quasar whispered teasingly, "The reason they're acting antisocial toward us is that now they know you're a psychic, and they're afraid you might latch on to their dark secrets."

She glanced up at Quasar and smiled at the jest. Considering Quasar was the guest of honor, very few people said anything to him. "You think that's what it is?"

"Yes, which is fine with me. I'd rather be alone with you than making small talk with any of them."

Taking a sip of her wine, she glanced around the room, and another female caught her attention. "Quasar?"

"Yes?"

"That woman standing over there in the blue dress. Do you know her? She keeps looking over here, trying not to be obvious that she's doing so."

Quasar looked across the room. "I've never seen her before, but I understand she's old man Carter's new wife. He's still robbing the cradle. I see. William Carter is older than my father, and his wife looks to be my age if not a few years older."

Randi noticed William Carter wasn't the only old man

there with a young wife. "Dinner was great, by the way," she said, being totally truthful.

The food had definitely been the highlight of the evening. A five-course meal had been presented by servers dressed in crisp, white uniforms with matching gloves. All twenty invitees had sat at a table set in a dining room with furnishings fit for a queen. It was hard to believe that all this wealth, elegance and prosperity had been a part of Quasar's past. A past he'd chosen not to return to.

"Before we leave, I will introduce you to Dori, the head cook. She's been at the Patterson Estates for as long as Barnes has." He paused a minute to take a sip of his wine and then added, "She makes the best peanut butter cookies."

Randi smiled as she listened to Quasar tell her about all his favorite dishes that Dori would prepare. Moments later she wondered if she was the only one who noticed Doyle, who'd been standing with a group of men, give a silent nod to William Carter's wife. As if on cue, the woman whispered something to her husband and then disappeared down a long hall. Moments later, Doyle excused himself from the men and moved down that same hall. Hmm. Interesting.

She looked for Lilly and saw her standing across the room with a group of people. Lilly's gaze was glued to the same hallway both her husband and the woman had disappeared down. Even from a distance, Randi could see anger flare in Lilly's eyes.

At that moment it became clear to Randi that Lilly was very much aware her husband had invited his mistress here tonight.

CHAPTER THIRTY-FOUR

QUASAR GLANCED AROUND his father's study. Other than new furniture, nothing had changed. He had the same expensive portraits on the walls and several artifacts acquired during his hunting safaris in Africa. Quasar was surprised to see that the huge painting of his mother still hung over the fireplace. She had been a beautiful woman. His mother had meant everything to him, and her death had left a void that it had taken him years to get over. He then thought about Randi. He believed Elaina would have liked her had they met.

While Quasar waited for his father, Lilly was supposedly giving Randi a tour of the place. He knew that was just Lilly's ruse to question Randi about the true nature of their relationship. He had all the confidence in the world that Randi could hold her own with the likes of Lilly.

"There had better be a damn good reason you pulled me away from my guests, Quasar." Louis entered the room with an irritated expression on his face.

Quasar had waited until the last of the guests had left before telling the old man to meet him in his study. So his father's claim was nothing but bluster. "I wanted to speak privately with you before I left."

Louis moved to sit in the chair behind his desk. "You wouldn't have to if you had agreed to spend the night."

Staying under this roof was the last thing Quasar

would agree to. "I have no reason to stay here. I have my home in Malibu."

"Then what's so pressing that you had to meet with me tonight? If you need to borrow money, the answer is no. I know about all that money Lucinda left you. If you've squandered it already, that's your problem, not mine."

Anger radiated through Quasar as he stared at the man who'd fathered him. "My only problem is regretting how I allowed you to treat me over the years. It was always obvious Doyle was your favorite, and I want to know why. You can't claim I'm not your biological son. So what the hell did I ever do to you to make you hate me?"

His father leaned forward as if to make to certain Quasar heard whatever words he was about to say. "You want to know why? Then I'll tell you why," he said in a steely voice. "What you did to me was be born."

"HE STILL LOVES ME, you know."

Randi turned her attention to Lilly. The woman had given her a tour of the monstrosity of a house…not that she'd asked for one. Now they were walking side by side in the brightly lit backyard where an Olympic-size pool as well as a tennis court were located. "Who still loves you?"

Lilly smiled over at her. "Quasar, of course. I saw it in his eyes the moment our gazes connected. Although it's been years, the love is still there."

"And you're telling me this…why?"

"Just in case you get any ideas about a future with him. I think I ruined him for any other woman."

She'd certainly done that, Randi thought. "You say that like betrayal is something to be proud of." She saw her barb land as Lilly flinched. "Why would you think he still loves you when you're married to his brother?"

"Once I talk to Quay, I'll explain everything."

Randi wondered what there was to explain. "Did Doyle force you into marrying him?" she asked, figuring there had to be something she was missing for Lilly to think she could be so disloyal to Quasar and he would still love her.

Lilly chuckled. "Of course I wasn't forced. Quay was gone, and Doyle was here. Besides, Quay would never have gone to jail had he stood up for himself and told the authorities the truth."

"The truth?"

"Yes. I'm sure Quay has told you he only confessed to the land fraud to keep Doyle from going to jail. Louis asked him to do it for the good of the family."

No, Quasar had not told her that. It was hard to believe his own father persuaded him to go to jail. How crazy was that? Quasar had alluded to the fact that none of his family visited him while confined. Not even Doyle, the brother he'd been serving time for? Unbelievable.

Pretending Quasar had told her, Randi said, "I agree that Quasar should not have served time for something Doyle did, but you did promise to wait for him."

Lilly shrugged. "Three years was a long time. Doyle began showing me attention, buying me stuff and taking me places. What was I supposed to do?"

"Keep your promise to Quasar."

Lilly stopped walking, and her spine became ramrod straight. "Well, I didn't, but he will forgive me anyway."

The woman certainly didn't lack any confidence. "You think so?"

"Yes. He loves me too much not to. I'll admit when I

saw the way he was clinging to you tonight, I was a little concerned. But then I overheard Louis tell Doyle that there was nothing serious between you and Quay. When Louis talked to him a couple of days ago, Quay stated he was in town on business. That means you're business to him and nothing more. We know what he does for a living now, so it made sense that he was hired to protect you."

Randi shook her head. Lilly thought she had it all figured out. "So you think business is the only thing between me and Quasar?" she asked as they resumed walking.

Lilly chuckled again. "Oh, I'm not saying the two of you aren't sleeping together since I, of all people, know how much Quay enjoys sex. All I'm saying is that you mean nothing to him."

Randi smiled, knowing the woman was probably right, but not for the reason she assumed. "Are you trying to convince me or yourself of that, Lilly?"

Not waiting for the woman to respond and deciding she'd tolerated as much of Lilly Patterson's company as she could handle, Randi excused herself and began walking toward the patio that led back inside the house.

Once away from Lilly, she paused to regain her composure before going inside, and she heard raised voices coming from a room off the patio. They were angry voices, and one them belonged to Quasar.

"WHAT DO YOU MEAN that what I did to you was be born?" Quasar roared.

"Just what I said. I never wanted any children. Elaina knew that when we married. But one night she used her feminine wiles on me, and the next thing I knew, I was agreeing to give her a baby."

Louis paused a minute as if he was remembering that time. "When Doyle was born, I was happy that she had changed my mind about fatherhood. The moment they placed Doyle in my arms, I knew it was meant to be."

Then Louis's expression changed. It went from contentment to anger. "But Elaina wasn't satisfied. When Doyle turned three, she tried to talk me into another child, and I refused to consider it. I told her then that I honestly didn't have enough love in my heart for another child. That Doyle was all I wanted. But your mother got pregnant anyway and lied and said it was an accident. I didn't believe her and told her to abort the baby. When she refused, I made it clear to her that I wanted no part of the baby when it was born, and I meant it."

Quasar couldn't believe what he was hearing. "Let me get this straight. All these years you've mistreated me because I was an accident?"

"You weren't an accident. Your mother knew what she was doing. She deliberately got pregnant."

"And you hardened your heart against the child? Against me? A child you helped create?"

"She was warned."

Quasar was furious. "You never gave me a chance. No matter what I did, it never met your satisfaction, was never good enough for you. Your whole world centered around Doyle. Dammit, you have two sons!"

"Yes, but only one has my heart."

His father's words cut him to the core. Sliced right through his heart. How could anyone be so cold, unloving? So damn cruel? He had this man's blood running through his veins, yet his father would never love or accept him. "Do you know what you're saying?" Quasar asked in a voice filled with rage.

"You asked and I'm telling you. I am being truthful. If you want to be angry with anyone, then let it be your mother for defying me and getting pregnant."

Quasar shook his head. No wonder his mother had gone out of her way to make sure he felt loved. This is what his godmother hadn't been able to tell him. She'd known but had felt he needed to hear it directly from his father. And he had.

"Now that I know the truth, I want closure. You can continue to live your life with the only son you claim you can love. By your own lips, you've admitted you don't love me."

His father waved off his words. "Regardless of that, you're my son and you're needed back here. To work for the company. To take Doyle's place since he's going into politics."

Quasar drew in a deep breath. What kind of sense did that make? This man had just told him that he didn't love him. That he could never love him because he didn't want to share any of the love he had for Doyle. That Quasar had been a baby he hadn't wanted. Still didn't want to this day. He'd always thought the situation between him and his father was crazy, but it was worse than crazy. It was royally fucked.

At that moment, Quasar knew he was not really Louis's son. At least not in all the ways that mattered. As he traced back all the years in his mind, living with his father's dismissive, demeaning, controlling behavior, he now knew that he had never truly been his son…except when Louis needed to use him to protect Doyle.

Quasar shoved his hands deep into the pockets of his slacks. It was either that or hit something. Rage filled him when he knew that it shouldn't. All his life he'd known his father was an asshole, but now Quasar saw him as worse than that. What father could not love a child who came from his own seed, regardless of the circumstances surrounding his birth? He would never allow himself to be used and mentally abused by his father and Doyle again.

"I refuse to love someone who could never love me. Who has, in fact, actively gone out of his way to hate me. Goodbye, Louis."

With those words, words that might very well be the final words he would ever say to his father, he looked into those I-don't-give-a-damn-about-you blue eyes and walked out of the study as deep pain ripped out his heart.

CHAPTER THIRTY-FIVE

RANDI HAD HEARD EVERYTHING and wasn't sure what to say. Quasar was quiet as they drove away from his family's home. Quasar's and his father's voices had been loud, and the words the men had spoken had carried for anyone close by to hear.

She was sure everyone had heard…and listened. She, Doyle, Lilly and most of the servants who had been bustling about, trying to straighten up and bring order after tonight's dinner party. They had heard Louis Patterson tell his youngest son that he didn't have room in his heart to love him. How cruel was that?

She had been standing outside the door, waiting for Quasar, when he'd walked out of the study. Lilly and Doyle were there, as well. When Quasar opened the door, his gaze immediately went behind her to his brother. She turned, hoping he would get some kind of support there, but instead Doyle had the gall to stand with a damn smirk on his face while twirling a glass of champagne between his fingers.

At that moment, she knew that Doyle Patterson was just as big a bastard as his father. She was not a violent person, but knowing now that Quasar had spent three years in prison for a crime he didn't commit, all to protect Doyle, a man who had the audacity to find what had happened between Louis and Quasar amusing, was almost too much. She was tempted to slap that grin right off Doyle's face.

Evidently the same thought had run through Quasar's mind, because she could see his hands tightening into fists at his sides. But instead of crossing the room to Doyle or even looking in the direction of Lilly, he said to Randi in a low, husky voice that was filled with emotions he was trying hard not to reveal, "We can leave now."

When they reached the door, Barnes was there, and Randi saw the sheen of tears in the older man's eyes. Quasar and the man exchanged a bear hug, and she heard Barnes say in a low, broken voice, "Take care of yourself, Mr. Quasar."

Instead of answering, Quasar nodded before walking out the door. She gave the older man a hug, as well, and nodded when he whispered in her ear, "Please take care of Ms. Elaina's boy, Ms. Randi. He's going to need you."

While waiting for the valet to bring the car, Randi wasn't surprised when Lilly appeared. Ignoring the fact that Randi and Quasar stood side by side, Lilly went to Quasar and reached up as if to stroke his face. Quasar caught her hand before she could touch him and pushed it away. "Don't do that, Lilly."

Lilly had the nerve to tell him, "Louis didn't mean what he said in there, Quay."

Quasar chuckled derisively. "Oh, he meant it."

Lilly frowned. "So you're leaving? What about me?"

As if her question didn't make any sense, he asked harshly, "What about you?"

"You still love me. I know it. Stay in LA. We can be together. Doyle has a mistress. She was here tonight and—"

Randi watched the anger in Quasar's face spread from his eyes to encompass all his features. Lilly must have observed it, as well, because she had the good sense to take a step back.

"What makes you think that I still love you?" Quasar demanded. "That is the most ridiculous thing I've ever heard. I stopped loving you years ago, Lilly. When I realized just what kind of person you are. For years I called myself all kinds of fool for ever wasting my love on you. Just look at you. You are Doyle's wife, yet you want me to hang around. For what? To play second to my brother like I've always done? Marrying Doyle was your decision, so you can deal with him and his whores any way you see fit. Personally, I don't give a damn."

Randi was certain Quasar would have said more if the valet attendant hadn't chosen that moment to deliver the car to them. Ignoring Lilly, Quasar opened the car door for Randi before settling himself in the driver's seat. Without giving Lilly a second glance, he pulled away.

Since leaving the party, Randi had endured his silence. She loved him, and it pained her to know the man she loved was hurting. She felt at a loss because she didn't know what to say to give him comfort. To take away his pain.

When he brought the car to a stop at a red light, she decided she couldn't take the silence any longer. "Quasar?"

He glanced over at her, and her heart swelled with even more love for him. His eyes, which were usually full of life and energy, now appeared dull and unresponsive.

"Please talk to me," she said. "Tell me what you're feeling so I can help."

Instead of saying anything, he turned his attention back to the road to stare straight ahead. A few seconds ticked by before he said in a defeated, lifeless voice, "You can't help, Randi. This is something I have to deal with on my own. There's a lot that you don't know."

She figured that much was very true. "I know you went to prison. Served three years for something Doyle did because your father convinced you that it was the right thing to do."

The traffic light changed and he moved the car forward. Without taking his eyes off the road, he said, "I thought you couldn't read me."

"I can't and I didn't."

"Then how did you know that? I never told you."

"No, you didn't. Lilly told me. She was under the impression that I knew already."

He was quiet for a moment, and then he said in a bitter tone filled with anguish, "You know what's so fucking funny, Randi? I came here for closure. I came here knowing Louis didn't give a shit about me. But still, I had to know why so I could move on. Nobody wrote or called while I was locked up. I had the good sense to know it was because they didn't given a damn. That hurt. When I left prison I refused to let my family hurt me again, so I cut them off. I didn't let them know where I'd moved. Then Louis hired a private investigator to find me, and I thought that maybe I'd been wrong. Maybe he had cared. I suggested we meet, away from LA or Charlottesville. On neutral ground, so to speak. He refused. And it then became apparent from his phone calls that it was merely about control. He didn't truly love me, but he wanted to control me."

Randi heard the pain in his voice, and a part of her was tempted to tell him to pull to the side of the road so she could wrap her arms around him. Comfort him. Tell him how much she loved him. How much she truly cared.

"I was determined to move on and make something of my life. I looked toward the future based on the premise that although you can't choose your family, you can definitely choose your friends. So I chose friends who became closer to me than Doyle ever could. On top of that, I befriended a man who was the type of father figure Louis could never be. I felt I no longer needed the Pattersons of Beverly Hills to be content."

He huffed out a frustrated breath and added, "Yet tonight, when I should have found closure, should have been strong enough to walk away and not give a damn, I let the bastard hurt me once again. I allowed him to have that much power over me."

Quasar didn't say anything else during the rest of the car drive back to Malibu, and a part of Randi could feel him withdrawing into himself. Putting distance between them. Even when they reached the house and went inside, he didn't say anything. After locking the door behind them, he moved toward his godmother's bedroom. The one they'd been sharing together.

Before opening the door he stopped, turned to her and in a pained and emotionless voice said, "I need time alone tonight. I'll see you in the morning."

He closed the door behind him. Shutting her out.

RANDI OPENED HER EYES, still unable to sleep. She could hear Quasar moving around in the bedroom below, pacing, as if he was trying to walk off his hurt and pain. She wanted to be there with him. She felt she needed to be there, regardless of the fact that he'd told her he wanted to be alone.

She shifted in bed to lie on her back and stare up at the ceiling. She didn't want to think about what an ass

Louis Patterson had been. Instead she wanted to focus her thoughts on Quasar. By closing the door on her tonight, he had rejected her. But a part of her understood.

She moved her head from side to side on the pillow. No, she understood but wouldn't accept it. She knew he was in pain, but she had to be there for him. What they shared this week counted for something. Granted, she had no reason to think he loved her like she loved him, but she did love him, and she would be there for him. Mind made up, she eased out of bed and grabbed her robe off the chair. He would have to look her dead in the eyes and tell her he didn't want her. That tonight he didn't need her.

Quickly moving down the stairs, within moments she was standing outside the bedroom door. Drawing in a deep breath, she knocked several times. She knew he was in there, and she intended to keep knocking until he opened the door.

She gasped when the door was snatched open and he stood shirtless in a pair of black boxer shorts. A livid expression was on his face as he braced his arms against the doorway. "What do you want, Randi?" he asked in an angry tone. "I told you that—"

"I know what you told me," she said, easing under his arms to enter the room. "But I'm not accepting it. You're mad. You're hurt. I get that. But what I don't get is you not letting me be here with you."

He turned, his expression even angrier. "I don't want you here. I prefer being alone tonight. Is that too much to ask?"

"Yes," she said, flopping down on the bed. "I'm telling you that's too bad, because I'm staying."

Suddenly he lunged toward her as if he intended to remove her physically from the room. He grabbed her around the waist, without much effort threw her over his shoulder like a sack of potatoes and headed for the door. She was convinced he was about to open the door and toss her out on her ass when he suddenly stopped. Lowering her to the floor, he pulled her into his arms and buried his face in her hair. "I told you I wanted to be alone," he whispered brokenly. "Why didn't you listen?"

"I couldn't," she said softly, holding on to him as tightly as he was holding on to her. "No matter what you said, I couldn't let you be alone, hurting. I wanted to be with you. I always want to be with you."

For the longest time they said nothing as they stood there, holding each other. He reached down, lifted her chin with his fingertips and said in a fragmented voice, "I need you tonight in a way I've never needed you before, baby."

She held his gaze as his term of endearment washed over her, making the need to love, protect and soothe him an urgency that plowed through her. "And I need you to need me tonight, Quasar."

Randi figured what she said didn't make sense to him, but maybe it did. He suddenly swept her into his arms and moved toward the bed.

The moment her body touched the bedcovers, he removed her robe and was frantically pulling her nightgown over her head, leaving her totally nude. She saw a look of need and hunger in his eyes as he raked his gaze over her naked body. And then, as if he couldn't take any more looking, he was quickly shoving his briefs down his legs and climbing on the bed with her.

She went to him. He was speaking in Spanish, and she understood everything he was saying, warning her of all the things he intended to do to her tonight. His words were raw, carnal and arousing.

He lifted her hips and buried his head between her legs. Before she could catch her next breath, his tongue had slid between her womanly folds and captured her clit, and he began sucking hard. Her juices flowed while sensations tore into her. He greedily lapped her up, only to start the process all over again.

She grabbed hold of his shoulders to push him away when the pleasure became overwhelming, but in the next instant she was straining, pushing her hips closer to his mouth. He'd never gone down on her before with this much intensity, greed and hunger as if this would be his last meal. His ravenousness was stoking her own, stirring it, multiplying it and generating even more desire and passion. She felt the increase in every pore, and the wildness of the sensations made her dig deep into his back with her nails.

She felt the first signs of orgasmic heaven when he began swirling his tongue around inside her with a tempo that had her vagina throbbing mercilessly. He made her moan. Made her say a few of her own lascivious words in Spanish. When he began sucking hard on her clit again, she couldn't stop from screaming when her body exploded in pieces.

As if he was addicted to her taste, he kept his mouth locked to her until the last spasm left her body, lapping her up and making sounds like he was enjoying every second doing so. When he finally pulled his mouth away, he licked his lips while pulling her up and turning her body around so that she faced the headboard.

She felt the thick head of his shaft rubbing against her backside and thigh before unerringly finding the target between her legs. Her feminine mound was still pulsating from the intensity of his tongue. She felt like she was on fire and needed him to put out the flames.

"I love you this way," he said, sliding his engorged erection inside her. He kept going deep until his groin was smack up against her buttocks. She could feel the thatch of hair covering him as he rubbed against her backside, causing an arousing friction. He kept a firm grip on her thighs as if to lock his body inside hers. He didn't move, giving her body time to adjust, and she understood why. She felt him grow even larger inside her, pushing against her inner muscles, pressing them in a way that had her senses reeling.

Then he began moving, slowly at first in long, languid strokes. Suddenly he picked up the beat, moving faster, pumping hard, hammering deep and thrusting his body into hers. She moaned and groaned. Said his name over and over, shuddering hard under the force of an orgasm that kept on coming and coming. Multiple climaxes ripped into her, making her tip her hips up for him to go deeper inside her. And deeper he went, holding tight to her hips as he repeatedly drove hard into her.

She heard him shout her name at the same time hot semen shot into her, coating every muscle inside her body in a heated warmth that had her groaning in ecstasy. He kept pounding right into another hard erection, and her inner muscles clenched him for more. Within seconds he ejaculated inside her again, and she whispered his name in total satisfaction. He slouched down in bed, pulled her into his arms and held her close with his penis still embedded within her. She felt his warm lips against her neck, and he spoke more Spanish softly in her ear, telling her not to be surprised if he awakened her later to make love to her again. Smiling at his warning, she drifted off to sleep.

QUASAR BREATHED IN Randi's scent as she lay asleep in his arms. They'd made love again. And he had unleashed all the desire he felt for her. The more she gave, the more he wanted. And the more he got.

She had to be the most giving woman he knew. In his eyes she so was special, so damn special. He couldn't help but recall the words she'd whispered before drifting off to sleep. Words he doubted she'd intended for him to hear.

I love you.

The sad thing was that he didn't want her to love him. He was a man a father couldn't even love, so why would she? He didn't need love and didn't want it. Especially from a woman. He'd been there before, and wouldn't ever go there again. And to think Lilly assumed he still loved her after all she'd done.

He rubbed a hand down his stubbled face and felt himself weakening where Randi was concerned. It was getting harder and harder to resist her, to keep her away from his heart. She could be the one woman who was his downfall. The one who could tempt him to love again. And he couldn't let that happen. He needed to put space between them. He needed to think and regroup, and there was no way he could do it here. Not while her scent surrounded him, her beauty captivated him and his sexual need for her overpowered him.

Slowly easing from the bed, he knew what he had to do. He headed for the bedroom door and refused to look back.

CHAPTER THIRTY-SIX

RANDI CAME AWAKE at the feel of someone touching her shoulder. She opened drowsy eyes to see a fully dressed Quasar standing beside the bed. The bit of light shining through the window told her it was the predawn hours.

She pulled up in bed and pushed her hair away from her face. When she focused on his features, she saw an intensity there that worried her. "Quasar? What's wrong?"

"Nothing's wrong. I didn't want to leave without saying goodbye."

Leave? She blinked, trying to grasp what he was saying. "You're leaving?"

"Yes."

"Going where?"

"I'm returning to Charlottesville."

She rubbed sleep from her eyes, certain she hadn't heard correctly. "But why?"

"There's nothing for me here."

I'm here, she wanted to scream. "But—but we have two more days to spend together."

He shook his head. "Trust me, you'll enjoy things more without me here. I wouldn't be very good company."

What he was saying didn't make sense. What would she do here without him? "But this is your house. You can't just leave me here."

"Sure I can, and you're welcome to stay. I left Paul's

number on the kitchen table. Let him know when you leave so he can call the cleaning crew. And I'm leaving you the car. Just turn it in at the airport. The bill was pre-paid. I've called a private car service to come take me to the airport. I'll be on standby."

Randi shook her head, not believing what he was say-ing. "But what about last night?"

He lifted a brow. "What about it?"

"We made love."

He shrugged. "We make love every night. What's the big deal?"

That question pissed her off, and she was out of bed in a flash to stand in front of him, not caring how she looked. "The big deal is that I thought… I had hoped… that I was beginning to mean something to you."

He took a step back. "Whoa! Hold up. I never told you that. In fact, I distinctly remember telling you the same thing I tell all women I bed. I don't do serious."

All women he beds? She shook her head, wanting to believe his words were no more than a front. It had been more than sex between them last night. It had been solace, and it had him running scared, falling back on old habits.

"Look, Randi," he said, breaking into her thoughts. "Evidently you got the wrong idea about a few things."

"Yes, evidently," she said, refusing to lower her pride for any man. Even one she thought had been fated to be hers.

"I enjoyed my time with you. It was great."

She broke eye contact with him or else he would see her wounded look. The sun was coming up now, and she thought of how they would sit beside each other near the water's edge, holding hands, leaning into each other while they watched it rise. She pushed the memory out of her mind.

His cell phone went off, and he pulled it from his jeans pocket and checked it. "My driver is here. When I get back to Charlottesville, I'll be working a lot, so I won't be able to attend your brother's birthday celebration with you, after all."

She nodded while hurting deep inside. He didn't mention not taking her to Striker and Margo's wedding, but she figured she would eventually get notified about that, as well. He was washing his hands of her. This was final. "Alright, I understand," she said, and this time she really did.

"Great. I'll see you around."

"Okay." Then, deciding to save him the trouble, she said, "And I just remembered I have something to do the weekend of Striker's wedding, so I won't be able to make it."

He nodded, and Randi thought she saw relief flash in his eyes. "Alright."

His phone went off. "That's probably the driver calling again. I'd better go. Take care of yourself."

She merely nodded. "You do the same, Quasar."

He walked out the bedroom door. She held her breath until she heard the sound of the front door opening and closing behind him. Then she fell back on the bed and started crying.

SPECIAL AGENT RIVIERA stared at the man sitting across from him. If anyone had told him that one day he and Wallace Conway would be on opposite sides of an interrogation, he would not have believed it. As far as he'd known, Wally had been a fine agent. Dedicated. Loyal.

And as honest as honest could get. It had been hard for him and some of his fellow agents to accept that Wally was none of those things. That he had betrayed them in the worst possible way.

"I know what you're thinking, Jarez," Wally said in a defeated voice. "You're wondering how I could have let Levan Shaw get to me. I have always been a clean agent."

Riviera nodded slowly. "Yes, that question has crossed my mind. But I figured the answer is obvious. Money."

"Yes, and the fact Levan was my cousin."

At the surprised look in Riviera's eyes, Wally smiled. "See, there are some things that do get past the Bureau. Levan made sure no one knew. And because we were related, I felt a loyalty to him."

Riviera tried to hold back his fury. "You knew what he was doing. Killing innocent people. Selling women and children into slavery. Trying to cause a gang war. Damn, you knew what he paid Constantine and Griffin to do to Esther Emiliano. As far as I'm concerned, you're as repulsive as he was to have gone along with it."

Wally stewed on that for a moment before saying, "I was greedy. Tired of fighting damn criminals who got away and often lived a hell of a lot better than we did. No, I can't justify all those horrendous acts Levan did. I won't justify them."

"Yet you harbored him as a fugitive. Fed him information so he could stay one step ahead of us. Men like you sicken me."

"I know, and believe it or not, for the past few months I have sickened myself. But maybe I can make it up by doing the right thing for once. I don't want anyone else's blood on my hands because of Levan."

Riviera straightened in his chair. "What do you mean?"

Wally drew in a deep breath. "Levan was a man who didn't believe in leaving behind unfinished business."

An uneasy feeling settled in the pit of Riviera's stomach. "And?"

Wally leaned back in the chair. "Order me a freshly brewed cup of coffee, and I will tell you everything I know."

RANDI STUDIED HER FACE in the bathroom mirror and winced at the puffiness around her eyes. She refused to shed any more tears for a man who'd made it clear that he didn't want her. Things would be okay. She was prepared to live a life without him, but it wouldn't be lonely. She had her family, a few friends, her work and of course Glendale Shores. She could always escape there. She'd been to the island for long periods by herself and the seclusion never bothered her.

But how would she manage to put out of her mind the feeling of being with Quasar? Of being held in his arms? Of being made love to all through the night? Of sharing intimate, oftentimes hot and steamy conversations in Spanish? Just being with him? Seeing him sitting across a table and looking at her in a way that made her wet?

She clenched her legs tightly together at the memories she hoped would sustain her through the lonely days ahead. She couldn't get over how in just a short time Quasar had come to mean so much to her. Granted, she'd known he was her intended, yet from the first there had been something about him that had gone beyond just sexual. Like his easy acceptance of her gift. Not once had he ever made her feel as if she was some type of freak. More than once he'd complimented her on it and told her

how special she must feel to have it. Knowing that was
his attitude had made her gift special.

She left the bedroom and was headed for the kitchen
to see what she could scrounge up for breakfast when
there was a knock at the door. Her heart began racing
and then she slowly calmed it down. There was no way
it was Quasar returning since he had a key.

Crossing the room to the door, she looked out the peephole and frowned. It was Kendra. What on earth could
the woman possibly want? Of course like the first time
Randi saw her, Kendra didn't have a hair out of place
and was wearing a cute shorts set, while Randi thought
she herself looked like crud in a pair of well-worn cut-
offs and an old T-shirt.

When Kendra knocked again, Randi decided to open
the door. "Kendra? May I help you?"

Kendra smiled brightly, looking behind Randi to see
inside the house. "No, you can't help me. I was looking
for Quasar."

Randi crossed her arms over her chest, annoyed with
the audacity of the woman. "He's not here." There was
no way she would tell the woman he'd left her and returned to Virginia.

"Phooey. I needed his help with something."

Randi could just imagine what. "Is there anything I
can help you with?" she asked sweetly, knowing there
wasn't.

"Um, not unless you know how anything about motorboats. I can't get it to move. It was fine when I took it out
yesterday."

Randi nodded. "Well, this is your lucky day, because
I do know something about motorboats. I own one myself." Randi thought of her beautiful motorboat docked

at Glendale Shores. It had been a graduation gift from her parents when she got her PhD.

Not surprisingly, Kendra didn't seem impressed. "Ah, that's okay. I'd rather have Quasar look at it. Please tell him to mosey on down to my place when he returns."

Without waiting for Randi to respond, Kendra walked away, deliberately swaying her hips as she did so.

Randi knew she should have told Kendra that Quasar wouldn't be returning, but eventually the woman would find out on her own when Quasar didn't mosey on down to her place. Too bad. Too glad.

"You're a celebrity, senor?"

Quasar switched his gaze off the beautiful scenery they passed to the driver of the private car. "No, I'm not a celebrity. I'm nobody."

"Oh, that's where you're wrong, senor. Everyone is someone, even if they don't know it yet. Take my Anita, for instance."

Quasar would rather not take his Anita. He was not in a talkative mood. Just his luck to get a driver who was chatty.

"My Anita was always a quiet child and got bullied a lot while growing up. We had no idea until we found a note she'd written when she'd planned to commit suicide by hanging herself. She'd gone so far as to purchase the rope and everything."

That got Quasar's attention. "What did you do?"

"We talked to her, told her that she should have told us what was going on. We had no idea what she'd been going through. She was only fourteen. And some of the things those mean-spirited kids did to her were heart-breaking. I admired her strength for persevering as long as she had. But I assured her that now that her mother and I knew what was going on, we would carry the load from here on out. She should not worry."

Quasar couldn't imagine someone so young having to deal with people so cruel. At least while growing up he'd had a lot of friends. But his bully was living right under his roof. Doyle. He recalled the number of ways his older brother made his life a living hell. When he'd complained to the old man, he hadn't done a damn thing about it. His mother, on the other hand, would scold Doyle and put him under punishment, which didn't last once Louis found out. "How is she doing now?" Quasar asked, sincerely wanting to know.

"My Anita is fine and is now twenty-seven and a medical doctor," the man said proudly. "She's married and has a wonderful husband and a little baby. She is happy. Her mom and I are happy. Happy ending for all."

"I'm glad," Quasar said, thinking it truly was a happy ending.

"My Anita is living proof that everybody is somebody. You should never let anyone define who you are. You have to love yourself, even if no one else loves you. It's their loss and not yours," the driver was saying. "We had to convince Anita of that to help her move on. We also stressed to her that a person has to be willing to accept love from others. That there are those who will come in your life who love you in spite of anything. In the end, they become your everything."

Quasar didn't speak as he thought deeply about what the man had said. He wondered if he'd allowed his father to define him even when he thought he hadn't. He'd stayed away for ten years. Three involuntarily and seven voluntarily. Yet the minute he returned and saw his father again, those feelings of inadequacy had returned twofold. Although he'd convinced himself what Louis thought didn't matter, in the end he'd proven that was a lie. And for his father to look him in the eye and tell him that he could never love him—that had broken him down when he should have been strong enough to deflect the pain. At least he should have been able to walk away and not give a damn about how the old man felt one way or the other. He should have been more like Anita and moved on. And he should have been willing to accept love. From Randi.

Randi.

Quasar leaned back in the seat and thought about the woman he'd left behind. In running away from the pain and humiliation caused by his father, he was also running away from her. And her love. He clearly recalled their last conversation and everything he'd said. His words had been spoken more to convince himself that what they'd shared had been nothing more than a fling.

Deep down he'd wanted it to be more than that, but he'd backed away as soon as things got real. What he'd said this morning had hurt her, and she hadn't deserved the pain. But he had wanted to convince her that she meant nothing to him…when he knew she truly meant everything.

Quasar had no right to leave the way he had, not when she had been there for him, given herself to him and supported him last night. When he had thought he hadn't needed anyone, she had been there to prove he'd needed her.

He would admit he *still* needed her. He would also admit something else. He loved her. What they'd shared over the past few days had nothing to do with sex…although he would admit it was the best he'd ever had.

It was about building a relationship based on respect and love. Randi was everything a man could want in a woman. Tough. Resilient. Sexy. He chuckled. Definitely sexy. And last night she had stood by him while facing his family in a way no one else had.

He thought about Lilly and how she still expected him to love her. And the fact that he hadn't indulged in serious relationships because of what she had done only proved she still had a hold on him and his life. A hold Lilly didn't deserve to have on him. Instead of moving on, he was stuck in the past. It was time he got over it and, like Anita, moved on.

He needed to talk to Randi. Tell her how he felt. Convince her that he loved her. "I've changed my mind," he said.

The driver met his gaze in the rearview mirror with a puzzled look in his eyes. "About what, senor?"

"Take me back."

"Sí señor."

They had ridden for twenty minutes, and Quasar had leaned against the backseat of the car with his eyes closed while thinking about what he would say to Randi when he saw her. He would do whatever it took, even grovel if he had to.

Suddenly he opened his eyes as a feeling of unease swept through him. He wasn't sure why, but he knew it had something to do with Randi. Why did he get the feeling that she was in danger? Just like he had before. He could call Agent Riviera. But what if he was wrong and nothing was amiss? Besides, the agent would have to come all the way from LA. That was nearly an hour's drive even on Sunday.

Quasar sat up straight in the seat and looked out the

window, recognizing the area. He was closer, less than a half hour from his home in Malibu. But still...

"Could you speed it up a little?" he asked the driver. "I need to get home as soon as possible."

CHAPTER THIRTY-SEVEN

DECIDING THAT THIS would be a do-nothing day, Randi planned to kick-start it with a swim. Since there was no reason to remain here another two days, she had contacted the airlines to see if she could get an earlier flight out. Preferably in the morning.

She would return to Richmond and reschedule that class she was to instruct at Quantico. According to messages from her personal assistant, a ton of magazines had called for interviews about the LA case that was making headlines everywhere. That would keep her busy.

Although she didn't want to think about Quasar, she was doing it anyway. She hadn't realized how attached they'd been. Very seldom had he let her out of his sight. While he was her bodyguard, they had eaten all their meals together, gone everywhere together and slept under the same roof and most nights in the same bed.

But Quasar had made his decision about them and she had to accept it. And she would.

Deciding to spend time on the beach, she had packed her beach bag with a good book, a towel, her wrap, a couple of bottles of water and a few snacks. When she got halfway to the shoreline, she noticed the small motorboat and wondered if it was the same boat Kendra alleged she'd been having trouble with. That made Randi wonder if the woman's claim was a ploy just to get Quasar alone. She wouldn't put anything past the woman.

Randi removed her sunglasses when she noticed how close Kendra's boat was to shore. She had to admit it was a beautiful black-and-gold motorboat, and the design was sleek with a smooth, shiny finish. It was the perfect size for a couple to sit comfortably without squatting.

Kendra's back was to her, and like Randi, she was wearing a huge floppy straw hat to protect against the sun. Randi removed her wrap, took off her hat and placed everything in her beach bag. She then raced toward the water.

Like she'd told Quasar, she loved to swim. She hoped one day he would triumph over his phobia and they would swim together. She scolded herself for even thinking such a thing when Quasar had made it clear that they wouldn't be seeing each other again.

Randi had swum back and forth in the water for a good fifteen minutes when she heard a cry for help. She glanced around and saw a few puffs of smoke coming from Kendra's motorboat. "What in the world?"

When Kendra's screams got louder, Randi began swimming toward the boat to offer her assistance. There wasn't a lot of smoke, which was good. Oftentimes boaters didn't double-check to make sure the gasket was on tightly to prevent water from seeping inside the fuel. The smoke could certainly be caused by that, which was a relatively easy thing to fix.

When Randi reached the boat, she pulled herself out the water and swung her legs over the side to get in. Before she could steady herself on her feet, she felt a sharp sting prick her right shoulder. She glanced over at the woman holding a tranquilizer gun and wearing a huge grin on her face.

That was the last thing Randi saw before everything went black.

QUASAR QUICKLY PAID the driver and rushed to the door. "Randi! Randi!" he called out at the top of his lungs.

When he didn't get an answer, he unlocked the door and checked the bedroom where they'd spent the night before. When he found it empty with the bed already made, he left the room and took the stairs two at a time to check the rooms there. They were also empty. Frustrated, he rubbed a hand down his face as he went back downstairs. Where was she? The rental car was still parked outside, so she couldn't have gone far. Relief filled him when he guessed she must be on the beach.

He moved toward the French doors that led outside. Standing on the patio, he looked along the water's edge. All he saw were two teens readying a pair of Jet Skis.

Quasar was about to go back inside the house to call Agent Riviera when, as if with a mind of their own, his eyes moved across the ocean to the small motorboat traveling farther and farther away from shore. Why that boat interested him, he wasn't sure. Stepping back inside the house, he grabbed the pair of binoculars off the table by the French doors. They were the ones Randi had purchased to use that day at the noontime concert they'd attended. He held them up to his eyes.

"What the hell!" He blinked rapidly to make sure he was seeing straight, and when he was certain he was, his heart began pounding. He kicked off his shoes and tore off his clothes as he raced toward the beach. The two teens were about to take their Jet Skis into the water when he reached out and grabbed one. "I need this."

The teen resisted. "No! You can't take my Jet Ski from me."

Ignoring the teen, he took it anyway. The other teen exclaimed, "That man is wearing only his underwear."

The observation that he'd stripped down to his boxer shorts made the teen stop resisting and all but shove the Jet Ski at him. Both boys took off, running away from him as fast as they could. He hoped they would tell their parents about the half-naked man who took one of their Jet Skis, and the police would be summoned.

Quasar got on the Jet Ski and headed out toward the boat. Dread filled him to the core at the same time an angry snarl curled his lips. His body began shaking, and he tried to remain calm and keep the Jet Ski steady as it sliced through the waters.

RANDI JOLTED INTO consciousness when a pail of water was thrown in her face. "Wake up, bitch. I don't have all day. I need to take care of you, then go back and take care of—"

"Why are you doing this, Lilly?" she asked, barely able to get the words out. Her tongue was thick in her mouth, and parts of her body felt as if they were not her own. She was very much aware that her hands were tied tightly behind her back with a rope and that her feet were bound, as well.

"I will tell you why. You killed Levan."

Randi's eyes lit in surprise. "You knew Levan Shaw?"

The woman's face filled with rage. "Of course I knew him. He and I were lovers for years. He set me up in business and taught me everything I know. He was my confidant and I was his. I promised him that I would kill you if he failed in his plans to do so."

"But that doesn't make sense, Lilly. You're married to Doyle and—"

"So? Doyle has several mistresses he thinks I don't know about. Or he doesn't give a damn if I know. One was at the party last night. I saw them disappear. Not the first time I've noticed such a thing, and it never bothered me before because I had Levan. But you ruined that. You should never have come to LA."

"I had to come."

"No, you didn't. And then I find out that you, of all people, are involved with Quasar. Last night he rejected me for you, which gives me another reason to kill you. I want you to know how it feels to be helpless. I'm going to push you overboard, and with your hands and feet tied up, you'll drown. You will know how it feels to have life slowly leave your body. By the time Quasar notices you're gone, what's left of you will have washed up onshore."

Randi intended to keep Lilly talking while she worked her hands free of the rope. With her skill in karate, even with her feet bound, if she could get her hands free, she could overpower Lilly.

"Where is Kendra?" Randi asked.

Lilly chuckled. "I gave her a shot from my tranquilizer gun, but a heavier dosage than I gave you, so she will be out for a while. Once I take care of you, I'll go back and take care of her. Imagine her surprise when she returned from her walk on the beach to find me in her house, waiting for her. I never liked the bitch. She bragged about being Doyle's first girlfriend, always saying she could get him back whenever she wanted."

Randi saw the evil in Lilly's eyes. "I plan to have a little present for her husband whenever he gets home. He's going find his wife cut up in little tiny pieces."

Randi was convinced Lilly Patterson was stone crazy.

Determined to keep her talking, Randi asked, "Does Louis or Doyle know about what you're into?"

Lilly rolled her eyes. "Of course not. All Louis wants is for Doyle to be mayor of Beverly Hills. All Doyle wants is to please his daddy. He had the nerve to tell me this morning over breakfast that his father wants us to have a baby. I don't want a damn baby to ruin my figure. He's crazy."

Randi wanted to tell her that she was the crazy one. She felt a little wiggle room in the rope and knew she was slowly loosening it but needed more time. If she kept Lilly talking for just a few more minutes, then she might be able to free her hands.

"Quasar loved you, you know," Randi said. "You hurt him when you married Doyle."

"I had to marry Doyle."

"Why?"

"Because I wanted the Patterson name and I didn't care which brother gave it to me. Then Levan came along and—"

All of a sudden, a loud hum rose above the waves. Lilly looked out over the waters. "Damn, someone is headed this way on a Jet Ski. I can't be seen."

Before Randi could react, Lilly rushed over. With a strong push to Randi's chest, she sent Randi tumbling overboard into the cool waters of the Pacific Ocean.

CHAPTER THIRTY-EIGHT

QUASAR KNEW THE MOMENT Randi hit the water. He quickly brought the Jet Ski to a stop and dove into the ocean after her. It seemed to take forever for him to reach her, and he didn't bother trying to untie her. He quickly grabbed hold of her around the waist and rushed to the surface. She sputtered out water and drew in a deep gulp of oxygen.

In between breaths she said, "I thought you'd left."

He took several deep breaths, as well. "I had. I sensed you were in danger." Before she could ask anything else, he said, "Turn around so I can get you untied."

Quasar had freed her hands and was just finished untying her feet when the sound of the motorboat got their attention. "She's coming toward us," he said.

"She has a regular gun and a tranquilizer gun," Randi informed him.

He quickly calculated the distance to the Jet Ski and knew they couldn't chance it. The motorboat would plow into them before they could reach it. However, he refused for them be sitting ducks. "Let's split up. I'm going to get her to come after me while you swim over to the Jet Ski. Take it back to shore and get help."

He could see the mutinous glint in her eyes. "I can't leave you out here."

"Yes, you can." He didn't have time to argue with her. "Do it, Randi. That's the only chance we have."

Randi nodded, and then they both dived underwater so Lilly wouldn't know what direction either of them had gone.

Moments later Quasar quietly resurfaced and saw the motorboat was idling while Lilly scanned the waters to see what direction they had taken. Luckily he had surfaced behind the boat. Quasar saw the waters stirring ahead. Randi was near the Jet Ski but had tossed something in the water in the opposite direction, causing it to ripple. Lilly took the bait and began firing her gun in the area.

Quasar knew he had to do something before Lilly figured out she'd been fooled. He moved to swim underneath the boat and with all the strength he had, pushed. The boat rocked a couple of times before toppling over. He heard Lilly's splash and after making sure she was no longer armed, he immediately swam over to her, ignoring her kicks and screams. Grabbing her around the waist, he lodged her hands between them. "Stop it, Lilly. It's over."

"No!" She continued to struggle. "I need to kill that bitch for killing Levan. I promised him I would kill her."

Levan? Was she talking about Levan Shaw?

Before Quasar could ask what in the hell she was talking about, they were surrounded by several boats filled with men wearing FBI jackets, guns drawn. He gave a sigh of relief when he recognized Agent Riviera on deck.

"You okay?" Riviera asked as agents jumped into the water to take Lilly off his hands.

"Yes, I'm fine," he said. He was more than happy to turn her over to the authorities.

"Where's Dr. Fuller?" Riviera asked anxiously, glancing around.

"I'm here," Randi said, swimming toward them. When

she reached them she said, "Lilly shot Kendra Biltmore with a high dose from a tranquilizer gun. Please send someone to her home. She's going to need medical treatment."

Quasar told Riviera where Kendra lived. The agent immediately used his phone.

"We got here as soon as we could," Riviera said when he ended the call. He and the other agents helped Randi and Quasar on board and handed them huge towels.

"How did you know what was going on? I figured that kid's parents would report I hijacked his Jet Ski, but I didn't figure they would send the FBI after me," Quasar said.

"We were already on our way. To clear his conscience, Agent Conway told us about the promise some woman made to Shaw to kill Dr. Fuller. Unfortunately, he didn't know the woman's name. When I couldn't reach either of you on the phone, I figured something was wrong. Then, when Sutherland told me they got a call about a naked man who fit your description on a Malibu beach commandeering a Jet Ski from a teenager and heading out in the ocean toward some motorboat, I put two and two together."

Quasar frowned. "I'm not naked."

Riviera chuckled. "Pretty close to it." Then, on a more serious note, he asked, "Either of you know the woman?" Lilly was behaving like a raving maniac with her screams and foul mouth.

Quasar ran a hand down his face. "Yes. She's Lilly Patterson. My brother's wife."

Riviera blinked. "Your brother's wife?"

"Yes."

"And she had connections to Levan Shaw?"

"Evidently," Quasar said. "Although I find it hard to believe."

"Believe it," Randi said quietly. "She bragged that they were lovers for years and blamed me for his death. Said he'd set her up in all kinds of illegal business operations. She promised him that if anything happened to him before he could kill me, she would finish the job."

Riviera shook his head. "What a mess. I hope your brother can afford her a good lawyer."

"His problem, not mine," Quasar said, glancing over at Randi. They hadn't had time to say a whole lot to each other, and he knew there was much he needed to discuss with her in private. Right now he was glad the nightmare was finally over and she was safe.

Another agent approached. "We're ready to take statements now," he said.

"Good," Quasar said. He was ready to give his. The sooner they could get this part over with, the sooner he and Randi could talk.

RANDI CAME DOWN the stairs feeling totally refreshed. It had taken longer than she thought for Quasar and her to give their statements to the federal agents. A lot of questions had been asked as they pieced together the depth of Lilly's involvement with Levan Shaw. Lilly, while verbally spouting her excessive anger, revealed more than she probably intended, and agents were following up on those leads, as well.

From all accounts, Lilly Patterson had been living a double life that no one, including Doyle and Louis, knew about. She had been Shaw's lover and protégé and was set to take over a number of his sleazy operations. It was rumored there was a list of businessmen, politicians and others included in the seedy operations, and Riviera and his agents were scrambling to uncover the list.

A group of numbers mixed with letters kept popping up in Randi's head. Not certain if the numbers could mean anything or were somehow connected to the case, before her bath she had phoned Riviera to pass the numbers on to him. He would be meeting again with Agent Conway to see if perhaps the numbers meant anything to him.

Kendra Biltmore had been rushed to the nearest medical facility and admitted for close observation. All reports indicated she would recover and was lucky to be alive. Since Randi had gotten shot with the tranquilizer gun, as well, she'd been checked over by paramedics and deemed okay. From what Kendra told the authorities when she finally came to, Lilly had been waiting inside her home when she came back from her walk on the beach and had come up with this plan to lure Randi on the boat to kill her.

Now, after a long bath, Randi felt ready to talk to Quasar. Before she'd headed upstairs, he'd said they needed to talk when they finished washing up.

The first thing she noticed when she descended the stairs was that it was getting dark outside. An entire day had gone by, and although her life had been in danger, another seasoned criminal was off the streets. If Agent Riviera had his way, there would be more. Because Quasar lived in a private community, the media hadn't been allowed inside, although reports were already popping up in the media. Randi had called her parents to assure them she was okay.

Her parents were glad she was safe and anxious for her to return home. Her father also mentioned he couldn't

wait to meet Quasar to thank him personally for protecting her. She didn't have the heart to tell her parents that
wouldn't be happening.

Randi rounded the corner, stepped into the huge great
room and stopped. Quasar had his back to her as he stared
out the floor-to-ceiling glass window that overlooked the
ocean. Soft music was playing in the background, and
the majority of the lights were either off or turned down.
The quiet room felt calm and tranquil.

The dimmed lights cast a soft glow over Quasar, who
seemed lost in his thoughts. He'd said in his statement
to the FBI that he'd come back after sensing she was in
danger. No one had questioned his ability to do that. Was
he now questioning it himself?

"Thanks for saving me yet again today, Quasar," she
said, deciding to get whatever talk he wanted them to
have over with.

He slowly turned to face her, and the look on his face
was unreadable. He shoved his hands into the pockets of
his slacks. Her gaze automatically went to his physique.
He was truly a masculine, well-built man. She could see
how many people considered him practically naked in
just his boxer shorts. Randi knew there were swimming
trunks that were skimpier, but she doubted any looked on
a man like Quasar's boxers looked on him. Sexy didn't
even come close.

"I would do anything for you, Randi."

His words touched her, yet she wished they could go
deeper than a touch, because she knew he wouldn't do
anything for her. The one thing she wanted him to do
that he couldn't or wouldn't was love her.

"You did it, Quasar," she said, smiling, reminded of
one obstacle he'd successfully faced that day.

He arched a brow. "I did what?"

"You went back into the water, and I'm happy for you."

He stared at her a minute before saying, "Honestly, I didn't think about diving into that water. All I knew was that I had to get to you. My fears of being in the water took a backseat to everything else. I couldn't lose you."

He couldn't lose her? Did he not realize that because of his words this morning, he had lost her? He'd made it pretty darn clear he didn't want her.

He walked over to the breakfast bar. "I poured glasses of wine. Would you like one?"

"Yes," she said, moving toward the sofa to sit down, folding her legs beneath her. "You said we needed to talk."

"We do," he said, handing her a wineglass and then taking the wingback chair across from her.

"Thanks." She took a sip of her wine. "I really don't know why we should talk. I think you said everything this morning, and personally, I don't have anything to add."

"I do." Quasar drew in a deep breath. He'd known he'd loved her when he'd asked the driver to turn the car around. He just hadn't known how much until he'd looked into those binoculars and seen her tied up on that boat.

"I now understand what you've been dealing with, Quasar," she broke into his thoughts to say. "With your fear of the water. When Lilly pushed me overboard, in my mind I knew I would drown, but a part of me refused to accept it. I held my breath underwater, not knowing how long I could, and knowing when I couldn't hold it any longer it would all be over. I prayed for a miracle. And then there you were, swimming toward me. I thought

I was hallucinating. I didn't believe you were real until you touched me."

He nodded. "I hope you don't have a fear of water after this."

She drew in a deep breath. "I don't think I'll have a fear, but more apprehensions. I won't be able to swim anywhere without remembering what almost happened. What could have happened had you not been there to save me. Let's just say I have no desire to go near that much water anytime soon."

Quasar was quiet. Then, after taking a sip of his wine, he said, "When I left this morning, I had no intention of ever seeing you again."

"I know. I regret that your intuition where I'm concerned put a monkey wrench in those plans."

Was that what she thought? If so, then he needed to straighten her out about that now. "It wasn't my intuition of you being in danger that made me come back, Randi. I had already instructed the driver to turn around and bring me back here even before I sensed you were in danger." Quasar could tell from the lifting of her brow that she was surprised to hear that.

"Why were you returning? Had you forgotten something?"

He chuckled slightly. Yes, he'd forgotten something. Something he hadn't been aware he'd left with her. His heart. "Yes."

Instead of telling her what it was just yet, he said, "I had a very talkative driver. He told me about how his daughter was bullied in school and how he and his wife had helped her through that difficult period in her life, but only after finding her suicide note. She had planned to end her life at fourteen."

"How awful."

"Yes," he agreed. "It was. But with their support, she got through it and is now a doctor, married and doing fine."

"Good. I'm happy for her."

"I'm happy for her, as well. What inspired me most about what he told me was the fact that his daughter was able to come out of the dark and into the light because she had someone who believed deeply in her. Someone who truly cared. In a way, that's what helped me through my years in prison. Sheppard Granger truly cared. And because he cared, he pushed for policies that would benefit the prisoners. He had our best interests at heart."

He paused before continuing, wanting to get this right. "The same thing holds true for Striker and Stonewall as well as a lot of the other guys. We were able to build a bond because of Shep. That's why we're still close today. Closer than any brothers could be. I never felt the affinity toward Doyle that I feel for those guys."

"From what I gather, Doyle never tried to be the brother you needed," Randi said softly.

"No, he didn't. His expectations of me were even worse than Louis's. Instead of a brother, he thought of me as nothing more than a scapegoat."

He paused a minute and stared into his wine before saying, "Both Louis and Doyle called while you were taking a bath. I wish I hadn't answered. Do you know what they asked me to do?"

"No. What?"

"Take part of the blame for Lilly's downfall. After all, she used to be my girlfriend. Louis felt it wouldn't make Doyle look so bad if I did. His political supporters are backing off. They feel if he couldn't manage his business at home and had no idea what was happening in his own house, then he couldn't manage a city like Beverly Hills."

"Does make you wonder. So what was your response to their request?"

He shrugged. "I told Doyle to shove it up his ass. I wasn't that disrespectful to the old man, but I basically said the same thing. And I warned them if my name gets linked to Lilly's in any way to take the heat off Doyle, then I will go to the media and announce to the world how I was railroaded into serving time for a crime Doyle committed."

"I'll bet neither of them was ready to hear that."

"No, they weren't. I don't see how, after our conversation in his study last night, Louis would ask such a thing of me. Evidently he didn't get the message. I think he did this time."

Quasar took a sip of his wine and leaned forward to rest an arm on one of his thighs. He looked at Randi, held her gaze and said, "As far as someone not being ready for something, I wasn't quite ready for you, Randi."

He wanted to cross to the sofa and kiss her, ask for her forgiveness for being so stupid, but he knew more than anything he needed her to understand why he'd been so determined to walk away from her this morning and not look back. And why, in the end, he hadn't been able to.

She broke eye contact with him, glanced down at her wine and then back at him. "You weren't quite ready for me in what way? I'm not a complicated person, Quasar."

"No, you're not complicated. What you are is too good to be real. Or at least I thought so. It was hard to believe there was any woman who could melt the cold casing around my heart. When it came to women, it was all about sex and nothing more. You proved me wrong and showed me there could be more. The sex was good. But in a way, the relationship we were developing between us was even better. You respected who I was and what I did. You didn't put me down. In fact, more than once you lifted me up."

She sat quietly for a moment and then, in a voice raw with pain he could he actually feel, she said, "Yet you wanted to end things. You walked out that door without wanting ever to see me again."

He drew in a deep breath. "Yes. Before drifting off to sleep, you whispered that you loved me…"

The lifting of her brow confirmed she hadn't known those words had slipped from her lips.

"I couldn't handle hearing that. I felt like I needed to get away from here. I was running, Randi. Running away from my fears and disappointments. And from you. I didn't think I was ready to give my heart to another woman. Not sure I could accept any more pain. But before I could get to downtown LA, I knew I had no choice. I admitted to myself that I had fallen in love with you, too, and asked the driver to turn around. What I had left behind was you. The one woman whom I knew deep in my heart I could trust. The one woman I knew was deserving of the love I tried holding back for so long. The decision to come back, grovel if I had to…beg for your forgiveness, was made before I sensed you were in any kind of danger."

Randi sat there, unable to move. She couldn't even speak. All she could do was fight the tears threatening to fall from her eyes. She drew in a deep breath and watched as Quasar put his wineglass aside, stood and crossed to stand directly in front of where she sat. She tilted her head up to meet his gaze.

"There are a million other words I can say, Randi. But I hope none are more profound than me saying I love you. I believe with all my heart that you and I were meant to be together. This thing between us might have started with all that strong sexual chemistry, but I know it ended with love. A lot of love. And I feel it here," he said, placing a hand over his heart.

He then reached his hand out to her. "Let me warn you, Randi. If you take my hand, you're also accepting my heart, and accepting my heart comes with a lot of obligations."

She lifted a brow. "What obligations?"

"To love me as much as I love you. To be there for each other, no matter what. Always to trust each other. If we do those things then I believe we will handle everything else, any obstacles and challenges that come our way. Together."

Randi set her wineglass aside and placed her hand in his. She believed they would be able to handle those obstacles and challenges, as well. He gently pulled her up, and she couldn't help the smile of happiness that touched her lips. Those same lips he was staring hard at right now.

"I love you, Randi Fuller, so damn much." He kept her hand entwined in his as he leaned down and opened his mouth over hers in a kiss that curled her toes. By the time he released her, all she could do was moan.

"So," he asked, licking around her moist lips, "do you love me back?"

Her smile stretched from one side of her mouth to the other. "Yes, I love you back, Quasar. I wasn't aware I'd spoken those words last night, but I'm glad I did. I meant them, and they were spoken from my heart. I do love you."

"And I love you."

He pulled her into his arms and held her tight. She closed her eyes and inhaled the scent of him, the man she loved so much. The feel of him. She loved every single thing about him.

He leaned back and looked at her. "So are we back on for Striker's wedding? Will you attend with me?"

She chuckled. "Yes. And what about Trey's birthday celebration? Will you be attending with me, or do I have to find a date?"

He brushed his knuckles against her cheek and whispered with meaning, *"Bebé, tus días de citas se han acabado. De ahora en adelante voy a ser el único hombre que estará cerca de tí."*

At that moment she felt wrapped in a silken cocoon of euphoria. He'd said the words in Spanish, but she clearly understood them.

"My dating days are over, huh?" she asked, wrapping an arm around his neck.

"Most definitely. But just in case I need to prove my point…" He swept her into his arms and headed straight for the bedroom.

CHAPTER THIRTY-NINE

"So you think you have a job to come back to after being gone for over a week? Playing in the sands of Malibu with a beautiful woman?" Stonewall Courson asked the man walking through the door of Summers Security Firm.

Quasar ignored his friend's comments. Instead he glanced over at Striker, who was sitting at a small table, eating what had to be the biggest cookie he'd ever seen. "I take it Stonewall still hasn't had a date with his detective, which is the reason for his foul mood."

Striker nodded. "Yeah, and I'm getting a little damn sick of his attitude. I think we need to take him somewhere and work him over."

"I'd like to see the two of you try," Stonewall said with an edge to his voice.

Quasar grinned as he eased into the chair across from Stonewall. "Where's Roland?"

"Meeting with a new client," Stonewall said, tossing on the desk the pencil he'd been rolling between his fingers in agitation. "So, Dr. Fuller has made a name for herself once again."

"Yes, she did," Quasar said proudly, knowing Stonewall was referring to all the national attention Randi had gotten in the media. Before leaving Los Angeles, Agent Riviera had called to thank Randi for supplying those numbers and letters to him. It seemed they were the password to get inside Shaw's state-of-the-art secret vault. The Feds had gotten enough incriminating evidence to put away ten politicians and several well-known businessmen for years. Agents were already making arrests.

He glanced back over at Striker. "Do you plan to share any of that cookie?"

"No. My woman had this delivered just for me."

"Greedy ass," Quasar muttered. He turned his attention to Stonewall, who was staring at him. "Why are you looking at me like that?"

"You seem different since I last saw you," Stonewall said.

Stonewall's observation got Striker's attention, as well. Quasar rolled his eyes. "You're imagining things."

"Um, and where's the psychic?" Striker asked, taking another bite of his cookie.

"Asleep, I guess."

Striker raised a brow. "Sleeping where?"

"Not that it's any of your business, but I left her sleeping in my bed. Do you have a problem with it?"

A smooth smile touched Striker's lips. "No. None whatsoever. So when's the wedding?"

Stonewall sat up straight in his chair. "Wedding? You're getting married, Quasar?"

"Eventually. I just haven't asked her yet. Waiting for the right time."

"But you will?" Stonewall asked, watching him closely.

Quasar met his friend's stare. "Yes, Stonewall, I will. She means too much to me not to put a ring on her finger." His friends didn't know just how much he meant by that. He hadn't been looking for love, but he'd discovered it anyway with a woman who meant the world to him. The woman he loved.

"Striker's getting married. You're thinking about getting married. And I can't get a date with the woman I want."

"Sounds like you need to step up your game," Quasar said, grinning.

Stonewall nodded. "I think I will. It's about time, don't you think?"

Striker chuckled. "It's past time."

A week later

"MOM. DAD. I'D LIKE you to meet Quasar Patterson. Quasar, these are my parents. Jenna and Randolph Fuller."

Randi had told Quasar her father was tall, but Quasar hadn't known he was just as tall as he was. He extended his hand to the older man. "Mr. and Mrs. Fuller. It's nice meeting you."

A huge smile touched Randolph Fuller's features as he took Quasar's hand in a strong handshake. "My wife and I are the ones honored to meet you. We know how diligent you were in keeping our daughter safe."

After shaking Jenna Fuller's hand, Quasar wrapped his arm around Randi's waist to bring her closer to his side as he smiled down at her. "I will always be there to keep her safe."

Randi beamed in pleasure. Quasar had all but told her parents that he intended to be a part of her life for a long time.

"Well, I for one am glad to hear that," Randolph said, grinning. "I don't want to think what would have happened to her if you hadn't been there, protecting her."

After conversing with her parents a little while, Randi introduced Quasar to those he hadn't met, like her great-grandparents, Robert and Julia Fuller, and her godparents, retired Senator Noah Wainwright and his wife, Leigh. She also introduced him to her godsister Noelle Wainwright.

Everyone was ecstatic about meeting Quasar, especially after hearing of all the times he'd saved Randi's life. The story about him diving into the ocean to save her from drowning was the one everyone wanted all the details about. Personally, Randi preferred putting the memories behind her.

"Miss me?"

She glanced up from the snack table when Quasar reappeared. After dinner he had been talking to her father, and the next thing she knew, the two had disappeared. Knowing her father, he'd probably taken Quasar into Trey's study to talk about his favorite football team, the Washington Redskins, which happened to be Quasar's favorite football team, as well. Her parents were season ticket holders.

"Of course I missed you. I thought maybe you'd forgotten about me."

"Never. What time do you want to head out in the morning?"

He would be spending a week with her at Glendale Shores. "Let's do it early," she suggested.

A sexy smile touched his lips. He leaned down and whispered close to her ear, "Baby, we can do it anytime."

She chuckled. "You know what I was talking about. I can't wait to get to the island to show you around and everything."

"And I can't wait to see it." He took a sip of his punch.

"Everyone I met here tonight is really nice. You have a wonderful family, Randi. Your father reminds me a lot of Sheppard. The way he carries himself and talks to people. Like he doesn't have a pretentious bone in his body."

That was a huge compliment coming from Quasar—she knew how much Sheppard Granger meant to him. "Dad's super. I wouldn't trade him for the world. Mom is super, as well. One day I'll tell you how they met and everything it took for them finally to be together."

"I can't wait to hear it."

Haywood got everyone's attention to announce that it was time to cut Trey's birthday cake. Randi had noticed that even Trey had taken off his big brother gloves around Quasar. That meant he really liked him. She glanced across the room and saw her parents smiling. Those smiles meant they were pleased about something. She would have to ask them about it later.

"Yes, Quasar, you're right. I have a wonderful family. I think I'll keep them."

He leaned down and kissed her forehead. "And, sweetheart, I intend to keep you."

She smiled back at him. "I'm counting on it, Mr. Patterson."

"READY FOR OUR SWIM?"

Randi smiled over at Quasar. "Yes, I'm ready." He had been supportive, giving encouragement and helping combat her fear of water since her near-drowning incident. And it was working. Since arriving on Glendale Shores, they had gone swimming every day. Sometimes twice in the same day.

A ferry brought them over, and having a car available made it easier to move around on the island. Quasar loved the big house that Trey and Haywood inherited from her great-grandparents, Poppa Murphy and Gramma Mattie. And on the drive to her bungalow, she showed him the homes her parents and Zach and Anna owned, as well. She could tell from the minute he pulled up in front of her place that he liked it. It was no way as large as his place in Malibu, but he said he thought the two-bedroom, two-bathroom cottage suited her. Inside it was open concept with a spacious living room and eat-in kitchen. He especially liked her huge screened-in patio. She told him about her family's annual Fourth of July celebration next month on Glendale Shores and invited him to come be a part of it. He said that he would.

"Race you to the water," Quasar said, grinning, before taking off at a fast run.

Although she knew she couldn't outpace him, she ran after him anyway. By the time she reached the edge, he was already in the water and swimming like a fish. And he looked good doing it. His hands and shoulders were expertly slicing through the water. She was glad he'd completely overcome his phobia.

She dove into the water and tried to impress him by doing several flips. "I'm glad you're okay with swimming again," he said, smiling over at her while swiping excess water from his face.

"Me, too. Although I can't brag about being captain of my swimming team while in high school and college, I always thought I did okay."

He smiled. "Those times in Malibu when I would sit in the sand and watch you swim, I thought you were a great swimmer."

"Thanks. You're not so bad yourself," she said, smiling back at him.

"Let's race."

She rolled her eyes. "Again?"

"Just to that marker over there."

Randi lifted her hand to shelter her eyes from the brightness of the sun. "Where?"

"Over there," he said, pointing out to her the marker near the bank.

That was his downfall, because she pushed against him, making him lose his balance, producing a huge splash. That's when she took off, swimming toward the marker.

"Cheater," he shouted.

She refused to look back, although she knew he was gaining speed and was not far behind her. He was an excellent swimmer, but she was determined that this was one race she would win.

Just when she thought she'd made it home free, she felt him grab her legs and pull her under the water. He went under with her, and they both came up moments later, laughing and spurting out water. "That's not fair, Quasar," she yelled, wiping water from both her hair and eyes.

"Oh, now you want to call foul play, huh?" he said, wrapping his arms around her.

"Whatever."

Despite the sun that had been shining brightly all day, the water was somewhat cool, and she loved the feel of his arms around her. When he pulled her even closer, she could feel his hard erection through his swim shorts.

"Do you ever not want sex?" she asked him, recalling how many times they'd made love and predicting just how many times he would want more. His libido should have been outlawed.

"I can go for months without sex and it wouldn't bother

me," he said, staring down at her. "But the thought of not being able to make love to you is definitely something I don't want to think about."

He reached down and gently traced her lips with the tip of his finger. "I love your lips."

"Do you?"

"Yes. I think it's time for us to get out of the water, don't you?"

She nodded. "Yes, I think so, too."

He had packed a lunch for them, and they had a picnic near the waters. She noticed after they'd eaten that Quasar had gotten quiet.

"You okay?"

He smiled. "I couldn't be better." He reached out and took her hand in his and said, "Spending time with you these past weeks has been simply wonderful. It's going to be hard when I leave to return to Charlottesville and you remain in Richmond."

She'd been thinking the same thing. "You have an open invitation to visit me whenever you want in Richmond."

His smile widened, and he returned the invitation. *"Mi casa es su casa."* He got quiet again and then added, "But I want more, Randi. I want forever with you."

He shifted positions to get down on his knees before her. "I want to spend the rest of my life with you. I don't care if it's in Charlottesville or Richmond or both places or neither of those. All I know is that I want to marry you, make a home with you and one day have a family. I will always love you and protect you and be there for you. I asked your father for your hand in marriage at your brother's birthday party, and he gave his approval. So now it's up to you. Will you marry me, Randi?"

She fought back the tears in her eyes. "Yes! Yes! I will marry you, Quasar. I can't believe it's just like my great-grandmother told me it would be."

"Your great-grandmother Julia?"

She shook her head. "No, my great-grandmother Mattie." She told him about her vision and the prediction for their future as well as the reason she hadn't told him before now. "You were chosen for me and I for you. But we had to earn each other's love. I earned yours and you earned mine."

He nodded, smiling. "Do you think that's why I have a sixth sense where you are concerned to protect you from danger?"

"I'm thinking that's why. You were able to know when I might be threatened when I didn't have a clue."

"I hope that's the way it will always be, Randi. I want always to be your protector."

She wrapped her arms around his neck. "And lover. Best friend and husband. You will be my everything man."

"And you are definitely my everything woman," he said, sliding an engagement ring onto her finger.

Her mouth widened. "OMG! It's beautiful." Randi couldn't believe her eyes as she stared down at the two-carat diamond solitaire engagement ring.

Quasar laughed. "You can thank your sister, Haywood, for knowing your taste in jewelry."

When Randi threw herself in his arms, he held her tight. This was the woman who'd brought him so much joy. The same woman who'd seized his heart by seducing the hell out of him. She was the one woman who would always and forever be there for him, the same way he intended always to be there for her. Like he'd told her, he believed there was a reason he was the man chosen to be a part of her life, and he intended always to make her happy.

"Want to go for another swim?" he asked her.

"No, I want to make love. Now."

He glanced around. "Right here? Out in the open?"

"Yes, right here. Out in the open. Not another soul is on this island but us. We can do whatever we want to do, and I want to make love."

Quasar pulled his future wife into his arms. He was more than happy to oblige.

EPILOGUE

"By the powers vested in me by this great state of Virginia, I now pronounce you husband and wife. Lamar 'Striker' Jennings, you may kiss your bride."

Striker turned to the woman whose life was now joined with his. Lifting her veil, he whispered words of love before lowering his mouth to hers, sealing the promises they'd made and the love they shared.

Sitting in the audience Randi dabbed the tears from her eyes. It was a beautiful outdoor wedding on the Connelly Estate, the home of the bride's uncle. During a portion of the ceremony, the bride and groom spoke their own words of love and dedication and pledges they'd included.

Since Quasar was a groomsman, he and Randi had arrived early, and he'd seated her in the spot where he wanted her while he and Stonewall ushered in the wedding guests. She thought her fiancé looked dashingly handsome in his black tux. She was happy to see a familiar face when Detective Joy Ingram arrived and sat beside her. The two of them had become friends while working together months ago on the Erickson case. From the first time they'd met, she'd thought Detective Ingram was as beautiful as she was friendly. And she was a top-notch police detective.

Randi recalled that upon their initial meeting, there

had been some unusually strong vibes radiating off the woman, ones that had indicated they would one day share a close friendship. She had felt those same vibes from Margo Connelly, as well, when they'd met. At the time she hadn't understood why she would feel such vibes from the two women. Now she knew and understood.

Joy congratulated her on her engagement to Quasar and *oohed* and *aahed* over her engagement ring. Randi had to admit Quasar had done a great job, and she'd gotten more than a few compliments on her ring.

Randi even got to meet Sheppard Granger, his beautiful pregnant wife, Carson; Sheppard's sons Jace, Caden and Dalton; and their beautiful wives, two of whom were also expecting. All three women were practically glowing, and Randi thought it was wonderful that three babies would be born within weeks of each other.

It was good seeing Quasar's boss, Roland, again. They'd met months ago at the crime scene. The same one where she'd first laid eyes on Quasar. A night she was certain she would never forget. A night that had been destined to change her life forever.

Like Joy had done, the Grangers and Roland congratulated her on her and Quasar's engagement, and she couldn't help but let them know how happy she was about it.

"Ready to be escorted to the reception, sweetheart?"

Randi glanced up when Quasar appeared by her side a short while later. "Yes, I'm ready."

The reception was held by the pool, and the setup gave Randi more than a few ideas for her own wedding. She and Quasar planned to have a September wedding on Glendale Shores. Her parents and her entire family were excited and happy for them. She would be keeping her home in Richmond for the time being but would be moving to Charlottesville, where she and Quasar would make their permanent home. She looked forward to all the changes in her life.

Hours later Quasar leaned down to whisper, "The bride and groom have left for their honeymoon. Are you ready to leave?" She smiled up at him. He had mentioned the couple would be honeymooning in Dubai. "Yes." She glanced around. "I was looking for Joy to say goodbye and don't see her anywhere."

A mischievous smile touched Quasar lips. "Joy has been kidnapped."

Randi lifted a brow. "Kidnapped? By whom?"

"Stonewall. I guess he got tired of things popping up whenever they planned dates and decided to take matters into his own hands."

"Oh," Randi said, smiling. She recalled months ago, right before leaving Charlottesville, that Joy had been excited about her first official date with Stonewall. A date that never happened because of a homicide Joy was called away to.

"Well, I'm glad they're finally going on their first date, but did he have to kidnap her?" Randi asked, chuckling.

"Evidently, he thought so," Quasar said, taking her hand. "Come on. I have plans for you tonight."

She smiled as he led her off, and her mind filled with all the plans she had for him tonight, as well. She was happy. The man holding her hand was her future. He was the person she was meant to spend the rest of her life with, and she couldn't wait to start.

* * * * *

If you enjoyed Quasar and Randi's story,
don't miss the next book in
THE PROTECTORS *series,*
featuring Stonewall and Joy,
LOCKED IN TEMPTATION.
Coming soon from
New York Times *bestselling author Brenda Jackson*
and HQN Books!

**In the third installment in *The Protectors* series,
New York Times bestselling author**

BRENDA JACKSON

**proves that some distractions are just too
tempting to resist.**

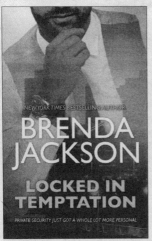

Police detective Joy Ingram's
connection to elite security
expert Stonewall Courson was
instant. Undeniable. Electric. But
her commitment to protect
and serve has always come first.
Everything else is secondary—
especially now that a killer is
tearing through the city. As
the body count rises, so does
the pressure on Joy to catch
the murderer. She can't risk a
distraction, not even one as sexy
as reformed ex-con Stonewall.

There are few things Stonewall
values more than a strong
woman. But when Joy's case draws her into a criminal's game,
he must convince her that he's the best man to protect her.
And while he puts his life on the line to save hers, the insatiable
attraction between them becomes the one danger neither of
them can escape.

Available July 25

Order your copy today!

www.HQNBooks.com

PHBRJ214

  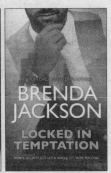

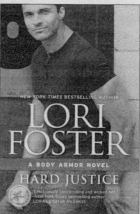

 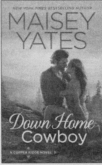 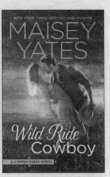

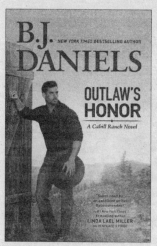